Eleanor's Answer

Andrew Croughton

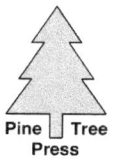

Pine Tree Press

2 Pine Tree Drive
Barnwood
Gloucester
GL4 3LJ

ISBN: 978-0-9526501-2-6

Preface

Schoolteacher David Anderson and Eleanor Jenkins have developed a close, but unusual friendship. Unusual because David is a widower with adult and married children while Eleanor is still at school in the sixth form. But they are not in the same school. Their relationship, although platonic at first, had been discouraged by their church pastor at the instigation of Eleanor's parents. However, circumstances had brought them together again, but now on a decidedly non-platonic level

When Eleanor's parents became aware of their rediscovered friendship, they told her in no uncertain terms that she must end it. Eleanor's first problem was should she obey or disobey her parents. But there was another decision to be made, this time by David. Should he end the friendship in the best interest of Eleanor? Things needed to be resolved, one way or another, and they were both invited to Sunday afternoon tea with James and Lucy Butler, James being the church pastor who had told David to cool the relationship months earlier. After some discussion, David reached his decision.

This is the sequel to "David Makes A Decision." If you haven't read that, then stop right now! This begins with that decision

Chapters

Chapter 1

The Decision

"I think that we should," David paused and looked up. "We should get married."

Eleanor's reaction was to utter a shriek, but she managed to hold it back. "Do you mean it?" she whispered.

"Hang on," Lucy said. "I mean, shouldn't you ask her properly?"

David looked her, and grinned. "You're right." He slipped from his seat onto one knee and turned to Eleanor. Taking one of her hands in his, he smiled at her. "Eleanor, would you marry me?"

Eleanor's reaction was to throw her arms round his neck. "Yes, of course I will," she gasped. Then, forgetting where she was, she kissed him passionately. David gently eased her off.

"Eleanor, remember where we are," he whispered.

"Oh, sorry!" She sat back onto her seat, looking embarrassed. "So, what now?" she asked.

"I think we should have a cup of tea," Lucy said.

"Don't we have anything better?" James asked.

"Darling, I think I should take Eleanor home soon, and how would she explain any alcohol on her breath?"

"Ah!" James said. "Good point. But wouldn't Eleanor prefer David to take her home?"

"Yes, you don't have to take me, Mrs Butler," Eleanor said quickly.

"And when your parents ask who brought you home?" Lucy asked, ignoring the reference to her surname.

"They'll probably ask if I saw David," Eleanor replied. "If Mum had known he was here, she would have taken me home again. She said she would pick me up after church."

"Yes, I saw her and explained that you were baby-sitting for us. I said I would get you home, so she needn't find out," Lucy replied.

"Lucy!" James said.

Lucy spread her hands, and turned to her husband. "James, look, it isn't going to be easy, and they will have to know eventually, but I don't think tonight is the time."

"I'm not happy," James said.

"Okay," Lucy said, turning to Eleanor. "What do you think?"

Eleanor turned to David. "What do you think, David?"

"I agree with Lucy, Sweetheart. We need to think about our options, I mean, are you prepared to tell them tonight?"

"No, not tonight," Eleanor said quietly. "Oh, David, what are we going to do?"

For a few moments there was silence. Then James spoke. "Let's call it a day, er, an evening. Skip the tea, and take Eleanor home now, dear," he said to his wife. "Eleanor, David, I think we need to talk. When can we next meet? I'm free on Thursday evening, could you both come round?"

"I can," David said quickly, looking at Eleanor.

"Yes, I can too! Goodness, I am seventeen!" Eleanor said with some passion.

"Good," James said, and then standing up.

"Why not come for a meal?" Lucy added.

They arranged a time for Thursday and then David followed Eleanor out to Lucy's car and kissed her goodbye. "Shall I see you tomorrow lunchtime, or after work?" he asked.

"After work – I'll try and finish early."

"So," Lucy said to Eleanor, as she pulled away, "quite a day!"

"What do you mean?" Eleanor asked.

Lucy glanced at her. "Well, it's not every day that a girl gets proposed to," she said.

"Do you think I was right to say yes?" Eleanor asked.

"Pardon?" Lucy said, somewhat surprised. "Why do you say that? Isn't that what you want?"

"I just wish I was older."

"Eleanor, never wish your life away. Why do you want to be older?" Lucy asked.

"For David's sake. Does he really want to marry a teenager?"

"I don't think he would have asked you if he felt like that."

"Unless he felt obliged to ask. He was just being nice," Eleanor whispered.

"Are you serious, Elly?"

Eleanor shrugged. "And if I was older, then my parents couldn't stop me from seeing him. I feel so mixed up. On the one hand I want to see David, but on the other, I know I am disobeying them. In fact, it's the deception that really makes me feel bad."

"Perhaps you shouldn't see him until after Thursday," said.

"Why should it be any better then? Perhaps I will tell them tonight."

"Would you like me to come in with you."

"No, but I may need you to come and rescue me. They said that I was not to see him while under their roof."

"Look, leave it at least for one more day. I don't think tonight is a good idea – it would be a bad end to a good day, agree?"

Eleanor smiled. "Okay."

"And I wouldn't worry about being asked to leave home, I'm sure they don't mean it."

Eleanor turned to Lucy. "I think they were serious, Mrs Butler," she said. "And that scares me."

"Eleanor, my dear, if that should happen, we know someone who would be happy to take you in, don't we."

"But don't you see, David can't do that," Eleanor burst out. "They already think we are having," she paused, "you know. That would just confirm it in their mind. And then they would report David!"

"In which case we will have to think of something else, Eleanor."

"But am I doing the right thing, Mrs Butler?"

Lucy didn't answer, but pulled her car over and turned off the ignition. Then she turned to Eleanor. "Eleanor, as a woman, and a bit of a romantic, I find it all very exciting. However, as a pastor's wife, I can't take sides, but I can offer support. Another thing, I can't give advice on matters of the heart. James once told a friend that the woman he was involved with was totally unsuitable as a life partner. The friend didn't agree and told James where to go! End of friendship. Anyway, the friend went ahead and married the girl, and it was a disaster. So, Eleanor, you must make your own decision, sorry. Oh, and I thought I told you to call me Lucy?"

"But you will be there for me?" Eleanor asked.

"Of course, but for what it's worth – and this is not advice to marry him – with a man like David Anderson, I don't think you would need support from anyone else."

Eleanor smiled. "Thank you, er, Lucy."

Lucy dropped Eleanor outside her house. As she walked up the path, Eleanor noticed that her mother had been watching out for her, no doubt to see who brought her home.

"Hello, Mum, hello Dad," she said, as she walked into the front room. "Mum, Mrs Butler told me you went to Church. I hope you weren't rude to David."

"I didn't see him," Sheila Jenkins replied. "Anyway, I only went at the end to pick you up."

"You didn't need to do that," Eleanor said. "You don't usually do that, so why this time?"

"Isn't it obvious?" her mother replied rhetorically. Eleanor felt indignation, or was it anger rising, but she controlled herself, and decided not to react.

"David?" she asked, as though it was not obvious.

"Of course."

"How long do you intend to chaperone me, Mum?"

"Until he's out of your system and you come to your senses," Sheila Jenkins said.

"What about when I'm eighteen?" Eleanor asked, keeping her tone as gentle as she could.

"That's irrelevant, my girl," her father broke in, and speaking for the first time. "As far as we're concerned, until you go to university. So long as you live here, you obey our rules."

Eleanor could not contain herself any longer. "Then perhaps I should leave home then," she said.

"Don't be stupid, girl. Where would you go?" He paused, and then continued before she could answer. "And don't say you could go and live with him – he's not that silly."

"What do you mean?"

"You don't think a mature man – a teacher to boot – is going to risk his career over a besotted teenager do you?"

It was on the tip of Eleanor's tongue to say that David had proposed to her, but she held it in. She took a deep breath. "I think I'll go up," she said, and then standing up. "Goodnight."

"Bit early, isn't it?" her father said.

Eleanor shrugged.

"And don't think of using your phone," her mother added. "It's for emergencies."

David rode his bicycle home – his head in a spin. He had just asked Eleanor to marry him, and she had said she would. And soon. But how soon? At the end of her school year? And what about her family? Or his family – he gulped – he knew her family would be against it, but what of his family. Was his family important? They couldn't stop him, but their disapproval might, no, would make life difficult. Then his mind switched back to Eleanor and her parents. Would she manage not to tell them? They had threatened to make her leave home if she kept seeing him. But they wouldn't, would they? And how much support could he expect from James and Lucy – after all, it was James who had first spoken to him about spending too much time with Eleanor. He reached home with his head still spinning. He needed to tell someone, but why? Did he want to be talked out of it? He was horrified by the thought. He picked up the phone and dialled his daughter's number.

"Hello, Jill speaking."

"Hello, Jill," David said carefully.

"Dad! Are you all right?" she exclaimed, wondering just why he had phoned. David had spoken to her earlier, before visiting James and Lucy.

"Yes, I think I am," David replied slowly.

"You think? Well, are you or aren't you."

"Jill, I've asked Eleanor to marry me," he said in a flat voice.

"And now you regret it?" Jill asked, misinterpreting his tone of voice.

"No, no. I do want to marry her," David said more animatedly.

"You're not winding me up?" Jill asked.

"Jill! Not on something like this," he said earnestly.

"So you've asked Eleanor to marry you – and what did she say?"

"She said yes, of course."

"Of course?" Jill repeated.

"No, I didn't mean it like that. I meant that she said yes."

"Right," Jill said slowly, "let me get this right. You're getting married again. Any idea when?"

"No, not at the moment. It all happened so quickly."

"Oh! Are you having second thoughts, Dad?" David hesitated, and Jill continued. "You are, aren't you?"

"No. Well, not about me. Oh dear, I'm not explaining myself. I know what I want!" David said.

"Dad, why not come over tomorrow and we can talk. You haven't spoken to Daniel about it, have you?"

"No."

"Then don't. What time shall I expect you? For lunch?"

"Do you mind, Jill?"

"Dad! Of course I don't. Isn't that what daughters are for?"

"To check up on prospective stepmothers," David said, and they both laughed.

"Tomorrow then, Dad. Bye."

"Who was it, love?" Keith asked, as Jill rejoined him, and shaking her head.

"Dad."

"What was it about," Keith said.

"You'll never guess!"

"He's getting married?"

"What?" Jill exclaimed. "How did you know?"

Keith laughed. "I didn't. But the only things he could do that would shock you are to resign or to marry. And it's not the time to resign! Anyway, do we know her?"

"Yes."

"Go on."

"She was at Danny's wedding."

"What?" Keith sat up straight as he realised who the lady in question was. "I thought you said she was at school!"

"She is."

"Has he lost his marbles?"

"Keith! Anyway, I remember you commenting on how," Jill paused, "er, how attractive she was."

Keith shrugged. "Did I?"

Jill grinned. "Yes, and I agreed with you."

"Well, well," Keith said slowly. "So, what now? Did he say when?"

"No, but I got the impression he wanted to talk, so I've invited him over for the day, okay."

"So you can sort out his problems?" Keith asked, and laughed.

Eleanor lay on her bed, staring at the ceiling. Despite what her parents wanted, she was engaged to be

married to David Anderson. Her mind wandered. Mrs
Eleanor Anderson. She repeated it aloud, well just
audibly. It sounded all right. If only she could tell
someone. Someone with whom she could share her
happiness. Then she had a worrying thought. Had she
forced him into it? With her ultimatum about having
children sooner rather than later? Did he really want to
start again, and with a teenager? Her heart lurched at
the thought. And what about his own children? Would
they accept her? Jill had been friendly, but she wasn't
sure about Daniel. And yet Stephanie had dropped hints
about her becoming family. Yes, Stephanie liked her,
she was sure but then, she wasn't a threat to Stephanie,
was she. There was a knock on her door which brought
her back to earth with a thump. It had to be one of her
parents – or even both – and they were the last people
that she wanted to speak to at the moment. She thought
briefly about ignoring the knock, but that would have
led to another argument.

"Come in," Eleanor called, resignedly. It was her
mother.

"Hello, Dear," her mother said.

"Hello, Mum."

"How was tea?"

"It was okay – just Sunday tea. Sandwiches and cake.
The usual."

"What did you talk about?"

"Pardon?" Eleanor was momentarily stunned by the
directness of the question. "Mum," she continued,
"don't you think that that's rather personal?"

Mrs Jenkins shrugged. "Only if it's something
unsuitable."

"Well, maybe it was. Maybe I'm planning to rob a
bank!" she exclaimed.

"Eleanor, don't be silly."

"Mum, do you expect me to tell you every detail about my life, who I want to see, and why? I've been invited round again next Thursday evening. Do you want to come with me?"

"No, but I may take you and collect you."

Eleanor sat up. "Are you serious?" she gasped.

"Well, how do I know you won't go in a different direction?"

Eleanor cocked her head on one side and smiled. This was too ridiculous to believe. "Well, yes, that is possible," she replied seriously. "Will you be taking me to school next term in case I do a runner?"

"There won't be anywhere to go in term time, will there?"

"In term time? Why should that be different?" Eleanor asked.

"On your own?" her mother asked pointedly.

Eleanor smiled and said nothing. Did her parents really think they could watch her all the time? David had decided to continue at his school on a part time basis and Eleanor knew that he would be free on Wednesday afternoons. He had talked about using the time to study, but it also meant he would be free if she did skip school – not that he would let her!

"Is that it, Mum?" she asked, as pleasantly as she could.

"Eleanor, we're serious about you not seeing David Anderson."

"I can see that," Eleanor said.

"Well?"

"Well what?"

"Do you think you should disobey our wishes?"

Eleanor swung her legs off the bed. "Do you think there might be circumstances where it would be okay to disobey you?"

"Don't change the subject, Eleanor."
Eleanor stood up and looked steadily at her mother.
"Mum, we're not getting anywhere. I think I would like
to go to bed now, please."
"You'll thank us one day," Sheila Jenkins said. As she
left, Eleanor bit her lip and waited. Then she flung
herself on the bed, and sobbed quietly. It had been so
hard to be nice to her mother. "David, dear David," she
whispered into her pillow. "Please come and rescue
me."

David woke up early the next morning – far too early to
go to Jill's. His term time routine had not survived the
holiday, partly because it had not been needed, and
partly because he had used any and every opportunity
to see Eleanor. He had fitted in school preparation
round those opportunities, but with the visit to Jill on
his mind, he knew he would not be able to settle down
to academic work. Standing in his kitchen, he suddenly
spotted his new cookery book, the present from
Eleanor. He picked it up and opened it randomly. Fruit
pies. Apple pies. Blackberry pies. Gooseberry pies.
Fruit pies. His mind moved on. He had two
blackcurrant bushes and two gooseberry bushes in his
garden. Jenny had been into flowers, but these four
bushes had been his. However, since Jenny's death he
had virtually ignored them. Well, apart from picking
the fruit, which had gone first into his freezer, and then
on to Jill. That was last year. This year's harvest was
still in his freezer. He looked at the book, and then
checked off the ingredients. An hour later he had two
small pies ready for cooking. Their size was determined
by the amount of flour that he had. And he had
substituted margarine for the butter, trying to make
allowance for the fact that it was soft margarine! The

rolled out pastry seemed very similar to what he had seen Jenny make, so he had continued. The next thirty five minutes seemed more like an hour, but the pies he eventually took from the oven did look like pies! It was still too early –not even nine o'clock, so he picked up his book again and made a list of ingredients for the next attempt. Finally, he put his still warm pies into the car boot, and left.

Eleanor wondered whether her mother was serious about taking her into work – she usually rode her bicycle. It meant her mother had to go in later than usual and would then have to finish earlier than usual. Eleanor made no comment, merely thinking she would have to phone David about the change in plan. Maybe they could have their lunch together. However, by the afternoon, when she still hadn't reached him, she began to feel panicky. David, meanwhile, was oblivious to this. His time with Jill had begun with coffee and small talk over the kitchen table. She had been very amused with his presentation of two pies, but had reserved judgement until lunch time.

"Right, Dad," Jill said, coming back from putting their mugs by the dishwasher to sit opposite him. "Tell me about your reservations."
It caught him out. "Who said I had reservations?"
Jill didn't answer for a few moments. "Dad, are you marrying for, oh, how can I put it delicately?"
"No, of course not!" David exclaimed. "Is that what you think?"
"Keith did raise it as a possibility," Jill said gently.
"Oh my goodness. Is that what other people will think? I didn't realise how naive I am. Oh, poor Eleanor. No, that's not the reason, I can assure you."

12

"Okay, do you not fancy her, is that the problem?"

"Jill, I am very aware of her charms in that area, I'm not made of wood!"

"Then what is it, Dad? Is it her age?"

"Not directly,"

"What do you mean, not directly?" Jill asked.

David smiled. "I know it sounds odd, but right from the beginning her age seemed irrelevant. Okay, yes, there were times that I worried, but when we were together we were just two people."

"In love?" Jill suggested gently.

"No. Just two people with common interests. In my case I didn't allow myself to develop those kinds of feelings, because I knew she was younger!"

"Tell me about her, I mean about your, er, friendship."

Beginning with the cup of tea incident, David told how their relationship had developed, the time spent in rehearsing, the time on hold and why, and then how they had rediscovered each other.

"That was when our feelings, well, my feelings, really grew," David said. "It was good just to be with her, but at the same time I worried about how and when things would have to end. I assumed that sooner or later she would meet someone more appropriate – and if not before she went to university, then definitely when she was there. Meanwhile, I just loved being with her, sorry."

"Don't be sorry. So, what is the problem?"

David hesitated. "Jill, she's giving up everything for me. Especially education."

"Like I did for Keith?"

"Yes."

"And you were so angry at the time, weren't you," she said, smiling and reaching for his hand.

"I was, Darling. You were a high flyer!"

"But you want Eleanor to do the same for you?"

"Yes and no." David then went on to explain Eleanor's viewpoint about having children as soon as possible. "Apart from that, would you be happy to wait, what, another four years?"

"No, Darling. As I said, I am a normal man. But there is something else. Her parents have banned her from seeing me – they didn't know we were seeing each other."

"What?" Jill exclaimed. "Didn't they ask her where she went?"

"We met secretly, after church, after school, then after work, or in lunchtimes. She didn't know about the wedding!" David explained how he had collected Eleanor from camp, and how he had bought her wedding outfit before giving it to a charity shop to be bought back by Eleanor. "And I still have the shoes and handbag!" David added.

"But they found out. When?"

"Saturday." David told her about them being seen by the neighbours and their subsequent visit to his house. "They said so long as she lived at home she could not see me."

"What did they say when you told them you were engaged?"

"We weren't – not then. I only asked her to marry me yesterday."

"I thought she was not allowed to see you."

"We were both invited to tea with the pastor, and I asked her there. Her parents didn't know about it. I'm going to meet her after work today. The problem is that Eleanor hates the idea of disobeying them."

"Which means she can't marry you, Dad," Jill said.

"That's why we went to see the pastor. He suggested

that the principle to marry over-rides the obey parents
principle."

"Okay," Jill said slowly. "Now what? How old is she?"

"Seventeen, eighteen in November. We're seeing the
pastor again on Thursday to talk about things. He said
he would marry us when she is eighteen."

"Even though she's not allowed to see you? I bet her
parents will really be chuffed! And what about school?"

"I don't know," David said. "But it's not just that. By
marrying me she loses her parents."

"No she won't. They'll come round. You did."

"It's not quite the same, is it. To start with, you did
finish the sixth-form. And at least Keith wasn't old
enough to be your father."

Jill laughed. "Nowhere near!"

"But he came between you and University."

"Are you still bitter?"

"No, not at all. Not now. In fact your mum said, just
before she died, that at least you were in good hands."

"She said that?" Jill asked

"Uhuh."

"Well, I agree."

"It was the right thing for you, I can see that now,"
David told her, squeezing her hand.

"And I think marrying Eleanor is the right thing for
you. As soon as possible."

"Sure?"

"Dad, I watched you both at Daniel's wedding. Any
one who didn't know would have assumed you were
engaged, if not newly-weds."

"But we weren't wearing rings."

"Dad! That doesn't mean a thing nowadays. In fact, I
did overhear a conversation, something like, isn't that
Dan's father."

"And?"

"It was assumed that the lady was your, er, partner, a new partner."

"Is that it," David asked.

"Well, no. But I needn't go further."

"People shouldn't make assumptions."

"Dad, I think some people assumed that I was pregnant when I married Keith. I could tell by the way they looked at my tummy!"

"Oh, Jill, I am rather naive, aren't I?"

Jill sighed. "If Eleanor thinks you're as lovely as I do, then you'll be fine! Right, tell me how you made your fruit pies. Are they safe to eat?"

Chapter 2

An Unexpected Development

Before leaving Jill's, David brought up his other worry, that of his own son's reaction.

"Maybe you should both go and see them, and tell them in person," Jill added. "I don't think Stephanie will be surprised."

"Jill, how shocked were you?" David asked directly.

"Who said I was shocked, Dad?" Jill replied. "I believe that is called begging the question."

"Okay, were you shocked?"

"No. I was shocked when I first found out about her. I mean, you becoming friendly with a young woman. And as I said, just watching you both at Daniel's wedding, I could tell it was more than just being friends. Come on, Dad, you don't walk around holding anyone's hand!" She laughed. "But, yes, I didn't expect this to develop this fast. As I said, Stephanie could see that she was special, but Daniel? I think he thinks it is just an aberration, and that you will move on. Dad," she said softly, "our own father is going to marry someone younger than his kids. It is unusual, you've got to admit."

"I know, I know. I tried not to fall in love, for her sake as much as mine."

"I think Daniel may see it as you trying to replace Mum," said Jill.

"Do you know, Eleanor brought that up on the way to Daniel's wedding. I remember, we had stopped for breakfast. She said something about would she be replacing someone who should be there, namely, your mum. I pointed out that replace was not the same as displace. I used a football analogy, you are expected to replace an injured player, but an under performing player is displaced. Your mum was taken – she has not been displaced."

"In our memories, Dad," Jill said quietly

"Oh, Jill, are you saying one should never remarry? Or is it too soon? I think, no, I know that Eleanor accepts that I have memories. That's another thing that endears me to her. But I can see that it is going to be hard for you and Daniel. Boy, what about Eleanor? Put yourself in her shoes. Suppose, and I say this carefully, but suppose you lost Keith and then met another man. A man older than me. A man with adult children. It could happen, Jill!"

"I know. We have talked about it." She paused, and took a deep breath. "Dad, you are going to see Daniel as soon as possible, and you are going to take Eleanor." She hugged David. "Now let's get you on your way. You have the shopping list, right?"

They had eaten one of his fruit pies at lunch-time, when David had then been told why he should have used butter, or at least a hard margarine in the pastry, and why the recipe included corn flour! They had laughed, and Jill had insisted that he took the other pie back to show Eleanor.

"But why?"

"It will make her laugh!"

"At me!"

"Yes, Dad, at you. But it will do her good, remember the saying, laughter is the best medicine."

Jill had added to his shopping list because he had insisted that he wanted to try again at making another fruit pie. However, because he was later than he had intended to be, he drove straight to Eleanor's workplace rather than go home or shopping first. It would mean that he would not be able to ride home with her on his bicycle, but he did want to see her. It also meant that he didn't find the

message from Eleanor on his answer phone! Leaving his car in the car park, he walked round to the door where she usually left, and not really looking where he was going.
"What are you doing here?"
He stopped short and looked up, recognising immediately the aggressive female tone of Eleanor's mother. For a moment he felt anger – who was she to challenge him? It wasn't her business. However, he managed to control his anger.
"I've come to meet Eleanor," he said calmly.
"Well, you needn't have bothered, I'm taking her home. I thought we made it clear that we don't want you seeing our daughter."
"You made it perfectly clear," David replied slowly.
"So, you may as well go."
"Sorry, Mrs Jenkins, but I have as much right to be here as you."
"I won't let her speak to you," she added.
David just smiled and then took up a position to wait in a better place than Sheila Jenkins.
"Have you been waiting long," David asked politely, and looking at Mrs Jenkins. She didn't answer, but David continued. "So you've had to leave work early, then?"
This time Sheila Jenkins turned away, which made David smile because she could now not see the exit so well.
David looked at his watch – any moment now. Wow, he had nearly missed her, and he would not have known. He meant to have kept his eyes on the door, but a movement from Sheila Jenkins distracted him. She was taking out her mobile phone, and …
"David!" It was Eleanor. "What are you doing here?"
Sheila Jenkins heard her and spun round, removing her phone from her ear. "Eleanor! Come with me."
Eleanor looked at her, then back to David. For a moment she hesitated, then she walked across to David. "I've been

trying to phone you – all day. Where have you been?" she said quietly.

"I've been to Jill's, Sweetheart. I'm sorry."

"Eleanor, I'm waiting!" It was a bark of a command.

"Have you told them?" David asked. "About us," he added quietly.

"No. David, do you still want me?"

"What? Yes of course I do, silly girl!"

Eleanor reached for David's hand, and turned back to her mother.

"Mum, I'm going to marry David," she said quietly, but firmly.

It was almost as if Mrs Jenkins did not hear. There was no reaction. "Rubbish, now come with me."

"Mum! You didn't hear. I said I'm going to marry David."

Sheila Jenkins ignored Eleanor and addressed herself to David. "If you had any decency, you'd tell her to do what I say. I thought Christian children were supposed to obey their parents."

"It also says not to provoke your children," David replied evenly.

"For the last time, will you come with me, Eleanor?"

"And will you let me see David later?" Eleanor replied, still holding onto David's hand.

"You heard what your father said. Not while you live with us."

"Then I'll leave," Eleanor said.

For a moment, David thought she would come across and try to physically drag Eleanor away. But she didn't.

"Right," she said. "So be it!" She paused, and drew herself up. "I'll put your things on the doorstep. You can pick them up later!" And with that, she turned and marched away.

David and Eleanor stared at the retreating figure of Sheila Jenkins.

"Oh David. What have I done?" Eleanor gasped.

"I think you have just burnt your boats, Sweetheart," David replied.

"Do you think she meant it about putting my things on the doorstep?"

"I don't know," David replied slowly. "Maybe she hopes you will beg to be allowed back in."

"I will only go back on my terms," Eleanor said bravely. David put his arm round Eleanor. "Then we won't rush," he said. "And when we do go, we'll soon see if the doorstep is clear! Meanwhile, we need to think about the alternative, oh, and eating."

"Eating! I don't feel like eating!" Eleanor gasped.

"All right, but we must think about what to do if they do put your stuff out. We need to find somewhere for you to stay."

"Won't I stay with you, David?"

David took his arm from her shoulder and turned her to face him. He then kissed her gently.

"Eleanor, one day you will, but not tonight. We're not going to give them more ammunition."

"Ammunition?"

"Yes, they will accuse me of taking advantage of you. If you stay with me they will assume that I'm sleeping with you."

"But David, I don't have anywhere else to go!"

"Let's go and talk to James. If all else fails, I'll take you to my daughter. Come on."

David still found it hard to believe that Eleanor would not be allowed home. His suggestion that Jill would be available was made in order to keep her spirits up. However, he did think that Eleanor had to establish her right to see him; so to rush her straight home would not be of benefit. He was not sure how James could help, but it would give them some breathing space. It did not take long to reach their house, but now a new problem presented itself. Neither James or Lucy were at home.

"Bother," David said, as they turned away from the front door.

"Now what do we do?" Eleanor said.

"Well, we could just drive past and check that nothing has been put out," David said.

"And if it has?"

"Eleanor, it won't be. We'll go and eat. Then I'll take you home," David said.

"Will you come in with me?"

"Of course. I wish you hadn't mentioned marriage though."

Eleanor looked surprised, then hurt. "But I thought," she began.

"I do, Sweetheart," David said quickly, "but I think maybe we should have moved more slowly."

Eleanor's eyes filled with tears. "I'm sorry."

David hugged and kissed her. "What's done is done. Come on, let's go and look."

They drove in silence, each deep in their own thoughts. David turned into her road, and held his breath as he approached her house.

"There's nothing there, David. She didn't mean it," Eleanor exclaimed.

"There, I said things would be okay. Right, let's go and have something to eat, then we'll go back to face the music."

David had eaten a cooked meal at Jill's, whereas Eleanor had only eaten sandwiches. David suggested that he took Eleanor out for a meal, but she said she didn't want that.

In the end, David bought fish and chips for them both, which they took to David's house. Eleanor was still subdued – until it came to eating his second fruit pie. As Jill had forecast, when Eleanor learnt how David had made two pies and had altered the recipe, she laughed.

"I should be hurt," David said seriously, "but at least it's made you smile." He paused. "Actually, I made them like that deliberately. Just to make you laugh."

Eleanor looked at him, then she burst out laughing again. "David Anderson, you're a poor liar."

"Well, I thought it was okay," David said. "I liked it."

"So did I," Eleanor said, but making a show of crossing her fingers and then laughing again. Then she suddenly became serious. "Do you think we should go."

"If you like," David said.

"I don't like," Eleanor said, "but I suppose we had better go and face the music."

Eleanor seemed to believe that she would be going home, but she was still worried by the situation.

"You will come in, won't you," Eleanor said, as they pulled into her road.

"If they let me," David said.

"I won't go in if you can't come in," she said.

However, the discussion was irrelevant.

"David!" Eleanor gasped, and seized David's arm.

"I don't believe it," he muttered. But it was true. There were two big cardboard cartons, three plastic bin liners, and Eleanor's bicycle by the front door step.

"Now what do we do?" she said.

"That's up to you, Eleanor."

"What do you mean?"

"I said that you had burnt your boats, well, you haven't – not quite yet. Maybe they're expecting you to knock on the door and apologise."

"Or I can ask you for matches!" she said.

"I don't have any matches, Eleanor. You're not thinking of burning their house down are you?" David said rather shocked.

"No, silly man. I was speaking metaphorically. Will you help me load the car?"

"Is that what you want?" David asked.

"Is that what you want?" Eleanor replied.

"You know I do, Sweetheart."

"Then let's do it."

It was the work of minutes. Eleanor didn't even examine the contents.

"What about your bike?" David whispered, even though they were standing by his car. He had closed the boot lid as quietly as he could.

"You go ahead, and I'll ride it. Meet you there."

"I wonder if they were listening by the door."

"So what," Eleanor said, with a shrug.

"You're taking it very calmly."

"What choice do I have?" she replied. "Now go, please. Just go!"

David arrived before Eleanor and unpacked the car. After a moment's hesitation, he carried her things up stairs and put them into Jill's old room, then into his study, and then back into Jill's room. He knew that his house would become Eleanor's new home, but as from when, he wasn't sure. His next concern was where Eleanor could stay that night. He had mentioned his daughter, but that wasn't the most convenient. Eleanor would need to sort out her possessions. There was also her work the next morning. He thought of James and Lucy and decided against it, but wasn't quite sure why. He heard his front-door bell ring, and his heart lurched. Surely her parents hadn't arrived already?

"Eleanor!" he gasped on opening the door. "Come in!"
He held her tight and kissed her, before he realised that
her cheeks were wet.

"Eleanor! You've been crying!"

"Sorry," she said.

"Don't be sorry," David said, pulling out a handkerchief
and wiping her cheeks. "Do you want to tell me about it?"
Eleanor smiled – the smile that still made his heart lurch.
"It was as I rode away – it just hit me. I cried and cried as
I rode – goodness knows if anyone saw me. Now I feel
better, much better. It won't happen again."

"It probably will, Sweetheart," David said gently.
"Anyway, why did you ring the bell? The door wasn't
locked. It's your home now." He paused. "I thought it
was your parents coming to take you home."

"Take me home? But you said this was my home!"

"You know what I mean. Wait a moment." David reached
across the hallway. "Here you are, your own key!" At
this, she collapsed into sobbing again and David held her.

"See," he whispered, "I said it would happen again."

"It's your fault," she said, pulling herself together, and
smiling at him.

"Yes, Dear," David said, in mock humility.

"We'd better check your things," David said.

"Oh, yes. Where are they?"

"I took them upstairs. There was no point in leaving them
in the car, was there?"

David followed Eleanor up, and directed her into Jill's
old room. The five packages were on the bed. Eleanor
looked into one of the cartons. "Oh. Things from my
dressing table, oh, and my top drawer."

"Such as?"

"Hair brush, make up, oh my driving licence – I wonder if

they realised, jewellery – well, not real jewellery, knick-knacks." She looked up and grinned. "Knickers. Oh, and ladies items."

"I know what you mean," he said quickly.

She turned to the second cartoon. "Ah, things from my desk. Ear phones. Books, ah, pens etcetera." She then looked into the plastic bags. "They have just emptied the contents of my three clothes drawers here. Tops. Tee shirts. Undies. Night clothes. Woollies. Shirts. All jumbled up – how could they?" she asked, turning to David.

"More tears?" David asked gently.

"No! I'm angry now. There's nothing from my wardrobe. My new dress – the one you bought. And no shoes. No dressing gown."

"There's a pair of your shoes here, remember?"

"That's not the point," she said. "They're my things!"

"We could go back tonight."

"No. I'm so angry, David, I would say things I shouldn't. Hey; I still have a key. Let's go back tomorrow when they're at work."

David hesitated. "Do you think we should? It sounds like breaking and entering."

"David, I have a key! They're my things!"

"Okay, when? You're at work tomorrow."

"Could you pick me up from work at lunch-time? Please?"

"I'm not happy," David said.

Eleanor put her arms round him. "Darling, if I leave them there, it's as if I still partially live there, isn't it?"

David grinned, and kissed her. "All right. Now we have to sort out tonight. But first a cup of tea!"

"Tonight?"

"Shush. Go and put the kettle on, woman!"

David waited until they were sitting in the lounge. "Right, I've been thinking."
Eleanor resisted the urge to make a facetious comment, and waited.
"As I explained earlier, I don't think you should stay here. It's too late to go to Jill's, and anyway, you're expected at work tomorrow. I did think about James and Lucy, but I don't want to put any pressure on them."
"Pressure?"
"Yes, I know they said they would support us, but just suppose, for a moment, that they thought you should go back home tonight. That would put them in a spot; to say that and upset you, or not say it, and go against their conscience. By Thursday, it will be too late, and there is the chance that your parents will back down."
"I'm not going back!"
"Sweetheart. Suppose they apologise and say that we can see each other."
"They won't!"
"Eleanor, stop it. I said suppose. Doesn't your vocabulary include the word forgive?"
"David, that was unfair!"
"I know," he said quietly. "If it helps, Sweetheart, I know a little of how you feel. We didn't want Jill to marry Keith. I was very angry and bitter at the time."
"You've never said."
"And maybe I shouldn't have been angry, sorry. Look, part of me hopes your mum and dad don't back down. It's like Saint Augustine's prayer, Lord, grant me chastity, but not yet. I hope they do relent, but not tonight. You couldn't take the emotional upheaval, and maybe, nor could I. So, back to tonight! I was thinking of a Travel Lodge, or similar."
"No!"
David looked at her. "We're not married, and even if you

were, you wouldn't be bound to obey me, despite what you told James about wedding vows."

"David, are you making me."

"No, I'm asking. I will take you, and collect you tomorrow morning."

"All right."

David just stopped himself from saying 'good girl.'

"Thank you, Eleanor," he said.

Eleanor sorted through her bag and boxes, and put a few things into David's cabin case. There wasn't much she could pack.

"It's mainly what I'm standing in. No wash things. No toothbrush or tooth paste. Just knickers, tee shirt and socks. Even my skirts and jeans are still at home – whoops, my parent's house. David, will I keep my clothes here and how long will I be staying in a hotel? Won't it cost you a fortune?"

"Look, love, if you have to move in here, so be it. But not tonight. Maybe up to a week, but definitely not until we have seen James and Lucy. You can have my toothbrush and toothpaste, oh, and shampoo."

"Share a toothbrush?"

"That's a point. No more kissing, especially French kissing. Too unhygienic!" he said, but with a twinkle in his eye.

"What do you mean – French kissing? What is it? Are you going to show me?" she asked slyly, and with a twinkle in her eye.

David smacked her bottom – gently of course. "I hope I don't regret this," he said.

"Regret what?"

"Marrying a modern bolshey Miss."

Eleanor put her arms round his neck, and kissed him hard on his lips. Then she touched her tongue on his lips.

28

David pulled away quickly. "Eleanor, no," he said. "Not tonight."

There was a Travel Lodge about twenty minutes drive away and David followed Eleanor in as she wheeled his cabin case. They had stopped on the way for David to withdraw cash from a cash machine.
"A room for the night, please," she said. "You have a reservation in my name – Eleanor Jenkins."
The receptionist looked at her, trying to sum her up. Eleanor did not look like a professional business woman, nor did she look like a woman who had an unsavoury occupation.
"Do you have any identification," she asked. Eleanor hesitated, and looked at David.
"Your driving licence?" he said.
"Oh, yes." She reached into her bag, the bag David had bought for the wedding. "Good job you made me bring it."
The receptionist looked at it, and did a mental calculation. "You're seventeen?"
"Yes,"
"How do you wish to pay?"
"I have cash," Eleanor said.
"Sorry, Madam, we only take cards."
"Can you charge it to me?" David said, taking out his credit card and stepping forward.
"Are you related, Sir?" the receptionist asked.
David looked her in the eye. "This young lady is a good friend of my daughter-in-law and has nowhere to stay. I made the reservation, what, thirty minutes ago. If you're not happy, then please get me the manager."

There was no more hassle and David followed Eleanor to her room.

"Have an early night, Sweetheart, and I'll call for you at about half-past seven," David said.

"Seven-thirty?"

"Don't you want to have breakfast with your fiancé?"

"Yes, or course," she said, with a smile. Then her face changed. "I do wish you would stay," she added.

"Eleanor!" David said, shocked by her suggestion.

"No, I don't mean for that," she said quickly. "Just as a friend."

"I'd like to stay as a friend, Sweetheart, but you're more than a friend. You're the woman I'm going to marry. Eleanor, a man's desire for his wife doesn't suddenly start on the day he gets married. Please understand."

Eleanor grinned at him, a wicked grin. "I do. Do you remember how embarrassed you were that time you had to rub cream on my back?"

"How could I ever forget?" David said.

"I haven't forgotten either. I liked it, I mean, I liked you touching me."

"Eleanor!"

She grinned. "I rather fancied you then, but I didn't expect anything to come of it. I told myself that I had a silly school-girl crush on you, like some girls did on their teacher." She paused. "Do you remember going to the lido?"

"Of course I do, silly. It wasn't that long ago!"

"What was I wearing?" Eleanor asked.

"You know what you were wearing!"

"I bought it especially."

"What? But you apologised for wearing it."

"I know. I was trying to be modest – in word, but not in deed! Did you like it?"

"Eleanor!"

"Well?"

"Okay, yes I did."

"Good. I did notice you looking at me."

"You did not!" David expostulated.

"Oh, David. You are funny. You must have noticed lots of girls, so if you didn't notice me, then I am very, very offended."

"I did, Sweetheart. But we weren't engaged then. I was in love with you, but I didn't want to be."

"Didn't want to be? Keep digging!" she said, and laughed.

"I'm going home," David said. He took her in his arms, kissed her passionately and then turned to go.

"Hang on, I'm coming to see you off," she said. "It's okay; I'll be your daughter's friend in public."

"It was my daughter-in-law, Stephanie! It suddenly came to me, thank goodness," he said, as they left the room.

Chapter 3

Mrs Hayes to the Rescue

Eleanor was already waiting outside when David arrived at seven twenty-five. She recognised the car, and walked towards him, pulling the almost empty case. David kissed her cheek, lifted the case into his boot, and then joined her in the car.

"Do I get a proper kiss now," Eleanor asked. "Now I'm not your daughter-in-law's friend?" It was a proper kiss, but still fairly brief. "Hm," Eleanor said, "perhaps you didn't miss me as much as I missed you." This time it lasted longer.

"The lady on reception asked me about tonight," Eleanor said. "I said I didn't know. Did my parents contact you?"

"No, Eleanor," David replied sadly. "That's one of the reasons I wanted you out of my house. Just in case."

"Can I come home, then? I can't live in a hotel for ever, can I?"

David sighed. "Don't rush me, dear."

"Okay, what's for breakfast?" she asked, changing the subject.

"Well, if I was alone, it would be cereal and coffee. But since I have an important guest, she can choose."

"David," Eleanor said quietly. "How long are you going to think of me as a guest? You gave me a key yesterday."

"Eleanor, Eleanor. I am sorry. Of course you're not a guest. Look, I had to get used to being married, then to being single again. I will change, honest, but it might take me longer than it should. What would you like for breakfast?"

"I'll have the same as you," she said.

"How does your mum organise breakfast," David asked, they walked into his house.

"It depends," Eleanor replied.

"On?" David prompted.

"What day it is."

"Go on."

"Okay. For years we all sat at the table, you know, together. On weekends we eat on our laps, in front of the telly. Why?"

"I sit in front of the telly! Your mum wouldn't approve." Eleanor laughed. "What's that got to do with it?"

"But we had family breakfast when the children were growing up," David added.

"So when we have a family, that's what we will do," Eleanor said.

"Eleanor, pet, not all couples can have children," David said quietly.

"Yes, I do know that. Okay, if we have a family," she said,

"I hope we do," David said.

"Do you, really?"

David took her hand and pulled her round.

"Yes, and for several reasons!"

"Several? What are they?"

"Okay, one. I think you are born for motherhood. Two, I think every woman has broody genes, as I call them. And three, well ..." he hesitated.

"Go on."

"Okay, by the laws of statistics, you will be a widow, rather than me be a widower."

"That's obvious."

"A relatively young widow. I hope you will find some comfort in having a family. It helped me."

"Then the sooner we start trying, the better," Eleanor said. "I'll be eighteen in November."

"I know that, pet. Mind you, I don't know the actual date!"

"Don't you? It's November the fifteenth. I was ten days overdue!"

"Good. That gives me plenty of time to look for a card."

"And a present?" she asked, with a twinkle in her eye.

"You'll have to give a list of ideas. I was no good at presents – didn't you hear how Nicola had to help me?"

"Yes," Eleanor said sharply.

"Eleanor?"

"Okay, so I was jealous,"

"Oh, Eleanor," he said laughing. "There was nothing to be jealous about. Anyway, make a little list!"

"I already have an idea."

"Which is?"

"I'll tell you later. Come on, I don't want to be late for work."

David dropped Eleanor off at work, and then drove straight round to see James. Lucy was surprised to see him, and showed him up to James' study. James was surrounded by books and in the middle of sermon preparation.

"Oh," David said, "sorry, I didn't realise." He remembered that James was usually unavailable on sermon preparation days.

James shrugged. "Problems?"

David nodded. "But they can wait until Thursday."

"Tell me now, and I'll have time to ponder," James said.

"No," David said, although hesitantly.

"David, from the look on your face, and the fact Lucy brought you up, I can tell something's on your mind."

"Okay." Starting with how he had met Eleanor from work, he told James the whole story up to the fact that she was now with him. "And we're planning to get the rest of her things this lunch-time," he added.

"Breaking and entering?" James said.

"Eleanor pointed out that since she still had a key, it won't be breaking in. I had half expected that her parents would arrive on my doorstep late last night. That's partly why I bundled her off to the Travel Lodge, so that they couldn't accuse me of seducing their precious daughter. But I don't think Eleanor will agree to staying there for ever, I mean until we can marry. I know you won't be happy, but I think she will have to move in with me – into the spare room of course!"

James grinned, which David thought was inappropriate. "Then my news will make you feel much better. Lucy and I were talking. We didn't expect Eleanor to be asked to leave, but we did make contingency plans. You know Mrs Hayes, she lost her husband, what three or four years ago? Lucy and I went to see her yesterday, and without mentioning names, we explained that we knew of a young woman who might need a home for a while. Not permanent!"

"And?"

"She said she'd be happy to help – and for nothing!"

"No, of course I will pay – that's assuming Eleanor is happy with the idea. So what do I do next? Won't she need to meet Eleanor first?"

"Of course. In fact she seemed quite excited. I said I would ask you to take her round as soon as possible."

"You mentioned me?" David gasped.

"Not by name. We said that her acting guardian would take her as soon as possible."

"Acting guardian? Is that legal?"

"Probably not, but what else are you at this moment in time?"

"So you think it's okay if we go and see Mrs Hayes today, well, after I've spoken to Eleanor?"

"As soon as possible. I hope Eleanor doesn't feel that it was none of my business," James said.

"I'm sure she'll understand. We actually came to see you yesterday! So," David stood up, "I'll let you get on again. Thanks James, you've made my day! Bye."

David met Eleanor as arranged at lunch-time, taking care to check that her mother was also not waiting. It wasn't that he thought that she might persuade Eleanor to return with her, he wanted to avoid unpleasantness.

He greeted her with a kiss. "Hello, Sweetheart, any chance of you having the afternoon off?" he asked.

"Why, are you going to whisk me off to Gretna?" she answered, laughing.

"We would need more than an afternoon. And they don't do same-day weddings. There's official paperwork, and a fifteen day period. And you need your birth certificate. Oh! Do you know where your birth certificate is?"

"There's a box with things like that. Yes, I know where it is. My passport is there too."

"Good, but back to you having the afternoon off. Any chance?" David asked.

"I did ask if I could have two hours. Do you think that we need more time?"

"Yes, but if it's not possible, don't worry."

"All right, I'll go and ask."

Eleanor returned in about five minutes, with a big smile.

"I explained that I needed to move home and Adam said I can take as long as I like," she said.

"Right, let's go."

David was dreading the operation, but it ran very smoothly. He made Eleanor go ahead and check that she could get in and that nobody was at home. She reappeared at the front door holding her guitar and waved him closer, so he then drove closer and parked outside.

"They didn't put my guitar outside," she said.

"That was a good thing, wasn't it?" David answered.

"Unless they wanted me to knock and ask for it! Anyway, can you bring the bags and boxes and help me?"

David felt very uncomfortable, but he knew it had to be done. Working fast, they emptied her wardrobe first. Then she took two pictures down. There were more things in her desk drawer, including photos and her CD player.

"What about your CDs."

"Oh, yes. Hand me another box, please David."

"Computer?"

Eleanor hesitated. "It's not really mine!"

"But the data on it is. Let's borrow it. Right, what about documents – passport, birth certificate?"

"Certificates!" She jumped onto a chair and took a box from the top of her wardrobe. "Certificates, and other stuff from the past," she said. Then she ran downstairs to find the box with her passport and birth certificate. Meanwhile, David began to take the boxes and bags to his car. Twenty five minutes later they drove away, and David heaved a sigh of relief.

"Wow, we've done it," Eleanor chortled.

"Not quite. The computer," David said.

"Oh."

"I'm going to a friend right now. Assuming he's at home, he'll be able to get the data off. And hopefully now!"

David was lucky. His friend was at home, and within minutes he had removed the hard drive, and copied it to his own. Then he deleted all her old files. It was an old computer, with a relatively small drive, so he sent several very large files of rubbish back to the hard drive, enough to over-write the deleted files and nearly fill the drive. David knew that deleted data was not in fact deleted from the drive. By saving new data over it, even rubbish, it made it impossible for any ordinary person to see what had been on the drive. David drove back to Eleanor's old house, and she replaced the computer in her old room.

"What about the posters?" David asked.

Eleanor smiled at David. "They're part of my old life. Goodbye bedroom," she said. "David, please take me home."

As they unloaded David's car, he noticed a difference. All the time they had been collecting her things, she had been tense, which was understandable, but now there was a lightness in her step. She hummed as they unloaded the car and took her things up to Jill's room. There were boxes and bags waiting to be unpacked strewn across the floor and on the bed.

"Where to start?" she said, with her hands on her hips. Then she turned and flung her arms round David's neck. "Thank you, thank you, David," she said. She looked at her watch. "I won't be too late back to work, will I?" she added. "Then I'll have to sort out all this. Will I be sleeping here tonight?" She paused, and her face dropped. "Please don't send me back to the Travel Lodge. I won't tell people if you let me stay here."

"You're not going back to the hotel, Sweetheart," David said.

Her face lit up. "Really? Am I staying here?"

"Not in the long term. I went to see James this morning, and, well, do you know Mrs Hayes?"

Eleanor wrinkled her face as she thought. "Yes, I think

so, why?"

"James asked her if she could help a homeless waif," David said, with a straight face.

"He didn't!" Eleanor said emphatically.

David laughed. "Okay, not those exact words. He went with Lucy and they said they knew of a young woman who might need a home for a while."

"Young woman? He didn't tell her that I was a school-girl?" Eleanor asked, opening her eyes wider.

"I don't know the details, it's just she said she would help."

"But what about school?"

"One thing at a time, Sweetheart. First, are you happy about staying with Mrs Hayes."

"Would she let me see my boyfriend," Eleanor asked, with a straight face.

"Oh. James didn't say if he mentioned anything about me. I hope it's okay."

"David," Eleanor said, laughing. "Of course it will be okay! James wouldn't arrange it otherwise, would he? When do I go?"

"Well, that's why I suggested that you took the afternoon off. We ought to go and see her this afternoon."

"Why the rush? I ought to go back to work first – Adam, my boss, is expecting me," Eleanor said. "And anyway, she may not be in!" she added.

"In which case, I'll take you on into work. I know, phone him now and tell him that something has come up. Do you want me to speak to him?"

"David, I'm not a child," Eleanor said, very sweetly.

"Sorry. I know you're not. I guess I've got things on my mind," he replied quickly.

"Okay, I'll phone him."

Although David was grateful for the offer of
accommodation, he was worried about meeting Mrs
Hayes. Although he knew who she was, he didn't really
know her well. He did remember her husband dying,
because at the time Mr Hayes had only just retired. Jenny
had sent a card on their behalf, he remembered. Someone
had mentioned to him that the couple had made plans for
their retirement together, and one year later, he had gone.
It should have focused David and Jenny's minds on the
frailty of life, but it did nothing to prepare them for
Jenny's death, what, just over a year later. Mrs Hayes had
sent a card, he did remember that, but he had never
thanked her. He wondered just how much information
James had given her. Did she know that Eleanor was a
schoolgirl, or even under eighteen? Would she want to
speak to Eleanor's parents, in which case she might
withdraw her offer. Then there was his own position –
what was it? Acting guardian! Perhaps Lucy should have
taken Eleanor round. Eleanor came back from the phone.
"Adam was very good about it. I even offered to work
late if he needed me."
"Oh?"
"Well, it could be a brief visit – all over by say three!"
she said.
"We'll see," David said, deliberately vaguely. He had
other plans as well. "Oh, one more thing, Sweetheart,
would you mind changing first?"

"What? I mean pardon?" Eleanor said.
"I was thinking of your new dress," David continued,
unabashed
"But I'm going onto work afterwards, aren't I? Adam will
think I've been out enjoying myself."
"Please!" David said.

"You explain to me why. Is it to impress Mrs Hayes?
She's seen me in jeans before."

"Eleanor, I'm just asking."

"Why can't you tell me?"

"Because, because – oh, Eleanor, please trust me. Look,
we'll take your jeans for you to change into."

"Is it because you don't like me in jeans?" she asked.

"You look very nice in jeans."

"But nicer in a skirt?"

"That's not what I was saying."

"But it's true?"

"Eleanor, okay, yes it's true. But that's not the reason
right now. I don't want to tell you why, so we'll leave it."

"David, where are the sandals, and the bag?"

"Upstairs, why?"

"Cos I'll need them with the dress, silly man. Go on, go
and get them."

Mrs Hayes lived in a small cottage about a mile away.
Her front garden was full of flowers, and she was out in
the garden when David and Eleanor arrived. She looked
at them with a detached look, but then she suddenly
smiled as she recognised them, and walked towards the
gate.

"Hello, it's Eleanor isn't it?" she said. "And Mr
Anderson."

"Yes, hello Mrs Hayes. How are you?"

"I'm very well, thank you," she replied. "And you?"

"I'm very well too, Mrs Hayes. Mrs Hayes, I believe the
pastor and his wife came to see you yesterday?" David
said.

"They did, yes." She turned to Eleanor. "And are you the
young lady?"

"Yes, Mrs Hayes." Eleanor said.

"Then you'd better come in, my dear," she said, opening the little gate. She looked at David. "Would you like to come in too, Mr Anderson?"
"Yes please, Mrs Hayes. Thank you."

David followed Eleanor and Mrs Hayes up her short garden path.
"I like your garden, Mrs Hayes," Eleanor said.
"It keeps me busy, my dear. It was my husband's interest and I have had to learn quite a lot since he passed away. Are you interested in gardening?"
"I've never had the opportunity, Mrs Hayes. My mum did the garden, Dad wasn't interested."
"So, have you fallen out with your mum and dad," she asked.
Eleanor stopped, and Mrs Hayes turned to her. "It's complicated, Mrs Hayes," Eleanor said quietly. "It's not possible for me to live there now, so if you don't want me, I'll understand."
"Is it anything to do with the young man behind us," Mrs Hayes asked.
"Why are you asking that, Mrs Hayes," Eleanor asked.
Mrs Hayes looked at Eleanor as if to say "well?" And waited.
"Yes," Eleanor whispered.
"I did wonder when I saw who brought you."
"Did you?"
"You sang together a few times, didn't you?"
"Yes," Eleanor said, and waited.

Mrs Hayes took one of Eleanor's hands, and held it with two of her own. "Eleanor, my dear, don't look so worried. If the pastor is happy about the situation, then who am I to say otherwise?"

"Er, I don't think anyone is happy with the situation, Mrs Hayes," David said, interrupting. "It's just that her parents said that we were not allowed to be friends."
"They put my things out on the doorstep," Eleanor said. Then she crumpled into tears. Mrs Hayes put her arms round her and held her as she sobbed for a few moments. Then she suddenly pulled away, and turned to David, who held her tight.
"I'll put the kettle on," Mrs Hayes said. "Just bring her in when she's ready, Mr Anderson."
David smiled and nodded. "I'm sorry, Pet," he whispered. "Do you want me to take you home, I mean, your home?"
"No, no, no! You don't understand! I'm not sad that I'm leaving; it's just that they made me choose! I would have been leaving anyway in a year's time."
"Why?" David said thoughtlessly.
Eleanor looked at him. "If I hadn't met you I'd have gone to university."
"Yes, yes of course," he muttered. However, it felt as though a knife had been plunged into his heart. He was responsible not only for breaking Eleanor's relationship with her family. He was responsible for the fact that now she would not be going to university – well, if they wanted a family. And the idea of a family with Eleanor, which once would have been unthinkable, was now something he was beginning to look forward to more and more. "Let's go in, Sweetheart," he whispered, gently manoeuvring her in the direction of Mrs Hayes' front door.

Mrs Hayes ushered them into her front room. "Make yourselves comfortable," she said. "The tea's nearly ready."
Eleanor and David sat together on her settee, and waited. Eleanor slipped her hand into David's and felt him

squeeze it. They waited for a couple of minutes, and then Mrs Hayes wheeled a tea trolley in, which also had a plate of cakes.

"Mrs Hayes," Eleanor said, "can I tell you my story before you begin?"

Mrs Hayes left her trolley and sat, her hands on her lap. Eleanor glanced at David, and then turned back to Mrs Hayes. "I got to know David, er, Mr Anderson, just over a year ago. He helped Tom and me with his guitar. Then, when Tom went off to University, David, I mean Mr Anderson took over. Well, eventually, someone decided that it wasn't a good idea that the two of us spent so much time practising, so the pastor spoke to David, and the singing was stopped. I really missed seeing him, but," she shrugged, "there was nothing I could do about it. Then, one day, something happened that brought us together, and we both realised how much we had missed each other, so we renewed our friendship. David was insistent that we were discreet, but mum and dad found out. They said that I could not see David and stay at home, so I chose David."

"Is this, er, friendship a serious friendship?" Mrs Hayes asked.

Eleanor looked at David. "Mrs Hayes, I am very, very serious about Eleanor. I wouldn't do anything to hurt her," David said.

Mrs Hayes looked at Eleanor again. "How old are you, Eleanor?"

Eleanor looked down. "Seventeen, Mrs Hayes," she said.

Mrs Hayes did not respond to this, but picked up a small china jug. "Milk, Eleanor, David?"

"Please."

"Yes please."

Mrs Hayes poured three cups and handed two to her

guests, and then took a sip from her own cup. David and Eleanor held their cups and waited.

"What is the situation at the moment, then?" Mrs Hayes asked Eleanor.

"They put my things outside their front door last night, so David took me to a Travel Lodge. But I hated it, so he said I could stay with him tonight." She paused. "But I know he's not happy about it."

"So would today suit you?" Mrs Hayes asked.

"Oh, Mrs Hayes, thank you," Eleanor squealed.

"Yes, thank you, Mrs Hayes," David said.

Twenty minutes later, David suggested that he ought to take Eleanor to work. The plan was for Eleanor to move in with a few clothes after work, and then sort out what she wanted to take and what she wanted to leave at David's over the next few days. When Mrs Hayes asked about giving Eleanor a meal that night, David said he would be taking Eleanor out for a meal. As they left, David turned to Mrs Hayes.

"Mrs Hayes, we haven't talked about paying you. You let me know, and I'll deal with it."

"Tush, young man. Who said anything about paying?" David took her hands in his. "I just did."

"I'll think about it," she said, smiling at him. "See you later, my dear," she then said to Eleanor.

"Sweetheart, I need to do something in town on the way to work."

"How long?" Eleanor asked, feeling dubious.

"As quickly as possible. Promise. And I'll come in and take the blame at work!"

Eleanor laughed. "You are so silly at times, okay. But you realise we haven't eaten, well, I haven't."

David struck his forehead with his hand. "Duh!" he said. "We'll buy a sandwich in Marks in town."

David parked in the multi-storey park and then took Eleanor's hand to lead her down the stairs. At the bottom, he turned right. Eleanor pulled him up.

"Marks is that way," she said, pointing in the opposite direction.

"Bear with me," he said, tugging on her arm.

She allowed him to lead her away, wondering what the urgency was. Suddenly he veered sideways, pulling her into a shop.

"Ow," she exclaimed. "David!" Then, "David," as she realised that it was a jeweller's. She pulled him back and took both of his hands. "Are you serious?" she whispered.

"Of course I'm serious," he said, feeling slightly aggrieved.

She recognised the hurt look. "Sorry. It just caught me out. I wasn't expecting it."

"What? Never?"

"Not never! I did think of putting it on my birthday present list though," she said, smiling at him. "You do realise I'm not used to getting engaged," she added.

"Good," David said. He took her hand and led her to the counter where an assistant was waiting. "We would like to look at engagement rings, please."

Chapter 4

Marriage Nerves

Twenty minutes later David glanced at his watch.
"Eleanor, do you think we should come back later?"
"Sorry, David. All right."
"Wasn't there anything you liked?"
"They're all very nice."
"When you said about putting a ring on your birthday
present list, did you expect me to choose it?"
"Well," she said.
"Go on, well what?"
Eleanor pulled David away from the latest tray of rings,
and away from the assistant. "I did see a ring I liked in a
shop down the road," she whispered in his ear.
"Why didn't you say?"
"You didn't give me a chance. I thought we were going
for a sandwich!"
David grinned. "I wanted to surprise you!"
"Well, you certainly did that," she said.
"Anyway, how far away is this shop?"
"Not far."
David turned back to the assistant. "I am very sorry, but
she can't find what she wants at the moment and," David
glanced at his watch, "this is meant to be in lunch-break
time."

"Why did you say at the moment? I didn't like any of
them!" Eleanor said as they hurried to the other shop.
"Well, I hope the one you like is still there, otherwise we
may have to go back. There must be loads more to look
at."
"At a price!"

David stopped her. "Eleanor, price is not an issue!"

She grinned. "So a hundred thousand is within your price range?"

"Okay, but then I would have to sell the house and we would live in a caravan."

"I almost feel like calling your bluff," she said laughing. "Come on, nearly there."

They reached the shop window and Eleanor scanned the display earnestly.

"Yes, I can see it," she cried excitedly.

"Eleanor," David said slowly. "Most of these are labelled 'pre-owned' in other words, second hand."

"Is that a problem?" Eleanor asked.

"Well, it's not what I had in mind! I can afford new!"

"Darling, I like it. And anyway, you're pre-owned," she said with a shrug.

"What?" David gasped.

"Sorry!"

"No. What do you mean?"

"It's all right."

"It's not all right. Now come on, you know the rules."

"You've been married before."

"Oh. You mean that you're my second choice?"

"No, I didn't say that."

"But you think it?"

"No, I don't even think it. David, all I meant was that, okay, you were with someone else – the ring was with someone else. You will be mine and the ring will be mine. I like you. I like the ring. Please can I have it?"

David blinked. "I'm not sure I follow your logic, but if that is what it takes to make you happy, then, after you, Miss," he said, indicating the door. Five minutes later they left, with Eleanor wearing her ring – it just happened to be the right size.

David delivered Eleanor to her work place and despite his suggestion of changing her clothes; she went in wearing her new dress. David suggested that she offered to work late and then phone him when she was ready to be picked up, but her boss said that his engagement present was to forget about her much extended lunch hour. It did mean that Eleanor was able to sort out most of her possessions as well as pack just a few clothes for that and the next couple of nights, together with her necessary toiletries and make-up equipment. These were delivered to Mrs Hayes and then David took her on to a restaurant.

"David, this is surreal," Eleanor said, halfway through the meal. "Tell me I'm not dreaming."

"You're not dreaming, Sweetheart. So what's surreal?"

"Perhaps you won't understand, but here I am; seventeen, engaged to be married, and due to go back to school soon!"

"I know," David said. "I don't find it easy. Here I am; a grumpy old man who is engaged to a beautiful young woman! Sweetheart, when I'm with you, I don't notice your age. That's what I found strange from the start. Right now, you don't look like a schoolgirl, and yet I know you are. You know, I compared you to the girls I taught and there was no comparison."

Eleanor laughed. "You're not a grumpy old man! If you were I wouldn't be here with you." Then she became serious again. "When do we talk about a marriage date?"

David took a deep breath. "Not tonight. As you say, tonight is surreal."

"We're seeing the pastor on Thursday, aren't we? Should we leave it until after that?" Eleanor asked.

"No. Come round tomorrow night. Better still, come and cook for me. Just to convince me that I should marry you!"

"I don't know about that. Suppose I don't convince you?"

Eleanor said, smiling.

"Perhaps I should order a take-away instead," David said, and laughed.

"Or I could give you another cookery lesson – we would make a fruit pie – a proper fruit pie!"

At this, they both laughed, so much that people at the next table turned and looked at them.

David delivered Eleanor back to Mrs Hayes at about nine. Eleanor let herself in with the keys she had been given, and was about to go up to her room.

"Eleanor, my dear, you don't have to go up," Mrs Hayes called from her lounge. She waited until Eleanor came to the door. "Unless you want to be alone," she added.

"No, I didn't want to intrude," Eleanor said.

"You're not intruding, my dear. Come and sit down and tell me about your evening."

Eleanor sat down, keeping her left hand out of sight. "Mrs Hayes, I have a confession." Mrs Hayes waited. "I'm going to marry David," she said in a rush and showing Mrs Hayes her left hand.

"Now why doesn't that surprise me?" Mrs Hayes said, with a smile.

"Did the pastor say anything," Eleanor asked immediately.

"No, my dear. It was seeing how you two looked at each other. Then I remembered wondering if there was anything between you when you sang together."

"There wasn't," Eleanor said quickly. "David was always a gentleman."

"As I would have expected. How long have you had the ring?"

"This afternoon, after we left here. I wasn't expecting it – it was a surprise."

"Is that when you decided to marry?"

"Oh no. David asked me on Sunday – at the pastor's house – in front of the pastor and his wife!"

"I thought you were still at school," Mrs Hayes said, after a pause.

"I am. I would leave tomorrow, but David thinks I should finish the sixth-form."

"He's thinking of your future, my dear," Mrs Hayes said soothingly.

"I know," Eleanor said. Then she sighed. "Mrs Hayes, what do you think? Am I too young?"

Mrs Hayes leaned forward and touched Eleanor's knee. "Why are you asking me, my dear? Are you having second thoughts?" she asked gently.

"No, not for myself. I meant am I too young for David? Does he feel obliged to marry me?"

"Obliged?" Mrs Hayes said carefully, jumping to the wrong conclusion. "You're not …?" she hesitated to say it.

"No, no. I don't mean that!" Eleanor said, looking shocked. "That will never happen!"

Mrs Hayes looked at her, and then replied quietly. "I'm sorry, Eleanor, I didn't mean to be offensive, but it does happen. Even within churches. So beware." She paused. "So what did you mean?" she asked.

"Does he feel responsible for my homeless situation?" Eleanor said

"Eleanor, my dear, you said he asked you on Sunday. You were still living at home then, right?"

Eleanor nodded.

"Then stop worrying," Mrs Hayes said. "Eleanor, I think you are tired – and too tired to think straight. Why don't I make you a drink, and pack you off for an early night?"

Mrs Hayes was right, Eleanor was tired – not having slept well the previous night alone in the hotel. Even so her sleeping pattern was erratic, probably due to yet another room in which to sleep, but also because of excitement. Mrs Hayes woke her with a cup of tea in good time for work.

"Mrs Hayes, this doesn't happen at home!" Eleanor protested.

Mrs Hayes smiled. "It's a one-off, my dear."

Over breakfast, Eleanor said that she would be eating with David that evening and with the pastor and his wife on Thursday. Mrs Hayes then replied with an invitation for David to join them on Friday. David met up with Eleanor at lunch-time and showed her the list he had been given by Jill. He then bought the items on the list and was waiting at home when she arrived on her bicycle. She was later than he had expected because she had gone home first to change.

"You went home?" David asked, surprised.

"Yes, to Mrs Hayes' of course."

"Oh, of course. Right, first I need order our supper, and then you are going to help me make a pie."

"Supervise, you mean," Eleanor told him. "You are going to do the work."

It was later that evening when Eleanor snuggled up to David, that she told him about her conversation with Mrs Hayes.

"Mrs Hayes thought I was pregnant," she said.

"What?" David exclaimed, sitting up and pushing Eleanor away. "Why?"

"It was my fault. I said I wondered if you felt obliged to marry me."

"What?" David repeated. "Why did you say that? Is that what you think?"

"No, I was tired and homeless. Maybe you then felt sorry for me."

"When I asked you to marry me, you were not homeless, Eleanor," David said firmly.

"I know, I know. Mrs Hayes pointed that out. Anyway, I said it could never happen," she said, snuggling back down next to him.

David kissed her forehead. "Sweetheart, when we are cuddling close like this, do you still feel so strongly that it can't happen?"

"What are you suggesting, David," Eleanor asked, struggling away from him, and facing him. "You're not suggesting that we ..." she stopped.

"Make love?" David filled in the missing words, and laughed. "Of course not. But are you saying the thought never crosses your mind?"

Eleanor did not reply, so David held her head and looked into her eyes. "It's what married people do," he said.

"I know that. Okay, yes, I did wonder what it would be like – but not seriously. I mean, I never dreamed that I would marry you, you know that."

"We've been engaged for nearly a week, dear," David said.

"And what a week too! David, I'm sorry, but it hasn't crossed my mind. Has it crossed your mind?"

"Oh yes," he said casually. "More than once."

"When, David? Cuddling just now?"

David laughed. "Well, obviously just now!"

"Go on, tell me, when else!" Eleanor persisted.

David laughed again. "Okay, when you joined me for breakfast yesterday and when you arrived panting on your bike this evening, oh, and when you sat on the bench telling me what to do with the rolling pin!"

"You're not serious – they were hardly romantic settings."

"Eleanor, that's a difference between males and females."

"So do I have to worry about my virtue?" she asked, smiling slyly at him.

"No, you know you don't." David sighed. "But it gets harder the longer you wait."

Eleanor snuggled down again. "David," she whispered, "it did cross my mind, especially because I suddenly remembered something that Mrs Hayes had said."

"Which was?"

"She pointed out that pregnancies do occur even in church situations."

"And did she also say that the road to hell is paved with good intentions?" David asked.

"No. She just said to beware."

"Darling, you told me you had boyfriends. Were you never tempted?"

"No way!" Eleanor replied, with some passion.

"And now?" David asked.

"A year is a very long time to wait," she whispered.

David gently pushed her away, and sat up. "That's something we must talk about. Does it have to be a year?"

"But I thought you wanted me at least to finish school," she answered.

"I do."

"So how do you explain that?"

"You finish school as Mrs Anderson."

"Are you serious?" she whispered.

"We had a girl in my school, what, about three years ago, who had a baby. She was fifteen. She left the baby with her mum and finished the year in school."

"When it happened in our school, the girl left and she was only fourteen," Eleanor said.

"You're missing the point! My girl, I mean the girl in my school, chose not to have home tutoring. If she was allowed to stay in school, then so could you – as a married woman."

"But schools aren't for women, they're for kids! That's what people will say," Eleanor said.

"Eleanor! People don't leave school on their eighteenth birthday, do they?"

"And I could get married on my eighteen birthday," Eleanor said slowly. "And then ..." she grinned.

On Thursday evening, David drove them both round to James and Lucy's house. Their twins were still up, and Lucy asked Eleanor if she would read them their bedtime Bible story. David and James strolled round the garden. David had asked Eleanor to hide her ring, and they had checked with Mrs Hayes that she had not mentioned the engagement.

"Has Eleanor settled in well," James asked.

"Yes, we're very grateful to you for suggesting it," David replied. "I still can't get over them banning her from seeing me let alone throwing her out."

"I was surprised, but I have come across it once before, oh, years ago."

"That's partly why I didn't want Eleanor staying with me – apart from the obvious. I expected them on my doorstep and accusing me of rape or something."

"Come on, they wouldn't do that!"

"Okay, but they could have made a scene on the doorstep," David said. "And that would have upset Eleanor. They still could come, I suppose. Hang on, have they contacted you?"

"No. Of course if they do come, I would have to offer reconciliation. You do understand?"

"Yes."

"And we can assume they haven't reported her disappearance to the police," James said.

"Why?"

"Well, the police would have asked about her friends and interest. They would have soon contacted me once there was a church connection. I wonder if they will hand over her birth certificate if one of us went and asked."

David laughed, and explained how not everything had been put on the doorstep and how they had gone back the next day. "We cleared the rest of her things including her certificates. We even took her computer away and a friend got her data from it. Then we put the computer back because Eleanor said that it wasn't hers!"

"And how are things between you?" James asked.

"Ask me after dinner," David said, smiling at James.

"So," James said, as they sat down for coffee, "how are you coping, Eleanor?"

"I think I'm coping, thanks to Mrs Hayes and of course my fiancé," Eleanor said, lifting her left hand on which she had replaced her ring. It was an obvious surprise to both James and Lucy, who looked at each other. Lucy recovered first.

"Eleanor, it's beautiful," she exclaimed, leaning forward to look at it.

"And you are both very sure?" James asked.

"Yes," David said, at once.

Lucy looked at Eleanor. "Lucy?" she said quietly.

Eleanor hesitated, and David also looked at her. "I still worry that I'm too young for you and," she paused, "whether I've pressurised you into it."

"I don't think you are too young for marriage or for me, okay? And I certainly do not feel pressurised."

"But do you have no reservations at all?" James asked.

"I worry whether I'm too old for Eleanor, but not enough to put me off marrying her. Then I worry about leaving her a widow, but no one's life is certain, is it? People will probably accuse me of being selfish though."

"Otherwise?" James asked.

"I also feel very bad about breaking up Eleanor's family."

"But you didn't," Eleanor cried. "It wasn't your fault!"

"Eleanor, if your dad's car had started, then you wouldn't be in this position," David said, referring to that time long ago when he had gone to collect Eleanor from the airport. "And we wouldn't be planning to marry."

"I mean we wouldn't have fallen in love, Eleanor."

"But we did, David." She shrugged. "And my parents should accept it!"

They sat in silence for several moments.

"So what now?" Lucy asked. "I mean, do you have any marriage plans – are you going to give up school?"

"No!" David said.

"David says there is no reason for me to leave school even if we marry," Eleanor said.

"What do you think?" David asked.

James looked at Lucy, then back at David. "Well, I can't think of a good reason why married people shouldn't go to school. University students can marry – not that many do, most just live together," he added sadly. "If you just lived together no one would turn a hair, would they."

"I'm not so sure about that," Lucy said. "Maybe if David wasn't a teacher himself."

"Anyway, I wasn't suggesting that," James said. "Have you set a day, then?"

"November the fifteenth would suit me – my eighteenth birthday," Eleanor said, with a smile. "Or as soon as possible afterwards. I don't want to wait a whole year. In fact, if we weren't Christians, I would suggest that we did move in together."

"No, sweetheart, I still wouldn't let you," David said.

"Why not? I thought that's what you would want!"

Eleanor said, surprised.

"Only because of the age gap. Living together wouldn't look good, me being a teacher!"

"Isn't that hypocritical, David?" Eleanor said. "I thought you …"

"Children!" Lucy said, interrupting and grinning. "May I make a suggestion?"

Everyone looked at Lucy. "Marriage requires planning. Are you sure that you could get your act together by the middle of November, even though it's three months away? Okay, so you have somewhere to live at the moment, but have you talked about where you will eventually live and," she paused, "sleep? And what about a honeymoon? I think a proper honeymoon is important. Could you both take a week off in mid-November? No; it would be back to work for you both the following Monday. I think that you should have a proper break together so that you can both learn to know each other properly, even if it does mean waiting a few more weeks." She paused, and looked embarrassed. "Sorry, it's one of my things. I'll shut up."

"No, Mrs Butler, I mean Lucy, please say what you like. I think I'm still in a bit of a daze anyway. I said to David yesterday that it all seems a bit like a dream. When it hits me, I shall probably end up in a right state – luckily, David's been there before."

"It was a long time ago, pet," David said. "This is where having a mum is a help."

"If orphans can cope, I'm sure I will," Eleanor said bravely.

"And you can turn to me, and I think Mrs Hayes will want to help. What do you think dear?" Lucy said to James.

"Well, I hadn't anticipated the rush, let alone the

engagement ring, and I was going to have a little chat about marriage in general, but somehow, it now seems irrelevant."

"I'm sorry, James. Look, let's pretend you didn't know about the ring," David said. "What did you want to chat about?"

"It's my 'are you sure' line. I should tell you that it is a bit tongue in cheek."

"Go on," said David.

"All right." He paused. "Do you both realise that you're unsuited for each other."

"We're not!" Eleanor exclaimed.

"Shush, Sweetheart. Go on, explain why," David said, realising that James was making a point.

"It's easy. It's not the age gap – it's the gender gap. You're a man and you're a woman," James said to them each in turn.

"I don't get that. I thought you believed in men marrying women," Eleanor said.

James smiled at her. "Be patient, Eleanor. I'm not talking about marriage, just relationships. Look, think of your best friends over the years, Eleanor. Boys or girls – don't answer yet. If David had two tickets to a cup final, who would he ask to go with him? A girl or another bloke? Who did you play with at play-time in school? Likewise boys. Can you see where I'm going, Eleanor? Who got Adam into trouble? Who got Samson into trouble?"

"Oh, come on!" Eleanor exclaimed. "Now you're being a misogynist!"

James smiled at her. "I hope you will regard David as your best friend, but at the end of the day you have to remember that he's a man. He has a man's brain. He won't think like you do. He won't act the way you might expect. He's different and he won't understand you and you won't understand him!"

Eleanor smiled slowly. "So why did God make Eve a woman?" she asked. "Because He knew what was best for a man." she added, to answer her own question. "But I do get the point, really."

"Just remember that, Eleanor, when David annoys you over something which he thinks is trivial and you think is important!"

Eleanor turned to David. "Did you know all that?"

"Sweetheart, I have been married. Women are impossible to understand – it's like they're from a different planet."

Eleanor's face lit up. "Venus and Mars, I've heard of the book!"

"You can borrow my copy, Eleanor," said Lucy who had kept quiet all this time. She smiled. "So has James put you off?"

"No, not now I realise he needs me!" she said with a grin. "Someone has to take him in hand, so it might as well be me."

"Which just leaves the question of when. You talk that over and then come back to me," James said.

"Does that mean you will marry us," Eleanor asked James.

"Yes, but I won't officially agree until you are eighteen, Eleanor. Then you will be an adult so if your parents approach me, I will point out that you are both of age."

"Thank you, Pastor," Eleanor said.

"So, shall we run over the main steps?" Lucy asked, looking at them both.

"Hang on, Dear. Don't jump in just like that," James said. "There's still time for Eleanor's parents to relent. If they do, then they may want to organise it."

"Do you think so?" Eleanor said hopefully.

"Well, once they realise that it will happen anyway, who knows what can happen? Look, give it another week or so and I'll go and see them. I could point out that you have found somewhere to live, and that once you turn eighteen, I won't have a reason to not marry you. What do you think?"

"I will only go back if they accept David," Eleanor said. "And I don't want to wait a whole year."

"There is another thing, Darling," James said to Lucy. "Assuming that Eleanor does not go home, then maybe Mrs Hayes would want to be involved."

David smiled. He had a feeling that more than one woman would like to be a surrogate mother to Eleanor. "Shall we get back to you when we've talked it over more fully?" David suggested. "Personally, I think that Eleanor's parents would have tried to sort things out by now, but, okay, James, please go and see them when you think it is appropriate. Have you had a family break this year?" David said, to change the subject.

Nothing more was said about the wedding, and the talking covered a range of topics. James and Lucy told them about their holiday; Eleanor told them how she had sent secret cards to David. They asked about her week at camp, and then heard the story of how David had collected her from camp well before breakfast to take her to Daniel's wedding.

"You didn't go in your camping clothes, did you?" Lucy asked.

Eleanor laughed, and told them how David had bought her outfit to the camp that morning.

"What did your mum think about that?" Lucy gasped.

More laughter as Eleanor explained the story of the dress, and its subsequent repurchase.

"If we hadn't been seen by the neighbour, then maybe I would still be at home," Eleanor said, after recounting how they had eventually been caught.

"I'm glad we were," David said. "I didn't like the secrecy. In fact, perhaps I should go and thank them, or invite then to the wedding!"

"I don't think that would be very tactful, David," Lucy said.

"But at least it helped us sort out our feelings," David said.

"Mine were already sorted," Eleanor replied.

"Okay, so I needed a kick to work out what I needed to do," David said. "I should have realised earlier!"

"But better late than never," Lucy added.

Chapter 5

Telling People

David met Eleanor at lunchtime the next day and they ate sandwiches together in the park.

"Do you remember Lucy saying that she thought that a proper honeymoon was very important?" Eleanor asked.

"Yes, why?"

"What did she mean when she said that if we really wanted to know each other properly, then it wouldn't help if we were both at work? I think I know you pretty well already."

David looked at her. "I think she was using an authorised version of the Bible phrase"

"There's nothing in the Bible about honeymoons, is there?"

David laughed. "In the A.V. it says something like 'Adam knew his wife and she conceived and bore him a son'," he said. "Modern versions are more direct – one talks about Adam making love to his wife!"

"Oh," Eleanor said. Then, "Oh! I nearly said that I knew you pretty well already! Is that really how people talked years ago?"

"I suppose so," David said. "Didn't you study Shakespeare?"

"Yes, of course. But I don't remember that phrase being used. Anyway, so do you agree?"

"Yes, I do."

"Oh," Eleanor said.

"What's the problem? Don't you want a proper honeymoon in a hotel?"

"Of course I do, but not enough to wait until next summer!"

"Eleanor, what's wrong with the Christmas holiday? It's not that long after your birthday, is it? I've already checked. Christmas Day is on a Wednesday, so I guess term would end on the Friday before. There are package holidays to the Canaries. Ideal. Marry on Saturday; fly on Sunday for a week in the sun. It would mean not having Christmas with the family, but would that bother you?" Eleanor stared at David. "David, you are amazing!"

"Well, I wouldn't argue with that," David said.

"Then that's settled. We'll get married in the holiday, and I'll go back to school as Mrs Anderson," Eleanor said.

"And hope it doesn't upset them, but we'll worry about that later. I'll go and check with James this afternoon, and if the day is free, I'll book the holiday too, okay?"

By the time David arrived at Mrs Hayes for dinner, Eleanor had already told Mrs Hayes about their plans, so they were desperate to hear the result of David's visit to James.

"He was free and he thought it was a good idea," David told them. "And I've booked the honeymoon."

"Where?"

"Do you really want to know?" David asked. "But you will need to pack your bikini," he added.

"Really? You won't be embarrassed?" Eleanor asked, at which Mrs Hayes gave them a look.

"Mrs Hayes, when David came with me to the Lido, he was embarrassed," Eleanor said, reaching out and touching his hand.

"Eleanor, don't tell the world," David growled.

"Your secret's safe with me, young man," Mrs Hayes said, laughing. She turned to Eleanor. "Right, you'll have to start making plans soon, my dear."

"Mrs Hayes, will you help me, please?" Eleanor asked.

"Only if you call me Molly, my dear," she replied.

Over coffee they talked about who they should tell, and
when. Molly suggested that it might be perspicacious for
Eleanor to keep very quiet at school about their
relationship.

"I know you want to tell the world, but I don't think you
should wear your ring to school, people might think you
were flaunting your position. Also, it could make it
difficult for your marriage to be accepted by the school
authorities."

"But what about church?" Eleanor asked. "Do you think
we should sit together?"

"That's up to you two," Molly replied, looking at David.

"Well, for one thing, Eleanor won't be in school uniform.
But," David said, and he turned to Eleanor. "No overt
signs of affection, Sweetheart."

"No snogging in the back row then?" Eleanor asked, with
a cheeky grin.

"No touching at all," David said. "Not even hugging, and
certainly no holding hands. I've seen some of the couples
holding hands in the hymns."

"But we will sit together, won't we?" Eleanor asked.

"And what about Lizzie?"

"Lizzie?" Molly asked.

"My friend Lizzie from school. She's been coming to
church, I can't not tell her. And she knows about David."

"Only that we're friends, Eleanor," David said.

"She knows how I feel about you, David," Eleanor said,
and turned to Molly. "She thinks it's funny and teases me,
but not in a bad way. I think she quite likes David – but
not the way I do! No, she will know something has
changed so I will be straight with her. She won't let me
down. It's your family I worry about, David." She
paused. "And I don't mean just your children."

"My parents?" David asked quietly, after a pause.

"And what about Jenny's parents? David, they will have

to be told. Have your parents not said anything to you since Daniel's wedding?"

"Not really. They did ask about you, something like who was that girl I was with. I repeated what I had told them at the wedding, namely, that your name was Eleanor and that Stephanie had invited you. I also reminded them that I had driven down to a camp especially to collect you. Then I threw in that Daniel's best man rather fancied you!"

"David! That was disingenuous. I thought Jill told you that she could see Cupid's arrows."

"My mum was probably more interested in her grandson than me," David said. "And remember, Jill had seen us holding hands earlier."

"Yes, that was embarrassing," Eleanor said. She went on to tell Molly all about the day, including the how David had collected her from the camp.

"I think the fact that we had to leave before the end helped. I didn't really spend a lot of time with them, did I?" David said.

"It's not just your parents, David. What about Jenny's. I think they could be upset. What do you think, Molly?"

"I don't, Eleanor, my dear. How close are you, David?"

"Maybe not so close as I ought to be. I know they talk to my parents, and to both Jill and Daniel."

"So they will find out, eventually," Molly said.

"You think I should tell them first?" David asked Molly.

"And when you do, don't take Eleanor with you," Molly replied. "That would be like firing both barrels at the same time. Who knows, they may have picked up something anyway at the wedding. If they did, would they ask you about it?"

"No," David replied quickly. "But they would ask my mum."

"And your mum did ask you, but you fobbed her off,"

Molly said. "David, you have some serious thinking to do. I think you should see your parents as soon as possible."

"And take Eleanor?"

"Yes."

"My parents, Jenny's parents, my kids, and in what order," David pondered.

"What about Eleanor's family?" Molly asked. "Do you have grandparents, Eleanor?"

"Yes, on both sides."

"Let's leave them out for the moment. After all, if this is a storm in a pudding bowl," David said.

"Pudding bowl? You mean tea-cup," Eleanor interrupted, laughing.

"Hardly a tea-cup, Sweetheart! As I was saying, if this blows over soon and fences are mended, then they needn't know, agree?"

Eleanor laughed again. "You and your metaphors, David. Were the fences broken by the wind?"

"Eleanor," David said impatiently. "This is serious!"

"Sorry."

"Right, Jill knows the most about us. I'd rather start there. I'm sure she would like to meet you again," David said.

"But what about Daniel?" Eleanor asked. "Shouldn't you ask him to be your best man?"

"Ideally, yes, but I'm not sure if he's embarrassed by our relationship. We'll see."

"Well, I think Stephie would like to be a bridesmaid," Eleanor said.

Mrs Hayes was looking confused by these names, so David explained who they were. Molly then turned to Eleanor. "Eleanor, bridesmaids are usually single. Stephie would be a matron-of-honour. But I agree, I also think you ought to tell your children as soon as possible, David. Why don't you phone from here about seeing one of them tomorrow, that's if it's not too late?"

"Eleanor?" David said.

"Are you sure, Mrs Hayes, er, Molly?" Eleanor asked.

"Yes, I think it's important. All right, I know David saw his daughter last Monday, but you were not officially engaged then, were you?"

"So who first, Sweetheart?" David asked.

"Jill," Eleanor replied, with no hesitation.

It wasn't too late, and they arranged to visit Jill and Keith the next day. David collected Eleanor after breakfast to drive to his daughter. It was a good visit – Eleanor was both pleased and surprised at how Jill had seemed genuinely pleased for them. When they arrived, Jill spotted the ring immediately and squealed. Then she gave Eleanor a big hug and a kiss, before hugging her father. Keith and David were not on hugging terms – they shook hands – but Keith also gave Eleanor a hug and a kiss. Jill's first question was about where and when they became officially engaged. Her second was to ask how many people knew.

"Molly, the lady I'm living with, and our pastor and his wife. No one else apart from you two," Eleanor replied.

"Not Gran and Grandpa?" Jill asked her father. "Or Daniel?"

"Not yet. I think we should go and tell them personally," David said. "And there are your mum's parents, Jill. I think that's going to be the hardest. Do you think they guessed anything at Daniel's wedding? You said it was obvious to you!"

"They did ask where you were, and I said that apparently, someone had to take Eleanor back to a Christian camp. I think they thought she was a leader."

"I think we, that is, both of us should go and tell Daniel. Can I phone him later, Jill? I'll invite myself, along with

Eleanor. I'm not too worried about that, but how do I tell my parents and your mum's parents, Jill?"

"Do you want me to tell them?" Jill asked.

"My initial response it to say yes!" David answered. "But that's just being a coward. Can I phone them as well, please?"

David phoned Daniel first and explained that he was phoning from Jill's house, but he did not say why he was there.

"I think I should come and check up on the two love birds, Daniel," he said, as a way of inviting himself after the usual exchange of pleasantries. "Are you free tomorrow?"

"Oh Dad. No, we've been invited out – all day. But what about next weekend?" Daniel said. "We would love to see you. Actually, we were talking about coming to see you, we want to ask you something, but if you're happy come to us, we'd love to see you. Could you stay over?"

"And where would I sleep?" David asked, knowing that they were in a small single bedroom flat!

"It's okay; we have been given a three-seater settee that can be used for sleepovers. It's actually very comfortable."

"Can I take a rain check?" David said. It was not the thought of the settee – there was nowhere for Eleanor.

"Don't tell me – you have a date! Are you still seeing your teenage friend?" Daniel asked with a laugh

"Yes, I am as a matter of fact," David replied rather stiffly.

Daniel laughed again. "Sorry. I shouldn't tease you, Dad."

"Actually, I was going to ask if I can bring her too."

"Oh!" Daniel said.

"Look, if it's not convenient, we'll leave it," David said quickly. Before Daniel could answer, he heard Stephanie call out to Daniel.

"Who is it, Love?"

"It's Dad."

"Have you asked about seeing him?"

"He was asking about coming to see us next weekend."

"Oh, good. Will he bring Eleanor?"

"That's what he was asking."

"Of course he must! Let me have the phone, Danny."

David smiled to himself as he remembered the times Jenny had taken the phone from him if one of the children were on the other end.

"Hello, Dad," a breathless voice said. "Of course you must bring Eleanor! Is she there with you now?"

"Yes," David said, "but it's not my phone. I'm at Keith and Jill's place."

"Oh. Well tell her I'm dying to see her again. And you as well!" she added. "You will be here for lunch, won't you?"

"But of course. I need to check up that you're feeding my son properly – not that I have any doubts," he added quickly, fearing she might not share his sense of humour.

"Well, he seems quite healthy," Stephanie said.

"I was joking, Stephanie, but if you remind me, I'll tell you a good story to remember if you ever have a daughter-in-law. Okay?"

The next phone call was to his parents. It was fairly brief; Eleanor had already agreed to ask for a day off work if his parents were free to see them.

"Hello, Mum. I'm with Jill and Keith at the moment, so this is just a quick call. I'd like to see you both about something; any chance of me popping over one day this week?"

"What about, David?"

"Mum, it's too complicated for a quick phone call. If you're not free, then some other time."
"No, this week is fine. Thursday? Will you be here for lunch?"
"Yes please. Oh, I'm hoping to have a friend with me. Is that okay?"
"What do you mean; a friend? What kind of friend?"
"How many kinds of friend are there Mum?" David asked, laughing. "I'll explain when I see you, bye."
David put the phone down. "Jill, she'll phone you and ask, you see! Please don't tell her."
"Dad!"
"Just say that I have asked you not to talk about it, all right?"

After dinner with Jill and Keith, they then returned to David's house in order to sort out Eleanor's things. When she returned to Mrs Hayes's later that evening, Eleanor took more clothes and some small personal items in order to make her room more homely. The next morning, Sunday, David was waiting at church when Eleanor arrived with Mrs Hayes. She walked across to David, but stopped just short.
"Hello, David," she said.
"Hello, Eleanor."
"This is weird, isn't it?" Eleanor said.
"Yes, it is. Whose gloves?" David asked, indicating her gloved hands.
"Mrs Hayes."
"Why?" David asked.
"Why do you think?"
"Oh. Are you wearing your ring?" David asked.
"Of course," she said with a smile.
"Good. Shall we go in?"
"No, I'm waiting for Lizzie. I phoned her this morning –

she's been on holiday. I told her I needed to see her urgently. Apparently she had phoned me at my old home, but they just told her that I wasn't there and they didn't know when I would be back."

"Didn't she text you?"

"Yes, but yesterday I left my phone at Molly's. I didn't expect her to contact me so I didn't check it when I got home."

"Are you going to tell her straight away, then?"

"I think I'll have to, sorry."

"No, if it has to be done, then the sooner the better. Look, she's coming."

Lizzie walked up to them, and smiled at David before hugging Eleanor. "Well," she said, "are you two still friends?"

Eleanor pulled off her gloves, and showed Lizzie her left hand. Lizzie just stared for several seconds.

"You're not!" she gasped.

Eleanor just nodded.

"To David?"

"Obviously."

Then Lizzie reacted. She suddenly hugged Eleanor – which was to be expected, but then she released Eleanor and threw her arms round David. Then she released him.

"Guys, you're not winding me up, are you," she said slowly.

"No, Lizzie, but it's got to be a secret," David said.

"From who?"

"School, of course, Lizzie. Okay? I won't wear my ring to school."

"Your ring! I still haven't seen it properly. Show me!" Lizzie cried, reaching for Eleanor's left hand. Before she could touch it, Eleanor pulled it away.

"Lizzie, wait! Not here, I'll show you later. People are looking."

Lizzie looked hurt, so David spoke to her. "Lizzie, please understand, we're trying to be discreet. Look, why not come to tea?"

"To tea? With who?"

"With us," David said.

"Are you living together then?" Lizzie asked, looking surprised.

"Of course not!" Eleanor exclaimed. "Lizzie!"

"Let's go in," David said, "and all will be explained later."

Apart from the misunderstanding, David was pleased that they had waited for Lizzie. He felt that to be seen sitting with both girls was less noticeable that sitting with Eleanor alone. There was coffee as usual after the service, where Lizzie was given the opportunity of seeing the ring. However, Eleanor took it off from her finger first and handed it to Lizzie, explaining that she didn't want other people to notice what Lizzie was looking at.

"Elly, you can't keep it a secret for ever – or do you want to?"

"No, people will find out, but gradually, we hope," David said. "Our main problem could be school, that is, Eleanor's school. She won't wear her ring to school."

"But they can't stop you being engaged, can they?" Lizzie said. It was a rhetorical question.

"We don't want to draw attention to the fact that we're getting married at Christmas," Eleanor said quietly.

"What!" Lizzie's response was far from quiet, and several people turned and looked at them. Then Tom and Ali walked over. Eleanor took her ring back and closed her hand over it.

"Hi," Tom said. He turned to Lizzie, "What are you shouting about then, Lizzie?" Lizzie didn't answer, so he turned back to David and Eleanor. "I see you're still friends then. Are you singing again?" he said.

Eleanor looked at David, who nodded slightly.

"Tom, Ali, I am going to show you something, but I don't want you to react like Lizzie, okay?" Eleanor said.

"Okay," Tom said, and shrugged, but Ali just looked at Eleanor.

"Ali?" David asked.

Ali smiled, and nodded. Eleanor slowly opened her hand, took the ring, and slid it onto her finger. Tom's mouth dropped open and his eyes opened wider, but Ali hugged Eleanor.

"So we were right?" she whispered.

"No, you were not right," Eleanor answered.

"I meant what was in your heart, Elly! So, how long? Oh, and when is the …"

"Shush!" Eleanor said urgently, and covering her left hand with her right hand. She had just noticed another friend approaching.

"Hi Nicky, have you heard the latest? Ouch!" It was Tom, then reacting to Ali's elbow.

"Hi all. Latest what, Tom?" Nicola replied, looking at them all in turn.

"It's a long story, and in here isn't the place to tell you," David said. "I'd ask you all to tea at my place, but I don't have enough bread, so let's go outside."

"We could bring our own tea, like we do for the young people's tea," Tom said. He grinned. "I was hoping we could come and see you, David," he added. "Can I bring my guitar?"

"What about biscuits," Nicola asked, with a grin, referring back to a previous time spent at David's.

"No, and I do have tea bags!" David said.

Eleanor went home with Mrs Hayes. David had been invited, but had declined. He felt he didn't want to impose on her. Eleanor cycled round to David's early in the afternoon. After a hug and a proper kiss, she stood back.

"David, when you invited them round, you didn't consult me."

David looked blank for a moment, so Eleanor continued. "And when you said it was, to quote, your place, were you being discreet? You said it was my home too."

David realised immediately. "No, Sweetheart, I wasn't. Oh, dear. I am sorry."

Eleanor laughed. "Actually, my home is now with Mrs Hayes. But you did ask Lizzie to tea with us, without consulting me."

"I know, I know!" David said. "Oh, Eleanor, I hope I cope with being a husband again. I suppose I've got used to being just me."

Eleanor laughed, hugged him, and then kissed him. "Maybe it's like riding a bike – once learnt, always remembered! Right; don't you think it would be nice to offer your guests some cake?"

"I don't have any – you know that. Um, I don't suppose …?" he began.

"You suppose wrong! But, dearest fiancé, I am prepared to supervise you. I know you have flour and stuff. Eggs?" He nodded. "Right, scones and or meringues? The problem is that both are best served with cream."

"No cream!"

"Can I use your phone, Dearest?"

"Go ahead," David said, looking puzzled. Eleanor phoned Mrs Hayes, and a minute later she replaced the phone, smiling broadly. "My foster-mum can lend you cream!" she said. "I'll see you start, then I'll bike and get it." Eleanor waited long enough to check that David knew what he was doing and how to use the oven, before disappearing. She returned and showed David how to whip the cream, just before the scones came out. They worked together and made a few sandwiches just before their guests arrived altogether driven by Tom – in his mum's car. Eleanor showed them into the lounge, waited until they were seated, and then went and stood by David. She slipped her hand into his.

"Right, first of all I want to say that Eleanor is not living here, and then for Nicola's sake, Nicola, did you know we were engaged?" David said.

"No! I guessed something was going on, but they wouldn't say anything. So. Is that it?"

"Oh, no," said Eleanor, "it's much more complicated."

"Because you're still at school?" Tom suggested, butting in.

"No. I've been kicked out of home," Eleanor said. Then she crumpled, and David put his arm round her.

"Because of the engagement, Elly?" Lizzie asked.

"Technically, no. Her parents said that she wasn't to see me. It was them or me, and luckily for me, she chose me. I asked Eleanor to marry me, so they then put her things out on the doorstep!"

"Where are you staying, then?" Lizzie asked.

Eleanor recovered enough to answer. "I'm staying with Mrs Hayes. She's a widow, Lizzie. The pastor arranged it."

"How long do you plan to stay there," Nicola asked.

"She says I can stay with her until we get married," Eleanor replied.

"Which is when?"

"Christmas!"

There was a long silence. Finally, it was Tom who broke it.

"But you're still at school, Eleanor," he said quietly, and using her full name.

"So what! We have a girl at uni who is married." Nicola said. "I didn't realise that you were already eighteen."

"She's not," Lizzie said, "not until November."

"When did all this happen, Elly?" Ali asked.

"Do you remember we used to sing, well, I sang and David played his guitar? Well ..." Eleanor told them the whole story, from being stopped from singing, through to becoming friendly again, and then how they were seen by a neighbour earlier that summer. Lizzie added the story of the dress and Daniels wedding.

"It was just over a week ago when things blew up. We went to see James and Lucy last week, actually, last Sunday afternoon. That's where I asked Eleanor to marry me."

"And I said yes!"

"But her mum suspected that something was up, so she went to collect Eleanor from her holiday job on Monday afternoon – and so did I. Eleanor came with me. Later that evening we drove round and saw her things on the doorstep, so, we picked them up. We brought her things here and later that night, I took Eleanor off to a hotel. And that's it."

"And haven't her parents come round to at least check up?" Tom asked, amazed by the whole story.

"Not as far as we know." David said.

"If I didn't know you, I would say that you have invented the whole story, Elly," Nicola said.

"I'd forgotten, but I remembered later that we had a girl at school who was kicked out of her home. But it didn't

last. The boy was no good, and she went home again,"
David said.

"What now then?" Ali asked.

Eleanor shrugged. "I will live with Mrs Hayes, and then
in January, or just before, I will move in here as Mrs
Anderson."

"And school?" Lizzie asked.

"She will continue to attend school as if nothing has
happened," David said.

"But people will see that she's married!" Tom protested,
pointing at his ring finger.

"I shan't wear it."

"Come on, you're getting married. It's public! Or is it
abroad? Someone will know. You won't get away with
it," said Tom.

"Tom, I have asked around, and looked on the Internet.
As far as I can make out, education is not denied to
married people. If Eleanor doesn't flaunt her new
position, then I don't think the school can legally object.
Lizzie, you must be discreet."

There was another period of silence.

"So what now?" Lizzie asked.

"We continue as normal. Go to jazz concerts and maybe
the lido next Saturday. Then school as normal. Marry at
Christmas and go back to school as Mrs Anderson."

"Are you really serious?" Lizzie asked, still looking
incredulous.

"Yes, Lizzie. Absolutely!"

Lizzie got up, went across to Eleanor and hugged her.
"Well, all I can say is that I hope you will be very
happy!"

This broke the ice, and the other two girls jumped up and
joined Lizzie, so it became a group hug. Tom looked at
David and grinned, got up and shook his hand.

"Guess I'm supposed to say congratulations," he said.
"You don't have to, especially if you don't mean it."
"I do," Tom said, and shook his hand again. "Well, well!
And all because I fell off my bike!"
"What do you mean?"
"Well, if I hadn't hurt my hand, then Elly and I would not
have needed your help. Need I say more?"
David laughed. "Okay, then thank you for falling off your
bike!" He looked at the girls now chattering. "Do you
want to show me your guitar then, Tom?"

David and Eleanor sat with Mrs Hayes that evening and
Eleanor kept her gloves on. There was a meeting for the
young people after the service, and Eleanor had two
choices. Should she go with her friends because she knew
Lizzie would go, or should she go home with David?
"You should do what you think is right, Eleanor," David
said, when she asked him. "I will see you every day this
week anyway. The only thing is, how will you get
home?"
"I'll walk if necessary – it won't be late."
"You can phone me if you need me," David said.
"How? No phone!"
"Eleanor," David said, feeling slightly exasperated, "what
is the point of having a mobile if you don't carry it
around?"
"It's not really my phone. They told me that it was for
emergencies, and they are the only ones who can top it
up."
"Oh, Eleanor, why didn't you say?"
"I thought I did. Anyway, you don't have one!"
"Right! I will get us both a mobile phone – and you can
teach me how to text." David said.

They stood looking at each other, still just inside the church entrance. People were still milling around.
"Goodnight, Sweetheart," David said quietly.
"Goodnight, future husband," Eleanor replied, and making a kissing noise with her mouth.
"Eleanor!" David exclaimed. "Be good!"
"Sorry," she said, but not looking at all contrite.
"See you tomorrow – lunchtime!" And with that, he turned and went.

Chapter 6

David's Parents

As David had forecast, they saw a lot of each other the following week. They met up to eat sandwiches together at lunchtime. He also met her from work, and cycled home with her, that is, back to Mrs. Hayes. On the Monday lunchtime David met Eleanor to look at mobile phones. Although most of David's colleagues carried mobile phones, only the younger teachers kept up to date in terms of the latest models. David was not interested in having the latest phone; to him a phone was a tool to communicate with another phone. He knew the difference between pay-as-you-go and contract use. He had a good financial deal on his land-line phone, so his mobile phone would not be used for long conversations. He wasn't sure what Eleanor wanted, however, she said that all she needed was something simple to call him, or Molly, especially if she was delayed at work. They left the shop within ten minutes. An added bonus was that the salesman put the small card from her old phone into her new phone, thus allowing her to keep the number.

"Eleanor," David said, when they were eating their sandwiches, "you said you needed the phone in case you were delayed at work. Why are you working?"
"For money, of course!" she exclaimed. "What other reason is there?"
"Why do you need money?"
"What?" she said, looking at him as if he were mad.
"Don't you get pocket money?" David asked.
"I did when I was younger. Why all these questions?"
"Just tell me, what do you have to buy?"

"You had kids, David. What did they spend money on?"
David grinned. "Music. Clothes. Tickets. Presents."
"Exactly! Plus I was saving up for university."
"Do you have a bank?"
"Yes, and a building society account. Oh! David!"
Eleanor suddenly gasped. "That's what I didn't collect.
My building society book!"
"Is there much in it?" he asked.
"Over a thousand," she said calmly. "And there are some
savings bonds in my name. Oh dear."
"Don't worry, they won't spend it. But back to work,
could you stop?"
 "I suppose so, but then I wouldn't have an income." She
spread her hands to illustrate her point.

"Listen, Sweetheart, you know Molly said she wouldn't
charge us, or you. I spoke to her about it again and she
was adamant. One of the reasons is that she thinks she
would have to pay tax, even though she wouldn't. What
I'm going to suggest is this – you help her around the
house and also tell her you want to contribute towards the
food. Tell her that students share food cost. I will
reimburse you and I'll also make up your lost earnings if
you need to give up your Saturday job."
"You want me to give up my Saturday job?" Eleanor
asked.
"Eleanor, do you expect to work on Saturdays when
we're married?" David said.
"I hadn't thought of that. So if I don't have a job, what
will I do for money?"
"That's one of the things to be discussed later. Right, how
do I use this thing?" He said referring to his new phone.

On the Tuesday afternoon she finished early and they
cycled back to their bridge. This time as they walked

along by the river, they held hands.

"David, so much has happened," Eleanor said. "Was it really a year ago?"

"More or less," David said.

"I still think about it," Eleanor said.

"So do I."

"What do you think?"

David pulled her round to face him. "I remember one of the things is that I was glad you were so young!"

"Really? Why?"

"You were too young for a relationship. I mean with me. I was safe being with you – no romantic complications. Just friends. I did like being with you, but then I worried about it. Was it normal, I mean, a middle-aged man being friends with a teen-aged girl. What about you?"

"I didn't really worry about your age, mind you, I didn't see you as middle-aged. No, I was aware that you were a recently bereaved widower, and not in a good place for a new romance. I did like being with you, but unlike you, I didn't worry about it!" She paused. "David, I am so pleased that my dad's car wouldn't start."

David pulled her closer. "So am I," he said.

As they were walking back towards the bridge and their bicycles, David brought up their wedding.

"Eleanor, Sweetheart, we ought to start thinking about wedding plans," he said.

"I know. Molly brought it up."

"So?"

"David, I know it went well at Jill's – I mean, they did seem genuinely pleased for us, but I'm worried about the rest of your family."

David was also worried, but this was not the time to share his worries.

"Don't be silly," he said lightly. "What's bothering you?"

"David! It's obvious. Suppose they don't accept me? I don't want to come between you and your family."

"Which family? My parents or Daniel?"

"Both."

"I don't think you should worry about Daniel. After all, you are a friend of Stephanie!"

"Okay, it's your parents."

"Would you rather not come?"

"I don't want to go, but what kind of wife would that make me. Of course I'll go! Should I wear trousers so they won't see my legs shaking?"

"Very funny."

"David, getting back to wedding planning. Can it wait until after I've met the family? Please?"

"Okay, but then we do start."

They spent Wednesday evening at David's. David noticed that Eleanor was unusually subdued as they rode back to Molly's together.

"You're very quiet," he said, by way of a comment.

"Am I?" she answered.

"What's on your mind?"

"Tomorrow."

"Tomorrow? Is that bothering you?"

"What do you think!" she snapped.

David kept quiet.

"Do you want me to cancel it?" he then asked quietly.

"Don't be silly."

They rode the rest of the way in silence.

"Say hello to Molly," David said, when they arrived. "I won't come in."

Eleanor suddenly leant towards David and kissed him quickly, and then wheeled her bicycle away.

"Hey!" David called. "Is that it?"

She stopped and faced him, still holding her bicycle. Then

she burst into tears. For a moment, David was nonplussed. His immediate thought was hormones – that time of the month! Jenny had never suffered serious physical discomfort, but she had been grumpy, albeit only briefly, and not every month. It was a thing they had learnt to deal with. He leaned his bicycle against the kerb and walked back to her.

"I could cancel it," he whispered, but wondering if it would make her snap another response. He stood wondering what he should say, if anything, when she suddenly turned and leaned her bicycle against Molly's fence. Then she turned to face him. For a moment, his heart lurched. No, it couldn't be, he thought.

"I am so sorry, David. Dear David," she said. He could now see her smiling rather weakly. "How do you put up with me? Of course we must go!"

"Is it," he hesitated, "is it the time of the month?"

This time she burst out laughing. "Is that what you thought? No, well, it's not PMT. Isn't that a personal question? Do you ask all your girlfriends that?"

"Eleanor!"

"I'm teasing you." She hesitated. "I suppose you will know about things like that."

"Of course I do – I have been married."

"No, I meant when we are married. Of course my mum knew, but I never talked about it in front of Dad!"

This time David laughed. "Of course I will know. Married couples do make love!"

"Do they?" He could see enough of her face to know she was teasing.

"Oh, Eleanor, for a brief moment back then, I thought you were about to tell me that there was no point in going. That, well …"

"David, kiss me. Properly."

David picked Eleanor up at half past nine. As she made herself comfortable in his car, she produced a CD from her handbag.

"David, I didn't sleep well, and I know I won't be good company, so can we play this?"

David grinned. "Sure. Stick it in."

The journey took over two hours so at one stage, they stopped for coffee. It was only a road-side caravan, but there were garden seats for the customers.

"Eleanor, you look beautiful!" David said, sitting opposite her.

She laughed. "David, don't tell lies. I saw myself in the mirror this morning."

David smiled at her.

"Now what are you thinking?" she asked.

David shrugged.

"Go on! I need to do my make up?"

"No, you look gorgeous."

"David! What is it?"

"Eleanor, this is going to be quite a bombshell," he said.

"I do realise that, David. We could go home."

"They're expecting us. Me and a friend. Not me and a young friend and certainly not me and his young fiancée."

"What are you saying, David," she asked.

"Do you think we should play down the fiancé part?"

"You mean, switch my ring?"

"Just to start with. Then if things go well, we can move up a gear, as it were," David said.

"And if things don't go well?"

"Then we'll both have parents who don't accept us."

David's parents lived in the leafy suburbs of a large town. As David pulled onto the drive, Eleanor caught a quick glimpse of his mother. She had been standing by the front window and waiting. Moments later, the front door opened and his mother stepped out.

"David, I'm not ready," Eleanor gasped.

"Too late, Sweetheart. Anyway, I said you look gorgeous!"

"I'm trying to look older!"

This time David laughed out aloud. "Eleanor, it's not your face! It's your demeanour. You are a mature person!" David said, opening his own door. He went to meet his mother and hugged and kissed her.

"Mum," he said, as he released her, "I want you to meet Eleanor." He turned to Eleanor, who was now getting slowly from the car. "Eleanor, my mum."

"Hello, Mrs Anderson," Eleanor said very quietly.

Mrs Anderson turned back to David. "Is Eleanor a shake-hands friend, or a hugging friend?"

"I think she would like a hug. She's feeling very nervous about meeting you," David said.

"Why are you nervous?" Mrs Anderson asked, before giving Eleanor a hug. She seemed genuinely puzzled.

"Because I'm going to marry her, and she's worried about what you will think," David said, before he could stop himself.

"Marry her? You're going to marry again?" his mother said, looking aghast. "But ..." She stopped.

"But what, Mum?" David asked gently.

"Nothing," she said quickly. "It's none of my business. Do the children know? I mean know that you're going to marry again?"

"Mum, let's go in, shall we?" David suggested. "And then we can talk."

David's mother showed them into her front room, and then went to tell her husband that David had arrived.

"He's bought his friend, but Ron, she's only a girl! And he's talking about marrying her," she whispered to him first. As his father entered the room, David stood up.

"Dad, how are you?" David said, as he hugged his father.

"Not too bad, considering," his father replied.

"Dad, this is Eleanor," David said.

"Pleased to meet you, Eleanor," his father said, extending his hand.

"And you too," Eleanor said, shaking the proffered hand.

"You were at Daniel's wedding!" David's mother said suddenly. "You were introduced as a friend of Daniel's wife, I remember now."

"Yes, I remember too," his father said. "Please sit down again, Eleanor."

"She is a friend of Stephanie," David said quickly. "We didn't want to draw attention to our friendship."

"I'm not surprised!" Moira Andersen said, before she could stop herself.

"Moira!" Ron Anderson said quietly, before turning to David. "So your friendship, is it longstanding?"

"Do you remember that was I helping someone with their singing last year," David replied.

"Yes, you went to an old people's home, right?"

"I was singing with Eleanor."

"But," Moira said and stopped. "But."

"Yes?" David replied.

"I thought the girl you sang with was at school. Then you were stopped. Are you saying you were, oh dear, how do people put it, going out? It was a bit early, wasn't it?"

"We were not going out, Mum. Not in the boy and girl sense, anyway," David said.

"In what way, then?" Ron said.

"Eleanor knew that I played the guitar, so when her singing partner hurt his wrist, they asked me to help. Then, when he went off to university, I took his place."

"And that's all there was to it?" Ron asked.

"No, we went to concerts. Eleanor, myself and another

friend because we happened to like the same music. We were just friends."

"You were friends with a girl half your age? Huh," his mother interjected.

"Actually, less than half. That isn't the point. I realised that it looked odd, but I was comfortable in Eleanor's company."

"But we were stopped," Eleanor said. "It was after the old people's concert. It was thought that our friendship was inappropriate, I think that was the word."

"And was it?" Ron Anderson asked his son.

"Dad, it probably was. But I missed her. We missed each other, so, after a while, we began seeing each other, but now very discreetly. This time I allowed my feelings to grow, and so we're planning to marry."

"And what about you, Eleanor?" Moira asked. "Isn't David old enough to be your father?"

"Yes, Mrs Anderson," Eleanor replied, looking steadily at his mother. "I am totally aware that I will be widowed, but I would rather spend some years with David than none at all."

"Really?"

"Mum, Eleanor is giving up a lot to marry me," David said.

"Then I hope you're worth it." She turned to Ron. "Ron, is the kettle on?"

It seemed that the interrogation was over and Eleanor began to relax. The conversation tended to be about the past – David, or David's children. This suited Eleanor because she did not want her youth to be the topic of conversation. Suddenly, however, the conversation changed.

"Well, Eleanor, are you a modern Miss?" Moira asked her.

"Modern Miss?" Eleanor repeated. "What do mean?"

"Well, what about a career?"

"I'm not sure what career I will eventually follow," she said carefully. "There are lots of factors to consider."

"Such as?"

Eleanor hesitated and looked at David for help.

"Whether we have a family," David said.

"But you've got children, David," his mother exclaimed.

"Grown-up children. You don't want to start again, do you?"

Eleanor held her breath. She accepted that children did not bless every relationship, but she did want children. And she assumed that David did too.

"Actually, I do," he said.

"What?" his mother gasped. "You want more children?"

"What's the problem?" David said. "That often happens with married people. Some people have lots."

"So I've noticed," she said, sounding slightly bitter.

"Mum," David said gently. "You only had me. Was that deliberate, or did it just happen?"

Moira lifted her head. "It was a decision. And I had my job to consider."

"Do you regret it?" David asked, surprising Eleanor by his boldness.

"Why should I? It meant you didn't go without."

"True," David murmured.

The conversation became general again – local news and events. The weather! The new bypass! Any subject but David and Eleanor's relationship. Lunch was served; a rather splendid lunch. David and Eleanor were left alone as his father and mother both found it necessary to do things together in the kitchen.

"So they can talk about us?" Eleanor whispered to David in response to his comment. "They're not happy, are they? How long do we have to stay?"

"Mid-afternoon?"

Eleanor smiled, and then nodded as David's father brought in coffee. Without warning, he suddenly addressed Eleanor.

"Are you into gardens, Eleanor?"

"No, I'm not," Eleanor replied. "I mean, I'm not into gardening. Mum looks after our garden," she said, before she realised that it was no longer her garden. "I mean, her garden. But I like looking at gardens."

"May I show you my garden after coffee, that's if there is time?"

"I'd like that," Eleanor replied. "Will there be time, David?"

David looked his watch, then his mother. "I'd like to go by mid-afternoon, Mum, if that's okay."

"Oh, well, all right," his mother said.

Eleanor followed David's father down the garden path. He showed her various flowering plants, and also his vegetables. Eleanor was following his guided tour with interest. She knew that David's interest in gardening was very limited. Two fruit bushes and the lawn. Suddenly he straightened himself and looked directly at Eleanor.

"Eleanor, are you serious about this relationship?"

For a moment, Eleanor was speechless. He had switched from growing peas to her marriage with no warning.

"Mr Anderson, do you think I would put myself through this if I wasn't?" she replied.

"Put yourself through what."

"Mr Anderson, it's pretty obvious that you don't approve of me."

"Eleanor, don't take it personally. It's not you. We think it's too soon, and well ..." He stopped.

"Yes?" Eleanor said, trying to look as if she did not take it personally.

"Do you think David might be too, er, mature for you?"

"Do you mean, too old? Or do you mean, am I too young," she said, forcing her self to smile sweetly.

"Eleanor, you are a very attractive young woman. Could that be the basis of David's infatuation?" he said carefully.

Eleanor paused. She could see the implied reasoning behind his comment. His son was infatuated, and it was her fault. Yes, she did try and look nice to please him, but what girl didn't?

"Isn't that rather insulting your son's judgement," she said calmly.

"He's just another man swayed by his hormones."

"Pardon?"

"Sorry. What I mean is, I don't think he is capable of making rational decisions yet. It's too soon!"

"Oh!" Eleanor said.

For a moment she thought that his father looked embarrassed. "Come and see my greenhouse," he said, as though the previous conversation had not occurred.

David's mother was not so blunt.

"David, you're making a fool of yourself!" she said.

"Is that why Dad has taken Eleanor into the garden? Is he telling her that she is making a fool of herself? No, Dad wouldn't be that rude."

"I'm not being rude, David. Someone has to say it!"

"Mum, you may well be right. That's the chance I want to take. Personally, I think it could be Eleanor who's making the mistake if any one is. She's giving up more than me."

"Tush! If you marry her, she will be able to take you to

the cleaners – half of your assets to start with. And
maintenance. Let's hope it's all over before we pass on."
"Sorry," David said, not sure how to take the last
comment.
"You are our only son. You will inherit this house. I don't
want it going to her!"
"In which case, Mum, leave it to charity!" David said.

They stood looking at each other, both breathing heavily.
Then David spoke again, calmly and deliberately.
"Mum, you don't know her. I know she's young, okay,
very young, but I know her character. I don't mind you
telling me what you think of me, but please take my word
for it; Eleanor is not in this for a quick buck! Her parents
have already disowned her."
"Really? Because of you?" his mother asked.
"They said she was not to see me. They put her things out
on the doorstep."
"You mean she's moved in with you already?"
"Mum!" David had raised his voice. "She has not moved
in. She is living with a friend, a retired lady who lost her
husband a few years back."

Neither spoke again for a few moments. Then his mother
spoke again.
"If you need to get married, I still think you should find
someone your own age, but there, who am I to tell you."
"Mum, I just wish you would give us a chance. I'm sorry
I announced it so dramatically. I had been worrying about
how to tell you."
His mother smiled. "When you said about bringing a
friend, we did wonder, but then when the friend was so
young, I think we were shocked. I was."
"Mum, I think we should leave. Shall I go and fetch
Eleanor?"

"No, maybe she's charming your father the way she charmed you!"

"Mum, leave it," David said sharply.

The uneasy truce between David and his mother continued until his father brought Eleanor back in twenty minutes later. Eleanor's face showed no indication of their discussions, in fact, she seemed enthusiastic.

"You've got a lovely garden, Mrs Anderson," she said. "I enjoyed being shown around."

"Eleanor, we need to leave," David said. They were already standing in the hallway.

"Oh, right." She turned to Mr Anderson. "Thank you so much for showing me round." Then she turned to Mrs Anderson. "Thank you for a lovely dinner."

"Bye, Dad, bye Mum." David kissed his mum's cheek, and opened the front door.

"Sweetheart, that went very badly," David said, as they drove away.

"I could see by your face," Eleanor said. "So what happened?"

"Put your ring back on, and I'll tell you."

Eleanor listened as David told her about his session with his mother and then she told him about her session with his father.

"So now we are both in the same boat," David said, by way of summary.

"Not quite. They are still talking to you!" Eleanor pointed out.

"Talking, maybe, but not saying nice things," David said. "I wonder if they will come round."

"Yours or mine?" he pondered. "I wonder how tomorrow will go."

"They won't be rude, David."

"No, but they will be hurt."

David set off alone on Friday morning to visit Jenny's parents. Although he had hidden his worries from Eleanor about visiting his parents, she knew he was worried about this visit. The journey was further, which meant more time for worrying. David thought that like their daughter, they would not want him to remain single. The issues were timing and age. Was it too soon, that is from their perspective? And would they be upset by Eleanor's age. As he pulled onto their drive, both parents came out. And both parents greeted him with a hug, and a kiss from Jenny's mother.

"How lovely to see you, come in," they said.

David had arrived in time for lunch and too late for morning coffee, so there was time for catching up on news. David didn't know how to bring up the subject, but Jenny's mother took the initiative. After about twenty minutes, and lunchtime getting nearer, she looked at David.

"David, we thought very highly of you as a husband and father," Jenny's mother said.

"Did you?" David replied, feeling nonplussed by this revelation.

"So if you want to tell us something, we won't be upset."

"Oh."

"Have you come to tell us something?"

"Er, yes."

"What is her name, David?"

"Eleanor," he blurted.

"Do you want to tell us about her?"

"How did you know?" David asked.

"We didn't, but we wondered, and then seeing you sitting there fidgeting, I guessed you had something on your mind that you were finding it hard to say. David, we are the parents of your late wife – what other news would be so difficult?"

"And you don't think it's too soon?"

"Did Eleanor know her?" Jenny's mother asked, ignoring the question.

"Not personally. But who she was – yes."

"So?"

"It's a long story, let me start at the beginning ..."

They listen with no interruptions.

"... so, I had to make a decision. Whether to stop seeing her and so prevent a rift between her and her parents, or ask her to marry me. I did the latter."

"And she said yes, we presume?"

David nodded.

"Right. So does that mean you're engaged?"

"Yes," he said quietly. "I am sorry if you are hurt, but I felt that I had to tell you. If you would rather I left, I understand."

"David, you will always be our son-in-law. Of course we don't want you to leave, but I do feel that lunch is now running late. Can you tell us the rest after lunch?"

The subject was dropped until after lunch. Jenny's mother waited until they had coffee.

"David," she said, "we are not hurt, but we are surprised. Was it the girl you were with at Daniel's wedding?"

"Yes, it was. It was Stephanie who insisted that she came, but I think she knew how we felt about each other, and that was why she asked her. I was in love, however, at that stage, I had no thoughts of marriage. We were friends, affectionate friends. I expected her to go to university and probably end up with a young man at college."

"And what about her parents threat?"

"They kept it. They threw her out. She's living with a widow from our church. Originally, we assumed that we would marry in the summer next year, that's two and a half years on, but now there seems no point in waiting. She has no proper home and I have a home waiting for her."

"Will she leave school?" Jenny's father asked.

"No. I can see no reason why she should. She will be an adult. People become adults in the sixth form. They drive to school. They can vote. Therefore they should be able to marry."

"I hope the school agrees," Jenny's father said.

David's heart was much lighter as he drove home. As he left, Jenny's father shook his hand and wished him a good journey. "And we would like to meet this Eleanor, David," he added.

"Really?" David said, surprised. "Does that mean you would come to the wedding? Or is that a step too far?"

"Let us think about it, David. But if not at the wedding, you must bring her to meet us."

"Or you can come to us!"

"We'll see."

Chapter 7

More Family

Friday night was jazz night, and he had arranged to pick up both Eleanor and Lizzie that evening. Before starting his journey home, David pulled into the side of the road and sent a text message to Eleanor. It was a laborious process, so it was a very brief message.

```
Good response just leaving will
pick you up as arranged
```

Things had gone so much better than he had expected, that he did not think about the next day's visit. It was to see his son and new daughter-in-law and he was looking forward to it – his first visit to their flat. His relief at way Jenny's parents had accepted his news banished any thoughts he should have had about Eleanor being worried.

Her first question on being picked up that evening was to ask about his visit.

"How did it go today?" she asked.

"Much better than I had hoped. They said they would like to meet you so I asked if they would like to come to the wedding."

"Oh, David, you didn't! What did they say?"

"They wanted to think about it."

"David that was tactless. They may want to meet me, but not at our wedding. Don't you see? It would bring back memories of your wedding with Jenny!"

"Oh, Eleanor. I am so stupid at times. You see, I do need a wife!"

"I've known that for a long time."

"Yes, you did say it soon after we met."

"I know, and that was tactless of me. I didn't want to say it, remember? You made me! Anyway, tell me about your visit."

He managed to tell Eleanor about the day before they arrived at Lizzie's house.

"I still can't get over it; you two getting married," Lizzie said, as she got into the car.

"You realise that you must take some of the blame," Eleanor said, turning to speak to her. "Don't you remember suggesting that he joined us at the jazz concert?"

"I do. I also remember suggesting going to the cinema!" David laughed. "Don't worry; I wouldn't have gone with Eleanor then either."

"Were you two serious when we went to the lido?" Lizzie asked.

"I was, he wasn't," Eleanor said laughing.

"So what happened, David?" Lizzie asked.

"What do you mean?" he replied.

"Come on, when did you get serious?"

"I discovered that she is a super-rich heiress, so I decided to marry her for her money!"

"What? You didn't!" Lizzie said, letting David fool her for a moment.

"Lizzie!" Eleanor howled with laughter. "Just ignore him."

Lizzie sat back in her seat, momentarily extinguished. Then she sat up again. "Huh," she said, "I think he's just a typical man. Doesn't know what's best for him – that or he's slow to make up his mind."

"Hey, stop running me down," David called, "or I'll press the ejector button."

The trivialities continued through the evening and right up to the point where they dropped Lizzie off. Then Eleanor went very quiet.

"Are you okay, Eleanor?" David asked. He knew it was a silly question, but he didn't like to ask what was wrong. Eleanor shrugged. "Was it because we included Lizzie?" he ventured.

"No! I'm glad she came with us, she kept my mind off other things."

"Other things? Parents?"

"Yes, now there are two sets of upset parents. I'm beginning to feel guilty about yours as well."

"Eleanor, Eleanor, it wasn't your fault."

"I know, but I feel bad. But I'm also angry and upset. It's very confusing. On top of all that, there's tomorrow. I wonder how Daniel will react."

David kept quiet. On the one hand, he could see there might be some embarrassment, but on the other hand, he was looking forward to seeing his son and new daughter-in-law in their new home.

"It can't be as bad as Thursday because Stephanie will be there," he said.

"That's true," Eleanor replied, but with little conviction.

It was over a two hour journey, so David picked Eleanor up at eight o'clock. They stopped for coffee at a road-side caravan where there were garden seats for the customers. The sun was shining. He could hear a blackbird nearby, even though it was near a road. David leaned back in his chair, feeling happy inside, and smiled at Eleanor.

"Now what are you thinking?" she asked.

David shrugged. He was thinking about his son. "The sun is shining, the birds are singing, and Eleanor, you look beautiful!" he said.

"Go on! I need to do my make up."

"No, you look gorgeous. I'm looking at the woman I'm going to marry – and I wish I was already married, okay?"

"David! Shush!" she exclaimed, as the implication struck her. Then she grinned. "So what could you do about it if we were?" she said, indicating the fact that they were among other customers.

"I'm sure there are plenty of deserted places further along

the road" he said, laughing.

"David!" She hesitated. "Have you, I mean?"

"I'll tell you when we're married," he said.

"But it will be winter then!" she replied, laughing.

"Not where we're going for our honeymoon! Come on, finish up. Time to go."

The stop was a bright interlude for Eleanor, and once back on the road, she descended into quietness again. Suddenly she sat up.

"David! What are you taking as a present?"

"I'm not. Sorry, it didn't occur to me," he answered.

"Can you turn round?"

"Why?"

"There was a flower stall by the side of the road. Please, David. I'll buy them with my own money." Seven minutes later they were back on the road. It seemed that buying the flowers made a difference to Eleanor, and now she chatted and helped David navigate the last few miles. They parked the car, but before leaving it, Eleanor moved her ring to her right hand. Then they began the climb up to the second floor. Stephanie must have been looking out of her window because she met them on the first floor landing. Eleanor was carrying the flowers, but she thrust them at David, and then the two girls almost ran into each other's arms. Finally they moved apart, with Stephanie taking both of Eleanor's hands in hers.

"I am so glad David brought you with him," she said. "I didn't really have much time to talk to you at the wedding, what with you having to leave early."

"Well, no doubt you'll make up for it today," David said. "Oh, these are for you, they're from Eleanor. I forgot."

"They're from us both, David," Eleanor said.

"Men!" said Stephanie, as she then embraced David. "I can see who Danny takes after!"

Stephanie led them back to her landing, where one door was ajar.

"Danny," she called, "they're here!"

Daniel came out, and embraced David. "Good to see you, Dad," he said.

"And I've brought Eleanor," David said, indicating Eleanor who had hung back.

Daniel hesitated as though he was not sure what to do. He nearly extended his hand, but then he bent forward and lightly kissed her cheek. "Hello, Eleanor," he said.

"Hello, Danny," she replied, using Stephanie's name for him.

"Anyway, come in, come in," Stephanie called. "Coffee?"

Daniel brought in the coffee as Eleanor sat next to David on the three-seater settee and then asked about the journey and his directions.

"It was fine – as were the directions. Eleanor read them and directed me," David answered.

"And how are you both?" Stephanie added, bubbling with excitement. "You're still friends then?"

Eleanor glanced at David, but he showed no response. David had told her that he wanted to settle in before he told them about the engagement. "Yes, of course," David replied. "Daniel, you said you wanted to ask me something, well?"

Daniel looked embarrassed. "It can wait. Finish your coffee," he said.

"Hey! I may only be a man, but I can drink and answer questions," David said.

"Later, Dad!"

"That's a beautiful ring, Eleanor. Can I see it?" Stephanie said.

"Sure," said Eleanor, pulling it off and holding it out towards Stephanie.

Stephanie took it and examined it closely. "It's lovely. Who bought it for you?"

"David did," Eleanor whispered, then looking at David. David smiled and nodded. Stephanie handed it back and Eleanor pushed it on to her left hand ring finger, all the while looking at Stephanie. Stephanie's mouth slowly dropped open. "You're not?" she said slowly.
"We are," Eleanor whispered, her hand then searching for David's hand.

This time Stephanie jumped up. "Wow!" she shrieked. Then she looked at David for confirmation. "Really?" she said.
David smiled, nodded and said, "Yes, really!"
Stephanie's response was to fling herself at Eleanor to hug and kiss her. Then she hugged David. "I am so pleased for you," she said.
"Are you?" Eleanor asked.
"Oh yes. How many girls get a mother-in-law they can relate to? Wow! Danny?"
Daniel got up and walked across to David. This time he shook his hand. "Congratulations, Dad, and to you too, Eleanor."
"Thanks, Daniel," David replied. "I can tell it's a bit of a shock."
"It shouldn't be. I told him it would happen," Stephanie exclaimed. "He'll get used to it."
"Eleanor's been so nervous about telling you," David told Daniel.
Daniel looked at Eleanor. "Do you understand, Eleanor? It's not everyday that a guy gets a step-mother who is actually younger than himself."
"Or a girl gets a step-son who is older," Eleanor replied. "It's really scary."
"He's not scary, Eleanor," Stephanie said, putting her arms round Daniel. "He's a pussy."
"I think Eleanor sees him as a lion," David said, putting his arm round Eleanor. "So, guess I'll have to find a lion tamer."

"I can do that!" Stephanie replied, laughing. "He'll get used to it," she added.

"I'm sorry, Daniel," David said. "Would you rather we went?"

"No, no," Daniel replied quickly. "Besides, we've been cooking for you. Sorry, look, Eleanor, I am pleased for Dad. I didn't expect it to happen so quickly, and especially to such a young beautiful woman. But I can't think of you as a mother, sorry."

"Danny, I'm never going to be your mother. I wouldn't know how to, but I think I can make your dad happy. Can you accept that?"

Daniel looked at her. "Come here," he said quietly. Eleanor went to Daniel and he gave her a long hug. "Welcome to the family, Eleanor," he said, whereupon Eleanor crumpled again, and turned back to David. David stood up quickly and held her as she sobbed. "Thanks, Daniel, you don't know how much that means," David said, as both Daniel and Stephanie looked puzzled by Eleanor's crying. "Eleanor has been kicked out of her home because of me," David said, to explain. "Her emotions are a bit tender. She'll be okay in a minute." Eleanor pulled away. "I'm sorry everyone," she said. "I keep doing that – but that's the last time." She took a deep breath. "Stephie, can I use the bathroom, please?"

Eleanor came back a few minutes later, and sat down next to David. "Sorry," she said again. Then Stephanie went and sat in the vacant place next to Eleanor, and put her arm round her.

"Dad has explained everything, Eleanor," she said. "I think you are very brave! So, tell us about the wedding plans."

"We have the date booked, and a honeymoon, but I couldn't face anything else until we had told you," she said. "I was wondering if you would be my matron-of-honour." Eleanor said, in a rush.

"Yes, of course. When is it?"

"The last Saturday before Christmas," David said slowly.

"What? Sorry, do you mean this Christmas?" Daniel exclaimed.

"Yes."

"But I thought Eleanor was still at school!" Daniel said.

"I am," said Eleanor.

"Can you do that? Is it allowed?" Stephanie asked.

"If mothers can go to school, why shouldn't wives?" David said. "Okay, education up to sixteen is compulsory, but it is a right after that. It will only be for two terms."

"Why don't you wait until she finishes school, Dad?"

"Why didn't you wait another year, Daniel?"

"There was no point. I had a job and we got this flat, so ... oh!"

"Exactly," David said.

"But will you cope with being a, er, student and a housewife?" Stephanie asked.

"You nearly said schoolgirl then, didn't you," Eleanor asked with a smile. "Look, girls can leave school and get married at sixteen. Why shouldn't I cope at eighteen?"

"And pass your exams?" Daniel asked.

"Daniel, Eleanor will come top of the class!" David said. Eleanor grinned. "You should see his whip!"

"Eleanor, it's not funny! It won't be easy!" Daniel said.

"Sorry. I agree, but I'd rather live with your dad than stay with Mrs Hayes, even though I love her."

Eleanor's statement obviously closed the matter, and for a few moments they sat in silence. Then Eleanor asked if they had their photographs back – they had. This took a long time. Then David wanted to be shown round the flat – all four rooms, counting the bathroom. There were five wooden crates stacked up in the bedroom, for which Stephanie apologised.

"They're my things, they're Danny's and they are presents that we can't find a space for," Stephanie said pointing at the boxes.

"I've got some of my things stacked up in David's house. I couldn't take everything to Mrs Hayes'. Don't you have a garage?"

"Yes, but we wouldn't leave things in it," Danny said.

"And isn't there anywhere else?" Eleanor asked. "Aren't there storage places?"

"We're trying to save money," Stephanie said, "so we put up with it."

"Until you get a bigger place," Eleanor said, innocently. She didn't notice Daniel and Stephanie look at each other.

"I'll go and check up on lunch," Stephanie said.

Lunch wasn't ready and they chatted generally until it was. After lunch, Stephanie suggested they went for a walk so that they could show David and Eleanor their local park. There was also a small café next to boating lake. As they walked there, they split into two groups, Stephanie with Eleanor in front and Daniel with his father behind.

"Stephie, will Danny really accept me into the family?" Eleanor asked.

"I think so, Eleanor, what should I call you by the way?"

"My friends call me Elly, my parents call me Eleanor as does David."

"So, what should I call you?"

"I thought you were my friend, Stephie,"

At this point they hugged; then Eleanor continued.

"You were saying – about Danny."

"I was pleased that his dad had found someone and I had a feeling that you and Dad were serious. I didn't know his mum, so," Stephanie shrugged, "obviously I don't have the same feelings. I think Danny would find it hard to accept any woman who takes his mother's place."

"Do you think I'm taking her place?"

"You'll be in her house, in her kitchen and in her …" She stopped.

"Bed?" Eleanor whispered. "Is that what you mean? The pastor's wife said something similar, but I didn't really think about it."

"Do you think you should?"

"Think about it or do something? There's nothing I can do, I mean, it's not my house anyway."

"Then you haven't talked about it?"

"We haven't talked about anything. I've had too much on my mind – sorting out where I should live, and worrying about coming here. But we will have to talk, I agree."

"I don't think Dad would consider moving while you're at school, do you?"

"Probably not – and is there time before we're married?"

"Hm, if you were lucky, just about. But you don't want that worry hanging over you. Imagine getting married and having to move on the same day!" She giggled. "Have you ever felt odd being in Jenny's house," she added.

"No, because it was never Jenny's house to me. And David sent me to a hotel the first night. Fortunately, the pastor found Mrs Hayes, otherwise I might have been in Jill's old room."

"But you are already in his heart!" Stephanie said.

"Danny can't begrudge me that, surely," Eleanor said.

"I haven't known his dad without knowing you. However, Danny has admitted to me that Dad is a different man, having met you. If you keep his dad happy, I don't think my husband will have any grounds to object. And you have me on your side, you know."

It was time for another hug.

David and Daniel were about ten metres behind the girls. "Daniel, can I ask, no, I will beg you. Please don't be unkind to Eleanor. Is it because she's young, or is it just that she's a woman? I mean, how would you cope if she were my age, your mum's age?"

Daniel hesitated, so David continued. "Or is it too soon?"
Daniel grinned, briefly. "Dad, too many questions."
"Sorry."
"Too soon?" Daniel repeated. "Dad, if I lost Stephie, I
don't know how I would cope. Stephie says we should
make wills, but the thought of her dying makes me, well,
I can't face it."
"If it's any help, we felt the same – it was having you and
Jill that pushed us into it. You don't have much to leave
anyway, do you?"
"You have a point, but that doesn't help. I just can't
imagine remarrying, sorry."
"So it's not that it's too soon, it's just that it's going to
happen."
"Dad, were you looking for a woman?" Daniel asked.
"Good gracious, no! I think I was coming to terms with a
new status – slowly. The job in my church helped. I
suppose there must have been a small hole, an Eleanor
shaped hole. It wasn't because she was young, no, in
many ways that helped."
"Helped? How?"
"Because she was nice to know and easy to get on with
and yet could not be a romantic complication. Daniel, I
taught girls of her age and no way would I ever have
considered being friendly with one of them, especially on
a one to one basis."
"Did you date her, Dad?"
"No! But we went on a bike ride – I offered to show her a
swan's nest that I had discovered. It was like we were
mates. Oh, I went to a concert, more than one, but with
her and a friend. There was no boy-girl thing."
"But something happened eventually, I assume."
"We had to spend time singing – you remember. And I
did enjoy her company. Yes, I was fond of her, but she
was still only a friend. Then the singing stopped and I
missed her. Things developed, I suppose after we began
seeing each other again, but strictly as friends." David

stopped, and faced Daniel. "Daniel, I had to make a decision. I knew how she felt. Either I had to stop seeing her for her sake so that she could begin again, and do it well before her exams, or tell her how I felt. Eleanor said that if we were to spend our life together, then on average, we would have less time together. So our life together should start as soon as possible and I will marry her as soon as practically convenient."

They began walking again. "Oh, and there's one other thing. Eleanor is filling a hole in my heart. She is replacing your mother, true, but she did not displace your mother. It could have been the other way round. If I had died, I would not have wanted your mum to live a lonely life. I told her that I would want her to remarry, okay. Good. Now what was it that you wanted to ask me?"
"I'm not sure if I can ask you now," Daniel said.
"Why? Is it anything to do with Eleanor?"
Daniel hesitated. "Possibly"
"Come on, it is or it isn't. What do you mean?"
"We're on a six months lease in our flat, however, we wondered about trying to get a place of our own. You saw how cramped we are. We have seen a place where they're building new houses, but they're outside our price range at the moment. If we leave it until we have a bigger deposit, we're frightened they may have gone up."
"And you'd like me to help?"
"We were thinking of a loan, but obviously things have changed now."
"You are still my son, Daniel."
"But I won't be your wife's son."
"I see. But tell me what your time plan was anyway."
"Are you sure?"
"Yes. It may be too ambitious regardless of whether I'm married, but I would still like to hear it."

Daniel explained that their six months finished in
January, and then they were on a month by month basis.
He said that a small deposit was required to reserve a
plot, and then to buy it would need a bigger deposit –
depending on how big a mortgage they would need.
"Do you know how big a mortgage you can get?" David
asked.
"Yes, but only approximately."
"And the deposit needed?"
Daniel said he did, so David fished in his pocket and
pulled out a scrap of paper. "Write both figures on there,"
he said. "To be honest, we haven't discussed anything
yet. We should have made a start this week – school starts
next week – but Eleanor was on edge about coming here."
"I'm sorry, Dad."
"Then will you come to the wedding?"
Daniel laughed. "Stephanie will insist on it!"
"Willingly?"
"Yes, Dad, of course willingly."
"Okay! I think Eleanor wants Stephanie to be a
bridesmaid. Well, a matron-of-honour to be precise,
which leaves me. It would mean a lot to us both if you
would consider being my best man."
"Oh!" Daniel gasped.
"I will understand if you don't want to."
"Dad, it hadn't occurred to me that you would want me."
"Hadn't it?"
"No."
"Look, there's no rush. As I said, I will understand. At
least you will be there," David said.
The subject was dropped, and they talked about other
things. Daniel's job. Football. Politics. Finally they
caught the girls up by the lake.

They spent an hour on the lake in two boats. For most of
that time they remained as they had been on the walk, but
now the two groups interacted by racing each other. For

the last fifteen minutes, they swapped places so that
Eleanor was with David.

"How are you now," he asked her.

"Much better. Stephanie is such fun. You seemed to be in
a deep discussion with Daniel every time I looked."

"Did I?" David said, not wishing to commit himself.

"This is nice," Eleanor said, a few moments later. "See
the swans over there? I wonder if they are ours?"

"Let's ask them," David said.

"Silly man." She smiled. He did like that smile.

They ate ice cream in the café, and then walked back.
When they left, after tea, Stephanie hugged Eleanor first,
and then David. Daniel embraced his father, and then
stepped over to Eleanor. However, instead of just a peck
on the cheek, he then hugged her. "Eleanor," he said
quietly, "thank you for coming. Dad said you were
worried. Please don't be. My dad has always been a good
judge of character, so I would like to get to know you
better."

As David and Eleanor drove home they discussed the
day, and Eleanor agreed that it hadn't been as bad as she
had anticipated. She was pleased that Stephanie had
agreed to be her maid-of-honour.

"What about Daniel? Did you ask him?" Eleanor asked.

"Yes. He said he hadn't expected it, so I've left him to
think about it."

"Good. What else did you talk about? Oh, didn't he want
to ask you something?"

"Yes, he did, but then he changed his mind."

"So you don't know what it was about"

"I do. I got him to tell me."

"Okay, tell me. Oh, sorry, was it personal?"

"It was about money – one of the things that we have to
talk about," David said. "I just have one question for the
moment. When we marry, where do you expect to live?"

"With you, obviously."

"Will that be a problem?"

"Not for me, personally," Eleanor replied, but wondering why he had asked. "I shall feel guilty though," she added.

"Of what?"

"Of being in a big house while your son and daughter-in-law live in such a small apartment."

David turned and smiled at her. "Shall we put that on our things to talk about list, Sweetheart?"

Chapter 8

A New School Year

David and Eleanor both approached the new term differently. Just over a year earlier David had been an uninspired, and therefore possibly an uninspiring teacher. It had been his church work and then the singing with Eleanor that had been something to enthuse over. He had finally made the decision to remain part-time, settling on a ninety-percent timetable. In reality, this gave him one afternoon off. Now he almost regretted not being full time. Okay, it was not important that people did not know the name of the capital of Mongolia, but it was important to understand how people interacted with other people, and with the environment. Why and how cities develop. In fact, he was surprised at how positive he was. Eleanor, on the other hand was surprised at how un-enthusiastic she was. She had always liked school, and coped well with its demands, both academic and social. Now she saw it as a temporary phase between her present time, and that of being a wife and mother. She had even made a chart showing all the days that could be ticked-off over the coming year. Mrs Hayes had seen the chart and was horrified.

David's term started one day earlier than Eleanor's. It was an in-service day, but his new positive attitude did not extend to an in-service day! However, it did allow him to sort his room ready for the next day. Eleanor spent the morning in town with Lizzie talking about weddings and wedding dresses. They separated after drinking coffee and it was then that going round a corner she came face to face with her mother. Both stopped and stared at each other.

"Hello, Mum," Eleanor said, speaking first.

"Hello."

"How are you?"

"I'm all right, thank you – and you?" her mother answered.

"I'm okay. How's Dad?"

"He's okay."

There was a pause. Then Mrs Jenkins spoke again

"Are living with that Mr Anderson?"

"Mum! Of course not," Eleanor exclaimed.

"Oh."

"I thought you knew me better than that!"

"Where are you living then?"

"I'm living with a lady from my church. She's a widow."

"Did you arrange that?"

"No, it was Lucy the …" She hesitated. "It was another friend from church."

"You're not telling me that it was already arranged?"

"No, it wasn't. When I saw my stuff on the step, we took it away and put it in David's house and then he booked me into a Travel Lodge for the night."

There was another pause. "So what did you think when I came and got the rest of my stuff?"

"Your dad was flaming mad. Why did you leave your computer?"

"It wasn't mine. It was a borrowed one from his work, right? Oh, and I've got my own phone now. We kept the little chip thing inside because it has my contacts, apparently. I will return yours sometime."

Sheila Jenkins shrugged. "It's up to you."

"Mum, why didn't you come looking for me?" Eleanor asked.

"Your dad said not to. He said we knew where you were
and that you would come back when he got tired of you."
"Is that why you didn't put everything out on the step?"
"Partly."
"Mum, he's going to marry me, look!" Eleanor said
showing her mother the ring.
"Don't be so naive, Eleanor," she said, waving it away.
"People his age don't actually marry teenagers. He's a
teacher, he'll be sacked."
"Mum, teachers don't get sacked for marrying. And we're
not having an affair!"
"Yet."
"Oh, Mum," Eleanor said, sadly. She paused. "Mum, do
you want to stay in touch?"
"Your dad said you will come back," Sheila Jenkins said
hesitantly.
"Okay," Eleanor said gently. "Suppose that's not soon.
Do you want to stay in touch until then?"
Sheila Jenkins nodded.
"Give me your shopping list," Eleanor said. She wrote
down Mrs Hayes' address and telephone number. "You
know my mobile number, so you can text me if you need
to, Mum. Bye." She leaned forward and kissed her
mother's cheek, then turned and walked away. A few
moments later she realised that she wasn't crying.

She told Mrs Hayes over dinner that evening. Mrs Hayes
quietly said that things would work out in time.
"Yes, but before or after the wedding," Eleanor said.
"That is out of our hands, my dear," was her response.
Later that evening Eleanor was drinking hot chocolate
with Mrs Hayes. She had sorted out all she needed for the
next day.
"Only about seventy days to go, and then another, oh, I
can't remember exactly, but I will be able to leave school.

Hooray," Eleanor said. "Have you seen my chart?"

"Yes, Eleanor," Mrs Hayes said quietly.

"What do you think of it?"

"Eleanor, if I were your mother, I would express an opinion. But you are a guest."

"You don't approve?" Eleanor asked, surprised.

"Whether or not I approve is immaterial."

"Mrs Hayes, I mean, Molly. Please tell me."

Mrs Hayes sighed. "Eleanor, my dear, what is the purpose of life?"

"Oh," said Eleanor. "Are you referring to the catechism that pastor James was teaching us?"

"Man's chief aim," Mrs Hayes prompted. "Remember?" Eleanor nodded.

"When I was young," Mrs Hayes continued, "I had to do a sixth month probationary period as part of my qualification. I counted the days off. It was like putting the days into a bin. They were not important. It took a few years before I realised, and then I regretted it. Eleanor, take each day as a gift from God. I can't tell you how to use your days – some days can be days of restful nothingness. But don't wish them away. I know you can't wait to marry, but wouldn't it be great to remember this time as a happy time. And as for the whole year, David wants to be proud of your academic exploits. It will be hard to achieve them if you resent school. There, sorry. I've said my piece!"

Eleanor stared at Mrs Hayes. "Thank you. Why am I so silly? It's times like this that I feel I'm too immature for David. Thank you for telling me, I will try to be positive."

"Eleanor, it's times like this that I think David is a very lucky man!"

"Do you?"

"I think he is going to be so proud of you, Eleanor."
"I wish my mum and dad felt like that," Eleanor
whispered.
"Just be patient," Molly Hayes said quietly.

Despite David's initial enthusiasm on the in-service day,
by the next morning he was back to normal! Because the
staff meeting had been held on the in-service day, the
school spent the minimum time on administration before
teaching the children. David spent the two periods of
form time with his form handing out time-tables and
homework diaries before teaching for the rest of the
morning. He was then going to go home. However, the
school secretary caught him at the end of the last lesson.
"Mr Anderson, the head says could you just pop in to see
him before you go?"
"Did he say what it was about?" David asked.
"'Fraid not, sorry," she said, and left.
David tidied up, packed his bag, and walked up to the
school office, his mind on the cooking he was planning to
do. Because of Saturday being spent with his family, his
normal term time Saturday routine had been missed, but
he had used Monday for that purpose. There was just time
to use Eleanor's cook-book before meeting her from
school.

"Go straight in, he's expecting you," the secretary told
him. Even so, David knocked before opening the
headmaster's door.
"Ah, David. Come in. Seat?" he said, indicating a chair.
"Good holiday?"
"Yes, thank you."
"Good start to the day?"
"Ye-es," David replied, wondering what this was all
about. Unless the head wanted to asked him to return to

full-time. Suddenly, the headmaster seemed to change. "I'll come straight to the point, David. I have been informed that you have a relationship with a schoolgirl." This was not at all what David had expected. They are words which strike fear to the very core of a teacher, regardless of whether there is any foundation of truth. But it did not do that to David. His first thought was that something had happened to Eleanor, so he sat and waited. "Well?" the headmaster asked.

"Would you mind telling me who gave you this information?" David asked.

"It was a phone call."

"From her school?" David asked.

"You mean it's true?" the headmaster seemed to gasp.

"Was it Eleanor's school?" David demanded.

The headmaster looked at David. Something was unusual. He had had this type of conversation only once before, and in that case the teacher had seemed to wilt in front of him. "I don't think so," he said slowly.

"You don't think so? Come on, you would know that!" David paused. "Are you saying it was anonymous?"

"I believe it was, but is it true?" he said, hoping to regain the initiative.

"Yes," said David, folding his arms, and leaning back. "It is."

"Oh!"

"Right, may I now ask you a question?"

"Well, yes. All right."

"If Jamie Rawson the head boy came to you and said that he had married this last holiday, what would you do?"

"What would I do?" the headmaster repeated.

"Let me remind you that when Annie what's-her-name had a baby the other year, you allowed her back after the birth. So?"

118

"Right, I would speak to him and ask him about the circumstances," the headmaster said.
"But would you let him stay and finish his education?"
"I would speak to his parents,"
"And if he were over eighteen."
The headmaster leaned forward on his elbows. "Is the young lady eighteen?"
"You answer my question first."

The headmaster sat erect again, and looked at David. "All right, assuming that his marriage does not cause disruption, I would have no reason to stop him finishing his time here."
"Thank you," David said. "I have become engaged to a young lady at another school. She has been kicked out of her home, and is living with a mature lady. She is not eighteen, but will be shortly and then we plan to marry. I can see no reason why it should cause any disruption here."
The headmaster blinked. "Is this serious, David?" he asked.
"Oh yes. First, let me assure you that there has been no scandal or indiscretion. Secondly, I have known her for over a year, during which time my opinion of her has risen steadily. Do you have a problem with that?"
"Well, no." He paused. "David, can I ask you something personal?"
"Of course," David said.
"Is this on the rebound?"
David smiled. "No, I don't believe it is. Why?"
"I did notice that you seemed to be a different person."
"When did you notice?" David enquired.
"Oh, I think someone mentioned it last Easter. And yesterday. I put it down partly to you being part-time."
"That does help," David said, smiling. "It also means I

can meet her from school later – discreetly, of course."

"I don't know what to say."

"Then say nothing. Please keep it quiet. My first thought when you spoke to me was that Eleanor was in trouble at her school. We both want her to finish the year," David said.

"Have you thought about waiting?"

"She's now with a landlady; I have a house, so why wait? She will turn eighteen in November, so we thought the Christmas holiday would be an ideal time."

"And she will go back to school as Mrs Anderson! Ah, now I see why you asked me the hypothetical question earlier. David, you are a rogue, oh, sorry, I didn't mean it like that."

David stood up, and grinned. "No offence taken."

The headmaster stood up and walked round his desk to see David to the door. He paused. "I do hope it works out. Congratulations," he added, shaking David's hand.

Eleanor bussed to school and met Lizzie outside the school. Of course they hugged, even though they had been together the day before. Then Lizzie made a grab for Eleanor's left hand.

"Lizzie, what are you doing?" Eleanor gasped, pulling it away.

"Just checking."

"Don't. Someone might notice," Eleanor said.

"But there's nothing to notice, is there?"

"There was a mark there when I took it off this morning, but I think it's gone now. Look, Lizzie, we don't know how the school will react, so there's no rush to tell them, okay."

"Elly, they're bound to find out sooner or later," Lizzie said.

"Then let it be later!"

Even as sixth-formers, there was a so called form time. Their school was a traditional school, with prefects and junior prefects. One of the first things, after completing their registration, was to hand out badges to the new senior prefects.

"You'll be the first married prefect. Elly," Lizzie whispered.

"Shush," Eleanor whispered back.

However, it was the next item that shook Eleanor. The careers teacher had dropped into their base for an announcement.

"College and university applications go off this term. I assume most of you have firmed up your ideas over the holiday, so I'm handing out some UCCA forms for you to familiarise yourselves with them. Then I will be conducting mock interviews soon. Any questions?"

"Please, Miss, suppose we don't want to go to college. My dad says we can't afford it," one of the girls said.

"Well Jacqueline, I do understand. Look, college isn't for everyone, I know that. But for those who can benefit, it is still an opportunity. If you think financial consideration will play a part in your decision, then please do come and tell me. There are sometimes ways and means to alleviate such problems."

Lizzie raised her hand.

"Yes, Lizzie?"

"Suppose I wanted to get married instead?" she asked.

Mrs Finch didn't turn a hair. For one thing, she knew Lizzie well, and knew she sometimes liked to be provocative just for the sake of it.

"Is that your plan," she said evenly, so that some of the girls laughed.

"No, Mrs Finch. I said suppose. Anyway, who knows, a knight in shining armour might ride in and whisk me off my feet."

"In which case, you could take your knight with you. University students can be married, you know," Mrs Finch said.

"Can school students be married?" The question came from Kylie King. Eleanor froze, and felt her stomach lurch. She looked at Lizzie, who shook her head slightly. "Is that going to happen to you, Kylie?" Mrs Finch asked her. Kylie was not gifted with prettiness, but she tossed her head defiantly.

"No. I read about it," she said.

"In a novel?"

Several girls giggled. Kylie was known as an avid reader of romance.

"No! It was in a magazine. There were two kids in an American high school, and they were married."

"America, eh. We're in Britain, Kylie. It's not likely to happen here, is it?"

"No, but could it?" she persisted.

"Can you see parents allowing it? Or were you thinking about people who elope to Scotland?"

Kylie gave up, but Eleanor was tempted to continue. As she began to raise her hand, Lizzie noticed.

"Mrs Finch," she called out without raising her hand. "Do you think we girls are disadvantaged?"

"Lizzie," she replied with feeling. "If you believe that, then you will be." Lizzie smiled. It was one of Mrs Finch's hobby horses, and once started, she could carry on for minutes. By the time she stopped, the topic of marriage was long forgotten.

"Why did you butt in, Lizzie?" Eleanor asked her later. "I thought you were going at ask a question."

"I was!"

"Eleanor, you're the last person to ask it. You don't want to draw attention to yourself, do you? Especially on this subject."

Eleanor grinned. "Thanks Lizzie," she said, and hugged her.

"Besides," Lizzie added, "I want to be invited to your wedding."

After school, Eleanor said goodbye to Lizzie, and walked up the road and round the corner. They had stopped meeting near the school entrance the previous term. She threw her bag onto the back seat, slipped into the front seat, and kissed David.

"Good day?" he asked.

"Yes, thank you. And you?"

"I got summoned to see the head. Apparently someone had told him I was having an affair with a school girl, well, the word he used was in a relationship, but I think he assumed the worst."

"Who told him that?" Eleanor asked.

"It was an anonymous phone call, apparently."

"Man or woman?"

"He didn't say, why?" David replied.

"I bet it was my dad!"

"No!"

"I saw Mum yesterday, in town," Eleanor said, before telling David all about it. "And I was so annoyed," she added, "I didn't cry. I think my dad wants me back just to prove a point. I bet he phoned your school. Oh, and I forgot to ask for my savings book!"

David gasped at the sudden change in topic. "That reminds me," he added. "There's a payment called child benefit isn't there. That should be transferred to Molly. She wouldn't object to that, would she? We'll phone your mum later. Right, let's go," he said, starting the engine.

Before they reached David's home, Eleanor had recounted the scene in her form room. "What bothers me," she added, "is what they'll say when I tell them I won't be going to college. They'll want to know why."

"Eleanor, Sweetheart, don't tell them. Look, you would have gone, wouldn't you? Just go ahead anyway."

"David!" she exclaimed. "That's dishonest! I'm surprised at you!"

"No, it's being wise. It's called keeping your options open."

"David, by this time next year I want to be pregnant!"

"But suppose you're not?"

"Then we'll still be trying. How can we make a baby if I'm away at college?"

"Eleanor," David said quietly. "Jenny and I had plans. Neither of us knows when we will be called home. You could even be a widow by this time next year. In which case, you would need that place!"

"David, don't talk like that," Eleanor said.

"Sweetheart, I don't expect it, but did the man who wanted to tear down his barns and build bigger ones expect it?"

Once home, David showed her his latest achievement – a gooseberry pie. Then, between them they cooked dinner, Eleanor having had sandwiches for lunch, as had David. After dinner, Eleanor said she wanted to phone her mum. "But tell me all about that phone call to your headmaster first. I interrupted your story earlier, sorry."

"Right," Eleanor said, when David had finished. "I bet it was my dad."

"You can't be sure, Eleanor."

"It must have been one of them," she insisted.

"Is that why you want to phone them?"

"No, I want my savings book, and I want my child money to go to Molly."

"Okay," he said.

"But I don't want to speak to Dad, so can you phone for me, please?"

David entered the prefix that blocks caller identification, and dialled the number. If he got her father, he was going to put the phone down again.

"Hello, Sheila Jenkins speaking," he heard.

"Ah, Mrs Jenkins, David Anderson here."

"Yes?"

"I've got Eleanor here, she wants a word," David said, handing the phone to Eleanor.

"So you are with that man," Sheila Jenkins said to Eleanor.

"Yes, for a meal. Now please listen, Mum. You have my savings book. I want you to post it to me, or I will report that you have stolen it."

"What?"

"And are you also still getting child income, or do I mean child benefit? It should now be going to Mrs Hayes because she is looking after me so I will tell her to claim, but you should send her the money you have claimed since you threw me out."

"You left! We would have let you back in if you had knocked!"

"Did you phone David's school?"

"Why would I do that?" Sheila asked. It sounded genuine to Eleanor.

"Then Dad did. I think it was despicable. Tell him that!"

"Anything else, Madam?" Sheila asked sarcastically.

"No, Mum."

"Then I think you should think about how you speak to your mother!"

"You're right. I'm sorry. But I still want my savings book. Please post it to Mrs Hayes' address, or drop it in here! Thanks."

There was silence from the other end.

"Is that it?" Sheila said.

"Yes Mum. I've got to go. Bye."

Eleanor put the phone down, and turned to David. He expected her to cry again.

"Mum said they would have let me back in if I had knocked. She won't admit to throwing me out. They want me to crawl back. How dare they?" she said, her voice steadily increasing in volume.

"Right, Sweetheart, time to start talking."

"Tonight?"

"Yes, but talks about talks. We will list all the things we need to do and talk about. The only thing that is certain is our wedding day and honeymoon! I'm going to do what James did, use a clipboard, remember?"

Eleanor grinned. "Are you going to get all officious?"

"No!" he answered quickly. "It just seems a good idea. We can then ask other people if we've missed out something."

"All right."

David went for a clipboard, and then sat next to Eleanor. "Okay, the wedding first. Building booked and the pastor booked. Exact time has not been decided, but it will have to be in the morning. Next, reception. Church hall – I have booked it. How many guests and who? Okay so far?"

"Best man – done. Bridesmaid – done. New suit. New dress. Bouquet," Eleanor said. Then she paused, partly to let David catch up.

"Car and photos," David added, and wrote them down.

"You said you had booked a honeymoon. How much can you tell me?" Eleanor asked.

"As much as you want to know, how much do you want to know?"

"All I know is that it's going to be warm, so it must be abroad. I don't know where."

"Do you want to know? I couldn't talk to you about it – I had to make a quick decision. I wanted to book a package in a hotel in a warm place, but the problem was availability and the time of the flights. In the end I booked a flight from Gatwick at nine forty-five the next morning. There was a flight at five o'clock on the Saturday night, but it would have been rather tight on time."

"So do we go home and then make an early start?"

"No!" David laughed. "We'll stay just off-site but check in the night before. Then we just turn up with our cabin bags. Anyway, that will do for tonight – oh – passport! You will need a new passport!" David stood up. "Come on, I'm taking you home. We'll finish the list another time."

"Are you fed-up with me already?" Eleanor asked, but not moving. "It's not late."

"No, of course not."

"Molly won't be expecting me," Eleanor added. She patted the seat next to her. "Come and sit down again." David sat, but with a noticeable gap between them.

"Am contagious? Do I smell or something?" Eleanor said, shuffling up to him. "The last time we sat on here you put your arm round me. We are engaged, you know."

David sighed. "You weren't a schoolgirl then."

Eleanor moved away, and sat straight. "What do you mean? Of course I was? Have you changed your mind about me – was my mum right?"

David moved up to her and put his arm round her. She tried to shrug him away, but he was too strong.

"Eleanor, Eleanor, calm down. Of course I haven't changed my mind," he said, sensing she was near to tears. "What's wrong then?"

"All this holiday you have been in casuals – pretty casuals. You were a young woman. Now I'm sitting with my arm round a school girl. I know it's still you, the same person, the same young woman, but it is bizarre. I love you, I want to marry you, but I'm going to marry a school girl. My wife will be a school girl. I will make love to a school girl. When a teacher runs away with a schoolgirl, the newspapers have a field day. Do you remember using the word surreal? It's like that. It's an odd feeling. How close is it to me being a paedophile?"

"Stop it, stop it," Eleanor exclaimed. "Don't say such things!"

"Can you see why I'm uncomfortable? I'll tell you this; you're in no danger of being seduced by me tonight!"

"You mean I was last time?"

"Well, no, not really." He grinned. "You know what I mean! Come on; please let me take my schoolgirl home."

Chapter 9

Marriage Preparation

Posh schools call the term that starts in September the Michaelmas term. David's school called it the autumn term. Either way, it was the longest of the three terms and many teachers dreaded it and began to long for the Christmas holiday long before it arrived. On top of the usual stresses and strains, David and Eleanor had a wedding to plan. Having taken Eleanor home early, David was invited to stay for a hot chocolate, and they showed their fledgling list to Molly that evening. Molly asked if she could help with the planning, and her offer was accepted eagerly. By the time David went home, it had been expanded, and firmed up.

One important issue was Eleanor's passport, that is, a passport in her new name. David had discovered that the Passport Service could issue a new ten-year passport post-dated into the person's new name up to three months in advance of their wedding. They obtained and completed the forms and submitted them within a week.

To Eleanor's surprise, her mother delivered her savings book at the first weekend. It was posted through David's door while he was at church, together with the investment bonds that she had mentioned earlier. They were in a sealed envelope, which David handed to Eleanor later. Although she knew about the bonds, she was not aware of their value, and gasped as she realised.
"David, this means I can pay for the wedding, well, for a good part of it."
"Sweetheart, I didn't expect you to pay."

"Well, I don't expect my parents will help, and isn't that traditional?"

"Eleanor, I had already worked that out," David said.

"And I wasn't expecting you to pay on their behalf."

"Well, I will buy my own dress!"

"Eleanor," David began.

"David, I want to. I don't want to be presented to you in a wedding dress that you own! Okay!"

"Calm down," David said. "But you have just brought up another thing. Who is going to give you away?"

"I will give myself away!"

"But," David began.

"You have arranged the day and the honeymoon. I will be responsible for presenting myself to you in my own dress. After that, then I will be an obedient little wife!"

Once school commenced, David and Eleanor knew that their life would return to the ways of the previous term with a few modifications, but with no secrecy. On Sundays they met at church. Then they alternated between David being invited to Molly's house, and Eleanor supervising and helping him cook Sunday lunch. She said it was a matter of principle that until she was married, it was still David's kitchen.

"Eleanor, will you feel at home in this house?" David asked.

"Why do want to know?" she replied.

David laughed. "Typical woman – I won't answer the question until I know the reason behind the question! Okay, since you didn't help choose this house."

"Or do you mean that because another woman lived here? I imagine that Jenny chose the curtains and cushions. And maybe organised the kitchen?"

"Well, have you thought about things like that?"

Eleanor nodded.

"Go on, then!" David said.

"You will probably laugh at me and you might be upset as well."

"I won't laugh and I'll try not to be upset," David said.

"Okay, when I first fancied the idea of marrying you – and I had no reason to think I would – I also thought I would change the cushions."

David wanted to laugh, but since he said he wouldn't, then he kept his face straight.

"You're laughing," Eleanor said.

"I am not!"

"You are inside!"

"That doesn't count," he said, but turning away.

Eleanor put her arms round him from behind. "Okay, you can laugh," she said.

A few minutes later when they were serious again, David reiterated the question. "And this time, tell me how you really feel now. Do you think we should move?"

"Move? I've never considered that!" Eleanor exclaimed.

"Really?"

"I have wondered if I should make suggestions about changing things here, but it's not just about you."

"Sorry?"

"Jill and Daniel lived here, didn't they," Eleanor asked.

"Well, yes."

"How do you think they would feel if I changed things around? Don't you still think of their rooms as Jill's room or Daniel's room?"

"All right, yes, sometimes. But I know they are not really their rooms anymore," David said. "So should we move?"

"No. Don't we have enough on our minds, what with marriage and then me doing my A levels? Maybe when I've left school."

On Wednesdays, David met and collected Eleanor from school. They prepared a meal together, and then Eleanor did school work before David took her home. Because she knew her fiancé was uncomfortable with her in school uniform, she arrived the second week with casuals in a bag. She went immediately up stairs and changed.

"Eleanor," David gasped as she came down.

"What?" she replied, looking puzzled.

"I've not seen you in that skirt before."

"I know, it's an old one. It's my dossing around at home skirt."

"It's a bit short," David said.

"I know. That's why I only wear it at home."

"Oh."

"What is it? Are my legs too skinny or something?" she asked. "You didn't like me in uniform, now you're complaining again."

"Sweetheart, come here," David said. He put his arms round her and kissed her nose. "I think you have gorgeous legs. When we're married, you can wear the shortest of skirts at home and I won't complain."

"Do you want me to change back?"

"No. It's me," David said. "I'll try not to look at you."

"Are you being serious?" Eleanor asked, looking worried.

"I'm joking, Sweetheart."

"About my legs or about looking at me."

"I like looking at you and I like looking at your legs. All right? Now let's sort out something to eat before I lose control and ravish you."

Eleanor giggled. "David, stop being silly," she said.

At the end of that evening, when Eleanor was having a bedtime drink with Molly, she casually brought up the short skirt topic.

"Molly, do you think this skirt is too short?"

Molly thought about it. "Who for?" she said in the end.

"Me, of course," Eleanor said.

"Isn't it all relative? When you said for you, I assumed you didn't mean for me, or do you mean around the house. I'm not offended. If I was much younger and had legs like yours, I'd ask to borrow it!"

"Molly!" Eleanor said, and laughed.

"Why are you asking? If you mean in the street, I wouldn't offer an opinion, okay?"

"No, I didn't mean out."

"Eleanor, my dear, why are you asking? Did David say it was?"

"No, not exactly."

"What did he say?"

"He just said it was a bit short," she said quietly.

"Is that all?"

Eleanor looked slightly embarrassed. "He said that when we're married, it would be fine."

Molly laughed again. "Oh Eleanor, Eleanor."

"What?"

"Don't be so naive. How can I put this? Just because David is, er, mature, it doesn't mean he is unaffected by female flesh! Marriage is more than just companionship."

"I know," Eleanor said quickly.

"Maybe it's like serving him up a nice dinner and then telling him he can only look and smell, but no tasting!"

"Oh," Eleanor said.

"And if David is a normal man, I imagine he's looking forward to tasting."

"Molly!" Eleanor exclaimed, shocked.

Molly laughed again. "Eleanor, I have been married. It's nothing to be embarrassed about."

"Sorry. Did you know we're supposed to be having a session on those aspects? I'm not looking forward to it."

"I thought they taught it in school, nowadays," Molly said.

"Yes, they do. We had a series of films which discussed the differences between boys and girls. Then we followed a pregnancy right through to the birth. The film of the actual birth was quite graphic – a couple of the girls vowed that they would never have babies – in fact, that they would never, you know, do it at all!"

"Did the films show how the baby is actually started?" Molly asked.

Eleanor laughed. "Oh yes, but it was a cartoon version, not real people. Then we followed the sperms up the fallopian tube to meet and penetrate an egg."

"What about contraception?" Molly asked.

"Yes, but that was done later. It didn't stop one of those two girls from having an abortion. It was supposed to be a secret, but we all knew."

Molly shook her head. "Do you think it was a waste of time?"

"No, or how else would I have known. Mum never talked about it."

"Well, since you've been taught at school you've got nothing to worry about," Molly suggested.

Their first 'marriage talk' or session was with James in his study. It was a Thursday evening, and David collected Eleanor from Molly's house in the evening after dinner.

"It's church policy that I have these chats with engaged couples," James said by way of introduction, "but I'm not sure everybody benefits. Especially in the case of mature people," he added, looking at David.

"I will try and pretend that I'm young," David replied with a smile.

"And I'm very young!" Eleanor added.

"Okay, so who in the Bible got married first?" James

asked, looking at Eleanor.

"Adam and Eve," Eleanor replied.

"When?"

"When God woke up Adam and showed him Eve?" Eleanor suggested.

"Let me read you what Adam said," James said. "Genesis 2:23: The man said, This is now bone of my bones and flesh of my flesh; she shall be called 'woman,' for she was taken out of man. That is why a man leaves his father and mother and is united to his wife, and they become one flesh." James paused. "What is odd about that?"

"Adam did not leave his father," David said. "So was he married?"

"Something to think about," James said. "Anyway, marriage can be thought of as a man and a woman both leaving their homes in order to set up a new home and become one flesh. Thus if you two set up home together and became one flesh, then you could be regarded as being married. In some societies, that is what marriage is. Everyone recognises the couple as being a couple, that is, as being married. They don't have a vicar to pronounce them as man and wife!"

"So if David and I just set up home together, it would save a lot of hassle, not to say expense," Eleanor said, tongue in cheek.

"And I personally would say that you were married in the eyes of God, as the expression is. But Paul wrote about acting decently in society. Also, our society has a system of registering marriages. It is the public nature of the event which is important. So, most societies have some form of public recognition. Bride price is an example. Feasting, singing and dancing, if they accompany the event, certainly make it a very public event. Everyone recognises that the man has taken a wife, in other words, they are married. Also notice the expression, became one flesh. Marriage is more than friendship, and in English Law, if there is no intimacy, then the marriage can be declared null and void."

James then went on to cover the New Testament teaching on the way that marriage helps people to understand the relationship between Jesus and his church, especially when the church is described as 'The Bride of Christ.'

"Did you know all that," Eleanor asked, as they drove home.

"More or less," David said.

"Then is it worth going to the other sessions? Won't you know that too?"

David shrugged. "We could refuse to go, but there is an advantage."

"Go on," said Eleanor.

"Well, it means you get a different perspective on things than from me. Who says that I am the expert? Suppose I have bad ideas or attitudes?"

"Be honest, do you think you have?"

"Well, no. But I'm prejudiced, aren't I. For example, I think I have excellent taste in women!" David said, with a laugh.

Eleanor laughed as well. "That's unfair!"

"Why?"

"Because if I tell you what I think, then I'm criticising your taste."

"Don't put yourself down, Sweetheart. For the record, I think you have lousy taste in men. You could have any man you wanted, but you're my woman."

"And you're my man," Eleanor said, patting his leg as he drove.

Their next talk was about finances. It was decided to arrange it as soon as possible rather than leave it nearer to wedding date. Edward and Susan Smithson, who usually hosted these sessions, were not fully aware of the situation when James approached them.

"Hi, guys, can you fit in another money management course?" he asked.

"Yes, of course, James. Who?" Susan replied.

"David and Eleanor."

"David and Eleanor?" Edward repeated. "Not David Anderson?"

"The same!"

"Well, well. I had noticed they seemed friendly," Susan said, "but marriage?"

"They're engaged," James said, "but they are not advertising the fact. You can ask them why."

There was a moment of silence. Then Edward spoke. "Is it really necessary? I mean, David has been married before."

"Yes, but Eleanor hasn't. Look, if you're unhappy, I'm sure they will understand," James said.

"James, what's your own opinion of the situation?" Edward asked.

James smiled. "Edward! You know better than that! But I would be interested in your opinion when you know them better."

"Two things, James. One, how old is Eleanor, and when is the wedding?" Susan asked.

"Eleanor is seventeen and the wedding is just before Christmas. Oh, and to save any embarrassment later, it is not a shotgun wedding! Still happy?"

They said they were still happy, so Susan approached David and Eleanor the following Sunday and invited them both for a meal. Although many people feel in awe of their church leaders, Eleanor had felt comfortable with James and Lucy – probably because they were present when David had proposed marriage, and had known about her resulting problems. However, as the forth person at the table together with David and her hosts, she was very aware of her youth and felt very nervous. Edward and Susan had been reminded that she was at school and that she was sensitive about it. However, it was David who mentioned it first in response to Susan's question about the actual date of the wedding.

"We both finish school at the end of term on the Friday then marry on the Saturday."

"Will you be leaving school, then?" Susan asked.

"No, of course not," David answered. "She wouldn't if she were a teacher, so why should she because she's a student?"

"Good point," Edward said.

"Does that make a difference, after all, I won't be working full-time," Eleanor asked.

"I beg your pardon? You will be working," David said.

"Oh, housework," Eleanor said.

"I meant school-work, Eleanor," David said.

"And no, it doesn't make a difference," Susan said, "but we'll talk about it later. So how do your parents feel about this wedding?"

"Didn't James tell you?" David asked.

By the time coffee was served, Edward and Susan were fully cognisant of the situation.

"Now I understand the rush," Susan said.

"Did you think she was pregnant?" David asked, in response to Susan's comment.

"No, we didn't. Not at all," Edward said.

"Do you think we're rushing?" Eleanor asked.

"Well, you are still quite young," Susan answered.

"But I'm not. We already have somewhere to live," David said.

"And we want to try for a family as soon as possible," Eleanor added.

"Eleanor!" David said.

"Well, it's true, isn't it?"

David looked at Susan. "It is true, actually, but Eleanor, Sweetheart," he added, looking at her, "one doesn't usually broadcast the news until there are results!"

After coffee, they settled down in the lounge. David had asked Edward to treat him like a young man with little experience, to make it easier for Eleanor. Edward then went over the basic concept of earning money, and how and why there were deductions. Then he went over the common expenses that almost all householders face, such as food, utility bills, rent or mortgage, clothing, transport and entertainment. He showed them a thrift money-box he had found in a second-hand shop, and explained how it was used.

"Of course, in those days, it was a cash economy. No money – no purchase."

He moved onto the use and dangers of credit cards, and other loans, before asking Eleanor to tell him about her financial arrangements. After this, he explained about the different ways to do saving and investing, including tax exempt savings. Then he turned to David.

"How do you manage your finances – cash or credit?"

David said that his utility bills were all paid by direct debit, and that his purchases was usually bought on a credit card, but that he settled his credit card every month. Then he added that he had a savings plan which received money by a standing order. Eleanor knew about credit cards, but direct debits and standing orders were new concepts.

Finally, Edward gave them some possible patterns for their domestic finances, including personal finances.

"Most couples have a joint account which receives the income, and pays all the household expenses. Some couples budget their housekeeping by means of an agreed weekly limit on the various different expenses, such as food or even transport. A modification is to have two accounts, one just for housekeeping, and the second account is fed by weekly or monthly standing order from the first. So far, I haven't mentioned personal money. Should both parties be allowed to dip into the central fund willy-nilly? We knew a couple who used their joint account to buy their Christmas presents for each other. There was only one cheque book, so they used it in turn. Alternatively, both parties could receive an allowance from the number one account so that the buying of presents for each other would be more personal. Have you talked about money yet?"

"Not really," David said. "I wanted Eleanor to hear what you had to say first."

"I do have some money of my own, and I am insisting on buying my own wedding dress!" Eleanor said. "I also have a Saturday job, but David wants me to give it up."
"Why?" Edward asked David.
"Well, originally, Molly Hayes said she would not charge Eleanor, so I suggested that Eleanor helped her."
"But we found out that Molly can claim child benefit for me. Anyway, my little job makes me feel independent," Eleanor said.
"So will you contribute to the household expenses when you are Mrs Anderson?" Susan asked.
"No, of course she won't," David said.
"Okay, so if you have a private income, what about David? Do you think his salary should belong to him," Edward asked her.
"Oh."

"So you have some talking to do!"

"Did you find that helpful?" David asked, as he drove her home to Molly's.

"Yes. Did you?"

"I knew it, Sweetheart."

"What did you do?" Eleanor asked.

"We had three joint accounts, number one was household expenses, number two was mine, and number three, in a different bank was Jenny's. All income went into number one, and then we used standing orders to send money to number two and number three."

"Oh, so if I keep working, is that what you would expect?"

"Eleanor, I don't really think you will need a Saturday job as Mrs Anderson? Look, think about it. Anyway, only one more pre-wedding session!" David said.

"And I'll be glad when it's over," Eleanor said.

Eleanor would have been surprised to learn that their session leaders were equally un-enamoured. Gareth and Fiona were still fairly new to the role. They had been married for ten years, and had a family of two, aged five and seven. Unlike Edward and Susan, Fiona had noticed that David and Eleanor were always together on a Sunday, and had mentioned it to Gareth over Sunday lunch.

"I'm sure there's something going on with those two," she added.

"No," Gareth said. "At least, I hope not!"

"Why?" Fiona asked.

"Do you fancy doing a session with a man old enough to be your father?"

"He's not!" Fiona said, laughing. "But I do see your point. He probably knows much more than we do!"

"And do you approve of middle-aged men taking up with teenaged lassies?"

"If we do get asked, Gareth, for goodness sake don't say that."

"Well, I don't expect to get asked."

James phoned that very afternoon. He spoke to Gareth, and after exchanging pleasantries, he came to the point.

"Gareth, did you know we have another engaged couple in the church?"

Gareth felt his heart lurch and his mouth went dry. "Do we?" he croaked. "Who?"

"It's David Anderson and Eleanor Jenkins," James said.

"Right," Gareth said. "Does that mean you want us to," he hesitated.

"Yes please, if that's okay with you."

"James, are you sure?"

James laughed. "Oh yes, I'm sure. They are very much engaged!"

"No, I don't mean that. Are you sure it's necessary?"

"Well, they've seen me, and they have seen Ed and Sue. They will be expecting you to contact them."

"Oh."

"Is there a problem, Gareth?" James asked.

"Are you happy about it, I mean isn't it a bit soon for David?" Gareth asked.

"I can understand your concern. Look, I have agreed to marry them. If you feel unhappy about their relationship, fair enough."

"When's the wedding, James?"

"Just before Christmas."

"This Christmas? It's a bit sudden, isn't it? She's not pregnant, is she?"

"No, and I don't expect her to be. Talk it over with Fiona, and let me know."

It was halfway through October, and a warm sunny Saturday afternoon. Eleanor was with David, sitting in his garden.

"Sweetheart, your birthday!" he said.

"Yes?"

"We should do something special."

"Like get married?" she suggested, with a laugh.

"I agree, that would be special. Do they sell birthday stroke anniversary cards? Hang on, it would also mean that if I forgot your birthday, I would be in double trouble for forgetting our anniversary! No, best keep them separate," he said.

"So what do you suggest, oh wise one?"

"Well, I don't think we can both take the day off, do you?"

"No."

"And I was thinking about how we have to keep a low public profile," David said

"Go on."

"So, how about a mini-break this half term? I know it's not actually your birthday, but we could still have a birthday tea on the day. It would be a chance to be out together, see a show, maybe buy you a present. What do you think?"

"Are you serious?"

"Totally. Either London or the seaside somewhere. I've seen offers on the Internet! What do you think?"

"I think you are a very clever man!"

Later that day, Eleanor was sitting with Molly as they drank their bedtime cocoa drinks.

"David wants to take me away on a mini break at half term," Eleanor said. "An early birthday treat. He wants to go where we won't be recognised."

"That sounds lovely; lucky you. Did he say where?"

143

"Maybe London, or by the sea. I think it depends on what offers he can find on the Internet."

They sat in silence for a few moments.

"I shall miss these times," Eleanor said.

"No you won't, my dear," Molly said, with a smile. "You'll be sitting and gazing into each other eyes."

"Molly!" Eleanor laughed. "I shall miss you; you have really made me feel at home. I think of you as my foster-mum!"

"Talking of which, have you and David talked about contraception?"

"Pardon?" Eleanor blinked.

"My foster-mother role, dear. Oh, I wasn't thinking of your break. No, oh dear. Whoops. Right, it's none of my business as to whether you want a family, or when, but, how can I put it; you don't want nature to spoil your honeymoon, dear! Things like that can be regulated. Mind you, a baby conceived on a honeymoon needs to be told not to arrive prematurely?"

Eleanor smiled at Molly. "We have our final session next week. Maybe they will bring it up."

"Possibly. Look, whatever you decide, if you need someone to go with you to the FP clinic, I'll be happy to go with you, alright?"

As Eleanor had said, their last marriage preparation was due the following week. Gareth and Fiona had agreed to run it, but had not wanted it to be based around a meal. The only free night was the first Saturday of the half term. David and Eleanor were invited for coffee and no sooner had it been served, when Fiona opened the conversation.

"Can we be honest with you? We're quite nervous about this. Okay, when we run theses sessions, we are well aware that many people may be experienced in this area, but we work on the assumption that we are starting from scratch, as it were. The problem is you, David. You will have more experience than us."

"We're not here for me, Fiona; Ed and Sue had the same problem, and they more or less ignored me. I'd offer to go, but I know Eleanor wants me to stay."

"Yes," Eleanor said quickly.

"All right," Gareth said. "You know this is not a biology lesson, don't you. We reckon that schools cover those aspects fully."

Eleanor nodded. She felt some relief.

"But is that enough? What are two of the biggest causes of problems in marriage? Money and sex! Agree?"

Eleanor nodded. "If you say so," she said.

"Right, Eleanor, what is the point of sex?"

Eleanor blinked. She had not expected such a direct question, and looked at David, as if for help. He smiled, and raised his eyebrows.

"To produce babies; to keep the species going?"

"Yes, good. So if a couple don't want any more children, or if they don't want any at all, what then?"

Now Eleanor was embarrassed. "It's a way of showing love?" she said hesitantly.

"Gareth, don't be so blunt," Fiona interjected. "Sorry, Eleanor. Let's start again. Eleanor, judging by the number of unwanted children, and the fact that money often changes hands, I would suggest that for many people, it's very often self-gratification. Either for gaining money, or for pleasure. And getting back to maintaining the species, it's a pretty undignified way of doing that. Look, Gareth and I have two children, but we haven't stopped making love, even though we don't want any more, well, not at the moment. So what does that tell you?" she asked gently, and with a smile.

"You like making love?"

"Exactly, but we don't always want to make love at the same time. Usually yes, but not always. And that will be the case for you and David. So, that's where you need to talk – we're not going to tell you how you resolve that. And sometimes things don't work as expected. I said it was undignified, didn't I, so learn to laugh at yourselves. It's not about scoring points; it's about pleasing each other. And if you're not pleased, then say so, tactfully, of course. Can I give you an example from the kitchen?"

Eleanor blinked again. Now what was coming?

"Gareth thinks, well, he says I'm a good cook. He often tells me he likes what I offer him, so when he says I've made a hash, I accept it! If things don't work in bed, then say so, tactfully of course. Maybe a slight change in technique somewhere will make the difference. Conversely, when they do, make sure you do say so!"

"Is that it?" Eleanor asked.

"We said this was not a biology lesson, but we usually offer to lend the couple some reading material for their honeymoon," Gareth said. "But in this case, we're not sure, I mean, what do you think, David?"

"I think it's a good idea. What are they?"

Gareth produced two books. "This one is rather explicit," he said, opening it and flicking through the pages.

Eleanor saw that it contained a lot of pictures, and even though it was a brief look, she saw that they were indeed explicit. She looked at David.

"We will borrow them, thank you," David said. "But put them in a bag, please."

Chapter 10

The Mini-Break

David had found and already booked a coach trip to London. The itinerary was to travel early on Monday morning, have free time and then a show. The Tuesday included a choice of tours or visits to the traditional sights. Wednesday morning was free, before taking the coach home. Molly then offered to drive Eleanor to the coach pick-up point, collecting David from his home. After their session with Gareth and Fiona, David had taken Eleanor back to Molly's and then stayed for a drink. Because he had then been invited to Sunday lunch at Molly's, staying there after lunch, they had not really talked about their time with Gareth and Fiona. David hoped they would be able to do this on their mini-break

Once they were settled into their seats and on their way, Eleanor snuggled closer to David, slipping her hand into his.

"Just the two of us. I feel married already," she whispered.

"Shush," David replied.

"Did you look at those books Gareth gave you."

"Yes, briefly."

"Well?" Eleanor said.

"Do you want to borrow them?"

"Do you think I should?"

David laughed. "Oh, Eleanor. I'm not your censor!"

"Well, would they offend me?"

"I don't know. I hope not; they are not meant to offend. Look, Jenny and I had similar books."

"Oh! They won't help you then."

"I said similar, anyway, I think you should look at them, and then you can decide, okay!"

"All right. But I won't keep them at Molly's – just in case!"

"Apart from that, I take it you have no further concerns based on last night?"

Eleanor sat up and looked around. There were people in the seats in front and behind. "Actually I have, but it's too public," she whispered. "I'll tell you later. Anyway, tell me more about this trip!"

Their coach deposited them at their hotel, where they also had a light lunch. Then it was into central London, the shopping part, namely Oxford Street.

"It's your birthday soon, right?" David said

"Yes, because this is my birthday treat!"

"I would like to buy you something special."

"You have!" Eleanor said, raising her left hand.

"For your birthday. A bracelet? Necklace? Watch – I mean a special watch. Do you have a gold watch?"

"No!" Eleanor laughed.

"Would you like one?"

"Are you serious?"

David pulled Eleanor round. "Sweetheart, this is a special birthday. I won't buy you a gold watch every birthday!"

Eleanor smiled at him, the smile! "Then I would like it, please," she said.

They didn't rush, and didn't find what Eleanor liked until the third shop. As it was being wrapped, Eleanor noticed the display of wedding rings.

"Look, David, is it worth getting our rings while we're in London?" she said.

"Eleanor – good thinking. That wasn't on the list!" David replied, before turning to the assistant. "We would like to look at wedding rings as well, please."

The assistant may have realised that there was a special relationship between David and Eleanor, but it had not extended to marriage. He obviously had not noticed her engagement ring, or if he had he had not associated it with David. For a moment he just stared at David.

"Well?" David said.

"Or course, Sir," he stuttered. "Can I measure you finger, Sir? And you, Madam?"

"Hang on a moment," Eleanor said, pulling David away from the counter. "Would you be offended if I bought you another wedding ring?"

"Sweetheart, I'm sorry, I just forgot about buying your wedding ring!"

"No, David. A ring for you! You used to wear a ring. You stopped when we were seeing each other – as friends. I didn't say anything, but I did notice. Would you rather not wear a ring now?"

"Sorry, why should I not wear one now?"

"David, stop being difficult."

"I'm not."

"David, you wore Jenny's ring. Then you took it off. Are you all right with having my ring?"

David's response was to kiss her. "Sweetheart, part of Jenny will always stay with me in here," he said, touching his chest. "You know that. But now I love you. Of course I want to wear your ring!"

"And will you let me pay for it? I can afford it! And I have my bank card."

"The ring and the dress. Okay!"

They left the shop with their purchases, and window-shopped along Oxford Street, then down Regent Street, past Piccadilly Circus, and ending up sitting on a seat in Trafalgar Square.

"What did you want to talk about?" David said. "On the bus this morning?"

"You know how Gareth was embarrassed having to talk to an older man?"

"Yes. I did understand. I got the feeling we had a cut down version."

"Did you? Well, I managed to grab a few seconds with Fiona later, alone. I asked her if she thought our age difference will be a problem."

"What did she say?" David asked.

"She said it could be a challenge!"

"Fair comment. Did you ask what she meant?"

"Yes." Eleanor hesitated.

"Go on, then."

"It's embarrassing."

"Sweetheart, one of their main points was that we should be able to talk!"

"Okay, she said that my youth might mean I was more, how did she put it?"

"Randy?" David said, and laughed.

"No, she said have a greater libido."

"Same thing," David said.

"But then she said something else."

"Go on,"

"She said you having a very young partner might affect your libido!"

"She said that?" David said and laughed.

"Does it bother you, David?"

"What, me having a randy young wife, or you having a randy old husband?"

"David! Shush! Don't talk like that."

"Oh, Eleanor. It is going to be a challenge, but some challenges can be fun. Don't you remember what they said? Sometimes things don't work as expected. It's not about scoring points; it's about pleasing each other. But one thing was being able to laugh. Look, it's an undignified activity, but take my word, it can be very enjoyable."

"Then I'll look forward to enjoying it with you, future husband," Eleanor said.

"David, did you and Jenny plan your family?" Eleanor asked, a few minutes later.

"Ah, that's something else I didn't put on the list," David said.

"Molly asked me if we had talked about it."

"Did she? Did she say we should?"

"She tactfully suggested that my cycle might need to be modified to avoid spoiling our honeymoon. She also said that a premature baby conceived on a honeymoon would raise eyebrows or something like that. I said the topic would probably be raised at our session with Gareth and Fiona, but it wasn't, was it? Anyway, she's offered to go to the family planning clinic with me. So, back to my question. Did you and Jenny use contraception?"

"Yes, we did."

"So shall I go to the clinic with Molly? Or should we talk about it first?"

"No, you go to the clinic and get ideas."

"Suppose they suggest the pill?"

"That's fine."

"But, David, I don't want to stay on it too long."

"Bearing in mind what you said before I proposed, and what Molly said about not conceiving on a honeymoon, I'm happy to leave it to you. But, Sweetheart, remember, babies don't always come on demand, and sometimes they don't come at all!" David looked at his watch. "I think we should be getting back to the hotel to change. They will have put our cases into our rooms by now."

The dinner and then the show were very enjoyable and it

was two tired people who arrived back at the hotel. David kissed Eleanor goodnight outside her room, after arranging what time they would meet for breakfast.

Tuesday was a full day. In the morning they visited the Planetarium and Madame Tussaud's. In the afternoon they took a boat trip to Greenwich and saw the Thames Barrage and the Cutty Sark. Dinner was taken back in their hotel, followed by a quiet evening in the hotel lounge. It was another opportunity for a chat.
"David, you said you had booked the church hall," Eleanor said.
"Yes, for a reception."
"Should you have booked caterers as well?"
"I have, well, in a way I have."
"Shouldn't I have been involved?"
"You will be. All I've done is to approach Mrs Mayfield. I said I was having a do in the hall, and if she was free, could I ask her to do the food. She asked what was involved, and I said it was some kind of reception. She asked about numbers and I said I didn't know, but I would let her know in good time."
"Oh," Eleanor said.
"So, Sweetheart, start planning."
"What? Right now?"
"Why not? We're not expecting a big do are we, Sweetheart? I mean, did you want to invite your headmistress?"
Eleanor laughed. "Mind you, it might bring her onto our side! Right, first of all, do we invite my parents?"
"Do you think they would come?" David pondered.
"No!"
"But it would be courteous to let them know. Let's go and see them together, next week."
"But we won't tell them the actual time. If it was my dad

who phoned your school, then he might cause an upset.
You know the point where the pastor asks if anyone
objects, then he would!"

"No he wouldn't, Eleanor!"

"I don't want him to know, okay."

David didn't believe a man would be that vindictive, but
he went along with Eleanor.

"But what about your parents, David?"

"Oh yes, Mum really approves of us, doesn't she?" David
said sarcastically. "But I'll ask her if she wants an
invitation, all right?"

"Eleanor, your grandparents. Would they cause trouble?"
David asked.

"Probably not. Actually, I do feel bad about them; I
would like to tell them about you personally."

"Then why don't we do that. Next weekend?" David
suggested.

"Stephie and Daniel are coming next weekend,
remember? Stephie and I are going shopping!"

"Okay, weekend after. I'll pick you up from work. Do
you have other family?"

"David, let's face it, if my parents don't approve of you, I
can't see any of my family coming, can you? So now to
your family. Five, including the baby."

"Agree. Let's move on," David said. "Friends."

"Lizzie, Tom, Ali," Eleanor said immediately.

"Nicola?" David asked. "And what about your other
friend from school? Jayne? Does she know we're
engaged, or even together?"

"Jayne doesn't know about this," Eleanor said, touching
her ring. "But she does know we're together. She asked
me if we were still friends and she meant more than just
friends. I know Lizzie finds it hard not to say anything
when she's with us."

"Then tell her, Sweetheart. She will be upset if she finds out afterwards. So can we include her and Nicola? I like Nicola, and she does know we're engaged."

"You like Nicola?"

"Yes. Not the way I like you, obviously. She might even want to bring a partner. I think she would be hurt, like Jayne, if she didn't even know about the wedding. Right, there's Molly, the four people who have seen us, plus their children. And there's James and Lucy, of course." David paused. "I would like to invite my neighbours, Mike and Rita, now that you have met them. They were very good to me when, you know."

Eleanor did some quick counting in her head. "That's about twenty. What about Mark Rogers and Philip, and their wives?"

"Yes, of course," David said. Mark was the assistant pastor, and Philip was the leader who had taken Eleanor to Romania.

"David, is cost an issue?" Eleanor asked.

"Why, are you thinking of inviting your class, or all the church?" David answered with a grin. "I thought we wanted to keep this fairly low key."

"No, but is it?"

"No," David said slowly. "Not for these numbers, why?"

"Well, I know we've had the money talk, but I have no idea at all about the cost of running a home. How much will I be involved? Will you want me involved at all? I know you wanted me to stop working, but I think I was right to carry on this term. Then I will stop!"

"Thank you, Sweetheart. Look, let's call it a day, or rather, a night. I will take you through my finances when we get home, okay. Tomorrow will be a full day, so let's go for a little walk, then an early night."

Their main itinerary for Wednesday was a tour inside
Buckingham Palace. David had booked the mid-day slot,
so he suggested that they had an eight o'clock breakfast,
and then visited the National Gallery. They travelled in
the tail-end of the morning rush, which was a novel
experience for Eleanor. She didn't mind being jammed up
tight to David, but she wasn't too happy being jostled by
unknown persons around her.
"Why do these people do it?" she asked David.
He laughed. "Well, maybe they wanted to stay in bed, but
then they would have been fired for turning up to work
late. In my case, I would have missed lectures."
"Did you go to university in London?"
"Yes."
Eleanor shuddered. "Ugh. Ghastly." she said.
"I was quite happy at the time," David said.
"Why are we so early?"
"It's not that early, Sweetheart. And anyway, I thought
you would like to spend as much time in the National
Gallery as possible before going to the palace."
"I do. Sorry to grumble!"

After the Gallery, they walked through Trafalgar Square,
down the Mall, and into Buckingham Palace for the tour.
It lasted over two hours, and what with all the walking
before that, they both felt exhausted. David suggested
taking an open top bus tour of London to fill the rest of
the afternoon. Although their tickets allowed them to
jump on and off, they remained on the bus. Finally, it was
time to disembark, buy some sandwiches, and make their
way back to their hotel in order to catch their coach
home. They were walking up Charing Cross Road
towards the tube station, hand in hand, when suddenly
David spotted a colleague walking towards him. Eleanor
was looking at David at the moment, and noticed his

expression change and felt his hand grip hers tighter. She looked to see the cause, and then gasped. It was one of her teachers, and she wondered why David knew her.

David was already back in control. He stopped, released Eleanor's left hand, and extended his hand to his colleague.

"Bob! What are you doing here?" he said, as they shook hands.

"I might ask you the same?"

"We're seeing the sights. Oh, Eleanor," David said, turning to Eleanor, "meet Bob. Bob teaches with me." David recognised Bob's wife from some function in the past, but couldn't remember her name. However, he could not speak to her because she and Eleanor were just staring at each other.

"Hello, Eleanor," the wife said.

"Hello, Mrs Finch," Eleanor said.

"You know each other?" Bob Finch said.

"Eleanor is a pupil at my school," Mrs Finch said. "We have great expectations for Eleanor!"

Suddenly her name popped back into David's head. "So do I, Valerie. So do I," David said.

"Did you, er, were you aware that she is at school?" Bob said, speaking to David.

"Bob, she has a name, and yes, I did know that Eleanor is at school. Incidentally, the headmaster knows as well." Then David turned to Valerie. "Valerie, I can see that you are shocked. I'm sorry, but I'm sure that you will agree that whatever Eleanor does, or who she sees out of school is irrelevant and none of the school's business. Although my headmaster knows about Eleanor, your school does not know about me, and I trust that you can keep this information confidential."

"But Eleanor is at school, and you are a teacher!" Bob said.

"Eleanor is at a different school, and is nearly eighteen, Bob. If she was working, would it make a difference?" Bob didn't answer, so David tried again. "Bob, if Valerie wasn't with you, you wouldn't have known, would you? So what would you have thought then?"

"I don't know, David, I don't know," he muttered.

"Well, when you get back, go and check with the headmaster," David said quietly.

Valerie Finch suddenly spoke again. "Eleanor! What is that ring?"

Eleanor had not been hiding her left hand, but nor had she placed it in front of her. Valerie either had very good eyesight, or she had looked deliberately at Eleanor's left hand. Eleanor pulled her hand away, and looked at David.

"It's an engagement ring, Valerie," David said calmly, reaching for the said hand, and holding it.

"But you can't be," Valerie gasped. "You're going to university!"

"People can do both, Valerie," David said, as he squeezed Eleanor's hand.

"Is that what you want?" Valerie said to Eleanor.

David squeezed her hand again and Eleanor took a deep breath. "Mrs Finch, who is the most important person in your life?"

"Pardon?" she said, blinking.

"I want what is best for both of us, Mrs Finch. If that involves university, then so be it."

"Yes, but," Valerie began again, but she was interrupted by David.

"Valerie, we're not in school at the moment, are we?" he said gently. He then turned to Bob. "Well, Bob, we have a coach to catch, so if you will excuse us?" He turned to Eleanor, "Eleanor? Coming?"

They walked in silence towards the tube station. "Don't let it spoil our day, Sweetheart," David said.

"She'll have another go at me on Monday, David. You don't know her. I've seen her go on at other girls who she thinks could do better for themselves."

"Can you put it out of your mind until then?"

"I don't know. You don't know her."

"Well, if she asks you direct questions, can't you decline to answer?"

"If it's one to one in her room, well, yes. But she had a go at one of the girls in public, I mean in the class. Poor Brenda, she ended up crying."

"She won't do that," David said quietly.

"David! She will!" Eleanor exclaimed. "She doesn't always do it directly. No, she talks about someone in this class, someone who is throwing their life away, someone who has no backbone. Everyone knows who she is talking about, even though she doesn't name that person."

"Let me think about it, Sweetheart. I'll come up with something."

Despite David's assurances, it did spoil the day and they sat in silence on the coach on the way home.

"I am sorry David," she said. "I have had a really lovely time – apart from that woman!"

"I've been thinking, Sweetheart. Tomorrow, I want you to text Jayne and Lizzie, and ask if you can meet them both for coffee or something. I have a plan."

"Tell me?"

"No, I need to see them too. Could you do that, please, and then, why don't you have a little snooze, princess?"

"You haven't called me that since that trip." Eleanor kissed his cheek. "It's a good job you're taking me home tonight."

"Why?"

"If we were staying at the hotel tonight, it would be like that night in the Travel Lodge. Only this time, I would be able to creep into your room!"

"Eleanor!"

"Sorry, but that woman really did upset me. Still, no doubt you would send me packing again," she said, with a wry smile.

"Eleanor, it is a good job I am taking you home! Now try and get some rest."

Chapter 11

Sugar Daddy

Despite David's protest, Molly had insisted on meeting them from the coach. She dropped David off first and then drove home with Eleanor.

"Well?" Molly asked, as she drove. "How did you get on?"

"Molly, it was fantastic – except for one thing. We met one of my teachers this afternoon."

"Oh dear. Was it embarrassing?" Molly asked.

"Not so much embarrassing as disastrous,"

"Disastrous? In what way, dear?"

Eleanor described what had happened and then remembered that David said he had a plan.

"Molly, please can I phone my friends tonight. I don't want to chat, just to ask if we can meet up tomorrow."

"Of course, my dear. Where will you meet?"

"Probably in a coffee shop, why?"

"When you were at home, did your friends come round," Molly asked.

"Oh yes, of course."

"Well, I want you to feel free to invite your friends here. And that includes your fiancé, of course!"

"Thank you, Molly," Eleanor said.

"Oh, I took the liberty of phoning the clinic. They have a session tomorrow evening. If you want to go, I could take you. Or would you rather David went with you?"

"From what you said earlier about planning my cycle, I would need the pill, presumably, so I won't need him. But I would like you to come with me, Molly, if you don't mind."

Molly patted Eleanor's knee. "Of course I'll come with you," she said.

Eleanor met David, and then Lizzie and Jayne the next morning. Lizzie, of course, knew about the engagement, and had kept Eleanor's secret. It had not been easy for her, especially when Jayne was with them. Jayne was the last to arrive and David bought her a coffee.
"Jayne, I owe you an apology," Eleanor said.
"Why? What for?" Jayne replied, looking puzzled.
"For not telling you about this earlier," Eleanor said, as she extended her left hand.
Jayne stared at it. "Is that what I think it is?" she said slowly, looking at Eleanor and then at David.
Eleanor nodded.
"David?" she said, looking at Eleanor.
Eleanor smiled. She was tempted to make a facetious reply, but because she felt guilty about not telling Jayne sooner, all she said was, "Yes, Jayne, it is."
"You're winding me up," Jayne replied, in a whisper.
"We're not, Jayne," David said. "The reason you didn't know is that it is a secret; except at our church. That's why Lizzie knew."
"How long?" Jayne asked.
"For a while. There's something else," Eleanor said.
"Go on."
"Mum and Dad don't approve, so I'm not living at home," Eleanor said.
"They kicked her out," Lizzie added.
"No!" Jayne paused. "You're living with David?"
"No, Jayne, of course not," Eleanor said, smiling at Jayne. "I'm living with a lady called Molly. And she says you're welcome at any time!"
"Does school know?"
"No. I suppose I ought to tell them my new address, but

they might ask questions, so I have kept quiet."
"Then why are you telling me now?" Jayne asked.
"Jayne, what are you doing on the last Saturday of this term, well, the first Saturday of the holiday?" David asked.
"Pardon," she said, puzzled by the apparent change of subject. "I don't know, why?"
"We would like you to do two things. One, keep our secret, and two, come to our wedding."
Jayne sat and stared at them. "You're not serious!" she said, finally.

It took five minutes to convince her, and that was with Lizzie's help! Then Eleanor told them about meeting Mrs Finch in London.
"I think she'll find a way to have a go at me on Monday," Eleanor said.
"That's true," Jayne said.
"But it's none of her business!" Lizzie exclaimed. "If she does, I'll tell her."
"The thing is," David interjected, "her husband is one of my colleagues. He was there too, and I asked her to keep the matter confidential. I don't think she will name Eleanor. It would be unethical."
"Yes, but you know how she does it," Jayne said. "She makes oblique references about you. Remember poor old Brenda?"
"If she does, try asking her who she is talking about, Lizzie," David said. "Or ask her if she has confidential information! See if you can embarrass her instead."
Lizzie grinned. "I will!"

Molly took Eleanor to the clinic that evening and went in with her to see the doctor. Eleanor explained that she was engaged, and that owing to personal matters, she was

living with Molly until the wedding and not at home, and
that was why Molly was with her and not her mother. The
doctor took down her details, including the name of her
own general practitioner.

"What do you know about contraception at the moment?"
the doctor asked, looking up.

"Quite a lot. We had a session at school with a nurse,"
Eleanor replied confidently.

"And what method are you using at the moment?"

"Pardon?" said Eleanor, not sure that she had heard right.

"Are you using contraception," the doctor asked.

"No! The wedding is in December," Eleanor replied.

"Right," the doctor said, thinking that this girl was
unusual. A good number of her clients were not even
considering marriage.

"And I'd like my honeymoon to go without a hitch, if you
understand what I mean," Eleanor added.

The doctor smiled. "I think I do. Are you regular?"
Eleanor nodded. "Yes."

"Right, so you want the pill?"

"Yes, please."

"Then tell me your dates, oh and the wedding date. Then
I'll tell you how to modify the regime if needed. But," she
paused, "what do you know about the injection method.
Then you don't have to worry about forgetting a pill."

"How long does it last?"

"About three months. Well, just over, we repeat the
injection every three months."

"What would happen if I didn't have the repeat
injection?"

"Your cycle starts again," the doctor said.

"Good!"

"Good? Most women call it a curse!"

"We want to get pregnant, Doctor, but not in the first
couple of months or so."

"May I ask why?"

"Easy. I don't want people to think we had to get married."

"Why should they think that?"

"If the baby is then born prematurely, what do people think?" Eleanor asked.

"I see what you mean," the doctor said. "But it means no injection. Your periods may re-start, but ovulation may or may not for maybe some months. We're back to the pill, so give me your dates, Eleanor."

The doctor loaded a spreadsheet onto her computer and entered Eleanor's dates.

"As you are at the moment, there's no problem with the honeymoon, look. However, just facing emotional upheavals can cause havoc with your cycle, so I suggest we start you here. It will give you time to get used to it and also you will then have no worries. I usually give three months first time, but I'll give you four. Let me explain. Start packet three here rather than stop. But just take another six or seven tablets from the packet to give you a few extra free days in the school holiday. This means that packet three will now be short, so then make a start on packet four on day seven. If you don't start packet four, you could conceivably, sorry about the pun, get pregnant in January. In which case you will take a folic acid supplement, won't you? You do realise that it's generally easier to prevent a pregnancy than start one. Mind you, there are some girls who do seem to find no difficulty at all – that is, in getting pregnant when they don't want to be!"

"Thank you, Doctor," Eleanor said.

On Friday morning David picked up Eleanor as arranged for the formal interview with the registrar of births and marriages in order to complete the pre-marriage documents. Since David was a widower, he needed Jenny's death certificate to prove he was now single! He also needed evidence of his age and place of residence. It was not so straightforward for Eleanor. She was glad that she had obtained her birth certificate but she could not complete and sign her form since she was still seventeen. It was arranged that she would sign it on her forthcoming birthday, which would still leave the required period of public notice. For evidence of residence, she used her driving licence, a rare document for a seventeen year old, and a bank statement.

David booked a limousine to take Eleanor and Stephanie from Molly's house to the church. Normally, the bride and bridesmaids meet at the church, but since Eleanor was going to give herself away, she wanted Stephanie to share the car. The reception would be in the church hall and so only the one journey was booked. Molly, who had already offered to make the wedding cake as a gift, showed them her work and then suggested that her friend should decorate it. She also asked if they wanted flowers in the church and reception, whereupon David asked if she would help, or better still, do it – but for a fee!

On Friday afternoon David had his financial session with Eleanor.
"Remind me about your current situation," David asked.
"You know I've had a bank account since I was seventeen, I mean, an account with a debit card. Before that I had a junior building society account – actually, I still have it. I opened the bank account when I was saving up for the Romania trip."
"And an investment bond?" David asked
"Several. They are government children's bonds. They

were begun when I was born, with various additions over the years."

"Who by?"

"Oh, parents and grandparents. Both grandparents made quite generous contributions when I was born."

"Do you know when they mature?" David asked.

"Yes, apparently I could access them when I was sixteen, but by then, some had been re-invested into ordinary bonds. They will mature next week!"

"Were you planning to re–invest them?"

"David!" she exclaimed. "I know nothing about investment, except that building societies give interest. Anyway, as I told you, I will need funds for my wedding dress."

"But, Eleanor," David began.

"David!" she said. "You know my feelings on the matter!"

"Okay, okay," David said quickly. "And you know my feelings about your Saturday job. I will not expect my wife to have a Saturday job! If you wanted to stop before then, I will pay you not to go to work."

"I have been thinking of stopping, David. And I definitely won't be working on the last Saturday before Christmas."

"Yes you will. Looking after me!" David said quickly, grinning.

"And there was me thinking that the idea was for you to look after me!"

"Then perhaps we will have to look after each other," David said. "Anyway, can I show you how I manage my finances at the moment? My finances will become our finances, and you will have access to them."

"Will I?"

"Sweetheart, I will change my account into a joint account – Mr and Mrs Anderson. In a few weeks time you will be the Mrs Anderson."

"It sounds scary," she said.

"What, being my wife?"

"No, just being a wife. Will I cope?"

"Eleanor, I have no worries at all," David said. "Come with me."

David switched on his computer and loaded his spreadsheet.

"This is a spreadsheet of my current account. I don't keep all my money in this account – for one thing, it pays no interest. Every month I have to pay council tax, water charges, electricity, gas, and the TV license. Look here." Eleanor gasped. "I had no idea that these things cost so much!" she said.

"There's more. Insurance – house and car. I must put you on my car insurance, oh, and tell the authorities about me having a wife."

"Why?"

"I get reduced council tax at the moment because I am a single person."

"So getting married will cost you?"

"Apart from my freedom – ouch – yes, but you're worth it," he said, laughing, and rubbing his arm where Eleanor had punched him.

"Is this your salary?"

"Yes."

"Will you get more when we marry?"

David laughed. "Why should I get more? Oh, as a reward for looking after a poor helpless female?" he said, jumping out of the way of a second punch.

"No, I'm serious. Don't you pay less tax, or something?"

"Unfortunately, no!"

Eleanor thought about it. "Okay. Will you expect me to use your account?"

"You mean our account!" David prompted.

"David, but it isn't."

"With my worldly goods I thee endow? Sorry, Sweetheart, don't you know the marriage lines?"

"Of course I do. But it all seems so theoretical, talking about it."

"Well, do you think you might go to the supermarket without me?"

Eleanor shrugged. "Well, yes, I suppose so."

"Then who will pay?"

"But you use a credit card, don't you?"

"Yes, and that's what you will use. And then you'll enter the details onto the spreadsheet."

"That's the one thing I can do – use a spreadsheet!"

"Well, that's a start," David said. "I'm sure you will cope with being a housewife."

"One more thing," Eleanor said, looking at the spreadsheet. "Looking at your income, can you afford the wedding?"

"Sweetheart, I can afford to marry you," David said, smiling at her. "I do have savings. The thing is, can I afford to keep you?" he added to tease her.

"What do you mean? I'm not an expensive woman!" she said indignantly.

"Then we will cope," David said, giving her a kiss.

Daniel and Stephanie were due to arrive late on Saturday morning. David met them at the station and took them home for coffee. The purpose of their visit was for Eleanor and Stephanie to look for dresses. Daniel did not need a new suit, but he said that his father did. Accordingly, David was also directed to go shopping with Daniel. Eleanor was working, but finished early and managed to join them about midday. After sandwiches, David drove them to a shopping centre some miles away.

Eleanor knew what she wanted and she also had an idea of the cost, but once they were on their own, she asked Stephanie about her own wedding dress.

"Stephie, I did like your dress. May I ask how much it cost?"

"I didn't buy it."

"Oh, sorry, I didn't mean to pry."

"No, you misunderstand. I hired it."

"You hired it?" Eleanor said. She had seen references to hiring in the magazines that she had been reading.

"Yes. I wasn't going to use it again, was I? I can tell you that it saved a lot of money."

"Oh," Eleanor said. "What did Daniel think?"

"He was happy about it, why?"

"I wonder what David would think?"

"Ask him – now you have persuaded him to carry a mobile phone. That really impressed Daniel, by the way. Anyway, it will save him money, won't it?"

Eleanor stopped and pulled Stephanie round.

"I'm paying for the dress myself. I insisted."

"Why?"

"Did Daniel pay for your dress?"

"No, my parents did. They also helped towards the wedding. So did Daniel's Dad."

"Well, I am giving myself away, in a dress that I bought."

"Then all the more reason to save money. Look, wait until you see what's available, then decide."

David and Daniel were in a different part of the shopping centre.

"This is the worst part about getting married," David grumbled. "I was never into buying clothes,"

"We all knew that, Dad," Daniel replied, laughing.

"Maybe I had better warn Eleanor what she's letting herself in for."

"Don't you dare!"

"I think Jill may be planning to have a word with her –
you know, tell her how Mum kept you in order!"

"Yes, she did at times, Daniel," David mused. "Anyway,
perhaps I mellowed with age!"

"Dad!" Daniel exclaimed. "You're not old."

"I hope I'm not too old for Eleanor."

"Dad! Cut it out. What's got into you?"

"Buying clothes, Daniel. That's what's doing it!"

"Dad, you're buying a suit for the woman you love and
want to marry. Need I say more?"

David stopped and faced Daniel. Then he hugged him.

"Thank you, Daniel," he said.

"What was that for?" Daniel gasped.

"You just referred to Eleanor as a woman!" David said.
"And you are right, I should not be grumbling. I'm
sorry."

An hour later, they met up as arranged at one of the
refreshment areas. David was carrying a box containing a
suit. Daniel was carrying two bags.

"What have you got?" Stephanie asked them.

Daniel answered, first pointing at David's box. "Three
piece suit, and," he then indicated his packages, "shoes,
shirt, and tie. Oh, and he refused to buy new socks! What
about you. I see no boxes!"

Stephanie looked at Eleanor, who answered. "Well, I've
seen three dresses that I like, and we found a bridesmaid's
dress that will go with all three."

"So?" David asked. "When will you decide?"

"It depends on what is available at the time."

"Sorry?" David said, perplexed by this comment.

"I'm going to hire my dress, David. I hope you don't
mind."

"Hire it? I suppose it does make sense – yes, what a good idea," David said.

"Anyway, I have reserved all three on the understanding that one will be available. It does mean that we will have to come back – they like to check the fitting. We will pick up Stephie's dress at the same time."

"So can we go home?" David said.

"Hang on, Dad," Stephanie said with a laugh. "I thought you wanted to buy Elly's going away outfit. And I heard that you like choosing her bikinis!"

David stared at her. "What do you mean?" he asked.

This time it was Eleanor who laughed. "Oh, David, she's teasing you! I told her how you had been embarrassed at the pool!"

"What's that?" Daniel asked.

"I'll tell you later, Darling," Stephanie told him, still laughing. "Dad, seriously, if you and Eleanor want to go home, we're okay, but it does seem a good opportunity to finish off while we are here. You are taking her away, aren't you?"

"Yes," David said. "Of course."

"Going away outfit, Dad?" Stephanie said.

"Oh, of course."

"Meet you back here in an hour, then?" Stephanie said. "Come on, Danny. Give Dad his things."

"Would you rather go home?" Eleanor asked David, when Stephanie was out of earshot,

"Sweetheart, I was never into shopping, but Stephanie was right, wasn't she? So tell me, what do you need?"

"How much can you tell me about where we're going," Eleanor asked.

"Somewhere warm and by the sea."

"Hotel?"

"Yes?"

"Evening meals?" Eleanor asked.

"Yes."

"Will I need to dress up?"

"Ah," said David. "Lead on!"

To David's surprise, they found a suitable dress within a few minutes. And then a pretty top and skirt.

"Feet?" David asked.

"The sandals you bought me for Daniel's wedding will go with both of these," Eleanor said.

"Daytime wear?" David asked. "I mean for when not on the beach! Shopping? Even walking."

"I'm okay, David."

"Stephanie mentioned a going away outfit, didn't she?" David asked.

"I was reading about those in a magazine recently. Originally, they tended to reflect the mode of travel, probably a coach pulled by horses, or a train. Something smart, yet useful. David, what did Jenny have – do you mind me asking?"

David smiled at her. "Of course not. She had what I think is called a two piece thing. It was a dress with a jacket – a matching jacket."

"Of course!" Eleanor answered, with a grin.

"Shall we look?"

This time it did take time. Eleanor was beginning to think there was nothing she liked when she stopped suddenly.

"David, look," she said, pointing at an outfit displayed in a window. It was a shop known for not being cheap!

"Wow!" said David, to encourage her. Then, "Wow!" He had just seen the price.

"Sorry, I hadn't seen the price."

"Hang on, do you really like it?"

"It is nice," she said wistfully. "Do you like it?"

"Actually, I do. Sweetheart, I don't expect to get married again. Come on, let's see if it fits."

"Well," said David, as they walked out carrying the outfit. "That's it, apart from the shoes." Eleanor had already told him that she would look for these at home. "There is something else," she said, slipping her hand through his arm. "Actually, two things. Stephanie's mentioned them."

"Bikini!" David said.

"Don't you want to help me choose?"

"Eleanor, do you think it is appropriate?"

"You mean because we're not actually married yet?"

"Well, no," he replied hesitantly.

She pulled away and stood in front of him. "David, you said we were never to talk about our age difference. In which case, it must not affect our behaviour. If you were my age, would you say it was inappropriate? You wouldn't, would you?"

"Probably not," he said.

"Are you interested in what I wear?"

"Eleanor!"

"Well?"

"Of course I am!"

"And in bed?"

"What? Shush," David said, looking around. "What's got into you?"

Eleanor laughed. "Stephie asked me what I wore in bed, and I said pyjamas. You knew I wore pyjamas, didn't you?"

"Yes. I did help you empty your drawers, remember."

"Do you think they are appropriate for a honeymoon?"

"Can we talk about this somewhere else? I am not going with you to buy a nightie! Bikini yes, nightie no!"

"Stephanie also mentioned lingerie!" Eleanor said, with a grin.

"Then perhaps you had better go with Stephanie," David said.

Eleanor kissed him quickly and then tucked her arm back through his. "There's a shop with swimwear back there. Come on we've got time. And we haven't talked about your holiday clothes, have we?" she added.

David sat with Daniel drinking coffee when the two girls went off together for their final shop. Items for Eleanor! The swimwear shopping had been less traumatic than he had anticipated. Eleanor had stopped him outside the shop.

"David, are you sure?"

"Yes, Sweetheart, I'm sure," he replied, forcing himself to smile.

"Would you rather I had a one-piece?"

"Why?" he answered, surprised at this apparent change of plan.

"What did Jenny wear?"

"When?"

"David! On holiday!"

"Sorry, I meant when, as in when in her life. When I met her she wore a bikini, but after the children she said it didn't suit her."

"So is it okay if I wear a bikini? I do find them more convenient."

Once inside the shop with rows and rows to choose from, he felt embarrassed again.

"Can you see anything you like?" Eleanor asked.

"They all seem okay," he replied, trying to avoid being involved too closely. "That's a nice colour," he added, pointing at one, but not looking at it closely.

"Do you want me to try it on?"

"Goodness, no!" he exclaimed, horrified by the idea.

Eleanor shuffled through the row, picked out her size and

led him across to the pay desk. Purchase completed, they left the shop.

"That wasn't too bad, was it?" Eleanor said, as they left.

"Did you see the way she looked at me?" David asked, referring to the sales assistant. "She obviously thought I was your sugar daddy!"

"Which makes me your sugar babe." Eleanor replied.

"Does that bother you?" David asked.

"David, if it did, I wouldn't be marrying you next month, would I?" she replied.

"Well, Dad, how's it gone? If I remember, you were never keen on shopping. I remember Mum dragging you out to buy something – can't remember what – I just remember the fuss you made!" Daniel said.

"And I think I've got worse with age!" David replied.

"Poor Eleanor," Daniel said.

"Yes, I agree."

"You looked happy when you came back just now. I assume you got what you wanted?"

"Yes, it is a very nice outfit. Not cheap."

"But she's worth it," Daniel said, with a grin. "What's in the smaller bag? Gloves?"

"She got me to help choose a bikini!" David said in a grim voice.

"Dad!" Daniel roared with laughter. "What is wrong with that."

"You should have seen the look the sales girl gave me. I bet she thought I was a right lecher."

"Eleanor's sugar daddy?"

"Exactly!"

"Dad, that's something you're going to have to live with," Daniel said soberly.

"I know, I know."

"But she's worth it?" Daniel asked with a grin.

"Very much so, Daniel," David said.

"Well, I just hope you appreciate what Stephie gets her to buy. I know I would, I mean if it was for herself."

"Daniel!"

"Well, if you don't, send them back."

"Them? I thought it was just for one thing; a nightdress. I drew the line at shopping for a nightdress."

"Dad, can I ask you? Weren't you interested in things like that with Mum?"

"Of course I was, Daniel. I'm very aware of those aspects in Eleanor, I'm not stupid. It's just with her being so much younger, it looks as if that is the reason that I'm getting married, and it's not. It would be much easier for you if she were older, I know." David shrugged. "Sorry."

"Don't be sorry, Dad. The more I get to know her, the more I forget her age. I think Stephie thinks of her as a sister. Maybe I will too, would that be okay?"

"Daniel, that's the best thing you've said today. Thank you."

Chapter 12

Invitations

On Monday David made sure he was early to school and waiting for Bob Finch.

"Bob, about London," David said. "As I said, our headmaster knows about Eleanor. Someone phoned him anonymously and he called me in. We chatted and he agreed that my personal life was my business. Presumably, Valerie appreciates that. Of course, were she to betray our confidence, I would regard it as a very unprofessional action. Eleanor may be at school, but as she is seventeen, nearly eighteen, and living with Mrs Hayes, there is nothing immoral or illegal, or even unprofessional about our relationship."

Bob looked at him and shook his head. "I can't say I understand what you are doing, David."

"Fair enough," David said.

"Actually, I think you've lost your marbles," Bob added. "At least she's not in our school."

"Bob, I didn't set out to fall in love with Eleanor. We were just friends! It happened."

"Well, I hope you don't end up regretting it."

David had another colleague to see later, and he went to the physics laboratory at lunchtime.

"Charlie, the first Saturday of the Christmas holiday. What are you doing?"

"Christmas shopping, I expect, why?"

"I would like you to keep this confidential, but I'm getting married. I would like it if you would take the pictures."

"You're getting married?" Charlie gasped.

"Congratulations!" he added, taking hold of David's hand and shaking it vigorously. "But why the secrecy?"

"I'm marrying a very young woman. Anyway, could you do it for me?"

"A young woman, eh," Charlie said, smirking. "Well, well. How young?"

"Charlie, very young. In fact a lot of people will mock me, okay. But I can see that you think it's funny, so we'll leave it."

"David, I'm sorry. Look, I suppose it caught me out. I mean, you've never mentioned her, have you?"

"That's because she's a teenager, Charlie."

"What? Come on!"

"Charlie, we are marrying in a church. She will be an adult. Will you do it?"

Charlie looked at David. "Is there anything else I should know? Why is it confidential? Do any other colleagues know?"

"The head knows about her. Bob Finch has met her."

"But why the rush?" Charlie asked.

"Personal reasons."

"Baby on the way?"

"Baby? No!" David exclaimed. "Look, yes or no?"

"Yes, okay."

David smiled. "Thank you, Charlie. One thing, please don't talk about it – to anybody."

Eleanor went to school on the Monday morning full of foreboding. It had been a fantastic weekend for her. Not just the shopping, but having Stephanie around. Because Daniel and Stephanie had stayed overnight with David, she had been invited to stay there too. It had meant tidying Jill's old room where some of her things were in storage, but that was a small price. Once home, she and Stephanie had retired to Jill's room and investigated their purchases. Stephanie had liked the going away outfit, but it was the swim-ware, lingerie and nightie that had been the cause of laughter and giggling.

"I hope David isn't shocked," Eleanor said, referring to the rather glamorous nightie.

"If he helped choose this bikini, he won't be," Stephanie assured her. "And you won't be wearing it to breakfast, will you? No one but David will see it."

"What about the hotel maid?"

"Tut! Stop worrying!"

Another aspect of the weekend was sharing the kitchen with Stephanie. Whereas with David, she always relegated herself to kitchen advisor, with Stephanie, she felt happy to assume some authority in that room. Together they cooked Saturday night's meal, and also the Sunday lunch. Then she went with David to see them off at the station. Although she was sad to say goodbye to Stephanie, she felt relieved that the time spent with Daniel had been free of stress. Indeed, she felt that Daniel was accepting her more and more. When David took her home at the end of the evening, she told Molly that the whole weekend had been fantastic. She showed Molly the outfit that David had bought, but kept the new nightie and lingerie hidden. However, by the next morning, she was back down on earth. It was Mrs Finch who then occupied her mind.

Mrs Finch did not appear on Monday morning and Eleanor breathed a sigh of relief. She left it until the afternoon and it caught Eleanor totally off guard.

"Just to remind you to be thinking about your UCCA forms." She paused, and then leaned on the front pupil's table. "A little bird tells me that someone here is thinking of throwing their life away!" As she stared round the room, Eleanor looked sideways, and caught Jayne's eye. Jayne winked and then immediately shot her hand up.

"Mrs Finch," she said. "Have you told the police?"

"Police?" Valerie Finch echoed. "What's it to do with the police."

"But you just said that someone was about to kill herself, Mrs Finch," Jayne said. "Didn't she?" she added, appealing to the class.

"Yes, you did, Mrs Finch," Lizzie said, having caught on to Jayne's comment.

"I did not!" Mrs Finch said.

"What did you say, then," Lizzie asked.

"I said that metaphorically speaking, one of you was throwing her life away."

"What do you mean, Mrs Finch?" Eleanor said.

"I think you know what I mean, Eleanor."

"Mrs Finch, you're speaking in riddles," Jayne said. "If you are accusing one of us, you should say so directly, not cast aspersions. Are you talking about me?"

"Are you engaged?" Mrs Finch said, looking triumphant.

"Who told you that?" Jayne said.

"Are you?" she asked.

"No comment!" Jayne said.

For a moment there was a stunned silence. Then Lizzie spoke again. "Mrs Finch, why does it concern you if Jayne or indeed anybody else is engaged? I thought it was a private matter!"

"Lizzie, I think you know what I am talking about," Mrs Finch said.

"Mrs Finch, are you saying that becoming engaged is equivalent to killing yourself?" Lizzie asked. "You must have been engaged once!"

"I wasn't engaged when I was at school!" she said.

"Are you saying that one of us is engaged?" one of the

other girls asked. "Who?"

"She knows."

"Mrs Finch, please tell us why it concerns you," Eleanor asked, speaking calmly.

"Because I don't like seeing a talented girl throwing her life away by marrying her sugar daddy!" Mrs Finch exclaimed, losing patience.

"Do you know who this, er, sugar daddy is?" Lizzie asked innocently.

"Yes, and I think he should be ashamed of himself," she said.

"Then I hope he doesn't mind being described as a sugar daddy," Eleanor said, looking at her.

Mrs Finch stared at Eleanor. Then she stood upright, and walked towards the door. At the door, she paused and turned. "Don't forget – UCCA forms."

Then she left. As soon as she had gone, there was a buzz of conversation, with the form mistress trying to complete her registration. Then the bell went, and the pupils dispersed to their classes.

That evening Eleanor rode round to see David and told him what had happened. His immediate reaction was to phone his colleague.

"Bob, it's David, can I speak to Valerie please."

He waited.

"Valerie, it's David Anderson. Eleanor has just told me what happened. I just want to say this. If you pull another stunt like that, I will personally see your head and make formal complaint about your unprofessional behaviour. Do you understand? Good. Goodnight."

He put the phone down and turned to Eleanor. She could see he was angry.

"I'm sorry that had to happen, Eleanor. In fact, I may visit your school and see the head myself."

"Calm down, David," Eleanor said. "Let's wait and see how it goes!"

David suddenly grinned. "Sugar daddy, eh? Well, well."

Despite David's apparent amusement at Valerie Finch's comment, he was still annoyed. He took several deep breaths and then tried to forget her. But Valerie Finch did the UCCA forms, and that was another area where she could find fault with Eleanor.

"Eleanor, how well are you doing with your UCCA form?" David asked, as casually as he could.

"Not well," she answered.

"Is there a reason?"

"Apart from not going to university, you mean?"

"Sweetheart, Jenny's death has taught me that none of us can plan for the future. Oh, I know we do have to plan, but we can't be certain."

"What are you saying, David?" Eleanor asked quietly.

"I think you know what I'm saying. Don't plan your life on me being around for ever."

"I'm not. I have thought about that, you know."

"I appreciate that it's highly unlikely, but this time next year you could be a widow," David said.

"David!"

"Which is why I shall top up my life assurance when I marry you."

"Don't talk like that."

"And which is why you should complete your university application forms. Added to which, Mrs Finch will now be looking for any legal way she can get at you. Sweetheart, don't make it easy for her." He paused. "When is the deadline?"

"Next Monday."

"Right, let's do the forms on Wednesday. I'll help you."

Eleanor smiled. "All right, and thank you, David."

"Good. Right, we were talking about seeing your grandparents, weren't we? This coming weekend?"

"Hadn't we planned to finalise and distribute the invitations?" Eleanor asked.

"Oh, Eleanor. We should go and see them. We don't even know if they know about me!"

"The following weekend?" Eleanor suggested.

"Your birthday weekend? I know Molly would like to give you a little party – tea party."

"How do you know?"

"She asked me about it."

"She is a dear. Now what do I do?"

"Phone your grandparents and see if they are available. They might not be."

"What shall I say? I feel bad because I haven't spoken to them since, since I left home!"

"Sweetheart, you will feel worse if you don't. And the longer you leave it, well …"

"I know, I know. Okay."

Eleanor phoned the Jenkins's first. It was her grandad who picked up the phone.

"Hello, Grandad, it's Eleanor," she said.

"Eleanor! Hello." There was a pause as they heard him call out to his wife. Then he was back. "How are you? We haven't heard your voice for ages."

"I know, and I am so sorry. How are you and how is Grandma?"

"We're alright; well, apart from needing a good squirt of WD40 into my joints. Grandma is beginning to whiz around on her little buggy."

"Her what?"

"Her electric buggy. Didn't your Dad tell you?"

"No" Eleanor replied quickly. "Grandad, can I come and see you next weekend. Will you both be at home?"

"Yes, of course. Oh, no, hang on, we've got a do. What about the following Saturday?"

Eleanor covered the mouthpiece and turned to David.

"They can't do this weekend, but they can do the following week. What do you think?"

David nodded. "Yes, that's fine."

"Yes, Grandad, the following weekend will be fine."

"Are you all coming? Your dad didn't mention it on Sunday," Grandad asked.

"No, just me, well, and a friend."

"A friend? A boyfriend? They didn't mention that!"

"Grandad, it's complicated. They don't approve."

"Oh. Alright. What about your mum's parents? Will you be seeing them, or shall we invite them over?"

Eleanor looked at David who had been listening. He nodded and then whispered. "But don't tell them why?"

"Grandad, that sounds a good idea. But one thing, please don't tell them I'm coming. Let it be a surprise. Oh, and don't tell Dad. That's very important."

"This sounds very mysterious! We'll expect two of you – when? For lunch?"

"Yes, that would be nice. But please keep it a secret."

"Curiouser and curiouser," he said, quoting from 'Alice in Wonderland'.

"Got to go, Grandad. I hope you're not disappointed."

"Disappointed? What made you say that?"

"Sorry, I shouldn't have said it. Forget it."

"Is there a problem, Eleanor?" Grandad Jenkins asked.

"Yes, but please, Grandad, please let me tell you. Don't ask Dad!"

"I won't my dear, but I did wonder. Every time we asked about you, they never said much, and you were always out."

"I know, and I will explain why. Thank you, Grandad. Got to go now, bye."

Eleanor handed the phone to David and let out big sigh.
"I know I haven't talked about it, but it has been on my
mind."
"Why didn't you talk about it, Sweetheart?" David asked.
"It wasn't your problem," she said.
"When will your problems become my problems?"
"When we're married."
"Wrong. In ten seconds time." He looked at his watch,
and waited ten seconds. "Time's up. Come here. Right,
now who shares in your problems?"
"You do," she whispered.
"You're a fast learner," he said, and kissed her nose.
"Now I have a problem. It's how to persuade you to go
home and study."
"I think you may need to bike home with me to make sure
I don't get lost," she replied, smiling at him.

David used the Wednesday afternoon to investigate
wedding invitations. By the time he left to pick up
Eleanor from school he had already produced three
printouts, however, since he knew the UCCA forms had
priority, he did not tell her immediately.
"Right, Sweetheart, let's make a start on the UCCA
forms," he said as they entered his house.
"Don't you want me to change first?"
"No, let's stay in character, as it were. If we can finish
this in good time, we can think about the invitations."
"All right, schoolteacher," she answered with a grin.
Eleanor didn't really need David's intellectual help. But
she did need his encouragement!
"It's very hard choosing a degree when your heart's not
in it," she said.
"Yes, but you already had an idea of what you wanted to
do when I first got to know you," David pointed out.
"But what you didn't know was that not long prior to that

I had been dilly-dallying between two other ideas!"
"So really, marrying me is saving you a lot of hassle,"
David said.
"Oh, I don't know. I think managing a husband is going
to give me hassle."
"Cheeky wench," David said. "You don't know what
you're letting yourself in for, whereas I do!"
"Well, it couldn't have been that bad the first time or else
you wouldn't try it again." She stopped, feeling horrified
at what she had just said. "David, I am so sorry, I didn't
mean to be flippant about your bereavement."
"Sweetheart," David said, putting his arm round her. "It
was so good the first time that I had to do it again. But it
meant finding the right person."
"It's very hard, David."
"What is?"
"My happiness is based on a sad event."
"Eleanor, if Jenny was still here with me, I would not
have spent time alone with you, would I? To start with,
there would have been no tactless comment from old Mrs
Teale. And no comment from you about flowers on a
grave. No spending time alone practising. No visit to see
swans. And if I had been the one picking you up from
Heathrow, no comment about missing you! You would
have been seeing another young man and looking forward
to university."
"I suppose so," she said.
"Come on, nearly finished. I'll go and phone for a pizza."

Dinner over and cleared away and with Eleanor now
changed, David told her about his afternoon.
"I hope you don't mind, but I went to investigate
invitation cards. There are, well, I think there are two
ways. One, have them done, and two, do them yourself."
"You mean hand write them?"

"No. The art and craft shop had both blank card and software, and a booklet of traditional and non-traditional invitations."

"Go on."

"Well, let me read you some invites." David read out about four or five. "What do you think?" he asked

"Well, since my mum and dad are not doing the invitations, the first one is out."

"Okay."

"And although we're not a typical couple, I think the quirky ones are out. I mean, I thought we wanted a low profile wedding?"

"Yes, I agree," David said.

"David and Eleanor invite you to their wedding?" Eleanor suggested.

"Yes, but we have to include time and place, and also tell them that they can join us at the reception, and where that is! Oh, an RSVP with our full names and addresses."

"Have you tried the software?"

David grinned. "Look at these." He handed over his three printouts.

Eleanor studied them and then looked up. "Shouldn't they be on card."

"Yes. I printed these on paper just to get an idea. I have done one on card, here."

Eleanor read aloud, "David and Eleanor request the company of dot-dot-dot to celebrate their marriage at etc, etc." She then looked up. "I like it. So you bought the card; what about envelopes?"

"It all came in one box – cards, envelopes, and the software on a CD. I've saved all three, but if you like, you can design another one. Then we'll print them."

"I like this one, so, print away, Mr Anderson. We'd better finalise the list."

"One reason I did it, Sweetheart, is so that we can take a couple with us. Even if your Grandparents can't make it, they might like an invitation."

"That's assuming they don't feel the same way about you as my parents!" Eleanor said.

"True!" David said.

"Come on; let's make our final and definitive list, David. Then you can print and I'll fill in their names. What do you think?"

"I think yes!"

By the time they had finalised their guest list, together with printing their invitations, most of the evening had gone! David took Eleanor home, and went in with her to give out their first invitation.

"This is for you, Molly," Eleanor said, handing Molly an envelope. "The very first one!"

Molly guessed what it was, and opened it with a smile. She hugged Eleanor first, and then she hugged David.

"I don't have an acceptance card, my dears, but I accept with pleasure," she said. "Your gain is my loss," she said to David, "I shall miss Eleanor."

"Molly, you will always be welcome in our house," David said. "I shall be ever grateful to you for looking after Eleanor for me."

David spent the rest of the evening as usual with Molly and Eleanor, and staying for a night-time drink.

David and Eleanor now sat together on a Sunday evening at church. However, they both felt that she should support both her friends and the youth leaders by staying on and joining in with the young people's meeting which followed on. At the end of the young people's meeting she would phone David in order to be collected and taken back to Molly's. On Monday, she handed in her UCCA form, which was accepted without comment. On Wednesday afternoon she was collected from school by David. They cooked their dinner together, and then after dinner he insisted that Eleanor settled down to work while he washed up.

"You're making me feel like a twelve year old," she grumbled.

"Stop grumbling, woman," he said, laughing at her.

"I think," Eleanor said slowly, "that since I shall be moving in with you as your wife and still have to do homework, then I should regard this as a trial. If I find that it doesn't work, there will be time to postpone our marriage until after my A levels."

"What?" gasped David.

"Or if I think you are too strict? Will you put me in detention if I don't work hard, Sir?" Eleanor said, flashing her eyelashes at him.

"Ha, ha," David said. "Very good. Listen, Sweetheart, if you were twelve, it would be easier for me."

"Why? Because I'd be less bolshey?"

"Well, there is that, I suppose, but if I remember, Jill had found her feet by then! No, it's because I would rather be enjoying your company."

"Can we enjoy each other's company later then," she asked, with a grin.

"You'll have to wait and see!"

Eleanor had a lot of work, but she finished it eventually and walked into the lounge. David had been marking and had long finished.

"I hate homework," she said

"And I hate marking. Come and sit down."

They watched the television together on the settee, and then David took her home.

Molly invited David to stay for a drink and they talked

about the forthcoming visit to Eleanor's grandparents as well as her birthday.

"Eleanor, my dear, something has come up. I'm afraid that I shall miss your birthday. My sister wants me to go and see her on Friday and stay until Sunday." She turned to David, "Could you look after Eleanor for me, well, feed and water her while I'm away?"

"Of course," David said.

"Will you be all right on your own sleeping here, my dear?"

"Yes, of course,"

"Unless you stay with David until I get back," Molly said.

"But won't that look bad?" Eleanor asked.

"You have just been away with David. Did that look bad?"

"No one knew, and anyway, we had separate rooms!" Eleanor said. "But I can guess what Mrs Finch thought," she added.

"And I assume David has more than one room," Molly said. "Anyway, it was just a thought."

"Well, it would be easier, true," David said.

"Are you serious?" Eleanor asked. "Then why am I staying with you?"

"Eleanor, you will be an adult on Friday. Look, you've spent the evening together tonight, haven't you? Were you chaperoned? Staying with your fiancé is hardly the same as living together, is it?"

"It also means that if I take you to work, I can then pick you up and go straight from work, Eleanor. It is going to be a rush to get there by lunchtime."

"One other thing, Eleanor, my dear," Molly said. "I was planning to offer you a little birthday tea-party after school on Friday. Would you consider Sunday? Would you like to invite your special friend, Lizzie, isn't it?"

"Molly, that would be lovely," Eleanor exclaimed.

"Please can I ask Jayne as well? She knows about us," she added, turning to David and holding his hand.
"Of course, my dear."

On Friday morning David drove to Molly's house first to collect Eleanor's overnight bag. They did not want Eleanor to draw attention to herself at school concerning her brief stay with David by carrying an overnight bag. Besides toiletries and night clothes, she needed clothes to work in the next day and clothes to wear to her grandparents. Eleanor then went directly to David's house from school that afternoon. They cooked their dinner together as usual and as they ate, David presented her with her birthday watch.
"Happy birthday again, Sweetheart," he said, giving her another kiss.
"I was wondering if you had forgotten, David," she said.
"Well, I might next year, but this year is special – you're a grown-up now, aren't you?" he replied.
"Which means I can sign my marriage form. Hooray!"
Since she was not being retuned to Molly's that night, they watched the news together on the settee.
"I like my watch," she said, "and I feel quite married already just being with you," she murmured, her head on his shoulder.
"If we were, I wouldn't be sending you up to Jill's room, would I?" David said.
"True. I'm so looking forward to sleeping with you," she murmured, sleepily.
"Me too," he said. "Perhaps you shouldn't have looked at those books so soon," he added.
Eleanor sat up. "I didn't mean for that," she said quickly. She paused. "Sorry, I am looking forward to that. What I meant was that I would just like to be near you all night!"
David kissed her on her forehead.

"I do understand. The problem is that if we went to bed, would that be enough?"

"David," she whispered, "when you said me too, you didn't mean just sleep, did you?"

"Shush, pet," David said.

"David, I do want you too. Is it wrong?"

"I don't have a problem with people marrying just for companionship, Eleanor. But if we both want more than just companionship, then those feelings won't wait until the I do bit, will they?"

"So it had better be separate beds!" she said, and smiled at him.

"And I'll give you another reason. My bed has history. We are going to buy a new bed, Sweetheart."

Eleanor was up before David the next morning and in the kitchen when he came down. He put his arms round her from behind and kissed her neck.

"Are you always as gorgeous as this in the mornings?" he whispered. "How did you sleep?"

She turned round and kissed him properly. "Better than I expected. I woke up a few times thinking about today."

"Is it worse than going to see Daniel and Stephanie?"

"Yes, much worse. I didn't think Daniel liked me, so I told myself I didn't care. But I did really!"

"Oh, Eleanor!"

"But I don't want to hurt my grandparents, David. I wonder how they will react. We could be on the road back within minutes of arriving."

"It depends on how much they know," David said. "They might have open minds."

"And they might not!"

"Let's be positive, Sweetheart. Anyway – breakfast, and then work!"

Chapter 13

Grandparents

When David picked Eleanor up from her Saturday job, she had already changed into what they called her wedding dress – the dress that she wore to Daniel and Stephanie's wedding. It was not really a long journey; but it was a rush to be there in time for lunch. David pulled up outside the house of grandparents Jenkins.

"You wait here, and I'll go and spy out the land," Eleanor said. "And maybe keep the engine running for a fast get-away."

"It will be all right," David said, but more in hope than belief. He watched Eleanor walk up the garden path. As she reached the door, it opened, and he saw her being hugged. It was her grandad.

"So where is the young man?" he asked, looking towards the car.

"Let me explain first," Eleanor said. "Where's Gran?" Her grandad led her into the front room where she saw that not only was Grandma Jenkins waiting, her other grandparents were already there. They had not been told about Eleanor's visit until they arrived some forty minutes earlier.

"I think he's shy," Grandad Jenkins said, referring to David still in the car, as Eleanor kissed and was kissed in return.

"So, is he coming in?" the other grandma asked.

"Only if you want to meet him," Eleanor said.

"Is there something wrong with him?" Grandad Jenkins asked slowly.

"Mum and Dad think so."

"Oh! Is he married, Eleanor?" the other grandma asked.

"No!" Eleanor exclaimed. "Of course not!"

"Divorced?"

"No! He's a widower."

"A widower? Not a young man then," Grandad Jenkins said.

"He is older than me; in fact you might think he's too old, but I love him, and I'm going to marry him!" Eleanor said in a rush, and holding up her left hand.

There was a long silence, and then Grandad Jenkins spoke. "What is his name, Eleanor?"

"It's David, why?"

"Then I will go and say hello," Grandad Jenkins said, moving towards the door.

"No," cried Eleanor. "Please don't …"

Grandad Jenkins turned. "Please don't what?"

"Please don't be unkind," Eleanor said quietly.

Her grandad hugged her. "Eleanor, he has brought you to see us. Of course I wouldn't be unkind. But it is very bad manners to let him wait in the car. We are all waiting to have lunch. Now are you going to fetch him, or shall I?"

Eleanor kissed him. "I will, Grandad," she said.

"David, they want to meet you," Eleanor said as she bent down to David's open window.

"To shoot me?" David asked.

"No, they won't do that. Otherwise they will have to pay someone to take me home, come on."

"What have you told them?"

"That we're engaged and that you are a widower."

"Wow, jump straight in at the deep end, eh," David said.

"Sorry, but they asked if something was wrong with you, and I said Mum and Dad think so, so then they made guesses – were you married or divorced?"

David was now out of the car, and he took her hand.

"Okay, lead me to the firing squad," he said.
"Shush, David!"

Grandad Jenkins met then at the door. "David, welcome. Thank you for bringing Eleanor," he said, extending his hand. "Come in."
Once inside the front room, David was introduced to the other three grandparents. "Grandma Jenkins, Grandma Thomas and Grandpa Thomas. This is David." He turned to David. "Right, we were expecting you for lunch, so are you ready to eat?"
Grandad J, as he was known, led them through to the dining room, where he tactfully put David next to Eleanor.
"Right, please sit down, David," Grandad Jenkins said. "We all want to know about you, but it can wait until after lunch, agree everyone? Right, let's eat! Eleanor, can you look after David, please?"
It was a cold buffet lunch, and everyone observed Grandad Jenkins's rule.
"Good journey," Grandpa Thomas asked from across the table.
"Yes, thank you," David replied.
"What time did you leave?" from somebody else.
"I picked Eleanor up from work, what," he glanced at Eleanor, "half an hour ago, if that."
The small talk continued until after the meal. David helped carry things out to the kitchen, where the two grandparent males then washed up. Grandma Jenkins took David and Eleanor back to the lounge and sat them together on the settee, before asking if they wanted tea or coffee.
"I've not been shot yet," David whispered to Eleanor as they waited.
"Shush!" she replied.

They sat until Grandad Jenkins came back in with the six coffees, handed them round and then sat down. He came straight to the point.

"Well, well. We have a situation. David, you want to marry our granddaughter, and her mum and dad don't approve, right."

"It's worse than that," David said, after thinking for a moment or two. "But that will do for starters."

"All right, why not tell us about yourself?" Grandad Jenkins said.

"You know, apparently, that I lost my wife. Do you know when?"

"No, we know nothing, as the expression goes."

"It was nearly two years ago." He noticed that the two grandmothers looked at each other. "Too soon?" David asked.

"When did you meet our Eleanor?" Grandma Thomas asked.

"I already knew, well knew who she was," David said.

"We go to the same church," Eleanor said. "So I also knew his wife, well, not personally."

"But at some time a spark must have been waiting to be ignited?"

"No! Nothing of the sort," David said. "I was very aware that she was a teenager."

"And I knew he was a grieving widower!"

"Then what did happen?" Grandma Thomas asked.

Eleanor told them about how she used to sing in the church with a lad called Tom, and how they had asked David to help them when Tom couldn't play his guitar. And then how they had continued when Tom had gone to university.

"It meant that we spent a lot of time together practising and got to know each other," Eleanor said.

"But that's as far as it went," David added.

"Anyway, at the end of the year we were asked to do a session at an old folks' home. Do you remember," David said, looking at one of the grandfathers, "one of you digitised some slides for me? Well, then suddenly, we were stopped."

"Stopped?" Grandad Jenkins asked. "Who by?"

"We, well, I think it was Mum," Eleanor said. "Officially, someone thought that it was not right for us to sing together, well spend time practising together, and the church pastor had words with David."

"Understandable," Grandad Jenkins murmured. "Didn't you feel odd spending time with a teenager?"

David looked at him. "I can see where you're coming from, and yes, I did think about it. But you have to remember that Eleanor is a remarkably mature young woman. I compared her to the girls I taught, and there was no comparison. There was another factor; I felt safe with Eleanor."

"Safe? What do you mean?" It was Eleanor.

"Safe from romantic expectations. I wasn't ready, or even looking for romance. Imagine what misunderstandings could have arisen if I had been closeted with a mature single lady. I assumed that romance was impossible with Eleanor! She was just a friend – a very young friend, but only a friend."

"A special friend," Eleanor murmured.

"Yes, a special friend. I didn't even notice her age at times."

"But things changed!" Grandma Thomas said. It was a statement, not a question.

Eleanor explained how she had thrown herself into the Romanian mission, and then what had happened on the journey back from the airport.

"So we began seeing each other, but discreetly. If I had tea with David on a Sunday afternoon, then we would cycle separately to church."

"Didn't anybody know?" Grandad Jenkins asked.

"Only my two best friends. I even went to Stephanie and Daniel's wedding, but from camp!"

"Are they your two best friends?" Grandma Thomas asked.

"Oh!" Eleanor stopped, and looked at David. He nodded.

"Daniel is his son," Eleanor said quietly.

There was a shocked silence.

"You have a married son?" Grandma Thomas said, to end the silence

"Yes," said David.

"Oh!"

"Can I tell you the rest?" Eleanor asked.

"Go on," said Grandad Jenkins.

Eleanor told then how they had been seen by a neighbour, who then told her mum and dad.

"They went ballistic," Eleanor said. "They drove me round to David's house and were rude to him. They told him not to see me. They even made an unpleasant accusation about us. Anyway, we went to see the church pastor because I felt guilty that I had gone against their wishes. We talked it over and David asked me to marry him." She shrugged.

"But then things went from bad to worse," David said. "They gave Eleanor an ultimatum. It was me or them. When I took Eleanor home, they had put her things outside on the doorstep."

"What?" exclaimed Grandma Jenkins.

"They had put my things outside," Eleanor said quietly.

"What did you do?" Grandad Jenkins asked.

"We took her things to my house, and I took Eleanor to a

hotel for the night," David said.

"You took Eleanor to a hotel?" Grandad Thomas asked.

"I took and left her at a Travel Lodge," David replied.
"She's now living with a friend, a widow from our church."

"And did they put all of your things outside?"

"No, not everything. I've seen Mum in town, and she told me that Dad expected me to ask to be allowed home. And not see David," Eleanor said.

"Did you know this?" Grandma Thomas asked Grandma Jenkins.

"No, we didn't," Grandad Jenkins replied for her. "We thought something was odd – she was always out when we talked on the phone."

"When was this?" Grandpa Thomas asked.

"Near the end of the summer holiday," Eleanor said.

"Have you been back to try and sort things?"

"I asked Mum why they didn't come looking for me?" Eleanor said. "She told me that Dad had said not to. They knew where I was and he said that I would go back when David got tired of me." She turned to David, and smiled. "And he hasn't got tired of me yet!"

There was another moment of silence, so David stood up. "Sweetheart, I think your grandparents have heard enough." He looked at his hosts. "Thank you very much for seeing and listening to us, but we won't embarrass you further. Eleanor, coming?"

Eleanor stood up, feeling disappointed that they had not really achieved anything.

"Wait a minute, David," she said, digging into her bag. She pulled out two envelopes and handed one each to her two grandmas. "I know you won't be interested in coming but since these have your names on them, I can't use them anywhere else. You may as well have them,

even if you just bin them."
Grandad Jenkins got up to see them out as Grandma
Thomas opened her envelope first.
"What?" she gasped. "So you're pregnant!"
"Pardon?" Eleanor said, spinning round.
"Just like your mother!"
"I am not pregnant!" Eleanor said, now facing them.
"You?" she added, looking at David.
"She is not pregnant. It's not possible," David said.
"You've had the …" Grandpa Thomas paused and was
then interrupted by Eleanor.
"You're no better than my parents! Of course he hasn't.
You're horrible!" Eleanor said, her voice rising. Then she
burst into years.

 David stared at them; then he wrapped his arm round her.
He looked at her grandparents. "Well?" he said.
"Can I ask you something?" Grandad Jenkins asked
David.
"Go on."
"Why are you getting married?"
David gave him what he thought was a withering look.
"For the same reason you got married."
"No, I mean so quickly. Isn't Eleanor still at school?"
"Because we want to have a baby!" Eleanor said, between
sobs.
"Are you serious?" Grandma Jenkins asked.
"Yes, we are very serious," David answered. "Oh, and
thank you for lunch. Eleanor, Sweetheart," he said to
Eleanor, "ready?"

"Please don't go!" It was Grandma Thomas rising from
her chair. "Eleanor?" she held out her arms. Eleanor left
David and went to her. "You knew about your mother?"
Eleanor nodded.

"That's why we thought, I mean, I thought. I'm sorry. But why do you want a baby? You're very young."

"Because my fiancé is not very young. I said yes to David on the condition that we married and started a family as soon as possible. I assumed it would be next summer but now I been kicked out, there's no point in waiting, is there? David has a house."

"And a grown up son," Grandma Jenkins added. "A stepson older than you?"

"Yes, and his son has a twin sister. But I'm not marrying them, I'm marrying David."

"And are these invitations genuine?" Grandpa Thomas asked.

Eleanor turned to him. "Yes, Grandpa, but only if you want to come."

"There is one thing though," David said. "Please don't tell Eleanor's father about our wedding,"

"Why?"

"Someone phoned David's school about us – anonymously. No one knew about us except Mum and Dad," Eleanor said. "I think he might try and stop it, you know, that bit when people are asked if they object."

"But you are eighteen."

"It would still spoil things," David said.

"David, Eleanor," Grandad Jenkins said suddenly. "Would you please stay for tea?"

David looked at Eleanor, but Grandad Jenkins continued. "We knew it was your birthday yesterday – Grandma has made a birthday cake. Please stay."

"Will you come to our wedding, then?" Eleanor asked.

"Wait, Sweetheart. Let them get used to me first," David said. "I don't think you realise how great a shock this has been." He turned back to Grandad Jenkins. "Yes, we would like to stay."

"Eleanor?" Grandad Jenkins asked. His answer was a
hug.

It was an interesting time for Eleanor. Although she knew
about her mother's rushed marriage and the reason, she
didn't know that her mother was expecting twins at the
time.
"No one told me that!" she exclaimed.
"Sweetheart, you told me that it was never talked about.
How did you know they had to get married?"
"I found a card saying something about losing a baby, and
I asked Mum. She said she was pregnant when she
married, and never wanted to talk about it again! And we
didn't"
"It was a dark time. Your mum had a breakdown."
"I never knew that," Eleanor said.
"They were advised to have no children for a while."
"But I was a long time after!" Eleanor exclaimed.
"That's biology for you," Grandma Thomas said.

They also talked more about David's life B.E. as Eleanor
called it – before Eleanor, as well as moving on to how
their relationship began, as well as the possible problems
they might encounter.
"Do you worry about stepping into Jenny's shoes, my
dear?" Grandma Thomas asked.
"Of course I do, Grandma."
"You're taking on a man already housetrained by
someone else," Grandma Jenkins said. "And I wish you
luck. It was bad enough starting from scratch," she said,
poking Grandad Jenkins at the same time.
"Are you going to move in with David?" Grandma
Thomas asked.
"Well, yes," David answered for her. "The main thing is
to keep her life as smooth as possible until after her

examinations next summer."

"And then?"

"We will think about it then."

"Hopefully, we'll be looking for nursery things," Eleanor said.

"My dear," Grandma Thomas said slowly. "Biology doesn't always do as it's told. After all, David is not a young man!"

"That's all the more reason to start trying as soon as possible," Eleanor said.

"But trying too hard sometimes hinders, my dear."

"I know. The doctor explained that."

"Doctor?"

"I've already been to the clinic. We don't want people to think we've jumped the gun as it were."

"She means a premature baby conceived on a honeymoon," David said quickly.

"Honeymoon? Where?" Grandad Jenkins asked.

"Somewhere warm, apparently," Eleanor said.

"And you have everything booked, I mean, wedding wise?"

"More or less. It's not going to be a big wedding for obvious reasons, but yes, we are now giving out the invitations."

"Who's giving you away, my dear?" Grandma Thomas asked, after a pause.

"I'm giving myself away. Stephanie will be my matron-of-honour," Eleanor said.

"Stephanie?"

"Sorry," Eleanor smiled. "Stephanie is Daniel's wife – the wedding I went to with David! She's like a big sister."

"But she will be your step-daughter-in-law." Grandad Jenkins said, with a laugh. "But seriously, what do they think of the situation."

"My son wasn't happy, I know, but he's going to be my best man, I'm pleased to say."

"There is the matter of inheritance," Grandpa Thomas said quietly. Even so, it stopped the conversation, and Grandad Jenkins shifted uncomfortably on his seat.

"You are absolutely right. But having a young second wife is no different to marrying a mature wife. And I'm sure we're not the first to have that problem," David said.

"Have you thought about the problem?" Grandpa Thomas asked. "A new will, for example?"

"Grandpa!" Eleanor interrupted. "I'm not marrying David for his worldly possessions."

"No, my dear, but if anything should happen to David once you are married, you become a significant beneficiary under probate laws. Unless David makes a new will with his forthcoming marriage in mind, then depending on David's estate, that is how much money and property he has, you might find you inherit everything."

"Is that true, David?" Eleanor asked. "That doesn't seem fair."

"Sweetheart, your grandpa is right." David turned to Grandpa. "Thank you for bringing it up. We have talked about money. I thought I had mentioned wills to you, Sweetheart, if I haven't then we will."

"But I won't need one, I don't have anything."

"Eleanor, the bonds," David said quietly. "And I shall add you to the house. Maybe we should have seen a solicitor at half term. I can go on my half day, I might just have to take you in school time, or immediately after school."

"Can we talk it about later, please?" she asked. "It makes me feel I'm marrying you for money."

"Sweetheart, I'm getting the best deal – I'm getting you!" David said.

Later in the afternoon, Grandad Jenkins suggested a little walk. "You could show David where you played by the pond when you were a little girl," he added.

"Are you coming too?" Eleanor asked.

"No, I think we old folks could do with a little rest," he said.

"David?"

"Yes, Sweetheart, that sounds great," David said.

"Well, things don't seem too bad now, do they?" Eleanor said as they walked towards the pond.

"True. You realise we were sent out so they could talk about us, don't you?" David said.

"No!"

David laughed. "Sweetheart, that's one of the things I love about you," he said. "Here truly is a woman in whom there is no deceit," David said, misquoting from the Bible.

"Don't you believe it, David," Eleanor said quietly. "Anyway, do you think they will come?"

"I don't know. If they do, it could build bridges to your mum and dad. That can't be bad!"

David was right; they were sent out so there could be a family discussion.

"We haven't got long," Grandad Jenkins said. "First impression?"

"Decent kind of chap," Grandpa Thomas replied immediately. "I hope he knows what he's letting himself in for."

"What do you mean?" his wife said.

"Well, a young woman with a young woman's needs."

"Arthur!" she said firmly. "Don't talk like that!"

"Fashion; interests," he replied lamely.

"But what about Len and Sheila? They're our kids."

"Len has always been stubborn; he'll come round

eventually. I say let him miss the wedding! Serve him right." Grandma Jenkins said.

"I feel cross they haven't told us. It sounded as though Eleanor had the bonds we gave her as a baby, but I wonder if she will get the card and cheque that we sent," Grandma Thomas said.

"Phone up and ask? Use our phone," Grandma Jenkins suggested. "You needn't tell them they are here, just ask to speak to Eleanor and see what they say."

"It doesn't seem right."

"Look," Grandad Jenkins exclaimed. "They haven't been straight with us. If you won't phone, I will!"

It was a fairly brief call, and they had it on speaker phone so they could all listen in. After saying hello to her daughter, Grandma Thomas asked for Eleanor.

"Is the birthday girl in?"

"No, sorry."

"Oh, well do you know when she will be in?"

"Not exactly."

"Oh, did my card arrive?"

"Yes, it came yesterday."

"Did she like it?"

"Of course she did. She always likes your cards."

"Did she get many cards?"

"Not here. I mean friends hand them personally, don't they. Her other Grandma and grandpa sent one as well."

"Oh good. Look, I've got to go, I'm phoning from a friend's place, bye dear."

Grandma Thomas handed the phone back.

"Why won't they tell us?" she said.

"Because they will have to admit to throwing her out," Grandpa Thomas said. "I say we let them stew in their own juice."

"And go to the wedding? That means we agree with it."
"Apart from their ages, what else worries you? They are obviously in love. Look, their pastor is prepared to marry them."
"Then we will go," Grandma Jenkins said, referring to herself and Grandad Jerkins.
"And so will we!"

Their discussion was over by the time David and Eleanor returned, and they were welcomed back as though there was nothing unusual about their relationship. It wasn't until after tea, with the birthday cake, that the hosts brought up the wedding.
"We've had a chat, and we would all be delighted to accept your invitation, Eleanor and David."
"That's fantastic," Eleanor exclaimed. "But will you tell Mum and Dad?"
"Do you think we should," Grandad J asked.
"I don't know. I was hurt and angry about the way they treated me, well, and the way they spoke to David when they met him. They made it clear that it was them or David, so what can I do? I half expected a text from Mum for my birthday. Nothing. Not even a card!"
"Sweetheart," David said, "you haven't been home since yesterday morning," David said.
"Not at home?" Grandma Thomas asked, picking up on David's comment. "Have you been going home?"
"David meant Molly's house. The lady I live with is called Molly. She's away at the moment, so last night I stayed with David. And I had my own room," Eleanor said firmly.
"Darling, where you sleep in your business," Grandma Thomas said quietly.
"Grandma, Dad more or less suggested that we were sleeping together," Eleanor replied.

"Then he is a stupid man," Grandad Jenkins said. "And I will tell him so."

"Grandad," Eleanor said. "I don't want to cause more problems, especially before my wedding."

"Then we won't tell him, agree," Grandad Jenkins said, appealing to the others.

Nothing more was said about the wedding until it was time to leave. Then Grandpa Thomas asked about the cost of the wedding.

"David, it's traditional for the bride's parents to contribute towards the cost of a wedding. I presume that in your situation, that's not happening, right?"

"It's not a problem, Mr Jenkins," David answered, "and it not going to be a grand wedding for obvious reasons."

"Which are?" Grandma J asked.

"Our age difference. It's not the kind of thing that one broadcasts, is it? We don't think it will go down well at her school."

"But are you ashamed of her?"

"No!" David exclaimed. "If you want to know, I'm proud of her!"

"And so are we," Grandma Thomas said.

"Back to my comment," Grandad Jenkins said. "We have been talking. We would like to contribute, that is, financially."

"Oh," David said. "That's not necessary."

"Are you paying for everything?" Grandpa Thomas asked.

"No," Eleanor said quickly. "I'm paying for my own dress."

Grandpa Thomas looked at David with a puzzled looked.

"She insisted," David said quickly. "It was a matter of principle for her."

Grandad Jenkins looked at Eleanor. "Eleanor, would you let us pay? It would be a matter or principle for us, for all four of us."

"Grandpa, that's not why we came,?" Eleanor said.

"I know, my dear, but it is something we would like to do, right Grandma?"

"I don't know what to say," Eleanor said.

"Try thank you," David whispered.

Eleanor thanked each of the four grandparents in turn, hugging and kissing them at the same time.

"And one other thing," Grandad Jenkins added. "We would like to give you a separate wedding gift."

"Thank you, Grandpa. We haven't thought about a wedding present list, but we'll let you know as soon as we can. The thing is, David's house is already fully equipped."

"Eleanor, my dear," Grandma Thomas said quietly. "We were thinking of money. We would like to give you something for yourself, that's if your future husband doesn't mind."

David smiled. "It's not a problem for me. I think Eleanor is a very fortunate girl."

"So do I, David, but not for the same reason," she said, and kissed him.

Chapter 14

Outed

Grandad T's comment about a wedding gift had reminded David and Eleanor that they had not thought about a wedding present list.

"The thing is, is there anything that we need?" Eleanor asked, as they drove home.

"Well, if we buy a new bed, we'll need bed clothes – under sheets, duvet, duvet covers."

"True."

"There might be things like ornaments that remind you of the day. Otherwise, some people ask for donations to a charity – such as your Romanian connection. Would you like new kitchen hardware?"

"I hadn't thought about it," Eleanor said, "but I will. Maybe a mixture of both." She paused. "David, I've been thinking."

"Danger ahead," David said.

"Where? I didn't see a notice," Eleanor said.

"From a thinking woman," David said.

"David, stop it. I'm serious."

"Okay," he grinned. "Go on."

"Well, I won't need my savings, and I'm about to be given some more." She paused. "And Daniel and Stephanie need help."

"Sweetheart, they're not your responsibility."

"Am I family or not?"

"Eleanor!"

"Well?"

"Yes, you will be."

"I know it's not much money, but as my mum used to say, every little helps."

David didn't answer.

"David," she asked, "you're not upset, are you?"

"No, Sweetheart, I couldn't think what to say. Except I think you are an amazing girl."

"Girl?"

David grinned. "Okay, woman,"

Molly returned from her sister's on Sunday morning in time to prepare the birthday tea-party for Eleanor. Eleanor had spent two nights with David, who then returned her after Sunday lunch and well before the tea-party. The first news they had was that someone had posted some mail for Eleanor through Molly's letterbox at some time during the weekend. They presumed that it was Eleanor's mother, since it had originally been delivered to Eleanor's old address. Eleanor opened her letters excitedly.

"Grandma and Grandad Jenkins," she exclaimed on opening the first, "Oh look, a cheque. Wow! Fifty pounds!"

Then the second. "Grandma and Grandpa Thomas," she exclaimed on opening the second one, "Oh look, another cheque – this time sixty pounds!"

She opened the third and last. "This looks like Mum's hand-writing. Oh, it is." She showed David and Molly. "Happy birthday Eleanor. Love Mum and Dad," she read. "I bet Dad doesn't know about this!" she added.

"Eleanor, you don't know!" David said gently. "You could text and thank her."

"She didn't text me!"

"Eleanor! This is not the Eleanor who helped a grieving widower!"

Eleanor looked at David. "Sorry David, but I'm finding rejection hard."

"Of course you are, Sweetheart. Would you rather I kept quiet?"

"No. I know you're right. As long as you don't say
WWJD. I do have the wrist-band, and I know the
answer."
"They'll come round eventually, my dear," Molly said.
"And when they do, I'm sure you will know how to
respond. Anyway, I'm still waiting to hear about the visit
to your grandparents."

With the visit to see her grandparents over, Eleanor felt
she was a new woman. This feeling was enhanced by the
reception and acceptance she had received from them.
Because of this, the small tea-party organised by Molly
was an anti-climax. Lizzie and Jayne seemed more
excited about her forthcoming nuptials than Eleanor.
They wanted to hear details of her wedding dress and
were disappointed when Eleanor said she didn't know
them.
"But you went to choose it, didn't you?" Lizzie asked.
"I saw three that I liked," Eleanor said.
"Three? You're not buying three!" Jayne exclaimed.
"No," Eleanor laughed. "I'm going to hire one of them.
Instead of reserving one, I'm semi-reserving three. One
will be available, but I don't know – or mind, which."
"Why are you hiring a dress?" Jayne asked.
"Because it's much cheaper. It's not as if I will wear it
again, is it?" Eleanor said, laughing.
"You could make it into a christening dress; that's if you
have a girl. Mind you, I don't suppose you will want to
rush into a family, will you?"

Eleanor looked at David, who made a shushing shape
with his mouth. Unfortunately, Jayne noticed.
"You're planning a family?" she gasped. "But what about
school?"
"Jayne, calm down," David said. "First, if we were

planning a family, we wouldn't tell anyone, would we? Secondly, we don't do christenings in our church, do we?"

"Oh," Jayne said. "Did you know that, Lizzie?"

"Yes," Lizzie said. "Our church does baptisms."

"What's the difference?"

"It's for people who know they are Christians already, as apart from hoping that they will become one."

"How did you know that, Lizzie," David asked.

"I've been to see Pastor James. He's going to arrange classes for me," she said quietly.

"Lizzie!" Eleanor shrieked. "Why didn't you tell me?"

Lizzie shrugged. "I didn't want to detract from your news."

"Lizzie, that's much more interesting – and important, isn't it, David?"

"What?" said Jayne, as David nodded. "How come?"

"Our news is about life now. Lizzie is thinking about eternity," Eleanor said.

"But don't you believe your marriage was made in heaven," Jayne persisted.

"In a way, yes, but it won't continue in heaven. Jesus said there is no marriage in heaven. Wouldn't it be complicated if there was? For example, who would David be married to, Jenny or me?" Eleanor asked.

"But didn't some people have more than one wife?" Jayne asked. "I remember something about King Solomon."

"Okay, what about a woman who marries twice. One of my aunts was widowed, and then remarried," David said.

"And some people, for example in Tibet, practised polyandry – that's more than one husband."

"Goodness!" exclaimed Jayne. "Who would know who their father was?"

"I don't think it was widespread," David added, "I think it

213

was when one husband at a time was away hunting, but I could be wrong. Anyway, as Eleanor said, it won't be a problem in heaven."

Later that evening David collected Eleanor from her after church youth group meeting – they had made a decision that she maintained contact with her peers. It was now accepted by them that not only was she engaged, she was engaged to an older man. However, apart from Lizzie and Jayne, no one in her class knew that she was even engaged. That was to change soon.
"I do believe the girls are more excited than you about the wedding, Sweetheart," David said, referring to Jayne and Lizzie.
"Sorry. I am excited, but it's not the wedding itself; I'm looking forward more to being Mrs Anderson. The wedding is the doorway, as it were. I want to be on the other side."
"A lot of people enjoy going through the doorway, Eleanor."
"Maybe it's because I'm on my own."
"You're not on your own – you have me," David said.
"I know I do, but don't you see, really, you are on the other side of the doorway. I'm in a hurry to get through."
"Then slow down, Sweetheart. I will still be there, and waiting. Don't wish away the days in between."
"Molly said the same thing," Eleanor said. "But it is hard."
"Sweetheart, why not give up your Saturday job. Spend Saturday mornings relaxing."
"You don't. One rule for you, but another rule for me!"
"Okay, suppose I did too!"
"When would you do your week's food shopping and things?"
"I don't know. Friday night? Eleanor, do you think I need

to?"

"Do you think I need to?"

"Sweetheart, why did I suggest it? And I did say you wouldn't lose out. Suppose I employ you for the last few Saturdays."

"Employ me doing what?"

"Eleanor! I don't know."

"I could come and help you – with your housework and stuff."

"All right. It's a deal!"

Eleanor worked the following Saturday, and told her boss that she wanted to stop as soon as possible. Of course he wanted to know why.

"I'm getting married, Sam."

"I know," he replied, pointing to her engagement ring.

"In a month's time."

"Be serious. Have you found a better paid Job, Elly?"

"I am serious, Sam."

"Eleanor, don't mess around. You're at school, right. Oh! You're not ..." Sam left it unfinished.

Eleanor smiled at Sam. "No, I'm not! Sam, I told you that I'm not living at home, didn't I. Well, I'm not living with my fiancé either – yet. But I'm moving in with him as his wife in four weeks time."

"And giving up school? Elly, I thought you were one of the bright kids, sorry, students."

"I'm not giving up school, Sam – at least, that's the plan. My fiancé won't let me!"

"What does the school think about it, Elly?" Sam asked.

"My school doesn't know!"

"Oh, Eleanor," Sam said. "They're bound to find out eventually, surely?"

"I know, Sam. If they kick me out I might ask you for a job."

"And I'd employ you like a shot. Eleanor, I'll miss you. Look, how long can you continue?"

"Next week, Sam?" Eleanor said. "Is that okay?"

The time was dragging for Eleanor. David was very disciplined about their time together. He met her from school on Wednesdays, provided that she brought her school work. They spent Sundays together, but alternating Sunday lunch with Molly. David could see that Molly enjoyed Eleanor's company, and told Eleanor that they should maintain contact when they were a married couple. On Saturday afternoons they either stayed in at David's or went to another town. The main exception to this was that they had continued to go to the jazz nights with Lizzie. Since they had continued going as a threesome during the development and blossoming of David and Eleanor's relationship, Lizzie was not at all embarrassed to be with them, besides which, David and Eleanor picked her up and took her home afterwards.

Following the end of Eleanor's Saturday job, with only a couple or so weeks to go, they went shopping for a new bed. When they were in public, they did not hold hands unless they were some way from their town, so that a casual observer would think they were father and daughter. What they had not expected was that a fellow pupil was also in the store with her parents. David and Eleanor were lying on a king-sized bed, with Eleanor having a fit of giggles.

"Is it called a king-sized because kings have them?" she whispered.

"Maybe," David said.

She rolled to face him. "You do seem a long way away, David. I think we should have a small double."

"And how many men have you slept with?" David asked

cheekily.

"Oh, I've lost count!"

"I know you're lying," he grinned. "Let me tell you, when your husband has a cold or cough, you will be happy to be in a king-sized."

They moved on, testing the different degrees of hardness or softness, when they were spotted.

"Elly!"

Eleanor sat up. Natasha was standing at the foot of the bed, on Eleanor's side.

"Tash!" Eleanor said. "What are you doing here?" It was a silly question, and Eleanor knew it. "Buying a new bed. And you?" Natasha said.

"Buying a bed," Eleanor said confidently.

"A king-sized?"

Of course she expected Eleanor to laugh and deny it, but Eleanor didn't. Now it was Natasha who was embarrassed. "You are?" she whispered. "Oh!" Then she spotted Eleanor's left had. "Oh! It was you!"

"What was me?" Eleanor said, getting off the bed. It didn't feel right lying on a bed next to David, talking to a classmate. David got off the other side.

"Mrs Finch and her comment about someone throwing her life away?" Natasha replied. Before Eleanor could answer, Natasha's mother appeared. "Natasha, dear, shall we go. The man said he will get your bed delivered on Monday."

"Mum, this is Elly," Natasha said. "She's buying a bed as well."

"Planning well ahead, are we?" Natasha's mum said, laughing. "She must have a big room," she then said to David, assuming that he was her father.

"No, mum, I don't think she is planning well ahead," Natasha said slowly, and stressing the word 'well'.

Natasha's mum looked at her daughter, then at David, as it sunk in what Natasha meant. "Right, we have a lot to do. Goodbye, Elly. Come along dear."

"Who was that?" Natasha's mother asked when they were out of earshot.

"Elly Jenkins, a girl in my class."

"And do I assume that wasn't her father?"

"Dead right, Mum. Eleanor Jenkins! Who'd have thought it?"

"Yes, he did look rather old for her," her mother said.

"It's not just that. It's the fact that she's sleeping with anyone. She's says she's a Christian, and that she doesn't believe in sleeping around."

"Natasha, dear, she may be sleeping with him, but that doesn't mean she's sleeping around."

"Okay, not around. Mum, there was a discussion last year, and she said she would wait. The hypocrite! Wait 'til I tell the others!" she said, fishing out her mobile phone, and bringing up the texting screen.

"Natasha, do you really think you should?" her mother asked.

The answer was a look!

"Oh dear, that's torn it," Eleanor muttered. "I bet she's already on the phone!"

"To who?"

Eleanor gave him a look. "David! Half the class will know in ten minutes."

"Sweetheart, they're going to find out eventually," David said.

"David, she thinks we're already sleeping together. Didn't you see the look on her mum's face?"

"Oh," said David. "Sorry, Sweetheart. Do you want to leave?"

"The damage has been done," Eleanor said, "so we may as well finish what we've come for."

"Sure?"

"David, Daniel and Stephie have already bought us a large duvet, and Jill said we were to buy covers and pillowcases. They won't be any use without a bed, will they? Meanwhile, I've got to think about facing Tash on Monday!"

"Tell her the truth, Sweetheart. Tell her why we were buying it. If she chooses not to believe you, then it's her loss."

"Tell her about the wedding? I thought our engagement is meant to be a secret at school!"

"Yes, Sweetheart, it is, but maybe no more. Tell her about the wedding. Better still, invite her!"

"David! You're not serious!"

"We'll talk about it later."

They chose their bed, and David arranged for it to be delivered on the following Wednesday afternoon. The next items were the duvet covers plus pillow cases. David left this entirely up to Eleanor. Eleanor said she was still worried about Natasha, so David suggested talking to Molly about it. They explained what had happened, and Eleanor told her what David had suggested.

"Think about it," David said. "Look, all your friends at church know about us. Most of the congregation seem to know. And for anybody who does want to check up, they can find out at the Registrar's office."

"I can't see Natasha doing that," Eleanor said.

"Can I make a suggestion?" Molly asked.

"Of course," replied Eleanor.

"Well, firstly, how long before the school finds out. Won't you be doing exam entries at some stage?"

"Well, yes."

"You've booked the wedding for half past ten and the reception at twelvish, or soon after, right? So, suppose you ask Mrs Mayfield to rearrange the reception for one o'clock, or slightly later."

"But that will leave well over an hour!" Eleanor said. "What will people do?"

"I think you've miscalculated on who will be there. In fact I think you will be surprised at how many turn up. Wouldn't you like your church friends to be there, I mean apart from your special close friends. Would it matter if some of your class-mates came? Then this Natasha would be able to see that you are properly married."

"But we have given Mrs Mayfield our numbers," Eleanor said.

"You're not having the ubiquitous disco, are you, right, so, offer a cake reception."

"Ah," said David.

"What's a cake reception?" Eleanor asked.

"What it sounds like!" Molly said. "A few cakes and cups of tea for all the guests, whoever they are. Then the proper reception after that."

"Would Mrs Mayfield agree," David asked. "And who will do it?"

"Leave that to me, young man," Molly said.

"But …" David began.

"David!" Her tone told David to stop! "So why not print a few more invitations, but with a variation – David and Eleanor invite etcetera, and to a cake reception immediately after the service. Give one to this Natasha girl as soon as you see her, and casually say that all are invited to the service. Do the same for the youth group. I know you've been loyal while engaged, but what will you do next term? It would be a nice gesture."

"Can it really be arranged, Molly?" Eleanor asked.

"If Mrs Mayfield is happy to move the reception back, I

can't see a problem."

"But what about the cakes, Molly?"

"We may have to buy some, but I'll phone around, all right. Now you stop worrying."

"Yes, Molly," Eleanor said, and hugged her.

The last few weeks went by quickly for David. He had end-of-term examinations to organise and mark. Then there were the reports – something that David hated. Once upon a time brief comments were all that were needed. David was firmly of the opinion that the more words that were used meant that less was actually taken in. Jonny is a pain in the neck and needs a kick up the backside was considered inappropriate but got to the point, in David's opinion. And how to let the parents of Soraya Patel know that their daughter would never become a brain surgeon? On top of this, there was the school play. In the past, David had been involved in these presentations. However, following his bereavement, and then his part-time status, he had not been asked. He had been asked for this term, but had declined saying he wasn't ready. This had been accepted without question, but David had felt guilty. It was his forthcoming nuptials that were the main reason.

The school play took place on three days, the Thursday to the Saturday of the penultimate week. It was tradition that the staff went on the last night, and then stayed on for the party. David had been to see Charlie earlier that week to firm-up a few details concerning the photographs. Charlie had taken the opportunity to tell David that he expected to meet the new wife-to-be at the party. David had laughed it off, but Charlie insisted that it was a serious suggestion. It so happened that the headmaster saw David in the corridor later the same day

"I take it that we will be meeting your fiancée on Saturday, David?"

"Er, we hadn't planned it," David stuttered.

"Well, please do. I want to meet her."

"Do you?" David replied.

"Of course I do. I want to thank her for bringing you alive again. Don't get me wrong, David, but at one stage, I thought we were going to lose you."

However, it was Bob Finch that persuaded him.

"I don't suppose you'll have the nerve to bring your teenage fiancée on Saturday, David?" he said with a smirk.

"And why shouldn't I?"

"So you will?"

"It depends on whether she is busy," David said to cover himself, but inside he now wanted to bring her. How dare Bob suggest he should hide her away.

David drove round to see Eleanor that night to ask about Natasha, and to invite her to his school play.

"Hello Molly, hello Sweetheart," he said, giving Eleanor a kiss. "How's things?"

"Hm, I had a reception committee this morning – who's sleeping with her fiancé then – and worse!"

"I'm sorry."

Eleanor shrugged. "It was to be expected."

"What did you do?"

"I looked for Natasha, who was obviously full of herself. I told her quietly that we were not sleeping together, but she laughed and said I must be more stupid than I looked. I asked why, and she said it was the oldest trick in the book. I asked her what she meant, although I thought I knew, and she said that men who can't get, er, well, you know, they offer marriage to get it. I then gave her the invitation." Eleanor stopped.

"Go on."

"Her face! It was a picture, she was almost speechless. She asked if I meant it. I said she would find out whether I was plain stupid or lucky if she accepted. She said she would be there. I then quietly told her friends who were gathering round that they were also invited to my wedding."

"Well done, Sweetheart."

"Oh, half of them laughed and said they didn't believe me, but then I saw Jayne and called her over. 'What are you doing on Saturday week, Jayne?' I asked. She looked me with a funny look because as far as she knew, it was still a secret. I said she could tell them, so then she confirmed it. You know what the next thing was, don't you?"

David thought he did, but didn't like to say.

"They said I must have a bun in the oven, to quote, sorry. I said if I did, I would be the only other woman beside Mary to have a virgin birth. Someone laughed, so I told them to wait and see if I was pregnant, after all, I should know. I hope the pill works on honeymoons, David."

"We could abstain," David said.

Eleanor stared at David. "You're not serious, are you?" she said at last.

David laughed. "Sorry, Sweetheart, I couldn't resist! Your face!"

Eleanor drummed her fists on his chest. "David Anderson – you're a bully. It's not too late to change my mind!"

"But then Natasha would have the last laugh," he said.

"Oh. So I suppose I've got to marry you now."

David laughed. "'Fraid so, Sweetheart. Anyway, I've come to invite you to our school play on Friday. The head specifically asked me to bring you."

"Don't tease me, David."

"I'm not. I ought to go anyway, but I would rather you

came with me."

"Do you mean it? Anyway, what would I wear?"

"Yes, I do mean it, and two, I have no idea what you would wear. Are you saying you need a new dress?"

"Are you offering?" Eleanor said. "I think I deserve something after all I've gone through!"

"One day after school?"

"I'm joking!"

"No, Wednesday!"

On Wednesday afternoon David took delivery of the new bed. He then moved into Daniel's old room, having decided that apart from having no duvet for it, the new bed would not be used by him alone. Eleanor later laid one of the duvet covers on it, because Jill had said that she would bring and fit the new duvet into its cover when they came for the wedding. David then rushed to meet Eleanor from school and took her directly to the shops.

On the Saturday evening, David took Eleanor to the play. He thought that Eleanor's new dress added years to her appearance, and they agreed that when asked about her occupation, they would give it as a student, rather than schoolgirl. It did leave open the question about where and what was her subject. Eleanor also guessed that she would see Valerie Finch again, and worried about it. However, the first person who came across to them was David's headmaster.

"David," he said. "So this is your fiancée!"

"Eleanor, meet Mr Banks, my headmaster. Headmaster, this is Eleanor."

"Eleanor, please call me Stuart, I regard myself as now being off-duty as it were. I am so pleased to have met you, the woman who has brought David back to life, sorry, no offence, David. I noticed the change, what, from last Easter, I think."

Eleanor did not know how to respond, but David did mention that there were just friends back then.

"Have you named the day, David?" Stuart asked.

"Yes," David replied cautiously.

"Well?"

"Next Saturday."

The headmaster hesitated, and David wondered if he had forgotten their conversation some time earlier. He had not.

"Does your headmistress know, Eleanor," he asked, lowering his voice.

"No, headmaster," she replied, and too embarrassed to use his name.

He raised his eyebrow, but said nothing. "Stuart, we would be honoured if you could attend," David said quickly.

Stuart looked at him for a moment. "Don't go away," he then said. "Let me ask my secretary, er, my wife." He grinned and excused himself and went cross to where his wife was talking to another colleague, a female.

"Susan, excuse me butting in, but can I borrow Joyce a moment," he asked. Then, as he led his wife away, he whispered quickly. "Joyce, remember David Anderson? He lost his wife about two years ago. Well, that's his fiancée – they are getting hitched on Saturday. Can we go, I mean, are we free?"

"Apart from shopping, yes."

"Good," he whispered quickly. Then, as they reached David and Eleanor, "Eleanor, this is my wife, and she says we are free. Yes, we'd love to come. Where and when?"

The information given and received, he led her back to Susan.

"She's obviously much younger than David," Joyce
observed on the way
"How old would you say she was?"
"Twenty five?"
"Yes, she could be, couldn't she? She's eighteen, Joyce."
"What?" Joyce stopped and turned to look again, but
David was being approached by Bob and Valerie Finch.

"Hello, Eleanor," Valerie spoke first. David and Bob
merely nodded at each other.
"Hello, Mrs Finch," Eleanor replied in what she hoped
was a confident manner.
"I've been hearing rumours, Eleanor," Valerie said.
Eleanor looked at David; it was obvious what she meant.
"Valerie," David said. "We had to make a decision. I
know you have strong feelings about girls and their
careers; in fact I feel the same. I was disappointed when
my own daughter chose to marry rather than study, but
she did the right thing – for her, and I now enjoy being a
grandfather. In our case there was no doubt about the fact
that we wanted to marry. I know you have children and
I'm sure you would want Eleanor to have children – one
day. The question is, given our unusual age disparity,
when should we become parents together, should it, of
course, be possible?"
Valerie Finch did not answer, and Eleanor could not
prevent herself from speaking.
"Do you really not understand, Mrs Finch?" Eleanor
entreated. Again it seemed that Valerie Finch's position
was immutable, but suddenly her demeanour wavered.
She leaned forward and hugged Eleanor.
"I hope everything works out for you, Eleanor," she
whispered.

They circulated for a while before going. Several of
David's colleagues came to see who his young

companion was, but none actually asked about her work. Several cast-members from the sixth form also spoke to David, but really hoping to make themselves known to Eleanor, probably assuming that she was David's daughter. However, when David introduced her as his fiancée, their interest waned. As David kissed her goodnight at Molly's she reminded him that there was only one more week.

"I'll be Mrs Anderson, and you'll be able to kiss me properly!" she said.

Chapter 15

French Kissing is Permissible

David was sitting at the front of the church with Daniel, relaxing. He had expected to feel very nervous, but in some ways, after the two hectic weeks he had endured, just sitting doing nothing was a luxury. The previous Saturday had been very busy. First of all, he had been with Eleanor to choose and order her bouquet, together with the two button holes needed for himself and Daniel. Then it was off to collect Eleanor's wedding dress and Stephanie's bridesmaid dress. Of the three that Eleanor had reserved, two were available, and Eleanor had to decide between them. The one she chose then needed minor alterations, so while that was in hand Eleanor took David shopping for himself. Eleanor decided he needed new nightwear, new beachwear and new swimwear as well as her. They also bought matching suitcases.

On the Sunday afternoon, Eleanor had raised the topic of Christmas cards.
"Are we sending joint Christmas cards, David?"
"Christmas! Sweetheart, I haven't even thought of Christmas!"
"Are you serious?"
"Yes."
A long silence. Then, "You do believe in Christmas?"
"Since you ask, I hate the big commercial razzmatazz that it's become!"
"So do I. But, well." For a moment Eleanor was lost for words. "Is that why you asked Nicola to help you last year?"
"I didn't ask her, she offered, and I was very grateful!"

"She offered? What made her do that?"

"If you want to know, I was going to ask you to help me, but you'd just been taken away by your mother. So I mentioned it, that I was going to ask you, and she offered. Look, it wasn't personal. I had no idea what to buy for my family. Jenny had always done that. I was clueless, well, I still am."

"I suppose she did the Christmas cards?"

"Well, yes."

"What about the one you gave her?"

"We didn't exchange Christmas cards – we lived together. Jill didn't get a card until she was married. Did your mum give you a Christmas card?"

"Yes."

"Oh!"

Another pause. "Would you have done anything this year?" Eleanor asked.

"I would probably have rushed into town on Monday or Tuesday afternoon and bought the same things as last year; whiskey for Keith, socks for Daniel, a scarf for Jill, oh, and Lego or something for my grandson."

"And Stephanie?"

"No idea."

"And me?"

David hesitated. "Sweetheart, I've had things on my mind. Would you mind waiting until after Christmas, and we can go looking together."

"A girl does like being surprised, David," Eleanor said.

"Even if it's something you hate?"

"It's the thought that counts!"

"Hmm. I remember buying my dad a tie which he never ever wore!"

"Okay, back to cards. Would you have sent any cards?" Eleanor asked.

"I didn't last year."

"What about this year?"

"I told you, Eleanor, what with our wedding and all the pressure at school, it simply didn't occur to me. I'm sorry."

"Would you like me to add your name to the ones I'm sending?"

"It depends on who to, doesn't it? I mean, if you're like the girls at my school, every girl had a card for every other girl in the class!" David said, laughing.

"Molly, James and Lucy, Edward and Susan, Fiona and Gareth, my grandparents," Eleanor said in a voice that showed she was not amused by David's comment.

"Molly? Yes – sorry, Eleanor. You're right, I didn't think. Yes, I would be grateful."

"I won't put your name on the card I'm sending to Mum and Dad."

"You're sending them a card?"

"Do you have a problem with that?"

"No, no, of course not," he said quickly. "Eleanor, Sweetheart, I'm sorry I'm grumpy. I'm like this at the end of term – and it's not finished yet! Please put my name where you think it ought to be."

During that last week, the word somehow got around that 'Sir' was engaged, with several classes summing up the courage to ask. It was usually one of the girls.

"Sir, is it true you're engaged?"

"Yes, Caroline."

"What's her name, Sir?"

"It's Eleanor, why?"

Caroline just shrugged.

"So when are you going to lose your liberty, Sir?" – That from one of the boys.

"You can let me know when you see the manacles, Lenny," David replied, which gained a laugh.

It was his sixth form class who were more direct and familiar in their manner.

"Smart lady on Saturday night, Sir," Phil said, who had been at the after school-play party. "In fact, a bit of a cracker."

David smiled. He knew that it was not meant to be anything but a compliment.

"Phil, it was his fiancée, you pin-head!" Gilly called out. Phil shrugged. "So?"

"Have you named the day, Sir," Gilly asked.

"Yes, Gilly."

"Will you tell us?"

"Why do you want to know, Gilly?"

"Because I would like to give you a best wishes card, Sir,"

"Oh," said David, her reason having taken the wind out of his sails. "All right, it's Saturday."

"Where?"

"In my church. We both go there."

The matter was dropped, or so David thought. It was later in the same day that Anne-Marie stopped him in the corridor. He liked Anne-Marie. She wasn't the brightest of his pupils, and had often struggled. He didn't teach her now, but she still smiled at him when she saw him.

"Sir, which church do you go to," she asked in her usual sweet manner. Without thinking, he told her. She followed this by asking which time the wedding was. David did not feel he could ask why she was asking, and anyway, she had always been one of his favourite pupils, so he told her. "I hope you have a good day, Sir," she said. "Oh, and happy Christmas, Sir."

"Thank you Anne-Marie, and a happy Christmas to you too."

During the rest of the week, with reports on his mind,
David accepted the occasional reference to his
forthcoming wedding graciously, along with the usual
best wishes for Christmas.

Because they expected to see each other only on
Wednesday and Friday before the wedding, there was an
exchange of text messages as the thoughts or ideas came
to them.

```
dont forget your new passport eleanor
xxx
I can't use the old one. It was
returned with the corner cut off! XXX
            *   *   *   *

dont forget to pack your pills xxx
David!
            *   *   *   *

lots of factor thirty we-re going to
stick out like sore thumbs xx
We won't be the only whities, David xxx
huh most people will b artificially
tanned xxx
Perhaps we should go to a tanning salon
xxx
if only there was time xxx
            *   *   *   *

David, have you wrapped Molly's
present? xxx
of course
Doesn't your phone do capitals?
I am waiting 4 u 2 teach me
            *   *   *   *

David, have you wrapped Stephanie's
present? xxx
grrrrr
```
On the Friday evening, David had collected Daniel and
Stephanie from the station and taken them first to his

home and then on to Molly's. After dinner they had a rehearsal with James – it was a very brief session. They had already agreed on the form of the words. There is a legal minimum, but most churches use more words than legally necessary. They had already talked to the organist, so they just ran through the order quickly.

"And don't forget that you can't ask who is giving the woman away," Eleanor reminded James.

"I know, and anyway, it's not part of the necessary wording."

"And you needn't tell us we can kiss," David said.

"Oh yes he can," Eleanor said. "Or don't you want to kiss me?"

"Eleanor! Don't you think it's unseemly? What do you think, James?" David asked.

James grinned. "I think it looks nice. You don't have to make a meal of it. Tell me, David, it may be a quiet wedding, but do you want it to be normal?"

"Well, yes, of course!"

"I know it's not necessary, but most new husbands are quite happy to be seen to be affectionate!"

"Okay," David said, with a distinct lack of enthusiasm.

"If you don't want to," Eleanor said, and shrugged.

David tried again, making an effort to sound enthusiastic, even though inside he did not feel it. "Sorry, Sweetheart, James is right. Of course you must say it, James."

With the rehearsal over, Eleanor wanted to show Stephanie and Daniel something, leaving David standing with James.

"David, did I say the wrong thing," James asked.

"No, it's just that I'm sensitive about her youth."

"And your maturity?" James added.

David nodded.

"David, I'm not a trained relationship counsellor, and I know you have both considered your age disparity, but for goodness sake, don't take your reserve into the bedroom!"

"Pardon?"

"You know what I mean. Or shall I bring Song of Songs seven-seven into my talk? Or one Corinthians seven?"

"No," David said quickly.

"I'm told it's like riding a bike," James said, with a grin.

"James, behave!" David said, as the other three re-appeared.

It was then back to David's after depositing Eleanor at Molly's. As he kissed her goodnight, she said that that was the last time he would kiss his fiancée. For a moment David was puzzled, then he realised what she meant, and he kissed her again. "And I'm looking forward to kissing Mrs Anderson tomorrow," he added. Daniel and Stephanie slept in David's new bed. There was no king-sized duvet for it, but David's old duvet was still available. Jill would fit the new duvet sometime after the wedding, ready for David and Eleanor's return a week later. Daniel used David's car to take Stephanie round to Molly's straight after breakfast so that the girls could prepare and dress together, before returning to David. They then had over an hour before it was their turn to set off – for his supposedly quiet wedding.

James met them by the door. "David, Daniel," he said, shaking their hands. David peered inside. To his amazement, he could see that the church was already half-full.

"James, have we got the right time?" David asked, thinking that they were the tail end of another wedding.

"More or less, why?"

"Something's going on. Is there another wedding over running?" he asked James.

"David, if there was, where would I be right now?"

"But all these people. I haven't invited them!"

"Well, it was announced on Sunday, David. They can come to a wedding service without being invited, you know."

"I thought it was going to be a quiet do. That's what we planned,"

"Do you want me to turn them all out except those with a personal invitation?" James asked, a trifle sarcastically.

"Don't ask, I might take you up on it," David replied.

"Dad!" Daniel gasped.

"I was joking, Daniel."

"And I wouldn't have done it anyway," James said. "You may as well come in – you've got the rings, Daniel."

Daniel grinned. "Yes, for the third time! Come on, after you, Dad."

David walked in, looked left and right and recognised people from Sunday. He began to walk to the front.

"Hello, Sir." David stopped and turned. It was Anne-Marie smiling broadly at him. And there were several more pupils, or students as the sixth form liked being called, with her. Boys as well as girls. Then he saw a group from the lower school, "Hello, Sir," they called. David returned their greeting, and then continued.

"Hello, David." He turned, this time to his left, to the Bride's side. It was Lizzie, with Jayne and a group of girls.

"Hello, Lizzie, Jayne. Who are your friends?"

"Classmates," Lizzie said, with a big grin.

Then, right at the front, he spotted the four grandparents. He stopped to say hello, and shake hands before he realised that Sheila Jenkins was at the far end of their row. She looked at him coldly. David moved slightly and whispered to Grandpa Thomas.

"What's she doing here? Is she going to cause trouble?"

"No, David. She won't cause any problems."

"But why is she here? How did she know?"

"We asked her?"

"So does Len know?"

"No. We asked Sheila to meet us on the other side of town, but we didn't tell her why. Then we asked if she wanted to accompany us to your wedding. She was shocked and didn't believe us at first. Then she asked if she could go home and change and we said there wasn't time. Either come with us or don't, we said. So, she came."

"Eleanor will be pleased," David said, before moving on. He had also noticed his headmaster and wife, so he went to speak to them. After greeting a few other friends, he took his place at the front next to Daniel – and relaxed! There nothing he had to do, except wait for his bride.

"Too late to run now, Dad," Daniel whispered.

"Very funny," David whispered back.

"You look very calm."

"I feel it. It's been quite a stressful time in a way – the last few days at school as well as preparing for the wedding."

"Well, now you can enjoy the day, Dad."

"I intend to."

It was ten minutes before a general stir in the congregation told David that Eleanor and Stephanie had arrived. He turned and looked back down the aisle and saw that Eleanor was standing alone just inside the door. He then had a sudden flash back to his first wedding. There was no reason for it – it was a different place, a

different church, a different woman, in fact the first
woman was with her father, this woman was standing
alone. But it was as though Jenny was standing there and
asking why he was remarrying. A feeling of guilt surged
through him. His legs went weak and he began to shake.
However, Daniel sensed something was wrong, and took
his arm.

"Dad? What is it?" Daniel whispered.

It was the pressure of Daniel holding his arm that brought
him back to reality, and he turned back to Daniel.

"Nothing. Nothing at all. It's Eleanor! She's here," he
said, as the organist struck up the wedding march.

By the time Eleanor reached the front, David was again in
control of himself. He stepped out to meet her, and then
as arranged, he lifted her veil to expose her face. But
then, and not as arranged, he bent and kissed her cheek.

"Thank you for coming, Sweetheart," he whispered.

Eleanor was surprised. "That comes later," she whispered
back. "Who are all these people?"

"Kids from my school, and some from yours, I think."

James coughed, to remind them that the music was still
being played, and that he should be the one in control.
The couple turned to face him.

"Sorry, James," David whispered.

"Eleanor, your bouquet," James whispered.

"Oh!" Eleanor turned and gave it to Stephanie to hold,
together with a white stole that she had wrapped round
her shoulders. She turned back to James. "Sorry," she
breathed. Then she took David's hand.

James waited until the music had come to the end, and the
congregation had seated themselves. Then he began.

"Dear friends and family, we are gathered here today in
the sight of God and in your presence to join together

David and Eleanor in holy matrimony," he began. David was waiting for one particular phrase which James eventually reached – "If any one can show a just cause why they may not be lawfully joined together, let them speak now, or forever hold their peace."
David held his breath, gritted his teeth and waited. There was no reason at all to worry, but having seen Sheila Jenkins, he was worried. James waited. No one objected and James continued as David breathed again. Eleanor was to tell him later that he was holding her hand so tightly, it hurt!

When it came to the vows, James picked up a roving microphone. This had not been part of the plan, but when James had seen the church filling up, he had quickly arranged for the sound system to be activated. David and Eleanor now stood facing each other.
"David Anthony Anderson, will you have this woman to be your wedded wife? Will you love and comfort her, honour and keep her, in sickness and in health, and forsaking all others, keep yourself only unto her as long as you both shall live?"
"I will."
"Eleanor Louise Jenkins, will you have this man to be your wedded husband? Will you love and comfort him, honour and keep him, in sickness and in health, and forsaking all others, keep yourself only unto him as long as you both shall live?"
"I will."
"Since it is your intention to enter into marriage, join your hands, and declare your consent in front of these witnesses."

James then held prompt cards in case they stumbled. David spoke first, glancing at the prompt card.

"I, David, take you, Eleanor to be my wife, to have and to hold from this day forward, for better or for worse, for richer or for poorer, in sickness and in health, to love and to cherish, till death us do part, according to God's holy law, and this is my solemn vow." David then turned to Daniel, who handed him a ring. Then David continued, at the same time as slipping the ring onto Eleanor's finger, "Eleanor, take this ring as a sign of my commitment and fidelity to you. With my body I worship you and I endow you with all my worldly goods."

Then it was Eleanor's turn.

"I, Eleanor, take you, David to be my husband, to have and to hold from this day forward, for better or for worse, for richer or for poorer, in sickness and in health, to love, cherish and obey, till death us do part, according to God's holy law, and this is my solemn vow." Eleanor now turned to Stephanie, who handed her a ring. "David, take this ring as a sign of my commitment and fidelity to you. With my body I worship you," she said as she pushed the ring onto David's finger. "And I endow you with my few worldly goods."

James then addressed the congregation. "David and Eleanor have declared their marriage vows in front of you. I now pronounce them husband and wife. David, you may kiss your wife."

David leaned forward and kissed Eleanor on her lips. It wasn't a quick peck, but it wasn't a meal! The congregation burst into applause.

The wedding then continued with a prayer, a hymn, a talk, a hymn, and a final benediction. Before James closed the proceedings, he announced that the formal reception had been delayed in order to offer everyone present some refreshments. It would be back inside the church after the photographs, because the hall was already set out for the formal reception. David then turned to Eleanor and offered his arm, and together they walked slowly back down the aisle. Eleanor took the opportunity to look around. From her position at the front, she had not been able to see the bride's side of the church; so of course, the first people she looked for were her four grandparents. She saw them immediately, and smiled back at them. Then she spotted her mother. For a moment she almost stumbled as they looked at each other. She recovered and was moved along as she clung to David with her heart beating faster. Now her worry was that her father might be there, but waiting outside. If it had not been for Lizzie waving from her seat next to the aisle, she might have missed her. She smiled back; and saw that Jayne was next to Lizzie. Another smile. Then she spotted almost all the rest of her class. Among them was Tash, who smiled very broadly and mouthed her congratulations. David spotted George from the old people's home and wondered how he knew. They had to pause twice in order for Charlie to use his camera. Then they were outside, in a cold, but very sunny day. David was in a suit, but Eleanor was in a wedding dress that left her shoulders and neck bare.

"There aren't too many photos, Sweetheart," he whispered.

But he was wrong. Charlie had been given a list by David, and he began working through it. Eleanor forced herself to smile, still wondering if her father would suddenly appear and cause an unpleasant scene.

"Eleanor and her grandparents," Charlie called. Standing in the middle of them, Eleanor felt safer, and now her smile was natural.

"David, you join them," Charlie called.

The next photographs were with Daniel, Stephanie, Jill, Keith and James. As far as David was concerned, these were the last ones. However, Grandpa Thomas then came forward bringing his daughter, Eleanor's mother.

"Can we have a Thomas family photo, please?" he asked.

Charlie looked at David, who looked at Eleanor.

"I don't know. Is Dad here?"

"No, he's not. He doesn't know about it, Sweetheart," David assured her.

"Do you want to be in a picture, Mum?" Eleanor asked.

Sheila nodded, so Eleanor looked at Grandpa Thomas. "Is it what you want, Grandpa?"

"Yes please, Eleanor. All five of us," he said, making it clear that David was included.

Even that was not the end. Anne-Marie then came forward.

"Could we have a picture with Mr Anderson, please?"

"My sixth form, Eleanor," David told her.

"Of course," Eleanor said. "And can I have Lizzie and Jayne?"

David and Eleanor were photographed surrounded by the boys and girls of his sixth form. Then David alone with his class. Eleanor's class then came forward to be photographed with her, after which Eleanor asked for Lizzie and Jayne.

"Sweetheart, we didn't think of Molly. Where is she?" David whispered to Eleanor.

"You're right. How did we miss her?"

David spotted Lucy in the crowd. "Lucy, where's Molly?" David called. "We must have Molly!"

It took a few minutes to locate and then persuade her to be photographed with Eleanor, but she agreed. By now, Eleanor was shivering, so Molly asked Stephanie for the stole and wrapped it round her shoulders and suggested that they went back in. Molly, of course, had been helping preparing the cups of tea about to be served. When Mrs Mayfield, who was organising the tea and cake session realised that the numbers were greatly exceeding her expectations, she had phoned her husband and made him do an emergency shop. He had arrived back just in time with a selection of cakes bought in the supermarket!

David and Eleanor circulated together and separately. Eleanor approached the girls in her class picking out Natasha.

"Elly, you look beautiful," Natasha said, giving Eleanor a hug before Eleanor could speak. "And your husband is very," she paused, and Eleanor wondered what was coming, "handsome."

"Thank you, Tash, and thank you for coming," Eleanor replied graciously.

Natasha drew her away from the others. "Elly, can I ask you something?"

"Yes, Tash."

"And you won't get angry?"

"I'll try not to Tash. Please don't be rude about David though."

"I won't. Elly. Are you really not pregnant?"

Eleanor took both of Natasha's hands and looked at her directly. "Tash, I've not done anything to get pregnant. Not with David or anybody, okay?"

"So why are you getting married?"

"Oh, Tash," Eleanor said sadly. "When you find your special person, you'll understand. You may have noticed that I was not given away by my dad. He won't speak to me now. I've been staying with a friend, so the obvious thing is to move in with David – but as his wife. I'm sorry if you don't understand."

Tash looked at her, and then suddenly hugged her again.

"I'm sorry I was horrible in the shop, Elly. I do wish you every happiness with your David."

"Thank you, Tash," Eleanor replied.

George, from the old people's home, found them and spoke to them when they were together.

"Well, well," he said. "Congratulations. I wish you both every happiness. I thought I noticed a degree of familiarity last year. It was a year ago, wasn't it?"

"There was no relationship, George," David said. "I can assure you."

"That's not what I said, David," George replied, with a grin. "Still waters run deep, eh, my dear?" he said to Eleanor.

"So I'm told," she replied, smiling at him.

"So, do you think it might be possible to come and sing to us again? Or have you not been singing at all?"

"George, would you mind if we told you after our honeymoon?" David asked.

"Then you're not saying no?"

"But it will be fifty-fifty. Secular-Christian, George," Eleanor said. "Agree?"

"Agreed," George said.

At the appropriate time, David and Eleanor said farewell to the first party, and then they moved on to the now delayed formal reception. Eleanor asked if her mother could be accommodated, but Sheila said that she had to leave as her husband knew nothing of her whereabouts. She added that she would not tell him about the wedding for the time being.

"But are you glad you came, Mum?"

"Yes and no. I still think you are making a mistake. I mean, have made a mistake, Eleanor."

"Sheila, I understand your feelings," David said slowly. "But in this case, you are wrong, and we are going to prove you wrong, if you let us."

"Mum, you have never replied to my text messages. Shall I text you when we come back?"

"Come back?" Sheila asked.

"Mum – honeymoon?" Eleanor said.

Sheila hesitated. Then she spoke. "Yes, dear. But when I'm at work so your dad doesn't find out."

"Bye, Mum," Eleanor said, holding out her arms. Again, Sheila hesitated. Then she allowed herself to hug and be hugged.

The meeting with her mother affected Eleanor. There was sadness in that there was still a barrier, but some joy in that it was smaller. It seemed that her father was now the main problem. However, she tried hard to contain her feelings, and by the way she smiled, not even David realised. Daniel made a short speech in which he admitted having reservations when he first met Eleanor, but adding that he was now looking forward getting to know his step-mother with great expectations, which embarrassed both Eleanor and Stephanie. (Stephanie gave him a good telling-off later). David recounted their initial meetings, and admitted that early on he had reservations about being friendly with such a young person. "But since I knew there could never be a romantic relationship between us, I continued to enjoy her company on what I assumed was a platonic level. Then, much later, when I knew that our feelings were more than just platonic, I had to decide whether to be selfish, and claim her for myself, or walk away and allow another man to be blessed. Eleanor allowed me to be selfish, and for that, I am so grateful." He smiled at his bride and sat down.

The party drew to a close, and Eleanor changed in the church office. Molly had brought her outfit, and was going to return the hired dress. There were hugs and kissing all round, and then another dousing with confetti as they got into David's car to leave. Suddenly, Grandad Jenkins pushed forward, and thrust an envelope into Eleanor's hands.

"Open that tomorrow, my dear," he said.

Eleanor looked surprised, and confused.

"It's nothing to worry you, Eleanor," he added, "have a nice time."

They drove away with Eleanor still holding the envelope.

"What do I do?" she said to David.

"Do as he says. Put it into your handbag, Sweetheart. Anyway, how did it go?" David asked.

"Better than expected. Did you know my mum was coming?"

"No. I did see her with your Grandparents before you arrived. I couldn't really tell you, but I felt your reaction when you saw her."

"Hmm," Eleanor said.

"Good and bad?" David asked.

"We'll see."

"But no regrets?"

"David Anderson, you do ask silly questions, don't you. Of course I have no regrets!"

They drove much of the way in silence, or listening to music. David felt glad it was over and was pondering over his flashback, but he knew he had no regrets. Eleanor was also pondering, but on her family situation. Support from her grandparents. Uncertainty about mother. Father? Did he hate her? Would he ever relent?

They reached the hotel with an hour to spare before dinner and booked in. Eleanor walked out of their bathroom as David removed his jacket.

"We don't need to unpack, do we?" she said. "Look, they even provide toothbrushes and paste."

"No, we don't. And it's an early start tomorrow, Sweetheart."

She came across to David and put her arms round his neck.

"Alone at last," she said.

"Sweetheart, we've been alone for over two hours!"

"What shall we do until dinner?" she added, ignoring his facetious answer.

"Whatever you like."

Eleanor kissed him, and touched her tongue to his lips.

"Weren't you going to teach me about French kissing," she said. "Assuming it is permissible now!"

"Me?" pause – a kiss. "What do I know about things like that?" pause – a hint of a French kiss. "You were going to teach me!" he said.

Chapter 16

The Canaries

It was about nine o'clock and they were cruising at about thirty-five thousand feet, according to an announcement. The hotel had woken them at five-thirty for breakfast and then a lift to the airport for a six-thirty check-in. They had brought the clothes needed for the flight in a separate bag, and now their smart going away clothes were stored in the boot of David's car.

"Now I really feel properly married," Eleanor said, leaning her head onto David's shoulder.

"Why because we're at thirty-five thousand feet?" David answered, puzzled.

"No, silly."

"You said something similar on the bus to London, if I remember."

"It's different, this time"

"What do you mean?"

"Last night."

"Shush," David uttered quickly, as he realised what she meant. "You don't have to tell the whole aeroplane."

Eleanor kissed his cheek. "I don't mind," she said, but this time in a whisper.

It wasn't the French kissing to which she was referring. Admittedly, it had led on to a more significant activity, but despite James' comment, David had been reserved. However, everything had worked and in Eleanor's case, according to the book they had both read, and they both had gone down to dinner with a satisfied feeling. It was what had happened after dinner to which she was referring. There was a lift, and they kissed in the lift, and in the corridor. Maybe it was the half bottle of wine, but they felt less inhibited, and decidedly more passionate as they moved from the lift to the corridor, and then from the corridor into their room.

"Were you nervous?" she asked, but in a whisper. "I was."

David looked around before answering. "Sweetheart, this isn't the best place to talk about it, is it?"

"Sorry," she giggled. "But the book didn't prepare me for the second time."

"Shush. What's got into you?"

She looked at him, and then giggled again. They were sitting in seats four and five. There was a woman in seat six by the window, and she looked up from her book.

"Eleanor, behave," David whispered.

"Or will you put me outside the room, like at school?" she asked cheekily. "I'm not wearing a parachute!"

"Eleanor, you're embarrassing me," David said.

"Am I? Sorry, David, I'm just feeling happy! I feel like a little girl whose just been given her first pink bike!"

"I thought you felt like a woman who has just," David stopped, and grinned, discretion preventing him from saying more.

Eleanor shrugged. "Okay, that as well."

"Right, no more on the subject until after dinner, okay?"

"It was before dinner yesterday!"

"Eleanor!" There was a slight sharpness to David's tone, but Eleanor just smiled. The woman in seat six looked up again, and glanced at Eleanor.

"I'm feeling happy!" Eleanor told her.

"Is this your first time?" the woman asked.

"Pardon?"

"Flying."

"Oh, yes. And to the Canaries."

"For Christmas?"

"Yes."

"With your father?"

"With my husband," Eleanor said, lifting her left hand into view. The woman looked at her two rings, wedding and engagement, and then by leaning forward, at David. She leaned back into her seat.

"Really?" she mouthed.

Eleanor smiled. "Yes, really," she whispered.

The woman leaned forward and this time she gave David a harder look before sinking back. Then she pointed at the rings. "When?" she mouthed.

"Yesterday,"

The woman looked down, shaking her head slowly, as if she didn't believe Eleanor.

"Don't you believe me?" Eleanor asked.

"Anyone can buy a ring," she said. "It's not as if people really care."

Eleanor sat back, not sure what the woman meant, and the woman went back to her book.

"David, can I see my passport?" Eleanor asked, after a few minutes.

"Why, Sweetheart?"

"Does it state that I'm married?"

"I don't think it does, why?"

"But it does have my married name."

"You know it has. What's the problem?"

"This lady thinks we're not married."

"Then leave it, Sweetheart. I'll explain later."

Eleanor picked up her puzzle book again, and tried to dismiss it from her mind.

"Tell me about our hotel," Eleanor asked some time later, putting down her book.

"I don't know a lot. I went into a travel agency and said three, no, four things. Not too far away. Warm. Beach. And adult."

"Adult? Doesn't that mean, you know? I mean I've heard of adult films."

"No, Eleanor. It means no kids. Mind you, I wouldn't expect many children over the Christmas period anyway. I would think it's people who don't have a family, or who hate Christmas, who go abroad at Christmas."

"Then you're not avoiding Christmas?"

"Eleanor! No! Would you rather have not had a honeymoon? I'm sorry if you are upset at missing it."

"To be honest, David, there was nothing to miss this year, was there? I know Molly wants to see her sister. You would have gone to Jill's."

"We would have gone, Sweetheart. She would have included you."

"But doesn't Keith have a family? When I was little we used to see Mum's parents one year and Dad's the next year."

"That's another reason to go abroad. It is Keith's turn this year, really. And Daniel is seeing Stephanie's parents." David hesitated. "We could invite both families for New Year – but I don't know if Daniel could stay overnight." Eleanor's face lit up. "David, that would be wonderful," she exclaimed. "Why don't we text them and ask."

"Text them? Will our phones work from abroad?"

"They should do. I know it can be very expensive to speak. For instance, if I phoned you, the call would go via England."

"But I could wish them a happy Christmas," David said. "We're both on pay-as-you-go. Did you top up?"

"Oh! No! It would just be a quick call!"

The plane droned on and Eleanor drifted into a semi-sleep

mode. Suddenly she regained full consciousness and reached for her handbag.

"Everything alright?" David asked.

"Yes. I suddenly remembered that letter, you know, from Grandad."

"Oh yes. You transferred it when you transferred your pills, I remember."

"Here it is. I wonder what it is. I hope it's not bad news," she said, holding it.

"Why should it be bad news?"

"Why was I told to keep it until today?"

"Sweetheart, the answer may be inside! Open it!" David said, laughing.

He watched as she carefully opened it, and then pulled out two single sheets, and two cheques. Both made out to Eleanor Anderson.

"David, look!" Eleanor was speechless for a moment.

"Both well over a thousand. Why?"

"Read the notes," David said.

Eleanor read the first one quietly. "Gift deed. We are giving the sum below to our grand-daughter, Eleanor Jenkins, on the occasion of her marriage to Mr David Anderson." She looked up. "Then it asks me to sign and date it as a receipt. Odd?"

"Sweetheart, are your grandparents comfortably off?"

"I don't know. Grandad Jenkins had a business, I believe, why?"

"They are giving it to you under estate duty rules; gifts on occasion of marriage are exempt."

"Are you saying it's a tax dodge?"

"No, it's fully legit. It means that were they to die in the next seven years, I think, then you, Eleanor Anderson, would not be asked to repay tax. Is the second one similar? Yes. I imagine they will leave the notes in with their wills."

"Wow, David. It's a lot of money!"

"It is. I hope we don't lose the cheques."

"Oh, David, I've never seen so much money. Suppose we do?"

"We won't. And anyway, they are made out to you!"

"To me as Eleanor Anderson. My account is still in my old name."

"We're going to be busy when we get back. Change bank details, including putting you on mine. We should have wills; I meant to see about that! Mine is now out of date, as from yesterday! Mind you, if anything happens to me, you will benefit under the rules of intestacy."

"But you have children, David," she said quietly, "and one of them could do with help!" She paused. "In fact, now I have some money, I would like to help them."

"Eleanor, Sweetheart, they're not your problem."

"You're right, they're not my problem; they are our problem. You said that my problems were yours, so yours must be mine. Ah!" she added as he was about to protest. "We'll talk about that as well when we get back. Now where's my magazine?"

They arrived eventually, had the hassle of collecting luggage, were shepherded by their representative to the coach, and finally arrived at their hotel at about one o'clock.

"Shall we find somewhere to eat, or unpack?" David asked.

"I'd like to change first, David," Eleanor said. "We left home in winter clothes!"

"Which means unpacking?"

"Not completely. Just enough. I want to get out of my jeans. Aren't you hot?"

"Yes. And I'm hungry! And I fancy a swim."

"I'll be quick."

She was quick, just throwing her jeans and sweatshirt onto the bed, and then rummaging in her case for a skirt and a top.

"Can I ask you something," David asked, now also changing into shorts and a polo shirt.

"Go on?"

"Have you always worn stockings?"

Eleanor laughed. "Of course not. Stephanie made me buy them. She said they would be more appropriate for a honeymoon. And she suggested the rest," Eleanor said, indicating her undies. "Do you approve?"

David smiled at her. "Of course. Should I thank her?"

"I don't know. But I bet she asks me if you noticed."

"Just say I did and leave it at that."

"Yes, Tiger," Eleanor said, and laughed. "Am I ready first?"

They walked down to an area near the beach and found a small pizza place, with an awning giving shade. David ordered a large pizza and two drinks.

"So, Mr Anderson, we've arrived," Eleanor said, looking around.

"So we have, Mrs Anderson."

"Did you bring Daniel and Jill here?"

"No, we stayed in England or Wales when they were young. We went to Spain when they were older, in a self-catering villa. Jenny and I went to Greece by ourselves when they were sixteen and at camp."

"A hotel?" Eleanor asked.

"Yes, one like ours. No children and half-board. What with the kind of breakfast and evening dinner available, we reckoned that we didn't need a big midday meal."

"Did you skip eating at midday?"

"No, Jenny brought plastic plates and cutlery with us and she would buy crusty rolls and fruit for a midday snack,"

David said.

"That sounds organised."

"Does it? I suppose it was. We also brought a small kettle and packets of drinking chocolate."

"From the way you are talking, it doesn't sound as if you've brought them this time," Eleanor said laughing.

"I didn't. But I did remember sun-cream! Factor fifty!"

"Ah, that reminds me," Eleanor replied, as their drinks arrived.

"Of what?" David said, after drinking half of the glass.

"Stephanie gave me some artificial tanning stuff. It's in my case."

"That doesn't protect you, Eleanor," David said quickly.

"I know; it's vanity – like using cosmetics. It will make me feel better! Can we apply it after lunch?"

"And then wash it off when you go swimming?" David asked.

"No, the box says it's permanent, well, nearly so. It only wears off as your skin wears away. Apparently it comes with thin plastic gloves. You shower, and then apply it all over."

"All over?"

"All right, nearly so. Do you know where your cossy starts?" Eleanor asked.

"I do when I'm wearing it!"

"David!" Eleanor laughed. "You can't wear it when you apply the stuff in case you get it on your cossy. I'm not going to risk getting it on my bikini!"

"So you put it on naked?" David said.

"No, you will!" Eleanor said, now laughing gaily. "You will rub it onto me. Oh. Your face!"

Just then their pizza arrived. It was on a big platter for them to serve themselves.

"Will you be mother?" David said.

"I hope so soon," Eleanor replied quietly.

"Eleanor, Sweetheart," David whispered earnestly. "It's not guaranteed."

"I know," she replied, picking up the spatula and putting a piece of pizza on both of their plates. They ate in silence for a while.

"David," Eleanor said, pausing in her eating. "Do you remember our first bike ride?"

"Of course."

"And me asking you to cream my back?"

"I will never forget!"

"Why?"

"Why? Eleanor, I was so embarrassed!"

"Why?"

"Eleanor! You were a sixteen year old girl! I didn't go around touching girls of sixteen!"

"But you're embarrassed now about touching your wife?"

David took another bite, and looked at Eleanor as he chewed. Then he smiled. "Sweetheart, yesterday?"

"You didn't answer my question on the aeroplane," Eleanor said slowly.

David took another bite and made Eleanor wait. "Okay, yes, I was nervous. And embarrassed. But I'm over it now."

"Sure?"

"Yes."

"But you seemed worried about painting on tanning stuff?"

"Did I? I think the problem will be the effect it has."

"What, in case we over do it and I turn out looking like an African?" she asked.

"No, sweetheart. The effect on me – I think I will find it erotic!"

Eleanor looked him and then smiled. "All the more

reason! Then you can paint me afterwards."
David looked at his watch. "Eleanor, it's early afternoon."
"David, you're not at school. We're on holiday, and there's no timetable!"

They worked carefully and slowly using the plastic gloves and making sure they followed the instructions. The artificial tan worked better than they expected; and there was enough for both of them to develop a light tan. They showered again afterwards; just to be sure it would not wash off, then used a tissue before the hotel towel, to make doubly sure it was permanent.
"Perhaps we should have unpacked first," Eleanor said, now standing wrapped in a towel.
"Eleanor, we're not at school. We're on holiday, and there's no timetable!" David said, grinning and using Eleanor's own words. "But we'll do it now!"
"Dressed like this?" she said.
David kissed her. "I think you look cute in a towel. In fact I'm thinking of burning all your clothes so you can live in a towel."
"I bet my school wouldn't like that, and anyway, it's winter back home!" she answered.
"Ah, good point," David conceded. "But I'm going to unpack now."

Five minutes later, their cases were empty and their clothes packed away in the drawers and wardrobe. There was a small pile of books and a folder on the dressing table. It was Eleanor's examination revision.
"How many brides take their homework on their honeymoon?" she grumbled.
David put his arms round her. "And how many schoolgirls go on a honeymoon especially just before their mock examinations? Would you rather we had

delayed the wedding until the summer?"

Eleanor put her arms round his neck and kissed him very passionately.

"There, that's your answer," she said.

"Sweetheart, seriously, if I wasn't in your life, would you have revised this holiday?"

"Yes."

"My kids revised over Christmas," David added.

"Did you make them?"

"Let's say I encouraged them!"

"Did they grumble?"

David grinned. "Of course."

"Can I grumble?"

"Of course you can. Do you know, I've never really thought of you as a grumpy person."

"I have my days," she said. "It's hard because I don't want to go to school anyway!"

"Eleanor, we have talked about that. Please try."

Eleanor smiled. "I will try, not for me, but for you!"

"Eleanor, whatever you do, work at it as if ..." David said quietly.

"I know. I know," she whispered.

"Let's go for a dip in the hotel pool," David said, to change the subject.

"Good idea. Hey, you haven't seen me in my new bikini. Turn round."

"What? I have seen you without clothes, Sweetheart!"

"I know, but I want to put it on before you see it."

"I have seen it. I chose it. It's stripy."

"David! Turn round! And put your trunks on."

"Yes, Mrs Anderson," David said meekly.

"Okay, you can look now," he heard her say.

"Eleanor!" he gasped, when he did look.

"What? Don't you like it?" Eleanor asked, looking

alarmed.

"It's very, er skimpy," David said at last.

"I know. I was surprised that you chose it."

"But that's not the one I pointed at," David said.

"Not the actual one. I had to look through and find my size. The one at the front was so huge you would have got two of me in it. Didn't you realise?"

"Not really. I went for the colour, well, the stripes."

"You like stripes?"

"Oh, Eleanor. I remember the last time I was with Jenny on the beach. We were talking about bikinis, well swim-ware in general. There was a woman in black with a rather gorgeous tan, and another woman in black with a white body. To wear white, black, or anything bold, you need a tan. Otherwise, something bland, or, we reckoned, something with stripes."

"Oh dear, what do I do now?"

"Just put up with people admiring you," David said.

"David! That's not the reason I bought it."

"So why do you wear a bikini!"

"Convenience! Well, and because that's what most people wear, but convenience is a major factor. It makes getting changed in public really easy, and going to the loo is easier, believe me. Anyway, what shall I do? Do you want me to buy another one?"

"What about the one you had last summer?"

"I forgot it. I'm sorry." She shrugged.

"We'll leave it, but if you feel uncomfortable, we'll buy another. Come on, to the pool, woman."

"Hang on; we need the sun-cream."

They spent the rest of the afternoon by the pool, alternating between sitting in the sun and sitting under a sunshade. The beach was about two hundred metres away, and it seemed that lots of guest preferred the hotel pool to the beach. David assumed it was the absence of children that was the main factor, but the proximity to conveniences was another. When they were not swimming, David and Eleanor studied the other guests. David also noticed that they were being looked at more than he had experienced with Jenny, and which he assumed was due to their age difference – but they were not the only dissimilar aged couple.

"There aren't many young couples, David," Eleanor whispered.

"Cost?" David said.

"Was this expensive?"

"Not very, I mean it's a package holiday. But newly-weds might find it expensive."

"They're not married, David," Eleanor whispered, indicating two couples opposite.

"How do you know? Ah, the men don't look drawn and haggard. Ouch!"

"And you're not the only cradle snatcher," she continued, having punched him.

"Sweetheart, I think you'll find they're not married either."

"Go on! Oh – that woman on the plane! She thought we were just pretending to be married."

"Probably."

"So why are people giving us the eye. Is it because they can see we are married?"

"Maybe, or perhaps because you look so fantastic."

"Stop it, David," she said.

"Eleanor, speaking as a man, you look incredible."

"You're biased, David."

"No, Sweetheart, I'm serious. I was always aware of your feminine charms, and I tried to ignore them."

Eleanor laughed. "Oh, David, sometimes you are so quaint."

"It was you as a person that captured me, oh, and your smile," David continued, earnestly.

"I seem to remember something about me wearing a mini-skirt," she said mischievously, "and we weren't married then."

"We were engaged!" David said.

"I asked Molly about it."

"About the mini-skirt?" David asked.

"Yes, about wearing it in front of you. She said that just because you were a mature man, it didn't mean you were unaffected by female flesh! She suggested it was like serving you a nice dinner and then telling you that you could only look and smell, but not taste. And she said that if you were a normal man, you would be looking forward to the tasting."

"She said that?" David gasped.

"She also said that marriage is more than just companionship."

"No problem there." He paused, and grinned. "But I have enjoyed the tasting!"

"Shush! Don't tell everyone," she said, poking him, and smiling.

After dinner, they went for a walk along the promenade, such as it was. There were bars and clubs in streets set off from the sea-front, and from where noisy Christmas music blared.

"Isn't it odd? All that Christmas music, yet it doesn't feel Christmassy," Eleanor said.

"It's the wrong setting."

"Wrong setting?" Eleanor asked.

"It's warm, and our hotel doesn't seem to do Christmas, well, not in a big way."

"It's the carol service at home tonight," Eleanor said, slightly wistfully.

"Do you wish we were there?" David asked.

Eleanor stopped. "Yes, but only a bit. We're only here because of yesterday, and I don't regret yesterday."

"I remember your mum dragging you away last year after the carol service."

"So do I. She thought Nicky was your girlfriend at first. Then it dawned on her that I had been seeing a single man. I think she would have prevented us singing at the old folks home if possible."

"I really missed you, Eleanor."

"And I missed you."

"I bought new socks, put them through the washing machine, and then gave them to the Romania project."

"What! Why?"

"I wanted to support what you were involved with," David said.

"I didn't know!"

"Of course you didn't," he said laughing. "Come on, time to go back!"

David had suggested that they didn't spend all day just being lazy, so after breakfast on Monday they went for a walk before it got too warm. Then they changed and went to the beach, partly to swim, and partly to see what other women were wearing. Eleanor thought many of the females on the beach were wearing even less, so they decided she didn't need a replacement bikini. But Eleanor said she would not be wearing it to the lido! After another light lunch, it was time for Eleanor's revision. David had intended to stay with Eleanor for her first revision session, but she said she was hot and he was a distraction, and asked him to leave.

"David, it's warm, I'm not wearing much, and there's a bed!" she said. "I would rather make love than work! So go, please!"

Andrew Croughton

"Will you be able to revise at home?" he asked.

"I won't revise in our bedroom wearing just a bra and panties, will I?"

David saw her point and went.

On Christmas Day Eleanor woke up first and crept out of bed to her drawers. However, the movement woke David. "What are you doing, Sweetheart?" he called.

She turned, and came back to their bed holding her hands behind her back. Then, kneeling on the bed, she handed him an envelope. "I know you think cards are for sending, but I've got this for you."

David opened it, took it out and read, "To my new husband, Happy First Christmas from his new wife. All my love, Eleanor. Kiss. Kiss. Kiss. Kiss." He looked up. "Thank you, Sweetheart."

As Eleanor got back into bed, David left from the other side.

"Where are you going?" she called.

David opened the wardrobe and took something down from the top. He turned, returned to the bed and handed her an envelope and a small package.

"David!" she gasped. "You said to leave buying a present until we got home!"

"I know. Sorry, but I thought of this when we walked through the shops at the airport."

"But when?" she said as she began to unwrap the small package.

"When I went to the loo," he grinned.

"So that was why you were a long time. Oh, David! Thank you!" She looked up. "Are you coming back to bed?"

"You haven't opened the card."

She put the present and unopened envelope on her bedside cupboard, and then patted the space beside her. "David?" she said, fluttering her eyelids at him in a very theatrical manner.

Maybe it was because it was an adults' only hotel, but they did not make a big effort for Christmas. However, possibly to accommodate the needs of their staff, there was only a simple breakfast, and no room service. Apart from the cards and the present, the rest of the day was decidedly non-Christmassy. So much so that Eleanor had to remind David that he was going to phone his children! It was only a brief chat to wish both families a happy Christmas, and also to confirm that both he and Eleanor were blissfully happy! It was when he had finished speaking that he noticed that Eleanor looked very sad.

"Sweetheart, Sweetheart, what's the matter?" he said, putting his arms round her.

"Nothing," she said.

David took his arm away and gently manoeuvred her to face him. "Eleanor," he said gently, "when we first became friends, we had a rule. Remember?"

A tear rolled down her cheek. "You have a family, and I don't," she whispered.

"You do have a family. You're part of my family," he said.

"But you didn't let me speak to them!"

David stared at her. "Eleanor! How could I be so stupid? I am so sorry. Look, you phone then now, please."

"No, that would look odd now, wouldn't it?"

"Okay, phone Molly!" David said. "I think she would like it!"

"David," Eleanor said after speaking to Molly. "Will we really have a proper Christmas next year? I mean, with all your family?"

"We could invite them, Sweetheart, but I'm not sure where we'll put them all."

"Oh!" She paused. "And there could be three of us."

"How did you work that out?"

"Well, I'm on my second batch of pills. The doctor told me to extend this month, then do one more month!"
"Eleanor, I think the average time taken to conceive is over six months. Okay, you could be pregnant, just. Anyway, thank you for saying what you said to Molly."
"What did I say?"
"That you were deliriously happy?"
"I am, apart from a few moments just now. I'm okay again now – in fact, I think I'll start planning for next Christmas."
"Eleanor?" David gasped.
"I'm joking," she said.

The week passed too quickly for them. On the final Sunday morning they were called very early and served a continental breakfast. Then it was off in the coach to the airport, a wait at check in, and the boring flight home. A taxi took them to their pre-holiday hotel to collect David's car. Because they had eaten on the plane, they drove directly home. Molly had already invited them to tea, assuming that their plane was on time, but they went home first.
"Do you want me to carry you over the threshold?" David asked, as he put his key in the lock.
Eleanor looked around, and giggled. It was still daylight, and most people's curtains were still open.
"Do you want to?" she said.
"Come here, wife," David said in a supposedly masterful way.
"Yes, Dear," Eleanor answered very meekly.
David pushed the door open, picked Eleanor up, and carried her in. He pushed the door closed and then put her down.
"Welcome to your new home, Eleanor," he said, and then they kissed.

It was a long kiss, and then she giggled again. "David, our cases are still on the door step! If we don't bring them in, you know what people will think!"

"So what?"

"David! That doesn't sound like you," she said.

"It doesn't, does it?" he said, kissing her again, but this time with more passion.

"Let's bring the cases in first," she whispered.

Chapter 17

A Disagreement

There was still time to unpack before going on to Molly's house, but before that, David remembered the two cheques and he suggested that Eleanor phoned her grandparents to thank them. She phoned Grandad Jenkins first.

"Hello Grandad, it's Eleanor," she said. *"We arrived back this afternoon."*

*   *   *   *   *

"No, not very long, we haven't even unpacked yet."

*   *   *   *   *

"Fantastic, Grandad. Grandad, I'm phoning to say thank you for that cheque. I've never seen such a big cheque! Thank you very much. I'll get the receipt part done ASAP."

*   *   *   *   *

"David explained, I understand."

*   *   *   *   *

"I do hope that you can come and see me next time."

*   *   *   *   *

"I will send you our address – and if you do the one-four-seven-one, you'll have my phone number."

After a few more minutes chatting with Grandad Jenkins, she phoned Grandpa Thomas. The conversation was very similar, but they also talked about her mother; Grandpa Thomas bringing it up.

"Eleanor, pet, did you mind us bringing your mum?"

"No, but I was worried in case Dad was around. How did you get her there?"

"When we met her we said we had come to see you, and
did she want to join us. She said she did, so we said she
had to promise not to cause any trouble. Then she asked
why we were dressed up, so we said it was for your
marriage. She said she didn't believe us, so we said she
had two choices – either to come with us and behave, or
one of us would stay with her. She said she would come."
"Do you think she was glad she came?" Eleanor asked.
"I'm not sure, but I'm sure she will be pleased
eventually."
"I hope so, Grandpa, I do hope so."

David and Eleanor continued with their unpacking, with
David showing Eleanor what to do with their dirty
clothes. However, it was her still relatively clean dresses
that were the next topic of conversation.
"David, I think this dress is still clean."
"Okay."
"Where shall I put it? And the clothes still at Molly's?"
"Oh!" said David, as the significance struck him. Their
bed was a new bed. It had never been slept in by Jenny.
But the storage space had been used by Jenny. "Are you
happy to use this wardrobe?" he asked, opening what had
been Jenny's wardrobe. "And these drawers? Or do you
want me to buy a new set?"
Eleanor laid her dress on the bed, and went up to David.
"David, dear David, how do you feel about it?" she said,
putting her arms round him.
"I don't know. It's odd – I mean you kind of grew into
the rest of the house. At first you were a guest, and you
only took charge in the kitchen when you had Stephanie
with you. But you're not a guest any more; this is your
place. It seemed obvious to buy a new bed for us, but I
just didn't think about your clothes. I'm sorry."
"David, I have never seen Jenny's clothes in this

wardrobe. For all I know, you could have replaced everything in the room. But if you don't want me to put my clothes here, I'll put them in one of the other rooms."

"Just give me a moment. You know Jenny and I talked about it. If it had been me, then I would not have wanted her to be alone. I thought about it; even about another man making love to her, and I accepted it. But I did not think about him putting his shoes in my wardrobe! And I thought I was a logical person!"

Eleanor laughed. "You are – you're from Mars. But you've got feelings, and I'm glad. I'll use the Jill's old room until you decide."

"No, you decide. If you're happy to use this room, then so am I. It will be your first decision in your new role, Mrs Anderson. We'll only change the furniture if we both see a need."

The house had been prepared for them in that David's children between them had fitted the new duvet into one of the covers, and made the bed. When they went back down, they found there was milk in the refrigerator and flowers in the lounge – courtesy of their neighbour Mike, or actually, Mike's wife. David's last job was to store their cases up in the loft.

"All done!" said David, as he came down from the loft. "I'll change, and then we had better go round and see Molly."

"And on to church afterwards?"

"As Mr and Mrs Anderson," David added.

"But no holding hands in the hymns!" Eleanor added, laughing. She knew what David thought about that.

"What shall I wear, David? My going away outfit, or a dress?"

"It's up to you," David said.

"My new outfit. It makes me feel married!"

"I thought you felt married already," David said,
laughing.
"You know what I mean! It makes me feel, well, more
mature."

Molly must have been looking through the window
because as they drew up outside, she was out the door and
down the path to meet them. She flung her arms round
Eleanor and kissed her, and then stood back.
"Well, well," she said. "You look good. How was it?"
"Fantastic, Molly."
"Everything?" she asked, more quietly.
Eleanor held her eye, and smiled. "Yes, Molly.
Everything was fantastic."
Molly then moved to David and hugged him. "You're a
very lucky man, David Anderson!"
"I know, Molly," he said. "And thank you for looking
after her for me."

After tea David offered to take Molly to church in his car,
but Molly needed her own car to drive home afterwards.
"This feels weird, David," Eleanor said, as they parked in
the church car-park. They were only just on time because
they had packed some of Eleanor's things into the car to
take back to their house. "The last time we came, we were
engaged," she added.
"And we left married."
"No, I mean on a Sunday. Can I hold your hand now?"
she asked. During their engagement, David had not
allowed any public demonstration of their affection.
"Of course, Sweetheart. But not in the hymns!" he added.
"I know!" she replied.
"What about afterwards. Will you stay on with the young
people?" he asked.
"No, of course not. Anyway, I could do with an early

night."

David squeezed her hand, and grinned at her.

"Calm down," she whispered. "I meant to sleep."

"Yes, it's been a long day. I feel tired too."

As they took their place, Eleanor spotted her school friend sitting with some of the other young people. "Look, there's Lizzie. Oh, and look, that's Tash with her," she whispered to David.

"Tash?"

"Natasha. The girl in the bed shop. The one who teased me at school."

"She was at the wedding, I remember," said David.

"Yes, but she's never been here before. I am surprised."

After the service several people wanted to speak to them to say how they enjoyed the wedding, or ask about their honeymoon. Eleanor could see Lizzie hovering with Natasha, so she excused herself and went to them. Lizzie threw her arms round Eleanor's neck.

"Elly!" she exclaimed. "You look fabulous! Have you missed me?" she added with a grin.

Eleanor grinned back. "Can I pass, Lizzie?"

"Oh, you haven't!" she said with mock disappointment. "Tell me, did you do any revision?"

"Yes, of course," Eleanor said.

Lizzie squealed. "No way!"

"I did! I did a couple of hours in the afternoons." Then she turned to Natasha. "Tash, I didn't expect to see you. Sorry, let me re-phrase. It's nice to see you here! You must meet my husband."

Lizzie giggled. "Your husband! It sounds funny!"

"I know it does, Lizzie. Sorry, Tash." She took Natasha's hand and led her back towards David, who turned to meet them. He said hello to Lizzie first, kissing her cheek.

"David, meet Tash. She's in my class, and was at the wedding," Eleanor said.

"Hello, Tash," David said, extending his hand in greeting. "Nice to meet you again."

"Hello, Mr Anderson," Natasha replied slowly.

"It's David," he said. "And I hope you enjoyed our wedding."

"Yes, I did. And you looked beautiful, Eleanor." She paused, and then spoke in a rush. "Elly, I'm sorry again about what I said in the shop."

Eleanor hugged her. "It's not a problem, Tash. Will you be staying on afterwards with the young people?"

"I don't know. Will you be staying?"

Eleanor turned to Lizzie. "Lizzie?"

"I can't, Elly. Mum's picking me up."

Eleanor turned to David. "David, what do you think?"

"Eleanor, you stay with Tash. Do you have your phone?"

"No, I didn't expect to need it."

"You can use mine, Elly," Natasha said. "What for?"

"To call David to pick me up. We'll take you home as well, if you like."

"Are you sure?"

"Sorted," said David. "Right, Sweetheart," he kissed Eleanor's cheek, "see you later, Bye ladies."

"What's it like being married?" Lizzie asked, as soon as David had left.

"You know," Tash added slyly, but not wishing to be too direct.

Eleanor smiled at Tash, and took her hand. "Tash, I've only been with one man, and that's David. But I'll tell you something that is special. It's waking up and seeing the man you love asleep next to you. Sorry, I didn't mean to sound all goody-goody, but you did ask me. Come on, let's find Tom and Ali. You haven't met them, have you?"

David picked Eleanor and Natasha up as arranged, and drove Natasha home first.

"How was it tonight, Sweetheart?" he asked later, as they made their bedtime drinks.

"It felt odd. Was I a young person or a wife? Being in my going away clothes didn't help."

"Did people comment?"

"No, everyone was nice. Several had gone to the wedding and said they enjoyed it. I hope you didn't mind me going tonight, after what I said."

"No, it was nice to be able to take Natasha home. She was quiet in the car. I assume she was not one of your close friends?"

"She's not!" Eleanor replied, emphatically.

"Why was she there tonight? Did Lizzie bring her?"

"She told Lizzie she wanted to see what kind of church I went to, so Lizzie suggested she came with her. I think she was surprised, and also surprised by the young people."

"Will she come again?"

"I don't know."

"Sweetheart, your feelings about being a young person or a wife. You're both. But you're a young person with a home – I mean; you're in the position of being able to offer hospitality. Remember that time you came after the pizza place? It's your home, Sweetheart, so if you want to invite the youth group, do it. And I do expect Lizzie to feel free she can come at any time!"

"Thank you Darling David. Hey, Lucy spoke to me after you left and asked me about the honeymoon. I said we got to know each other really well, and enjoyed doing so."

"You didn't!" David gasped.

"And I asked her to tell James that you took his advice."

"Eleanor, Eleanor." David said, groaning. "No!" He paused. "Is there anything else I don't need to know?"
"Um. Oh yes. George asked Pastor James if we could do another session at the old people's home now that it's respectable to be seen together. In fact, James said he would like me to sing one Sunday evening, and also the next time he does a Sunday afternoon at the home. What do you think?"
"What did you say?"
"I said it depends on you, after all, we're an item!"
"I think we should wait until after your mock exams, Sweetheart."
"All right. But aren't you glad we have been singing for ourselves last term. Another thing – I've been thinking. I think we should ask Lizzie to help. She plays the flute, and she can sing."
"But not at the same time!" David said, laughing. "Come on, busy day tomorrow."

Despite Eleanor's comment to Natasha, David woke up first. He wondered whether he should let her sleep on, but couldn't resist kissing her neck.
"Is there no peace for a girl?" she said, waking up and giggling and turning to kiss him in return.
"Not when there's work to be done." he replied.
"Tell me about it later after breakfast. Are you in a hurry to get up?"
"Not if you can persuade me to stay!"

"Right," David said, after breakfast. "Shall we make a list?"
"I've got a little list," she sang. "Are you a list person?"
"Sometimes," he said, taking an old envelope from his waste bin.
"David!" she cried. "Do it properly!"

"This will do. Okay. Wills. Car. Council Tax. Banking. House. Surgery. Child benefit."

"Child benefit!" Eleanor exclaimed. "You're not claiming child benefit!"

David grinned. "Sweetheart, it needs to be stopped from going to Molly. I don't know if I'm eligible, but if I am, why not?"

"Hmm!"

"I would get it if you were my daughter," David said, laughing.

"And do I really need a will. I understand about you, but me?"

"Eleanor, if our plane had crashed into the sea, your parents would now own this house."

"Go on, how did you work that out?"

"There was no valid will, so you would have inherited from me," David began. "You would have owned this house."

"Hang on," she interrupted, "but I would be dead too."

"The law presumes the older person died first. You then die. No husband. No children, but you do have parents. They inherit. And anyway, you have money – those two cheques!"

"Those two cheques! I'd forgotten. That's another thing; I want to help Daniel and Stephanie. Is there any reason why I shouldn't lend them some money?"

"No," David said slowly. "I've got savings too. But I didn't want to commit myself in case."

"In case of what?"

"In case you said you couldn't bear to live here."

"David, we've talked about that!"

"At the time we hadn't. And anyway, it's still early days."

"No it isn't. I feel totally at home. Especially in the kitchen," she said, laughing.

"I thought we were going to share the kitchen," David said.

"We are! But don't you think that there should be a boss and an assistant?"

"Eleanor!" David laughed. "And I assume I'm the assistant?"

Eleanor just smiled.

David wondered how many offices would be open and staffed for the days between Christmas and the New Year, but to his surprise, there was someone at the council office. David explained that he had just remarried, and that now there were two people in the house. The lady in the office said she could not deal with it there and then, but she would send David a form to declare his situation. David then added that his wife was in fact a student, and asked if she should be exempt from council tax. The lady said that he was to put all the relevant information on the form, and someone would deal with it.

The next call was to his car insurers.

"I wish to add my wife to my policy," he said, having been through their security process. It seemed that it would be straightforward until he was asked for Eleanor's date of birth. When he gave it, there was a silence. Then the question was repeated. David repeated. the information. Another pause, then – "did you say ..."

"Yes," said David. "She passed the test early last year, while she was still seventeen. Do you want details of her driving licence?"

"Yes please."

"Hang on a moment," David said. He turned to Eleanor. "Eleanor, can you get your driving licence please?" He waited and then read out the details of her licence.

"And the name on the licence, Sir?"

"Eleanor Louise Jenkins," David said.

"And you say she is your wife. Is this a wind up?"

"No, that's her maiden name."

"When were you married, Mr Anderson."

"A week last Saturday. Her name is now Eleanor Anderson. Look, can you deal with it, or can I speak to a supervisor?"

"Can I put you on hold, Mr Anderson?"

David fumed and fretted for over four minutes until …

"Hello, Mr Anderson? No problem, but there will be an excess to pay due to her age. We'll send you a new policy, but it probably won't get done until the new year."

"But she is on as from now?"

"Yes, Mr Anderson."

"Have you put me onto your car insurance David? I haven't driven for months and months."

"I thought you drove your mum's car."

"Only when she was with me. And your car is bigger!"

"And you're a year older now. I drove a van when I was eighteen."

"But you were a boy."

"Eleanor!" David exclaimed. "Don't let Mrs Finch hear you talk like that!"

"Nor Lizzie," Eleanor said, laughing. "Anyway, thank you. But I would like you to give me some refresher lessons."

Eleanor looked at David's list.

"Wills," she read. "All right, I now see the point of me having a will, but I haven't thought about who to. David, what does your will say – the one that is now invalid."

"I've got a copy in the desk, but basically, most is left to Daniel and Jill. There are some legacies, for example, there's a charity that Jenny supported, there's a charity to do with her illness, and there's the church. There are phrases such as when to sell shares, but I left the house to them both. They could then decide when or if to sell."

"So if you died today, they would lose everything?"

"Well, yes."

"Until you make a new will to replace the old one."

"That's right."

"Do they know what was in it?"

"Yes, of course. They are the executors. The people who see that it is followed."

"Oh."

"I'd like you be an executor now."

"Me? I couldn't do that!"

"Sweetheart," David said gently, "one of us will probably die before the other. People rally round and help. I will put Daniel as well, but also a phrase that you can employ a professional."

"Did you do Jenny's will, David?"

"Yes. It was short – she knew she was dying. She gave a few personal things to the kids before she died, otherwise everything came to me, except a couple of legacies. Both the children had some money."

"So will you leave everything to your children?"

David stared at her. "Eleanor, you're my wife! Do you think I would leave you destitute and homeless?"

"But I was before you married me."

David was very tempted to be flippant, but he could see that Eleanor was serious.

"No, Sweetheart, I won't leave everything to my children."

"But then it's not fair on them!" she exclaimed.

"Eleanor, if Jenny had died say in childbirth, then assuming the child would have lived, immediately their inheritance would have been reduced. And what if we have children?"

"Oh," she said.

"Sweetheart, you don't expect me to outlive you, do you?" David asked gently.

"No. I have thought about it, you know that. But on the law of averages, we should have quite a while together." She paused, and then continued before he could interrupt. "But I know there are no guarantees."

"So maybe my solicitor will suggest something," David said.

"Or we could ask Edward and Sue if they have suggestions," Eleanor said.

"But we'll put your cheques in your bank first."

The cheques were made out to Eleanor Anderson, and the account was in her maiden name. David assumed that it would a mere formality to change her name on the account, but no, the bank said they should make an appointment.

"All right," David said, quite equably, "please take a photocopy of my wife's marriage certificate, and change the name on her account when it suits you. She has two large cheques that need to be paid in to her married name, but we'll open another account in my bank if it's too inconvenient today."

It was suddenly convenient! They left fifteen minutes later with Eleanor's account now under her married name and with her new address, and with the promise of a new cheque book. The cheques had been paid into Eleanor's current account on a temporary basis. It was then onto David's bank, which fortunately was more accommodating. They were happy to add David's new wife to his account. David then opened a second account, as already planned, to be the equivalent of Eleanor's account.

"Good, now we'll drop in at my, sorry, I mean our

solicitor's and book an appointment, even though we want to talk to Edward and Susan. Basically, we want to add you to the deeds of the house and talk about wills. We'll ask about existing children. And possible more children."

"Hopefully more children!" Eleanor said, as they reached the door of the bank. Then she stopped him.

"Wait a minute, David. There's nothing in your new account."

"Yes, we'll talk about it."

"When? Why not now?"

"Well," David said. "Do we know how much we want to put in?"

"Do you mean regularly, or to start with?"

"Both."

"Well, to start with is easy. I've got a lot in my account. You've got none – let's split it," Eleanor said.

"Eleanor! That's not what your grandparents intended!"

"I didn't mean what we've just put in. I meant what was there before that."

"But that was your money."

"Okay," she said slowly, "then just write a cheque for that amount from our joint account to your new account."

"But then our money is just given to me! And anyway, it is rather a lot."

"Okay, split what is in my account."

"I'm not happy," David said.

"And I'm cross!" Eleanor took David's hand and pulled him back into the bank and into a quiet corner. "What did I bring to this marriage? What assets did I have?"

"Well, you. You brought yourself," David said, trying to inject some humour into the situation.

"What do you mean, me?"

"Your love, your care, your personality, your companionship!"

"They are all intangible assets."

"Okay, your physical self."

"My body?"

"Well, yes," David said slowly, wondering where the conversation was leading.

"Which you like!"

"Eleanor, shush!" David said, dropping his voice.

"Last night, did I give or did you take?" Eleanor continued, unabashed.

"Eleanor!" David said, feeling desperate?

"Well?"

"You gave," he said in a flat voice.

"Well, if I can't give you part of my monetary assets, I may not give you my body tonight!" she said, folding her arms. "Of course, I won't stop you if you want to take it!"

"Eleanor, can we talk about this outside, please?" David asked.

"Yes," she said. "But I want you to know that I will still feel strongly about it. David, we both talked about endowing each other with our worldly goods. I am accepting a share in your house. You won't accept a share in my pocket money!"

"Are you serious about it?"

"David, I wouldn't argue with you if I wasn't serious. I know I'm young, but I do feel passionately about some things," she said, her eyes beginning to fill with tears.

"But you do agree to ring-fence your grandparent's money?"

"Ye-es. But does that mean you won't allow me to lend it to Daniel and Stephanie."

"No, of course not. That's something else to talk about."

"Can we go home and talk about it now?"

"But what about the solicitor?"

"They won't see us until the new year, will they?

Anyway, I'm still feeling upset, I'm sorry, David. Please can we go home?"

David wanted to press on and sort things out in town, but he agreed to go home. In his mind, he thought they would try again in the afternoon.

"David, you sit at the dining room table, and I'll bring in some coffee," Eleanor said. "I shall want to put things down on paper; it helps me get a proper understanding. Do you mind?"

"No, Sweetheart, but I want to make a quick phone call first, okay?"

He phoned Edward on the off-chance that he could be at home – and he was. He had to make some general chit-chat about the wedding and the honeymoon first. Then he brought up his question.

"Edward, I'd like an opinion or a comment, please. Just a quickie. Because of the rush, Eleanor and I didn't get around to making a will. My will, of course is invalid now. I need to consider Eleanor's future, but she is concerned about Daniel and Stephanie – you see, my invalid will left them the house. Until I make a will, Eleanor would inherit under the laws of intestacy. I intend to put Eleanor's name onto the deeds, and I know she would then inherit as a shared owner. Is there another way?"

"Quickie answer, part one, David. Leave the house in your name, or, quickie answer part two, own it as tenants-in-common. Do you know what that is?"

"Edward, you're brilliant! Of course I do! Why didn't I think of it? Okay, thanks, got to go!"

When Eleanor came in with two coffees! David was sitting at the table with a couple of sheets of A4 paper.

"Right, Sweetheart, look. A proper sheet of paper! And look, three columns. ELEANOR, US, and DAVID. Under

ELEANOR, I've put your bonds, your savings book, your two cheques, and your pocket money. Under DAVID, I've put car fund, ISA, savings plan and pocket money. Under US I've written salary and expenses. I showed you that on the computer, but we'll go over it again. When I was first married, we were hard up and we gave ourselves an allowance. I just buy what I need now. I don't have to worry about money."

"You don't worry about money?" Eleanor asked.

"No, I earn more now and have no mortgage."

"Doesn't everyone have a mortgage, unless they are paying rent, I mean?"

"Do your parents have a mortgage?" David asked.

"I don't know. I've never thought about it. Why don't you?"

"Jenny was insured, and the money paid off the mortgage."

Eleanor gasped as she realised. "Oh, David. I'm sorry! Me and my mouth."

David smiled. "Anyway, to continue. I will change the car fund and savings plan into joint names, and then move them to the US column. An ISA has to be in a single name – individual savings account. There's no tax paid on the interest."

"Does that mean I should have an ISA?" Eleanor asked

"Not necessarily. You're not a tax payer, so there's no advantage. What I want to do here is work out how much we could lend to Daniel and Stephanie, considering what we have in the various columns."

Fifteen minutes later they had the problem sorted. It was based on a combination of the gifts from her grand parents, her bonds, the car fund, and some of David's ISA savings. Eleanor got off her chair, and took David's hand.

She led him into their lounge and pushed him down onto the settee.

"David," she said, as she sat on his lap, "I'm sorry about earlier. It's just that all last week you treated me as an equal."

"I know, Sweetheart. It's me that has the problem. You're half my age!"

"Then why did you marry me?"

"I told you at the reception. I'm selfish. I love you and want to spend the rest of my life with you." He paused, and kissed her. "On top of that, I think you're a very attractive woman and I'm not used to having attractive women on my lap," he added, kissing her again.

Chapter 18

A New Year

Apart from the minor hiccup on the Monday, sweetness and joy returned to their relationship for the rest of that week. Unfortunately, there were two clouds which did cause a shadow, but these were nothing to do with David. One cloud concerned her parents. She intended to text her mother, but since she was not sure when her mother would be back at work, she put it on hold. The other cloud was school, and how they would react to her new status. Part of her did not really care if her school used its ultimate sanction and excluded her. However, she knew that David wanted her, not only to finish the course, but to finish well. As a result, she spent much of the week doing revision because David asked her to. His suggestion, which he recommended to his own pupils, was two sessions of two and a half hours a day, and Eleanor followed it. David's contribution was to be responsible for the meals. Eleanor agreed, but on condition that she decided the menu – she did not want marmalade sandwiches everyday midday, and spaghetti every evening. The result was that after breakfast they sat down with his cookery book, and Eleanor suggested a simple meal for that day.

David kept himself out of Eleanor's way in order not to distract her and also not to be distracted by her – she had taken note of his earlier comments about wearing her skirt once they were married! He also had some school preparation to do so he suggested that she used the dining room to work, while he used his study. Because he knew that arrangement was not really fair, he set about modifying Jill's old room to add a desk and shelves for the use of Eleanor to do her homework. In the evening they made a point of doing something together just to make a change from studying. An evening entertaining Lizzie and Jayne – where they did a lot of singing, both Christian and secular. A visit to the cinema. An evening with Molly. And an evening at the church New Year's Eve party. They both intended to keep a low profile because they felt they didn't fit in. One of them was young and one was older – older than young – as they put it. Although they had been asked to sing a year ago, it did not occur to them that they would be asked again. It was James who suggested it, and he had an ulterior motive.

"A year ago, someone suggested that Eleanor sang to us, and we were delighted that she did. I'm hoping that she will use her talents again in church, but meanwhile, I wonder if she and David would sing again."

"But we haven't sung in public for a year," Eleanor protested.

"And we don't have a guitar," David said.

"Here's one," someone called.

"Can you remember that Jazz number?" David whispered.

She did. James watched them perform together. Even though it was a year ago, he was sure there had not been that sparkle between them that he could now see. He glanced at his wife, and knew that she could see it too.

On New Year's Day itself, they went to spend the day with Keith and Jill. They took late Christmas presents, and since the decorations were still up, it was just like a real Christmas for Eleanor. Jill even served Christmas pudding at midday, and there were Christmas crackers! On the return from their honeymoon, David and Eleanor had found the disc containing the wedding photographs that David's colleague Charlie had posted through the front door, so they had taken it with them. They also had the pictures from their honeymoon. After lunch, David phoned Daniel and Stephanie to wish them a happy New Year. He had the phone on speaker mode so that Eleanor could follow the conversation.

"We were hoping to see you both as well," David said, "but the beginning of term will be pretty busy."

"Come this weekend. Can you stay? Our three seater settee converts to a double bed."

David turned to Eleanor and she nodded.

"Daniel!" Stephanie interrupted. "They will have our bed! We'll sleep on the settee!"

"No, it's fine," David said.

Stephanie took the phone from Daniel. "Dad, when my parents came, they had our room, so, yes, you must too! No argument. When can you come? Friday? In the afternoon? I could get home early from work?"

"That would be lovely, Stephanie, but I think Saturday morning would be better, if you don't mind. Friday is already booked."

While at Jill's, Eleanor also enjoyed playing with her step-grandson, James, who was beginning to speak. David was 'ganpa,' but what was he to call Eleanor?

"What do you want him to call you, Eleanor?" Jill asked, at one stage.

"What's wrong with Eleanor, except I suppose it's too difficult at the moment?" she replied.

"Jill, Darling," Keith said. "Suppose Eleanor was Dad's age?"

"What do mean?"

"I know Eleanor is not his real grandmother, but if Eleanor were Dad's age, then many people would think that first names were inappropriate."

"But she's not Dad's age."

"But she is ganpa's wife," Keith said, mimicking his son. "And what about any future grandchildren who might arrive, say by Daniel and Stephanie? For the record, I think that Elly is undignified. I mean, your dad doesn't shorten her name, does he?"

"What Keith is asking, Dear, is would it upset you?" David asked.

Eleanor thought that Jill looked undecided, so she spoke again. "Let's leave it, it's not important."

"Ah, but it is, Eleanor," Jill said. "You see, Keith wasn't thinking only about James." She paused, and reached for Keith's hand. "We're expecting."

Eleanor reacted first. "Wow! That's wonderful," she exclaimed before hugging Jill. David looked surprised, but then shook Keith's hand before kissing his daughter.

"I think you should be Grandma," Jill said slowly.

"Are you sure?" David asked. "What about you, Eleanor?"

"I'll fit in with whatever you all want," Eleanor said.

At one stage during the day, it came up in conversation that not only did Eleanor have a driving licence, but David had now added her to his insurance policy.

"Have you driven his car yet?" Jill asked.

"No, of course not," Eleanor answered.

"Of course not? Sorry?" Keith said. "So he didn't get you to drive here today."

"I didn't ask," she said.

"And I didn't think of it," David said. "We did talk about me giving her a refresher lesson first."

"Is that wise, Dad? Husbands and wives together – recipe for disaster," Jill said, laughing.

"That's true," David said. "Perhaps I'd better get a proper instructor."

"But then it won't be your car," Eleanor pointed out.

"Dad," Keith said slowly. "It's a nice day, still sunny. I could take her for a short run in your car. It will start getting dark in an hour or so."

"No, it's okay," Eleanor said quickly.

"Keith, that's brilliant," David said. "Sweetheart, I wish you would! Best you crunch the gears without me hearing!"

"Yes, Eleanor. I think you should, seriously. Just fifteen minutes will make a world of difference to your confidence," Jill said.

"Really?" Eleanor asked.

"Yes, really. Thank you, Keith. And take as long as necessary," David said.

They drove home early in the evening, but after Eleanor had helped to bath and put James to bed.

"Well, Sweetheart? A good day?" David asked

They were still in a built up area with street lights, and to his surprise, a tear rolled down Eleanor's cheek. He pulled over and stopped. "What's the matter?" he asked. "Why are you crying?"

"Nothing. Honestly. I'm happy! They were so kind to me." She wiped her cheek. "People do cry when they're happy, you know,"

"I don't."

"You're a man! Didn't Jenny?"

"No, she didn't," David said. "But she didn't have the same roller coaster ride as you, well, not until." He stopped. He was going to say until she found out about her illness.

Eleanor touched his knee. "I understand. I shouldn't have asked. Come on, let's go."

The weekend with Daniel and Stephanie was another high spot. Because she had intended to revise on Saturday morning, she did extra work on the Friday. They made an early start, and Eleanor drove some of the way. The session with Keith had lasted half an hour, and although she still felt nervous, she handled the driving well, and drove for nearly an hour. To Stephanie's delight, they arrived mid-morning. Stephanie had intended to take her Christmas decorations down, but left them up for the occasion.

"And you know about Jill's news?" Stephanie said as they had their coffee.

"Yes, and apparently, I'm to be called Grandma, or gamma as James says," Eleanor said.

"How do you feel about that?" Daniel asked.

"I'm rather pleased, actually."

"Why," he asked with a smile.

"It makes me feel, well, that I'm not just a wife, I'm part of a family."

"Daniel," Stephanie said sharply, "you know we're the only family Eleanor has!"

"Yes, sorry. Maybe they'll relent. Your mum came to your wedding, didn't she?"

"Yes, and she says I can text her, but only when she's at work."

"But you do have your grandparents, Sweetheart," David reminded her. "Which brings us to something." He looked at Eleanor for confirmation. "Do you both remember asking about money?"

"Yes, we should have realised that you two were moving towards marital harmony; sorry," Stephanie said.

"Well," David continued, "we have been talking. First of all, Eleanor has come into some money, and with that and some funds that I have no immediate need for, we can help you. The only condition that I am insisting on is that you pay some interest to Eleanor. You see, the money was given to her for her own use." And with that, David handed Daniel a slip of paper. "Would this help?"

Stephanie leaned across to look at it and then she looked up. "Really?" she whispered.

"Both of you?" Daniel asked.

"Eleanor was given a significant gift by her grandparents on the occasion of her marriage. Under normal circumstances she would invest it, but she is very conscious that while she has a comfortable house, you both live in a tiny flat. She wants to help, and is happy for me to help."

"I don't know what to say," Daniel said.

"I think the word is thank you," Stephanie said. She jumped up and went round to hug Eleanor and then David.

"Yes, thank you, Dad, thank you Eleanor," Daniel said. He got up and bent over Eleanor and kissed her cheek, and then he hugged David.

Stephanie suddenly rushed to a cupboard and rummaged in a bag. She came back with a brochure, which she handed to David. "We've been on a mailing list, but we have been binning them without looking. Now we can look!"

"Would this help?" David asked, pointing at the slip of paper.

"You don't know how much," Stephanie said. "This is simply amazing!"

They spent the next half hour talking about what Daniel and Stephanie might look for, and where. Suddenly Stephanie stopped. "But we haven't heard about your honeymoon," she exclaimed.

"After lunch," Eleanor said. "We have the rest of the day!"

David and Eleanor drove home on the Sunday afternoon. Eleanor was again very happy, but this time she didn't cry.

"David, you know we talked about having your families to stay next Christmas?" she asked.

"They may not want to come!"

"Stephanie and Daniel would come, I asked her, sorry."

"You invited them?"

"No, I asked her if she would like to if you agreed."

David laughed. "I've got to agree now, haven't I. Otherwise I will look like the bad guy."

"No, it's not like that at all. Wouldn't you like it?"

"Yes, Sweetheart, of course I would. But where would we put them?" David asked. "And are you including Jill and Keith – and their two?"

"I thought of that. There's our room. If we bought a bed-settee, or air beds, there's the lounge."

"What about us?" David asked.

"Well, we would have to sleep apart, me in Jill's old room, and you in Daniel's. Unless we shared a single bed!"

"Or unless we move – or re-adapt the house. Turn Jill and Daniel's rooms back into one double bedroom."

"Or extend. But we've just given our money away!"

"Yes, but lent it, Eleanor. Anyway, we do nothing until after your exams."

"Which ones?"

"Your mock exams."

"But suppose there are three of us by next year?" Eleanor asked.

"Some people think that just hoping to get pregnant is a good contraceptive!" David said.

"Okay. I'll give up my next course of pills," Eleanor replied, laughing at him.

"Don't you dare!"

On Monday, David went to work – a staff training day – but as Eleanor's school also had a staff training day, she stayed at home. She had a lot to do. She sorted out her new study. She popped into town. She revised. She cooked dinner. And she welcomed her husband home from work, after showering and changing! David asked her later if this was another of Stephanie's suggestions. "No!" Eleanor replied indignantly. Then she giggled. "It was a film on telly, years ago. I was too young to appreciate it at the time."

"Well I appreciated it, Sweetheart," David replied. "Is it setting a precedent?"

"No, it was a special occasion. My first day as a wife whose husband was at work."

However, her main achievement was to text her mother. It was a short text. She said she was home from her honeymoon, and that it had gone well. She wished her mother a happy new year. She also said that her mother would be welcome at her house at any time, but understood if she didn't want to come. Her mother did reply. An even shorter text, thanking Eleanor for hers, and for the invitation. She added that maybe just the two of them could meet for coffee in town some time soon. When she told David, he suggested a Saturday, or a Wednesday afternoon after school, and said he would take her.

On Tuesday, Eleanor went back to school. She was with Lizzie and Jayne when Natasha came up to her before school and welcomed her.

"Hello, Mrs Anderson?" she said, with a genuine smile.

"Hello, Tash," Eleanor replied. "Good break?"

"Huh. Revision!" she said.

"And me!"

"You? But aren't you a housewife?"

"Married to a teacher!" Eleanor said.

"Oh, poor you!" Natasha said. "Still somebody has to be, I suppose."

"I hope it doesn't get me kicked out. David will be upset. Tash, don't make a thing of it in class, please."

"Is that why you aren't wearing your ring?"

Eleanor nodded. "I wanted to, but David said it was provocative. But I will have to tell them my new name sometime because of examination entries."

"And then the balloon will go up. Poor you."

However, there was no balloon. Even though between them the whole class knew about her, Eleanor and her friends had persuaded everyone to keep quiet. However, Eleanor had forgotten one thing. At the start of every term, Mrs Jones, her form tutor, had to check that their addresses had not changed.

"Right girls," Mrs Jones said, after greeting them and taking the register, "Has anyone moved?" She had asked the same question back in September, but as Eleanor still hoped then that her parents would accept David, she had kept quiet. At the end of the term, her termly report had been given to her to take home, supposedly, as the school thought, to her parents. She had shown it to Molly, but not as a parent. Eleanor was aware that every girl knew she had married, and therefore, had moved. She raised her hand.

"Eleanor?"

"I have a new address, Mrs Jones." She paused, and tore a sheet of paper from her general note book. "I'll write it down for you, Mrs Jones," she added.

"Thank you, Eleanor. No change in phone number though?"

"Oh yes, sorry." Eleanor added her new number.

"Oh," said Mrs Jones, "I thought people could take their number with them. I suppose the emergency contact numbers are the same?"

Eleanor felt herself go hot and cold. "Oh. What do you have?"

"They're held in the office, Eleanor."

"Oh yes, of course," Eleanor said.

"I'll leave you to sort it, then, Eleanor, okay?"

"Yes, Mrs Jones."

Throughout the day, a few more girls asked her about whether she was married or not. After the first time before school, Eleanor was ready for the next questions.

"Why are you asking," she would answer.

"Oh, we just heard. Someone said there was a girl in the sixth-form who was married."

"And you think it's me?"

"Well, is it?"

"Why do you want to know?"

"Oh."

At this stage, Eleanor would quietly admit it was her.

"Yes, it is me, but please don't make a big deal about it, alright?"

Mrs Finch saw her in the corridor and called to speak to her. She led Eleanor to a quiet place.

"Hello, Eleanor, how was your honeymoon?" she asked.

"It was very nice, thank you. Oh, I did take revision with me!"

"You what?"

"David made me do revision every afternoon," Eleanor said. "Mrs Finch, I may not go to university at the end of the year, but I do want to do well at school."

"Oh!" Valerie Finch said, suddenly wondering if there

was something odd about the marriage. "But you are properly married, aren't you?"

"Yes, Mrs Finch. Is that it?"

"No. Eleanor, I think the whole school knows about it, except the staff and headmistress. Look, someone is bound to tell them. I think you should tell the headmistress as soon as possible."

"And then get expelled?" Eleanor asked.

"No, Eleanor. David's headmaster told Bob, that is, my husband, and me about the hypothetical questions David had asked him. We had a girl here some time ago who left to have a baby, and then returned to take her examinations. She even went on to university."

"What happened to the baby?"

"She kept it. Well, her mother looked after it. What I'm trying to say is that I think you won't be excluded. But I do think you should see the head soon. Better it comes from you than from a parent."

"Thank you, Mrs Finch."

Eleanor worried about Mrs Finch's suggestion for the rest of the day, so instead of going home, she went to the school office.

"Excuse me, Mrs Philpott, is it possible to see the headmistress?"

"What, now, Eleanor?"

"Yes please."

"Sorry, Eleanor, but she is seeing the chairman of governors. Is it urgent? Do you want me to interrupt them?"

"No, no! Don't do that!" Eleanor gasped.

"What about before school tomorrow, I mean early? Could you get here early. I know she's free first thing."

"How early is early, Mrs Philpott?"

"She gets here at about eight o'clock, Eleanor. Shall I

book you in?"

Eleanor gulped. "Er, yes, Mrs Philpott. Yes please."

David did not expect the same welcome as he had experienced the day before, but seeing Eleanor still in her school uniform did surprise him. She was standing in the hallway and the look on her face told him something was wrong.

"No they haven't," he gasped, as he hugged and kissed her, "have they?"

"Haven't what?" she answered.

"Kicked you out."

"No." Eleanor smiled briefly. "Well not yet."

"Then what's wrong, Sweetheart?"

"I'm seeing the head tomorrow – before school. At eight o'clock."

"At eight o'clock? Why so early?" David asked.

"That's what Mrs Philpott suggested."

"Mrs Philpott? Sorry, Eleanor, you've lost me."

"She's the secretary. She arranged for me to see the head tomorrow at eight o'clock. David, I wish she hadn't!"

"Sweetheart, start at the beginning and tell me about it."

David led Eleanor into their lounge and sat her down. She told him what had happened in her tutor group first.

"So you went to the office?" he asked.

"Yes, but not about that. Mrs Finch said I should."

"Valerie Finch!" David exploded. "I will have words with her husband."

"No, no! It isn't like that. She stopped me in the corridor and asked about our honeymoon. I said that I had taken work with me – which surprised her. Anyway, she said that although all the girls seemed to know, the staff still didn't. She said that I ought to tell the head before she finds out from a parent. Oh, and she also said that she didn't think I would be expelled."

"Oh."

"So," Eleanor continued, "I plucked up courage and went to see the head after school. She wasn't available, so Mrs Philpott suggested first thing tomorrow. Now I'm regretting it!"

"Do you want me to come with you?" David asked. Eleanor smiled at him. "Part of me says yes, part of me says no."

"Do you want to explain?"

"It's scary going to the headmistress, don't you remember? But I am eighteen – an adult. And a married woman!"

"Which is what it's all about," David said. "Look, Sweetheart, do you have any homework?"

"Not as such. My examinations start on Thursday so I should revise."

"Okay. Look, do an hour or so, then change and we'll go out to eat."

"But we were supposed to be going shopping and planning the meals, David," Eleanor reminded him. That was because staying with Daniel and Stephanie had disrupted their planned routine for the Saturday.

"We'll do both, I mean all three," David said. "Shall I take you to school tomorrow morning?"

"That would help."

"Right, then an early night tonight."

David left Eleanor to work and went up to his study. His plan was to phone his own headmaster at home to ask for advice. He explained the situation, adding that Eleanor was about to take her mock examinations.

"Not a good time for an upset," his headmaster replied. "But David, I can't see that the school has any grounds to expel her."

"But they could exclude her just to make a point!" David said.

"Yes, but not when she's about to do exams. David, if the worst came to the worst, I would take her into our sixth form."

"Come on, that wouldn't work!" David said. "Not now half the school seem to know I married a schoolgirl!"

"Oh. Well, I'm sure another school would take her. David, it was a risk you took."

"I realise that. Do you think I made a mistake?"

"David, that time I asked to see you, you were quite forthright in your views. Now having met her, I can see why. Look, apart from this hiccup, any regrets?"

"Not at all!" David replied.

"Then tell your wife that if her headmistress wants to exclude her to ask for a delay until after the exams. If that happens, we talk about what to do next. Does that help?"

"Yes, thank you."

At seven o'clock, having phoned first to check there was a vacancy, David drove Eleanor to a restaurant in the country. While they were waiting for their meal, Eleanor glanced around.

"David, isn't this a bit up-market?" she asked.

"Yes, I suppose so. Call it next year's birthday treat," David said, with a grin.

"And the year after?"

"Yes, why not!" David said.

"I feel a bit like the condemned woman having her last meal!"

"Rubbish!"

"What do I do if she expels me?"

"She won't. You haven't stolen anything, sworn at anybody or hit anybody. And believe me, even then it's hard to expel you. The worst she could do is exclude you for a short while."

"Okay, suppose she does that?" Eleanor asked.

"Then you point out, very nicely, that you are about to take your mock exams, and could you please come and take them at school in a separate room until you can appeal to the governors."

"Oh."

"And meanwhile, why don't we write out our shopping list and plan the week's food?"

"Now?"

"Yes."

By the end of the meal, Eleanor was feeling mellow. This was the result of preparing the weeks menu and shopping list, then eating a nice meal including a sticky toffee pudding. The glass of wine also helped!

"David, you are brilliant," she said, smiling at him.

"I know, but what made you say it?"

"You've distracted me totally! And I didn't even ask about your day!"

David shrugged.

"Did you get asked about the wedding?" Eleanor asked.

"Yes."

"Well?"

"Not so much about the wedding itself."

"Go on," she said.

"My sixth form asked where we went, and was it a long flight?"

"Why did they ask that?"

"They were being cheeky."

"I don't get it."

"Eleanor, they were making a comment about my alertness."

"Alertness?"

"Sweetheart, they were suggesting that I was tired."

"Of me?"

David laughed. "No, Sweetheart. Because of you. Even Anne-Marie – remember sweet Anne-Marie – made a comment. But at least it wasn't in public."

"What did she say?"

"She asked me about the honeymoon, and then asked how I was coping."

"Coping with what?"

"It wasn't what she said, it was how she said it. All wide eyed and innocent; and with a straight face. How did I cope with having a teenage – she paused – having a teenager in my – another pause – house."

Eleanor smiled. "What did you say?"

"I thanked her for her interest, and pointed out that my own two children had been teenagers not so long ago, so I was coping."

"I wouldn't have dared speak like that."

David shrugged. "Come on, shopping and then home."

"With your teenage bride, Mr Anderson?" Eleanor asked.

"Shush," David said.

Chapter 19

Fantastic News

David deposited Eleanor outside her school at five minutes to eight. At eight o'clock she was in the school office.

"Hello, Eleanor, how are you?"

"Nervous," Eleanor replied.

Mrs Philpott looked surprised. She was used to seeing some younger pupils looking petrified as they waited outside the head's study, but didn't expect it from sixth formers.

"Nervous? You're not in trouble, are you, Eleanor?" she said, as she picked up the internal phone to speak to the headmistress. "Eleanor's here now, shall I send her in?" She turned to Eleanor. "She says go straight in."

Even so, Eleanor knocked before she opened the door.

"Hello, Eleanor," the headmistress said, smiling. "How can I help you?" There were only two reasons why a senior girl would want to see her, she thought. One, to say she was leaving, or two to say she was expecting! She didn't think Eleanor would be in either of those two categories, so she waited with interest.

Eleanor's mouth went dry, so she unfolded the marriage certificate, and without a word, handed it to the headmistress. The headmistress read it, and looked up. "Yours?"

Eleanor nodded, and then croaked, "Yes."

"Have a seat, Eleanor," the headmistress said, indicating the chair. Eleanor sat and for a few moments, neither spoke. Rather than thinking what she should say next, the headmistress was thinking of a phone call she had taken the evening before.

"Eleanor, do you know a Mr Stuart Banks?"

"No," Eleanor replied immediately.

"Are you sure? He works in a school."

"A school? Oh. Sorry, yes, if he is the same Mr Banks who was at my wedding."

"How well do you know him?"

"I, er, I met him and his wife at their school play. He's a headmaster."

"Do you know him well?"

"No, my husband knows him," Eleanor said.

"Is your husband also in the sixth form?"

"No," Eleanor whispered.

"What does," she paused and looked at the certificate; she had only looked at Eleanor's details on it and not read the name of he husband. Suddenly she realised that David was over forty. She rephrased her question. "Is David a teacher?"

Eleanor nodded.

"And are you pregnant?"

Eleanor found her voice. "No! Of course not. Why did you think that?" she exclaimed with passion.

Mrs Clark considered her next question. She had nearly asked if Eleanor was sure, but something about Eleanor's response stopped her. "Tell me about David," she said quietly. "How long have you known him?"

Eleanor thought about it. "I've known who he was for over two years, but I didn't really meet him until after his wife died. At first he helped me and a boy in our church sing together. Then when the boy went to university, he helped just me. We sang in church."

"Is that when your relationship began?"

"Oh no. We were just friends."

"But something happened at some stage?"

"I think we both liked each other for a long time, but we

both assumed that our ages were a barrier – that and my education."

"What about your parents? What do they think?"

At this stage Eleanor's eyes watered, and she crumpled. She had not expected to have her parents brought into it. The head's nickname among some of the girls was The Rottweiler. However, she got up and came round to Eleanor's side, reaching for a tissue from a box on her desk.

"Eleanor, my dear, what is it?"

"They kicked me out," she whispered.

"And is that why you married," she paused to take another look at the certificate on her desk, "David?"

"No, that's why they made me leave. Because I wanted to keep seeing David."

"When was this, Eleanor?"

Eleanor blew her nose. "Last Summer. They put my things out on the doorstep."

The head found this hard to believe, and was trying to remember if she had met them. She was sure she would have remembered if they had struck her as being awkward or unreasonable.

"That sounds a little extreme," she suggested gently, having returned to her seat.

"They expected me say sorry and give up David. But I went to live with a lady from the church. We would have married next summer if not before, but since I was eighteen and David has a house, there was no point in waiting."

"And you were quite sure it was the right thing to do?"

"Yes, Mrs Clark."

"Why didn't you come and ask me first?"

Eleanor blinked. "I didn't know I had to. And anyway, suppose you had said no?"

"Then why tell me today?"

"Mrs Finch said I should. And anyway, you would have found out when the examination entries were filled in."

"You're not wearing your ring, Eleanor," the headmistress said, suddenly changing the subject.

"We thought it would be best not to, but," Eleanor hesitated, "everyone knows. Well, all the girls in my class. Several came to the wedding!"

"But you didn't want The Rottweiler there, right?" Eleanor stared at Mrs Clark who slowly smiled. "I do know my nickname, Eleanor."

"I was shopping with David in a bed shop, and Natasha Spriggs came in. She thought that we were living together, so I suggested she came to the wedding," Eleanor said, to explain how the girls knew.

Mrs Clark sat looking at Eleanor. She now understood the point of the conversation she had had with Stuart. He had reminded her about a pregnant girl who had remained in her school, and then said he had had an enquiry about having a married student, and asked her opinion. Her opinion had been to do what was best for his school and that person. She smiled to herself. Stuart was a wily old fox! He obviously knew about Eleanor and that she was an asset to her school.

"Eleanor, I just want to say two things. Thank you for telling me, and two, I think you should wear your ring, don't you?"

"You mean? Oh, Mrs Clark, thank you, thank you so much!"

"Oh, and let the office know your next of kin details, Eleanor."

"Yes, Mrs Clark. Of course. Thank you again."

Eleanor left, and the headmistress picked up her phone.

"Jane, I need to speak to Stuart Banks. He's the

headmaster of ..."

Eleanor walked out in a daze and waited for Lizzie to
arrive. Lizzie knew about the meeting
"How did it go?" she asked after hugging her.
"She's told me to wear my ring!" Eleanor said.
"What?"
"She was really kind to me. All I've got to do is update
the records, you know, next of kin stuff." She giggled.
"My husband!"
"No more clouds in the sky!" Lizzie said. "Look, there's
Jayne. Come on, tell her your good news."
Eleanor smiled and followed Lizzie. There was still one
cloud. Her parents.

Eleanor texted her mother at lunchtime.

        Hi Mum. Good news. I can wear my
        ring to school. Exams start
        tomorrow. Looking forward to seeing
        you. Eleanor xxx

Then she texted David.

        Darling I can stay here. Love you.
        Eleanor xxxxxxx

She had a single word reply.

        fantabulous

It was David's half day and he picked her up from school.
On the way home she told him all about her interview.
"At one stage she asked me if I knew a Mr Stuart Banks. I
said I didn't"
"Yes you do, dear," David said, interrupting.
"Yes, it came back to me, and I said he came to the
wedding. I told her that you knew him. Then she asked if
you were in the sixth form and I said you weren't.
Suddenly she asked if you were a teacher."

"Right," David said.

"Then she asked if I was pregnant! I soon put her right. Then she asked all about you – how long had we known each other. I think she thought I married you to leave home, and when I explained about that, she was very kind. In the end she said that I ought to wear my ring. Amazing!"

"You tamed The Rottweiler," David said, laughing.

"But whatever made her ask me about your headmaster?" Eleanor mused.

"You should have asked her," David said. "We ought to celebrate, but I've made a start on dinner. And you've got an exam tomorrow, haven't you?"

"Maybe another early night?" Eleanor said, patting his knee and smiling at him. "But don't tell your sixth form!"

*　　*　　*　　*

It was about two weeks later and a Saturday morning. The exams were over. David and Eleanor had changed the bedding, had loaded the washing machine, had sorted out the next week's menu, and were just about to go to the supermarket. Suddenly her mobile phone rang, displaying her mother's number.

"Hello, Mum," Eleanor said.

"Eleanor," a breathless voice said. "I'm in town. Where are you?"

"I'm at home, Mum, just about to go to the supermarket."

"Oh."

"Is anything wrong?"

"No. It's just that I thought that we could meet. Never mind."

"Mum, do you know the Happy Hours coffee shop?"

"Yes, why?"

"Meet me there."

"When?"

"Hang on." She covered the mouthpiece. "David, can you get me to the Happy Hours?"

"What, now? Aren't we going shopping?" David asked.

Eleanor paused. "Alright, sorry."

"No, I'll take you, but you'll have to walk the last bit. It's in the pedestrianised area, isn't it? Twenty minutes?"

Eleanor uncovered the mouthpiece. "David said it will take at least twenty minutes, is that okay?"

"Alright. But don't bring him."

Eleanor took a deep breath. She felt like telling her mother where to go!

"See you soon," she said, and pressed the end button. She turned to David. "She was rude about you. I don't feel like going."

"But you ought to go, Sweetheart, even if I have to carry you! Come on."

Eleanor walked towards the coffee shop with mixed feelings and emotions. It was the first time she had heard her mother's voice since the wedding. Her mother had replied to text messages, albeit briefly. Eleanor's text sent following her interview with her headmistress had elicited four words – best wishes for exams. Now she had summoned Eleanor, and Eleanor had gone running – at least, that's how it seemed to Eleanor, and she felt resentful. But she knew she should not feel resentful, and so she felt guilty. On top of that was her mother's comment about not bringing David. That made her angry – with more guilt!

"Just be calm, Eleanor," she said to herself. "She is your mother."

As Eleanor entered Happy Hours, she saw her mother sitting alone. She slowed up, breathed deeply, and walked across to the table.

"Hello, Mum," she said quietly, leaning forward and kissing her mother's cheek.

"Hello, Eleanor."

Eleanor sat down, and there was an awkward silence. Eleanor spoke first.

"How are you?"

"I'm fine. And you?"

"I'm okay," Eleanor said. What she wanted to say was a lot more – that she was very, very happy and enjoying married life, but she didn't think her mother really wanted to know. "How's Dad?" is what she did say.

"He's fine."

"Does he know you're here?"

Her mother looked alarmed. "No, Of course not."

"When did you tell Dad about the wedding? Does he know I'm married?"

"Yes."

"Well?"

"I didn't tell him. Your grandad did."

"What? When?"

"That same day. They came round after the wedding. Your dad was surprised to see them, especially as they were all dressed up, so he asked why they were so smart. 'We've been to a wedding,' your Grandad said. 'Any one we know?' your dad asked. 'Yes.' 'Who?' 'Our granddaughter.'"

"What did Dad say?"

"Nothing at first, he didn't seem to realise they meant you. Then the penny dropped. He asked me if I knew and when I said I did, he went spare. He was rude about you and said horrible things to me. Then Grandad joined in and told him he was a stupid man, plus a lot more. There was an almighty row!"

"Oh, Mum, I'm sorry. What happened then?"

"Grandad and grandma went and your dad had another go

at me. I'm not to mention your name at home. That's why I said to text me in work time; then I can delete it before he finds out."

"What about Grandma and Grandad?"

"Grandad phoned on Christmas Day and apologised. He said he was apologising for the way he spoke, but not for what he said. They've come to a truce about you – Dad says he won't talk about you, so they needn't bother to ask him. Not that he knows anything about you. One of the things that made Grandad so angry was that they had never been told about you, and they said that was wrong."

"What about your mum and dad?"

"They don't talk to Dad, they talk to me. They ask about you – oh, they were pleased to get your card."

"I must phone them sometime; the last two weeks have been busy. I told you I had exams, didn't I?"

"You did."

There were another few moments of awkward silence, and Eleanor stood up.

"Mum, I ought to go. David will be waiting for me, but thank you for phoning. Next time, can you give me more notice? You would be welcome at our house, but I suppose that's asking too much."

"Your Dad wouldn't like that!"

"I didn't mean Dad, I said you."

"Here would be better. Next time maybe you will stay longer?"

"In which case I would bring David!"

Sheila Jenkins opened her mouth to speak, but then thought better of it.

"Bye, Mum," Eleanor said. She kissed her mother quickly and left.

"How did it go, Sweetheart," David said, as she slipped back into the car. He had been waiting in a limited-time waiting area.

"I'm not sure. Let's go, and I'll tell you all about it."

Eleanor slipped back into her normal school routine.
Since she was known by her first name, her new surname
made no significant difference. She wore a wedding ring,
but not her engagement ring – jewellery was not allowed.
She had performed well in her mock examinations, and
now did her homework in her new study. Since David
regarded them as a working couple, they followed his
pre-wedding plan, but only in outline. On Saturday
mornings they cleaned and did housework together. They
planned the weeks meal's, but these were now quite
different to David's. They cooked together in the
weekday evenings, but at weekends, Eleanor took over. It
was about a month after her meeting with her mother that
she received another call, but this time on a Friday
evening. Actually, David had taken the call.
"Hello, David speaking," he said.
"Hello, David," a quiet voice said. "May I speak to
Eleanor?"
"Yes, of course. Who is it?"
"It's her mother."
"Oh. Hang on a moment." He covered the mouthpiece,
and called Eleanor. Then he uncovered it again. "She's in
the loo. No, I can hear it being flushed. So, how are you,
Sheila?"
"I'm very well, thank you."
"Sheila, thank you for coming to the wedding. I'm sorry
it caused an upset, but Eleanor was pleased."
"Oh."
"Ah, she's on her way. Here she is." He handed the phone
to Eleanor, and started to leave.
"Don't go, David," Eleanor said, taking the phone. She
then pressed the speaker button, meaning that David
could listen in.

"Hello, Mum."

"Hello, Eleanor."

"Where are you phoning from?"

"From home."

"Oh."

"I'll explain later. Eleanor, are you free tomorrow?"

"Well, tomorrow is housework day."

"All day?"

"No, not all day!"

"Could we meet for coffee again, I mean properly this time?"

"All three of us?"

"I meant just the two of us."

"Mum, don't you remember what I said last time?"

"Yes. But. Oh, dear ..."

David waved his hand to get Eleanor's attention. "You go," he mouthed.

"Okay, Mum. But just this once!" Eleanor said.

"Yes, Dear," Sheila said, in a small voice.

They discussed the time and place before Eleanor put the phone down. She turned to David, who hugged her.

"You're winning, Sweetheart."

This time Eleanor was there first. She stood up as her mother arrived at her table, and kissed her cheek.

"Latte?" Eleanor asked.

"No, I'll get them."

"Mum, sit down. Anyway, you look harassed. Latte?"

"Yes please."

Eleanor came back with two lattes and two tea cakes.

"So, you phoned from home!"

"Yes, Grandma Thomas had a word with your dad. She said it was one thing for him to cut Eleanor out of his life, but he shouldn't expect me to. It was unreasonable behaviour!"

"What did dad say?"

"He couldn't say much to my mum, could he? Anyway, he agreed. He knows I'm here now. He's still not happy though. Oh, and your grandparents were really pleased that you went to see them again."

"Yes, we enjoyed it too. They seem to like David. At least, they're not rude."

"Maybe next time," Sheila Jenkins said, referring to another meeting for coffee.

"Don't you want to see where I live, properly, I mean?"

"I would like to, but, well – maybe one day."

"Hey. Mum. Look, David's got to go away for a few days in March – some kind of sixth form conference. Would you be allowed to come and stay for a night? We did talk about having one of my girlfriends to stay. Tell Dad I need someone to stay with me!"

"Eleanor!" Her mum laughed for the first time. "He'll say you shouldn't have left in the first place!"

"Mum. I didn't leave." Eleanor said quietly, but firmly. "You know that."

"I know. The plan totally misfired."

"Plan? What plan?"

"You were supposed to have knocked on the door. Then when you let yourself in the next day to get the rest of your stuff, he was so angry."

"Mum, you gave me the ultimatum."

"I know, and I've regretted it ever since."

"Oh, Mum."

"I feel I forced you into his arms."

"No, Mum. I would have married him anyway, but not so early, true. In fact, that suited me."

"And are you really happy? Your grandparents seem to think you are."

"Yes, Mum," Eleanor said, smiling at her.

"But he's much older than you."

"That's not a problem."

"What about, you know, intimately?"

Eleanor smiled again. "I can assure you there are no problems in that department."

"I can understand why he fancies you."

"Mum, I fancy David, not just because of what he is, but because of who he is!"

Sheila smiled. "Sorry, Eleanor, it's none of my business."

"You're right," Eleanor said, but speaking very graciously.

They then talked about Eleanor's school. She had brought her last report with her. Then Eleanor told her about her home routine, that is cooking and cleaning, and how it fitted in with her homework. They talked about Eleanor's friends.

"You remember Lizzie? Well, she was baptised last fortnight. And did you meet Jayne? Well, she comes to church now, oh, and another girl, Natasha. She was in the shop when David was buying our bed, and she was horrible to me. She jumped to the wrong conclusions."

"Like your dad?" Sheila said quietly.

Eleanor shrugged. It was a very bad memory.

"Darling," Sheila said, carefully. "This is not meant to be inappropriate, but would you like to have children?"

"We would both like a family, Mum."

"But doesn't he have children already?"

"Mum, try and say David – doesn't David have children already! Well, yes, he does. And I think they are happy about the idea. Why did you ask?"

"It's something that Grandma Thomas said. If children are a blessing, grandchildren are a double blessing. I think she would like great-grandchildren!"

"Mum. Stop counting chickens! Anyway, David said that hoping for children can be a good contraceptive! So, stop hoping for grandchildren!"

"Are you on the pill, Eleanor?"

"Mum!"

Sheila shrugged. "I thought one could talk to a daughter about things like that."

"Okay, I got put on the pill in time for my wedding, all right."

"Good. At least you can finish your schooling?"

This time when they separated, it was with a genuine hug.

"Mum, one last question. Do you think Dad will ever come round?"

"I don't know, dear. I'm still finding it hard."

Eleanor hugged her again. "But we're making progress," she said.

She told David all about it later that day.

"She asked me if I was on the pill," Eleanor said indignantly.

"So what? Jill talked to Jenny about things like that."

"But I'm not. I don't want her to know we're trying."

"Eleanor, we're not trying, we're just not un-trying!"

"Yes, sorry."

What David didn't know was that Eleanor was secretly taking her temperature every morning. She knew that the readings rise following ovulation. Some people use it to avoid pregnancy. Eleanor intended to use it to tell her when passion was required! She didn't expect to have difficulty in contriving an appropriate situation. Even so, she didn't expect success and she also didn't expect to return to her normal rhythm immediately. The fact that she appeared to be late did excite her, but as David didn't seem to notice, she did not mention it. And anyway, he was about to go away for a few days. Lizzie was going to stay on the Thursday night and her mother on the Friday night, with David returning sometime in the late afternoon.

The Thursday night arrangement grew. David only agreed to Jayne and Natasha joining Lizzie on condition they actually did some school work. He pointed out that Thursday was not the weekend.

"Sweetheart, when I was doing my A levels, we actually got together, me and three mates, just to study!"

"Yes, you've told me. But you were all doing the same subjects. We're not."

"You can't party the whole evening, surely?"

"It's not a party. It's a sleep over!"

"What will you do?"

"David! Eat. Talk. Watch a film. Talk."

"And sleep?"

"No, one doesn't sleep at a sleepover."

"Eleanor!"

Eleanor put her arms round him and kissed him. "I know why you're being grumpy!"

"Eleanor!"

"I'll make up for it when you come back. As long as you're not too tired," she added cheekily.

"Eleanor, you're behaving like a teenager."

"That's because I am a teenager. I thought you like being married to a teenager."

He kissed her. "I do."

"Even when she's being silly?"

He kissed again. "Uhuh."

The evening with the girls was a great success. They cooked their own meal. They did some work. They had times of silliness. They watched a rom-com and giggled. And they talked. They talked until late. The later it got, the more serious was their conversation. At one point, Natasha, who knew about Eleanor's problem with her parents, brought up the fact that Eleanor had gone against their wishes.

"Don't think it doesn't bother me, Natasha," Eleanor said. "That doesn't make it right. I thought Christians should obey their parents."

"So if my parent told me to kill you, would that be right?" Lizzie said.

"That's a silly example," Jayne said. "Come on, murder is obviously wrong!"

"Not to kill is a higher principle than obeying them," Eleanor said.

"Okay. Now apply it to your situation," Jayne said.

"Jayne, it was a problem for me, so I went to see the pastor. He talked about different principles being higher or lower. He said that to leave one's parents to start a new family was higher than staying at home just because they say so."

"But you were only seventeen, Elly. For goodness sake!" Natasha exclaimed.

"I know. I was nearly eighteen, an adult in law here in England, and probably older than Mary when she had Jesus."

"The Bible also tells parents not to provoke their kids. I think your parents were provocative, Elly," Lizzie said.

"I still wish it had never happened," Eleanor said.

"Do you?" Jayne asked. "Even when you're snuggling up to your husband?"

Eleanor sighed. "No, I like being married to David. But if we were still engaged, would I have missed what I didn't know about? We would have married when I left school."

The topic became serious again and they were talking about the Bible, and whether Jesus was relevant. Natasha thought he wasn't, Jayne wasn't sure, and Lizzie was a new Christian. Eleanor had one eye on the clock, but didn't want to end the conversation. Eventually Jayne gasped as she noticed the clock.

"Look, it's nearly two o'clock."

Then Natasha said something that surprised Eleanor. "When I was a little girl, my gran always said prayers with me. Elly, can you say a prayer for us?"
"Are you serious, Natasha, or is this a wind up?" Lizzie asked.
"I'm not messing, Lizzie."
"Jayne?" Eleanor asked.
Jayne nodded.
Eleanor waited a moment, then she prayed a short prayer thanking God for their fun time together, and also for their talking time. She also asked God to give them a good sleep, even though they were late. She said amen, and there was a silence. Suddenly Lizzie spoke. She thanked God for Eleanor and for her home which they had enjoyed being in. Then she thanked God for adopting herself into his family. Another amen.
"What did you mean by that," Natasha asked. Eleanor looked at the clock. To sleep, or talk about Jesus.
"Natasha, if you really want to know, come to tea on Sunday. Why don't you all come? I think we should honour God. I asked him to help me sleep just now. That means I should go to bed."
"I agree," Lizzie said. "Goodnight!"

None of them felt good the next morning. Natasha felt sick, and Eleanor was sick.
"Did we cook those prawns properly?" Jayne asked.
"I think so. I think I ate too many," Natasha said. "What about you, Elly?"
"I didn't think I did. Was it the chicken?"
"Whose idea was it to have a Thursday sleepover anyway? I vote we skip school today. Pretend it's a Saturday!" Jayne said.
"Very funny. I've got a test today! I've got to go in." Natasha said.

"I'm sorry," Eleanor said, "I shouldn't have invited you."
"Don't beat yourself up, Elly, I'm glad you did. Is that invitation for tea still on?" Natasha said.
"So long as you don't tell David I was sick!"

Friday evening was much quieter. Eleanor and her mother cooked together and then had a quiet evening watching television. They had an early night, which pleased Eleanor. She had confessed to her mother that they had been late to bed the night before and her mother had laughed.
"When the cat's away the mice will play," she said, and laughed.
"We weren't playing late, we were talking."
"Surprise, surprise," Sheila said.
"Serious talking," Eleanor said.
Sheila smiled. "Yes dear."
"Mum, I want to go to bed, do you mind?"

"Mum, I've been sick," Eleanor said at the breakfast table.
"Yes, I heard you. First time?"
"Yes, I mean no. I was sick yesterday morning, but we thought it was the prawns."
"Are you late?"
"Ye-es."
"Could you be pregnant?"
"Pregnant? You mean I could be pregnant? Wow. First time. We thought it could take several months. That's fantastic news."
"You mean you want to be?"
"Yes, Mum, I want to be pregnant. Okay?"

Chapter 20

An Apology

Sheila sat and stared at her daughter. "But you're on the pill."

"I was. This is my first free month."

"Well, don't get too excited. It could be a bug. Have you eaten anything this morning?"

"No, I still feel a bit sick."

"Right, you should try and eat something, especially if you are pregnant. I found that dry toast was good. Some people keep cracker biscuits by the bed." Sheila Jenkins paused. "And what about school? You'll have to leave school."

"No, why should I?"

"Because that's what happens, Eleanor!"

"Mum, it doesn't happen every time. It won't happen with me. Everyone accepts that I'm Mrs Anderson. What difference will having a baby make? Suppose I was at work? Anyway, as you say, it may be just a bug."

"Do you have a test kit?"

"No. I didn't want to get too expectant," Eleanor said, then adding, "if you'll excuse the pun."

"Right, we'd better get you tested – first thing after breakfast – and I want you to try eating something!"

By half past nine her mother had been out and returned with a test kit. By nine forty six, they had the two blue lines. Eleanor sat down on a chair in the kitchen.

"Mum, it's suddenly hit me. I'm going to be a mother."

"Eleanor, don't get too excited. Wait for three months before you tell the world."

"Why?"

"Eleanor, dear Eleanor, they say that one in ten babies doesn't make it that far. Didn't you know?"

"No. They didn't say that in school."

"What were you taught, as a matter of interest?"

"Why?"

"I'd like to know."

"Okay. Where sperms are made, where eggs are made. How the sperms get into a woman, and where they meet an egg. Fertilisation, implantation, foetus, and a video of an actual birth – nine months later."

"Nothing about the egg not being fertilised, or if it is, not being implanted, or if it is, nothing about wrong development and a subsequent miscarriage?"

"No, Mum. Is that what happened to you? I know I wasn't your first baby."

"It might have been better if you had," Sheila said quietly.

"Mum, you've never talked about it, and I know you had to get married, didn't you."

"Not now, dear."

"Mum, we must talk about it, later, if not now."

"Eleanor, it's not a suitable topic at the moment. Maybe, if everything goes well, and I'm holding a healthy baby, all right?"

"Yes. But there is one thing; if I am pregnant, then my baby will have two parents. I am so happy that we're friends again, but Mum, if we're to remain friends, then you must accept my baby's father. You must accept David. No rush, but don't take too long thinking about it." She paused. "Oh, I can't wait to tell David."

"Will he be pleased?"

Eleanor stared at her mother. "Will he be pleased?" she echoed. "Of course he will. Whatever made you ask that?"

"Eleanor, he's got two children – two grown-up children. And he's not a young man!"

"Mum!"

"And don't you ever wonder why he married you? Men have needs."

As this inference sunk in, a wave of anger swept through Eleanor. Anger at her mother. It was followed by a very brief moment of doubt, and then guilt; guilt that she had even entertained doubt.

"Mum, what time is Dad expecting you?" she asked in a controlled voice, and standing up.

"I said after breakfast."

"Then perhaps you'd better go home. We don't want to upset him, do we?"

"But ..."

"Dad will be expecting you! And I have work to do. I'll get your coat and bag."

Eleanor was already sobbing as her mother drove away. She remembered David talking about her life being a roller coaster. She had been so emotionally high. First the meetings in the coffee house with her mother. Then she had just come to stay overnight – admittedly while David was away. Then a possible, no, probable pregnancy. Wow. But then the suggestion that not only would David not want a child, but that he had married her just for his physical attraction to her youth. As if he was that kind of man! How could her own mother say such a thing?

"I have work to do," she muttered to herself. "Come on, girl, get on with it."

There was her mother's bed to strip, the washing machine to start, the week's menu to do – all things she and David normally did together. The hardest part was shopping. She sat in the car and then hesitated. This was the second time that she would use the car unsupervised. They had practised this on the last two Saturdays in preparation for this. She knew that she could do it; but in the light of that mornings event, was she in an emotionally unsuitable mood to drive? Suddenly her mobile rang. It was David. "Hello, husband," she said, hoping that her voice did not give her away.

"Morning, Sweetheart, are you at the supermarket?" Eleanor took a deep breath. "No, I'm running late. I'm just about to go. What are you doing?"

"It's coffee break here, then one more session, lunch, and away. Can't wait to see you. I'll let you know when we're nearly home, alright?"

"Yes, of course."

"Bye Sweetheart. Love you."

"And I love you."

She put the phone down and began to cry again, and then she began to tremble as her mother's aspersions about David resurfaced. Without thinking, she started the engine, but then she realised that there was no way she was fit to drive. But what to do? Suddenly a flash of inspiration. Lizzie might help. She dialled Lizzie. They usually communicated by text messages, or land-line. A direct mobile call was very unusual and it rang an alarm bell in Lizzie.

"Are you all right, Eleanor?" Lizzie said, as her opening words.

"I'm not good, Lizzie. Are you free?"

"Yes, why?"

"Lizzie, I need you. Can you come?"

"Yes, where are you? Have you had a crash?"

"I'm at home. Please come soon."

"On my way!"

Eleanor was still sitting in the car when Lizzie arrived.
She had asked her mother to take her, but without being
able to explain why?

"I don't know, Mum. All she said was please come as
soon as possible. Maybe she's fallen down the stairs!"

"No, she'd have rung for an ambulance! Perhaps she's
had a row with her husband." Her mother knew about the
marriage, and was still rather cynical about the
relationship.

"David's away."

"So she's missing him and can't cope!"

"She coped on Thursday night." Lizzie said and then
suddenly gasped. Today was Saturday, the morning after
Friday night – Eleanor's mother's night. "Oh no!" Lizzie
said quietly.

"You know what it is?" Lizzie's mother asked.

"No, but her mother was there last night."

"I thought they were friends again." Although Lizzie's
mother thought that the marriage was bizarre, she had no
sympathy for Eleanor's parents and blamed them for the
situation.

"I thought so too," Lizzie replied.

Lizzie jumped out of her mother's car and was about to
run past David's car when she realised that the engine
was running. Then she saw Eleanor sitting inside. She ran
round to the passenger side and let herself in.

"What's the matter?"

"I've got to go to the supermarket and I can't move."

"Elly, turn the engine off," Lizzie said quietly. She
waited. "Elly, you have driven on your own. You took
David to the school. You can drive."

"It's not that. I know I can drive. I can't drive right now!"

"Okay," Lizzie said slowly. "Do you want to tell me
what's happened? I thought maybe you'd fallen down the

stairs, or," she paused and took a deep breath, "you'd crashed the car!"

Eleanor forced herself to smile. "Oh, Lizzie, now that would have been really terrible."

"Obviously."

"No, no, because I'm pregnant."

Lizzie looked at her, not sure how to react. Was it a good thing or a bad thing? She knew that ultimately Eleanor wanted a family.

"Is that why you can't drive?"

"Lizzie, I'm pregnant," Eleanor repeated.

"I heard you. And I found you sitting here trembling, and I can see you've been crying. I don't know how to take it."

Eleanor turned to Lizzie. "Lizzie it's wonderful."

"So?" Lizzie said, now bewildered. "What's this about?"

"Mum's upset me," Eleanor said, and started to sob again.

"Eleanor, let's go back inside."

Eleanor let Lizzie take her back indoors and put the kettle on. Lizzie waited until Eleanor had a cup of tea (Lizzie had coffee, but she knew about Eleanor's special tea bags). "Why not tell me about it?" she asked quietly.

Eleanor told her everything, including her mother's comment about why David was attracted to her in the first place.

"Well, don't worry about that. After all, he chose you and not me," she said, tongue in cheek.

"I know," Eleanor replied, quite seriously.

"I was joking. Look, Nicola is pretty attractive, isn't she? He didn't ask her out – and he could have done." Lizzie knew about the shopping trip. "Elly, stop being silly. He loves you because you're Eleanor!"

"I know that, Lizzie. No, it was just that I thought I was building bridges again with Mum. And then she said

that!"
"Elly, you knew that lots of people would think that,
didn't you?"
"Did you?"
Lizzie hesitated.
"You did!"
"No, I don't think I did. David didn't seem to be that kind
of man. What I was thinking was that I knew how you
both felt before you did."
"You didn't know about me!" Eleanor said.
"I knew how David felt. It was obvious to me!"
Eleanor laughed. "Lizzie! Why didn't you say?"
"Maybe I was hoping ..."
"Lizzie!"
Lizzie laughed. "See, it's made you laugh. Right, Mrs
Anderson, finish that tea and go and wash your face.
You're going to take me shopping!"
"You?"
"Okay, us!"

No one would have guessed what had happened as they
pushed the trolley round the supermarket. They had just
passed the Pharmacy and were now giggling. Lizzie had
pointed at the contraceptives.
"You won't need those," she said.
"I was on the pill, Lizzie! You know that."
"Are you saying it failed?"
"No, I stopped last month."
"So David does know?"
"Only that I've stopped."
"Haven't you phoned him with the news?"
"Lizzie, I didn't know until this morning. I put it down to
the prawns yesterday, didn't I?"
"If I had known you were trying, I would have said
something yesterday morning."

"Lizzie, we weren't trying. Well, oh dear."

"What do you mean?"

"David said it could take six months to conceive. But I was taking my temperature, secretly," she giggled.

"And you still didn't twig?" Lizzie asked.

"Natasha didn't feel well, remember?"

"The question is, how are you going to tell David? Candlelit dinner. Bottle of wine. Pretty frock. Nice music. David …" Lizzie giggled.

"Stop it, Lizzie!" Eleanor giggled too.

"We must look like two silly schoolgirls," Lizzie said.

"We are schoolgirls," Eleanor replied, and giggled more.

"Come on," Lizzie said, wiping her eyes. "Let's go and look at the clothes. We need something for you to welcome your husband back from his travels."

"I've got those already!" Eleanor said, thinking of her honeymoon clothes, which started her giggling again

"What?"

"Lizzie, I'm a married woman. My sister-in-law took me shopping before my honeymoon."

"You haven't a sister-in-law!"

"Okay, my step-son's wife!"

At this, they both fell into each other's arms again, almost helpless with laughter.

"Can you stay for lunch, or is your mum expecting you," Eleanor asked, as they waited to pay. Lizzie took out her phone.

"Mum, I'm having lunch with Elly, okay?" She looked at Eleanor. "Lunch or dinner?" she asked.

"Something light. I'm cooking dinner tonight, remember?"

"Just a light lunch, Mum, is that okay?" Lizzie told her mother.

She put her phone away, and turned back to Eleanor.

"You didn't buy the wine or the candles!"

Eleanor giggled again. "Lizzie, stop it."

"Or …"

"Lizzie!" Eleanor said, wiping her eyes, and then taking out her credit card.

"That's another thing I can't get over."

"What?"

"You shopping with a credit card!"

"What are the other things?" Eleanor asked.

Lizzie leaned across and touched her left hand, or rather, her rings, then she patted Eleanor's tummy.

"Lizzie, don't tell people. Mum said to keep quiet for three months – things can go wrong."

"I know. It happened to my sister."

"What? You didn't say!"

"Exactly. I didn't know at the time."

"Oh, Lizzie, I do hope …"

"So do I, Elly. Come on; give the lady your card."

"Have you worked out how you're going to tell David?" Lizzie asked, as Eleanor drove her home. She had stayed with Eleanor until it was time for Eleanor to go and fetch David. She still thought that Eleanor should tell him over a candlelit dinner. "I could buy you some candles. There's still time," she added

"Lizzie! That's so corny. You've been reading too many romantic novels!"

"I don't need to. I just follow my best friend's activities."

"I will probably just blurt it out when I see him. Hello darling, I'm pregnant."

"I bet you don't," Lizzie said laughing.

"Why?"

"Because there will be other people around. At least you've dressed up!"

Lizzie had suggested that Eleanor wore the dress David

had bought her for Daniel's wedding.

"But it's a summer dress!"

"I think he will find you, er, scrumptious in that dress. It's not too cold, and the sun is shining! I'm surprised he didn't propose to you at that wedding!"

"Oh, Lizzie, you are such a romantic," Eleanor laughed.

She sat in her car as she waited – it was colder than she had expected – and her mother's comments kept going through her mind, especially the one about a man and his needs. There was plenty of information in magazines which meant Eleanor was not totally ignorant on that subject before her marriage. But it had been theoretical knowledge. As a married woman, she now had practical knowledge of the subject; however, as far as she was concerned, the comment could be applied to both sexes. She smiled to herself as she thought having David back home. There was a meal in the oven, a meal that would not be ready until some time after they got home. And there was her news! Maybe she would keep her news until afterwards.

The minibus pulled in, and the sixth formers began tumbling out, each carrying a bag or wheelie-case. Parents began exiting cars to meet their offspring, and as they met, goodbyes were exchanged between the sixth formers. Eleanor got out and walked across. It seemed that the two staff members were in no hurry to get out; presumably they had to check that nothing was left inside. Then David stepped out, also carrying his case. Eleanor walked across, wondering what the protocol was for a wife meeting her husband. David looked up and saw her, smiled and hurried towards her. With his free hand, he hugged her and kissed her on the lips, albeit briefly. There was a whistle, and someone called out that he could do better than that.

"Hello, Sweetheart," David said, ignoring the comment and taking her hand. "You look fantastic, but aren't you cold."

"Maybe I need warming up," she said quietly, smiling at him.

"Well, you look hot!" he grinned.

"Shush! Don't tell the world!" she said as they approached his car. Some pupils were still standing by the cars, chatting.

"Goodbye, Sir. Goodbye Mrs Anderson," someone said.

David looked towards the voice. "Goodbye Anne-Marie."

Eleanor handed David the car keys.

"No, you drive, Sweetheart."

"Me?" she said, her voice making a squeak.

"Well who drove it here?" he asked. "Besides, I've just been driving a mini-bus."

"All the way?"

"No, I shared it with Sue. She's going to take the keys home," he said, putting his case onto the back seat, and then going to the passenger side.

"I feel like waiting until the others have gone," Eleanor said, with a worried look.

"Well, we could just sit here and snog, I suppose," David said casually.

"David!"

"But I'd rather you took me home first," he added.

"Okay. But I thought we could make a start on painting the kitchen," she said, as she started the engine.

David laughed. "In that dress?"

"Oh. Well I would take it off."

He laughed again. "Now that sounds interesting."

"Calm down," Eleanor said, "I've got to concentrate."

"Sorry, Sweetheart. It's just that seeing you reminds me of how much I missed you."

"And I need you too," Eleanor said.

"I do like that dress," David said, as Eleanor slowed to pull into their driveway. "I like the way it zips up the back."

"I think you mean the way it un-zips," she replied.

"And I like the feel of the cotton, or whatever it's made of," he said, touching it above her knee. "Do you realise it's not totally opaque?" he added.

"So? Lots of clothes aren't. That's why I'm wearing a slip.

"And what else?" he said, slowly pushing the hem of the dress up her thigh.

She smiled at him. "That's for me to know and you to find out. Race you upstairs!" She turned off the ignition, and jumped out.

"Hang on; I've got a bag to get!"

"Later!"

"So tell me about your week," David said, as she snuggled back into his arms.

"It wasn't a week! It was only three nights."

"It seems like a week. Did you work on Thursday night?"

"Yes. And we talked."

"I can believe that," David said, laughing.

"Actually, some of it was very serious."

"Really?"

"Yes, at the end of the evening, Natasha asked me to say a prayer."

"She was joking, right?"

"I think she was serious. I've invited her for Sunday tea."

"Good."

"We were quite late, and the next morning she felt unwell, and I was sick."

"But you're better now."

"Actually, I was sick this morning as well," she said casually.

She felt his body tense, so she added, "But I feel fine again now."

She felt him relax slightly, so she waited a moment. "Do you suppose I could be pregnant? Mum said it could be a bug."

"Maybe," David said.

"But we did get the two blue lines."

"What are you saying, Eleanor," he said. She could feel the interest in his voice, so she waited.

"Eleanor?"

Eleanor pulled away and knelt up to face him. "I think we could be pregnant. Mum went out and bought a preggy test kit."

David stared at her for a moment, then he scrambled up to face her, throwing his arms round her and hugging her very tight. Then he kissed her.

"Are you pleased," she said, when she could breathe again.

"Pleased? Of course I am. Eleanor, that is amazing. You! Pregnant. Wow."

"We. It took two of us!"

"That's true, Sweetheart. But now you will do all the work. It won't be easy," David said, snuggling back down, and pulling Eleanor down with him.

"My mum said not to get too excited. It's very early days. Apparently, a lot of babies don't survive the first three months."

"Not a lot, Sweetheart. But some, I agree."

"We don't usually know, because many people don't announce it until things settle down."

"Fair enough. But didn't the girls say anything," David asked.

"No, because they thought it was the prawns – we made a

prawn and chicken curry!"
"Prawn and chicken!"
"It was my idea, I fancied both. And we had frozen prawns in the freezer."
David laughed. "Oh dear, does that mean we're going to have to live off prawns for the next nine months?" David paused. "So nobody knows except me and your mum?"
"Lizzie knows."
David laughed. "I might have guessed that you would have to tell Lizzie."
"It wasn't like that," Eleanor said very seriously.
"What do you mean, Sweetheart?"

Eleanor pulled away, and lay on her back. Speaking dispassionately she told David most of what had happened. Then she rolled towards him.
"I phoned Lizzie after you phoned. She's been with me all day, up to collecting you. So she knows."
"Come here, Sweetheart."
"It was Mum's remark about you marrying me because you had needs!"
"Sweetheart, my desire for you didn't suddenly start the day I married you."
"I know that. And I understand about needs now, my needs. But it sounded so sordid the way she said it. I thought we were getting along so well."
David took a deep breath. "And all because of me. I am so sorry."
"Don't be silly, David." She kissed him and pulled closer, and kissed him again.
"What about dinner?" David said. "Will it burn?"
"That's a good point!" She wriggled out of bed and ran down the stairs. "Don't go away," she called. "I will return!"
The girls arrived at about three o'clock on Sunday

afternoon, Jayne and Lizzie both carrying a bag.

"You didn't have to bring your tea with you!" Eleanor exclaimed.

Jayne shrugged. "I know, but we do if we go to the young people's tea."

"And you didn't buy those cream doughnuts, so I got my mum to get some," Lizzie said.

David was in his study, and came down.

"Afternoon, ladies," he said.

"Afternoon, David," Lizzie and Jayne replied together.

"I gather you spent the night eating and talking!"

"We did not!" Lizzie replied indignantly, "Did we Tash."

Natasha was too embarrassed to reply at first. She didn't know David the way Jayne and Lizzie knew him. "Er, not all night, Mr Anderson," she replied quietly.

"You can call me David," David said to her.

"Tash has a question," Jayne said. "Elly would not explain it to us."

"It was late, Jayne," Eleanor protested.

"True and you were unwell at the time."

"Was I?" Eleanor replied without thinking.

"You were sick the next morning, remember?"

"Oh yes."

"I told my mum," Jayne continued, "and she asked if you were pregnant!"

"That's a point." Natasha said. "Could you be?"

Eleanor didn't answer.

"Elly," Jayne whispered. "Are you?"

Eleanor moved across to David, and took his hand. "I might be," she said to Jayne.

"Might be? One either is or one isn't. Don't you know?" Natasha asked.

"Tash," David said quietly, "What she means is that she probably is, but we don't want people to know yet in case it turns out to be a false alarm."

"I tested positive, Tash. But not every positive test results in a full term pregnancy. Most miscarriages happen in the first trimester," Eleanor said. "So we're trying not to be too excited."

"When did you test?" Jayne asked.

"Yesterday morning. I was sick again."

"And your mum was here, wasn't she. What did she say?"

"Basically not to get too excited," Eleanor said.

"Do you want this baby?" Natasha asked. "I mean, you're at school!"

"Yes I do, I mean, we both do. I only just gave up the pill and it's happened already. We didn't really expect it so soon."

"I don't know what to say," Natasha said.

"You're supposed to say congratulations," Lizzie said, giving Eleanor a hug and a kiss. She looked at David, wondering what to do for a moment. Then she smiled, and kissed his cheek. "Congratulations, David."

"And is this what you really want?" Jayne asked.

"Yes, Jayne."

"Well then, congratulations!" Jayne gave Eleanor a big hug and a kiss. Then she looked at David.

"You don't have to kiss me," he said with a little laugh.

"What's sauce for the goose," she said, and kissed David's cheek. "Congratulations."

Natasha then followed suit, except she shook David's hand and called him Mr Anderson.

"So, what was your question, Tash," David asked, when all had calmed down.

"It was about being adopted into God's family," Lizzie said.

"Is it being baptised," Jayne asked.

"No, it isn't the same," Lizzie said. "That was my way of showing it."

"Why don't you tell us how and when it happened," David asked Lizzie quietly.

"All right," Lizzie said. "It began like this ..."

"I knew something had happened, Lizzie," Jayne said, when she finished. "I could see a difference."

"I'm not sure I get it," Natasha said.

"Not everyone does, Tash," David said. "For some people it seems obvious, for others, it's a struggle. That's why Jesus told stories, like the one about the woman who lost something very precious, she looked and she looked until she found it."

"Are you saying that I haven't looked?"

"No, Jayne. I don't know if you've been searching, or how hard. All I can say is that there are people around who can help you if you want it," Eleanor said.

"Like the pastor?"

"I was thinking more like Lizzie or Eleanor," David said. "Or some of the other young people at church." He shrugged. "But in the end, it's not what you know, it's who you know?"

The silence was broken by the doorbell.

"I'll go," David said, wondering who it could be. He closed the lounge door behind him and opened the front door. He nearly gasped audibly.

"Sheila!"

"Hello, Mr Anderson. Is Eleanor in?"

"Yes, of course. Please come in. Is Len with you?"

"No, I'm on my own."

"Please go through. She's in the lounge," David said, closing the front door. He couldn't see Eleanor's face, but he heard her gasp.

"Mum; what are you doing here?"

David followed her in. "Have a seat, Sheila," he said pleasantly.

"No, I won't be staying long."

"You said that once before," Eleanor reminded her.

"I know. I'm not here for the same reason."

"Then why are you here?" Lizzie asked.

"Lizzie!" Eleanor said.

"Sorry, Elly, but your mum should know what a state you were in when you called me yesterday. I found you sitting in the car, shaking, and with the engine running. There was no way you could drive to the supermarket on your own."

David turned to Eleanor "Is that true, Sweetheart. You didn't mention that!"

Eleanor nodded. "That's why I phoned for Lizzie. I knew I wasn't safe."

"But you did go in the end."

"I made her turn the engine off and we went back inside. Then, after a cup of tea, we tried again," Lizzie said.

David turned to Sheila Jenkins, and just looked. Then he spoke. "Are you proud of this? Eleanor had already told me what you said to her. My goodness, if I treated my daughter half as badly as you have treated my wife, I would be much too ashamed to show my face!"

Nobody spoke. Eleanor had never heard David speak so forthrightly. Lizzie's mouth was open. Jayne and Natasha were embarrassed. Then Sheila spoke – in a small quiet voice.

"Lizzie asked me why I was here. I am ashamed. I'm very ashamed. I just came to say sorry. I'll go now, if you don't mind. " She turned to the door.

"Mum!" Eleanor's voice was sharp. Sheila stopped and turned. "Mum, who are you apologising to?" Eleanor asked.

"Why, you, of course."

Eleanor walked to David and took his hand, still looking at her mother, and waiting.

"And?" Eleanor prompted quietly.

"Your husband," she whispered.

"He has a name," Eleanor said.

Sheila turned to David. "Mr Anderson, I want to say sorry for what I said about you."

"And?" Eleanor said.

There was a pause. "And for my behaviour last summer."

Again, there was a silence. "Sheila, I will accept your apology if you will stay and accept a cup of tea," David said.

"Please say yes, Mum," Eleanor whispered, her voice trembling.

"Yes, thank you," her mother replied, "er, David."

At this, Eleanor burst into tears, and rushed across to her mother. Sheila also began to cry.

David looked at the three other girls. "Why don't you three help me in the kitchen?"

Chapter 21

Nine Months

"I would like to tell Molly," Eleanor said to David that evening. She had given up going to the young peoples' after-church meeting.

"I can understand, Sweetheart. But wait a few days, just in case."

"And what about school?"

"No. I know they have been very accommodating, but wait until you have to. No, we've got a bigger decision to make."

"Not baby names yet!" she replied laughing.

"I was going to make a start on un-converting Daniel and Jill's rooms at Easter. Do we still need to do that?"

"What's the alternative," Eleanor asked.

"Do nothing, move or extend."

"Move?" Eleanor said. "But you know I'm happy here. And we did hope to have a baby!"

"I know. But the speed with which it has happened has made me think again."

"David, did you think of moving after Jenny had passed away?"

"No. There were more happy memories than sad ones."

"Has that changed?"

"No, not really. There's even more now."

"There are for me too."

"Extensions can be very disruptive. And is it feasible?"

"David, there's a house round the corner; a house like this in fact, which has been extended."

"That's true."

"Can we afford it?"

"Probably."

"Probably? Don't you know? Is it because we have helped Daniel and Stephanie?"

David looked serious. "Sweetheart, either way would mean taking out another mortgage. Not a huge one like Daniel, but it would mean borrowing money. How much depends on the cost. It could mean a return to watching our pennies."

"Daniel and Stephanie have to watch theirs, so why should I be exempt. No; it's how you feel about it. After all, four of you lived here, so three of us should cope if we do nothing."

David laughed. "Three of us. A year ago, there were not even two of us!"

"And all because my Dad's car wouldn't start," Eleanor said. "Isn't it sad. In some ways, he's responsible for our happiness."

"He'll come round eventually, Sweetheart. Your mum did."

Over the next two weeks, David spoke to colleagues about extensions. They both spent some time in an estate agency looking at four bedroom houses. They also knocked on the door of the house that Eleanor had noticed and asked about the extension. Eleanor's morning sickness developed over the month, and lasted for about two months. She managed by getting up earlier and eating toast. She found that toast and strawberry jam was better than toast alone. David modelled his morning routine on Eleanor's just to show some empathy. She went to school with make-up – not mascara or eyeliner, but extra foundation, to cover what she thought were obvious signs of strain. The Easter holiday was reached with nobody at school, apart from the three girls, realising what her situation was. There were only two people at church who knew, Molly and Lucy. Three weeks after finding out she was pregnant, David and Eleanor were invited to Sunday tea with Molly. She showed them into her lounge and waited for them to sit.

"How are you, Eleanor?" she asked, her eyes twinkling.

"I'm fine, thank you, Molly,"

"Enjoying married life?"

"Oh, yes."

"And coping with school, in the circumstances?"

"In the circumstances?" Eleanor repeated. "Do you mean being married?"

"No, being pregnant."

Eleanor gasped. "How did you know?"

Molly smiled. "Who else knows?" she asked.

"Only four people; Mum and three of my friends," Eleanor said.

"Two more. Lucy and James."

"But we haven't told them!" David protested.

"Lucy confided in me this morning. She told me what she thought and asked what I thought."

"I expected Mrs Mayfield to say something," Eleanor said. "But, Molly, how did you know?"

Molly smiled knowingly. "For the last three Sundays, you've been using more make-up, especially in the mornings. And today I thought your dress was slightly tighter."

Eleanor immediately touched her tummy. "I'm not showing yet, am I?"

"Not tummy, my dear. I have been watching you and waiting! Anyway, how far are you?"

"Five or six weeks, I think."

"Have you been to the clinic yet?"

"No, I'm trying not to get too excited. And it's a case of when it's convenient, so probably in the holiday. Fitted in between my revision."

"And how's that going?"

Eleanor shrugged.

"I think she's working hard," David said, "probably harder than my own kids did. I just wish my kids at school could see her."

"I'm not surprised," Molly said. "I'm so proud of you, my dear."

"And so am I," David added.

David's colleagues had given him the names of various builders that they had used. He also had the name of an architectural technician. Over the Easter holiday they made the decision to extend, and invited the technician to visit. She made a quick rough diagram of their house, and then used a series of transparent overlay sheets to sketch various ideas, based on their own initial ideas, or her ideas. She was there for over three hours, and when she left, they had a good idea of what they wanted. The only remaining issue was the cost, and the technician said she could provide three possibilities for three different prices. David had financial interviews to investigate his borrowing requirements. He had already asked to go back onto a full timetable, which would improve his income. Otherwise, the bulk of the holiday was given over to Eleanor's revision.

There was one other event that happened which caught them both out. The visit by David and Eleanor to David's parents had not been a success. Ever since then, whenever David spoke to them by phone, they had never asked him about Eleanor. The one conversation between David and his mother that did mention Eleanor included a simple question from David. It was when he and Eleanor were finalising their list.

"Mum, I am getting married."

"To that girl you brought to see us?"

"Yes. Would you like an invitation?"

"David! We think you're making a big mistake," his mother replied.

"Oh. I take it that the answer is no."

"In the circumstances, don't you think that is for the best, David?"

"I'm sorry you feel like that, Mum."

"Sorry, David, but that's how we feel."

However, they did ask Jill about her. The first time they had asked Jill if she had met her father's new girlfriend, she had affirmed that she had, and quickly added that she approved of Eleanor. His mother had sufficient tact to refrain from offering her own opinion, but they used Jill to keep themselves informed. Thus, although they were not invited, they knew about the wedding.

It was Easter Saturday. Although it was school holiday time, David and Eleanor were following their normal routine. They had just returned from the supermarket, and were unpacking when the doorbell rang.

"Can you go, Sweetheart?" David called.

"Okay," she called.

"Hello, Eleanor," the elderly lady said. "Is David in?"

"Yes, who shall I say it is?"

"Don't you recognise us?"

Eleanor stared. There was something, but she could not place them. "I'm sorry," she said. "Should I?"

"You came to visit us last summer."

The penny dropped. "Oh!" she gasped, "David's parents. Please come in." She called back into the house. "David, it's your mum and dad."

David came from the kitchen, and stopped. "Mum, Dad, what are you doing here?" he said in amazement.

"David!" Eleanor said quietly. She turned to his parents, "Please excuse my husband. Would you like coffee or tea?"

"Are you sure? We don't want to put you out."

Eleanor smiled. "Tea or coffee?"

"Tea, please," his mother said.

"Good. And you, David?"

"Tea please, Sweetheart."

David took his parents into the lounge, while Eleanor put the kettle on. Then she rushed upstairs to change and brush her hair. Back to the kitchen, lay a tray, make the tea, and carry it through.

"Here we are," she said, putting the tray down on the coffee table. She looked up at Mrs Anderson, senior. "Milk? Sugar?"

"Just milk, please."

"Mr Anderson?"

"The same, please."

Eleanor poured out four cups and handed two of them to her guests, one to David and left one for herself. Then she sat on the vacant seat, and waited. She wanted to know why they had visitors, but nobody spoke.

"Well, this is a surprise," Eleanor said. She wanted to add that they were the last people she expected!

"Yes, sorry," his mother replied. "We were just passing."

"On the way back from a few days at Oxford," his father added.

"Oh," said Eleanor. She knew where Oxford was; she knew where his parents lived; and she knew that they were not just passing. In fact, it was a significant detour. "Well, thank you for calling in. We've only just got back from shopping."

"Yes, so David was telling us," his mother said.

"Next time you must telephone us first," Eleanor said.

"Just in case."
"So, tell us about Oxford," David said.

Twenty minutes later, Moira Anderson stood up. "Well, look at the time, Ron. We ought to make a move."
Eleanor looked at David and raised her eyebrows. She mouthed the word "lunch." David nodded.
"Mrs Anderson, why don't you stay for lunch? We were planning to cook this evening, so it would only be a light lunch, but you are welcome to stay." Eleanor said.
"Yes, why don't you stay," David added quickly.
"Well," his mother said.
"Unless you have other plans," David said.
"No, we'll accept your kind offer, thank you."

When it came to lunchtime, David contrived to get his mother helping Eleanor in the kitchen. He took his father outside.
"Right, Dad, I'll come straight to the point. This place is not on your route home from Oxford."
His father smiled. "You're not stupid, are you?"
"Well?" David said. "You wanted to check up on us, didn't you?"
His father shrugged, but did not speak.
"Dad?"
"Okay, yes," his father admitted.
"I know Mum quizzes Jill about us. So, why?"
"Jill has stopped telling your mum everything. She says we should ask you!"
David laughed. "I know. Jill does tell us about it. So, you had to come yourself. Satisfied?"
His father looked embarrassed. "I still think the age gap is too great, but I must admit that I am impressed." He paused. "You still have a picture of your first wife on display. Isn't that tactless?"
"Dad, that's why Eleanor is so special."

Eleanor was mildly amused by the situation. But she was also annoyed. Here was this woman who did not seem to acknowledge her existence now having to help her in her kitchen.

"Right, Mrs Anderson, could you lay the cutlery please. It's still in the same drawer," she said.

"Doesn't that bother you?" Moira Anderson asked.

"No. Why should it?"

"But," Moira began.

Eleanor stopped and faced her. "Because that is where Jenny kept it, Mrs Anderson? When I met your son, he was still grieving for Jenny. I don't want him to forget his first happiness, but I do hope that I make him happy again."

"Is that why there are still pictures of Jenny?"

"Partly, but also because his son and daughter want to look at them as well. Mrs Anderson, I can assure you, it is not a problem. I know that David loves me, and I'm sorry that you think he has made a mistake."

"Then it's up to you to prove me wrong."

"No, Mrs Anderson, my job is to be a good wife. I hope you recognise that, but if you can't see it, I'm sorry."

Even after that exchange, by the time they left, Eleanor thought that maybe David's mother and father were more accepting of her. They had talked about the proposed extension, and then about the finances that were involved. They knew about the financial help to Daniel and Stephanie, but had not realised that some of it was from Eleanor. It was also news to them that because of it David now needed to borrow money. They knew that Eleanor was studying at school, but not what subjects were involved. The only thing they did not know was that Eleanor was pregnant.

"Why didn't you tell them I was pregnant?" Eleanor
asked David, as they watched his parents leave.
"I would have if they had asked, Sweetheart. Are they
really interested?"
"Do you know why they came? I mean, it wasn't really
on their way home, was it?"
"Ever since they knew about the wedding, they've been
pumping Jill, and Daniel to an extent. Jill told me, and I
asked her to limit the information she gave. They would
ask her about you, but not ask me. I think their curiosity
overcame their reticence. Anyway, how do you feel it
went?"
"Better than expected. My heart sank when I realised who
they were, but then I wanted to show them what I could
do. I bossed your mum around in the kitchen!" Eleanor
said, and went on to tell David about their verbal
sparring.
David laughed. "Maybe it will be an annual check up,
like the car MoT check."
Eleanor laughed. "So will they send us a certificate –
marriage MoT – pass?"
However, they did get a letter a few days later. The
envelope was addressed to Mr and Mrs Anderson, and
inside it was addressed to David and Eleanor. Not only
did it thank them for their hospitality, there was an offer
to help them financially.
"Wow!" said David. "You know what this means, don't
you?"
"Go on," Eleanor said cautiously.
"You've been accepted!" He picked her up and kissed
her.
"Just my dad now," Eleanor replied quietly.
"It will happen, Sweetheart. It will happen."

Eleanor's final term began with her feeling reasonably
confident academically and excited maternity wise.

Academically because she had worked very hard during the holiday. Maternity wise because she was booked in for her first anti-natal appointment. The only problem was that the first appointment was in school time. On the first day back, she went to see Mrs Clark, her headmistress.

"Hello, Eleanor, have a seat. How was your holiday?"

"It was spent revising, Mrs Clark," she replied.

"Good. That's one advantage of marrying a teacher, I suppose," she said with a smile. "Have you changed your mind about university?"

Eleanor hesitated. "No, Mrs Clark. And I have another reason not to go."

"You're pregnant?"

Eleanor nodded. "Yes, sorry."

"Sorry for being pregnant? Or sorry you can't go?"

"Oh, I'm not sorry I'm pregnant. I'm pleased. But I didn't expect it so soon, so I'm sorry if it upsets you."

"How far are you, Eleanor?"

"Nearly three months. I was coming to ask if I can go to the ante-natal clinic on Wednesday, Wednesday afternoon. My husband will be free and can take me – it will be my first scan!"

"It's games, isn't it?"

"That's not the reason, Mrs Clark, honestly. I don't think athletics will suit me, but I think I will be able to enjoy playing tennis. Wednesday afternoon is the first free slot."

"So what would you do if I said no?"

"I would have to cancel it. It's provisional."

"All right, so long as this is the only one in school time. Oh, and on condition you let me know the result."

"Yes, Mrs Clark. Thank you."

Eleanor was both excited and nervous about the scan. David said she was radiant and blooming, and apart from morning sickness, she was feeling very well. She hoped that this was a good sign, but she kept her mother's initial comments in mind. David held her hand as the doctor smeared the jelly on her abdomen and applied the device. Eleanor kept her eyes on the screen, but unable to see a recognisable pattern among the streaks.

"Are there twins in your family," the doctor asked casually, as she studied the screen.

"David has twins," Eleanor replied.

"Identical?"

"No," David replied. "A boy and a girl."

"Your side, Eleanor?"

"My mother had twins – it was never talked about, and then she had a breakdown. That's all I know. Why?"

"Because, Eleanor," the doctor said, turning back to her and smiling. "I think you are going have to buy a double buggy!"

"Are you saying I'm going to have twins? Oh, my!"

"I'm pretty sure. It will be easier to be definite as time passes, so don't buy the double buggy yet!"

"Is this to do with David or my mother?" Eleanor asked.

"David's twins came from two eggs – nothing to with David. It's a pity you don't know about your side. Will you be able to find out? Mind you, there's no rush, is there?"

"What is the significance?" David asked.

"Well, if your mother's twins were identical, there could be a genetic tendency for you to have identical twins. Ditto, non-identical. Or, maybe you don't want to know?"

Eleanor looked at David. "Do we want to know? Did you and Jenny know?"

"No, we didn't, but as the doctor said, there's no rush."

"And Mum said that she wouldn't talk about what happened to her until after the birth. Actually, she said until she's holding a healthy baby."

"Or two babies!" David added.

Eleanor's mother was now a regular visitor to their house and called in one Monday evening when David and Eleanor had the architectural technician's plans on the table.

"Excuse me being nosey, but is it an expensive extension?" her mother asked.

"It depends on how much we extend," Eleanor said. "It could be done in stages, but in the long run, that would cost more money. Would you like to see the rough sketches?"

"Will you extend your current mortgage?" she asked David.

"Mum, we don't have a mortgage," Eleanor said.

"Then you must have won the football pools," her mother said, without thinking.

"Sheila, Jenny was insured," David said quietly.

"Oh," gasped Sheila Jenkins, putting her hand to her mouth. "David, I am sorry."

"It's not a problem," he answered.

"Would you be offended if I asked how much?"

"Not at all," said David, picking up another piece of paper. "These are only her rough estimates. Of course, the builders might say it is a lot more."

"And would you need to borrow all this?"

"Mum!" Eleanor said.

"It's all right, Sweetheart," David said. He turned to Sheila. "What happened is this. We have just lent a tidy sum to Daniel and Stephanie," David said.

"But you need it!" Sheila exclaimed.

"Mum, they are living in a pokey one bedroom flat. I live in a three to four bedroom house. Their need is greater than mine! They are now in the process of buying a two bedroom house, which is still smaller than this one."

"But they're not your responsibility," Sheila said.

"Mum, they are my family. They accepted me when you

349

didn't. Of course I want to help them!"

"As I was saying," David continued. "We have helped them, but it may be repaid sooner than we expected."

Eleanor looked at David. This was news to her.

"Rearrangements within the wider family, Eleanor."

"The reason I asked," Sheila said, "was that I am also in a position to help you. Not all of that," she added, pointing to the biggest sum, "but some of it. Just bear that in mind."

Eleanor was too surprised to respond, but David leaned over and kissed Sheila's cheek.

"We will, Sheila. Thank you very much!"

The next phone call between David and his mother was initiated by his mother.

"Just a quick call to see how you both are," she said.

"Yes, we're both fine," David replied.

"You're not working Eleanor too hard?"

"I hope I'm not, why, did you think I was?"

"I thought she looked tired," she said.

"Well, that's blunt!" David said.

"And from something Jill said, before she clammed up."

"Go on," David said carefully.

"Is she expecting?"

"Who, Jill?" David said, erring on the side of safety.

"No, David. Eleanor!"

David paused. "Yes, she is."

"Were you going to tell me?"

"Mum!" David exclaimed. "When I brought Eleanor to see you, you made it quite clear what you thought of me having more children. Remember?"

His mother paused. "Yes, I do. But looking back, I think I was being hasty."

"Or tactless?"

"All right. Yes, I was."

"So, yes, we are expecting," David said.

"And are you pleased?"

"Yes, Mum, I am pleased. I am very pleased. I didn't expect it to happen so quickly, but there it is."

"What about Eleanor's school? How are they taking it?"

"Very well. I know some of the staff are disappointed by the fact that she has chosen motherhood above university, but on the other hand, they have an expectant mother who is married. How many other pregnant eighteen year olds are?"

"I see your point, David. When is the baby expected?"

"About mid-November."

A pause – his mother was calculating. "So you knew when we came!"

"Yes, but we didn't know whether you would be pleased. Well, are you?"

"David, if that's what you want, okay, yes I am."

"But you're not so enamoured about being a grandmother again?"

"I didn't see it coming David. But I coped last time, so no doubt I'll cope again."

As the term progressed, Eleanor moved into her second trimester and her sickness ceased. However, as her abdomen began to swell it was inevitable that someone would notice, and by half term it was common knowledge in her school that she was expecting. Only she and David knew that there were two babies growing inside her. She needed to purchase a new school skirt, but over half term, she wore what David called, a preggy dress, even though it was not really needed. Her final examinations arrived and were taken. Finally, it was end of term, and time to think about the extension. The plans had been finalised much earlier and a recommended builder had been hired. To enable the builders to work unhindered, David had decided to take Eleanor away for some of the time. Through a contact at his school, David had hired a cottage in west Wales. Eleanor was still in her second trimester, becoming rounder, but not over lumpy, and still fit enough to enjoy walking and swimming. Apart from the weather and views, and lack of a hotel service, it was like a second honeymoon for them both.

Once back at home, they found that their extension was nearly finished and the house was already habitable. However, there was something else on Eleanor's mind – her examination results. The following week she joined her year group to collect them; results that reflected all the hard word she had done, and justified David's faith in her ability.

"Now I can finally relax and concentrate on being a full time wife," she told him as she met him waiting outside the school. "Let's go home and celebrate."

Eleanor was now down to fortnightly scans. Her doctor now knew she was carrying twins, and even offered to let Eleanor know what she thought would be the sex. Sheila wanted to accompany Eleanor to a scan, so Eleanor had to explain to her doctor that she did not want her mother to know about twins. It was hard to explain why because Eleanor did not know herself, but she did manage it. The holiday ended, and David returned to full time work, leaving Eleanor as a full time housewife. Eleanor's friends knew they were welcome and the house was often full of young people – Lizzie, Jayne, and now Natasha especially. They were all going to university.

"Any regrets, Sweetheart?" David asked one evening after the girls had gone home. They had been talking about leaving home.

"Not at all. I've got everything I want – you and," she patted her rounded abdomen, "what you gave me in here."

"We'll have to be talking about names," David said.

"So long as we don't let on that we need four names!"

By mid October, Eleanor was very big and uncomfortable. Half term came and went.

"Where do you want to go for your birthday treat?" David asked.

"Hospital!" she said. "It feels as if there's a whole football team in here."

"Then show them a red card," David joked.

"I'm not in the mood for jokes!"

"David, Eleanor's phoned." It was the deputy headmaster. He had come to David's classroom at the end of morning lessons.

"Well?"

"She's in labour, and has taken herself to the maternity unit."

"Taken herself?" David exclaimed. "How?"

"She didn't say, but she did say she won't be cooking your dinner tonight!"

"Ha, ha!" David replied. "Is that it?"

"That's all I know. David, if you want to go off this afternoon, I can cover you!"

"Right, I will go. Thanks. I'll leave some work in the office on the way out."

Eleanor was surprised to see him.

"What are you doing here," she said.

"What do you mean? Isn't it obvious? I've come because you're having a baby! When did it start?"

"Calm down, David," she said, laughing.

"When did it start, Eleanor?"

"I had a twinge before you woke up, then another at

breakfast time."

"Why didn't you say?"

"David! Stop worrying. I thought you were used to this."

"Eleanor, answer my question, please."

"Okay. Two twinges – I wasn't sure if they were real. Then, just after you left, they began again, and then my waters broke about mid-morning, so I phoned for a taxi. I told your secretary to let you know where I was. They reckon several hours yet. Aaaah." She gritted her teeth for a few seconds. "You haven't had lunch yet, have you?" she said.

"No, I came straight here. I've been released from teaching this afternoon."

"Now I do feel guilty! Look, why not go back, have lunch, teach your classes and come after school?"

"Eleanor! I won't be able to teach now!"

"Then go and have something to eat. I don't think I'll be cooking tonight, do you?" she said, with a grin.

"Eleanor, it's me that's supposed to be making the jokes."

"Sorry. But I'm serious about you eating something now. But, would you mind rubbing my back first?"

David was back by mid afternoon. This time, Eleanor was in a gown, and looking slightly strained.

"How are things going?" David asked. "I see you have changed."

"I think things have speeded up. They say I'm dilating well. Aaaaaaah. Sorry," she panted. "My back needs rubbing again. Was it like this the first time?"

"Oh, it's always hard for the man."

"David Anderson! If I wasn't tied up having your babies, I would slap you. How was it for Jenny?"

"She started late afternoon, and the kids were born in the early hours. Then she went to sleep, and I had to drive home! Can't remember that much now."

"Oh, poor you."

A nurse arrived to check on Eleanor, so David chose to keep quiet.

"Well, Eleanor, everything is progressing like clockwork. The way things are, I expect both twins to be born vaginally."

"As apart from?"

"Sometimes, the second is by caesarean section. But as I said, I'm not anticipating that. We'll give you an epidural nearer the time. I'll leave you in the capable hands of your husband."

Eleanor looked at David. "Don't say a word."

Adam arrived soon after nine o'clock, and Matthew, his identical brother a few minutes later by the same route. Both babies were cleaned and then put to the breast as quickly as possible just to initiate bonding. It took a few minutes for Matthew to latch on before both babies were taken away from an exhausted Eleanor to allow her to sleep.

"Drive home carefully, Darling," she said to David. "And I'll see you in the morning. Oh, bring Mum, if you can."

David did not leave immediately, and once home, there were a number of phone calls to be made. His deputy headmaster – he would be late tomorrow. Family. Friends. The last call was to Eleanor's mother. Fortunately, she picked up the phone first.

"Hello, Sheila …" he began.

"David, I've been trying to phone you. Any news?" she panted.

"Yes, good news. Can you skive off work tomorrow morning? Eleanor's asleep right now, so come here and I'll take you in with me."

"Boy or girl?"

"Boy."

"Weight?"

"Satisfactory."

"David!"

"Sheila, just be here at eight, or soon after! I'm tired and I want to go to bed. Goodnight."

Chapter 22

Shocking News

"Well?" That was Sheila's first word as she arrived on David's doorstep at eight fifteen the following morning. "Hello, Sheila, come in." That was David's reply.

"The weight?" she said, as she entered.

"Somewhere between five and ten ounces, no, I mean pounds. Sorry."

"David! Be serious."

"Sheila. Just be patient."

"She was big, David. At least ten pounds, I would say."

"Sheila, when I left, Eleanor was asleep, and everything was fine. Let me finish my coffee, and we'll go. Then you can get all the answers you need. I just want to text Eleanor to see if she's awake."

> Sweetheart about to come with your
> mum okay

He did wonder whether Eleanor would be sufficiently awake to receive and then respond, but this was all part of their plan. It took five minutes before he had a reply.

> Will be feeding in half hour

David turned to Sheila. "Everything is fine, but not quite ready. We'll go in fifteen minutes."

"Why can't we go now?"

"Grandma, calm down," David said.

Sheila smiled. "It's all right for you, you're used to it."

"Yes, Jenny was on edge for the first grandchild, but we couldn't go and see Jill for two days, Sheila."

"So he was born before …?"

"Yes. I suppose that was the last time that Jenny was excited about something."

Sheila was silent for a moment. "Did Jenny know Eleanor?"

"Not personally – neither of us did. But we both knew who she was, and we both thought highly of her as a young person in the church."

"I wonder what she would have said if she knew?"

"Sheila, we both talked about what we would want the other person to do. I would have wanted Jenny to begin again, assuming she found the right person. Mind you, if you had asked me then what I would do, I would have said nothing. I didn't expect to find anyone, let alone start a new family. Especially with a teenager. I would have considered that to be totally inappropriate."

"Then why?" Sheila asked quietly.

"I think I had come to terms, as well as one could, with being a widower. Then, I was suddenly faced with losing Eleanor. I didn't want that. Sheila, it wasn't easy. As far as I was concerned, it was selfish; I was depriving Eleanor of a university education, and maybe marriage to someone of her own age. Don't you think I don't worry about her being left a widow? At least, now she will have a family."

"Oh, so you want more than one, then?"

David smiled. Eleanor had managed to hide the fact that she was carrying twins from her mother, and now she was about to find out.

"Would you like more than one?" he asked, parrying Sheila's question.

"What about you? You've got two already."

"Two is a nice number," David said, acting thoughtfully.

David knew roughly where Eleanor would be, but not the actual room.

"Is Eleanor ready to see us," he asked.

"I'm sure she is."

"Would it be possible to tell her we are here? I know it is a cheek, but there is a reason."

The nurse gave him a strange look. "Alright."

She was a few minutes. Then she returned, and winked at David. "They're ready for you both. In here."

The nurse stood back, as did David to let Sheila in. Thus, they did not see her face. Eleanor was sitting up in bed, with a baby in each arm.

"Mum!" Eleanor cried as she saw the blood drain from Sheila's face. David saw Sheila's legs begin to buckle. He managed to grab hold of her as she sank down, and prevented her head from hitting the door post. The nurse quickly came to his aid, and rolled Sheila sideways into the recovery position, before feeling for her pulse. The nurse turned and smiled.

"Only a faint. What's her name?"

"Sheila," David replied, scrabbling up to go to Eleanor. "She fainted, Sweetheart," he said, as the nurse slapped Sheila's cheeks gently and called her name. "Wake up, Sheila love, wake up."

"Oh David, oh David, what have we done?" Eleanor whispered.

"Come on, Sheila love, try and get up," the nurse repeated. Then she looked at David. "Can you help me? We'll get her to that chair."

A few moments later, they had Sheila sitting in a chair, looking bewildered, and still panting.

"Why didn't you tell me?" she said, looking accusatively at David.

"It was me, Mum. You said you wouldn't talk about what happened to you until you were holding a healthy baby. I knew it was something to do with twins, so I decided not to tell you, sorry. It was quite hard at times, especially when you kept commenting on my size. David, hand them to Mum, can you?"

David picked up the nearest, and carried him to Sheila.

Then he returned for the second.

"You're very honoured, I haven't held them both together yet," he said, as he placed him in Sheila's other arm.

"Are they both well?" Sheila whispered.

"As far as we know, yes," Eleanor replied.

At this, Sheila burst into tears, waking both babies, and making one of them cry.

"Take them, take them," she uttered, looking at David. David took them both back to Eleanor, who opened her bed jacket and put them both to breast. Then Sheila leaned forward and cried, almost uncontrollably. David was embarrassed and didn't know what to do. Both babies latched on, and began to suckle contentedly, so Eleanor suggested that David went to see if he could obtain a cup of tea for Sheila.

When David returned some seven minutes later with a cup of tea, Sheila was sitting composed. David handed her the cup, and looked enquiringly at Eleanor.

"I'll tell you later, David," she said quietly. "Here, do you want to hold your sons. They've gone back to sleep, so they'll be put into their cribs again. You just missed the doctor doing the hip joint test. It looked excruciating."

"How do we know who is who. They both look the same to me. Are they officially identical?" David asked.

"They're tagged. Look. This is Adam. This is Matthew. I was telling Mum how we named them. Their second names will be their maternal granddads, Mum."

Sheila just smiled.

"How are you feeling now?" David asked.

"I'm fine"

"Do you know what day it is tomorrow?" David asked her.

"It's Eleanor's birthday," she replied.

"We're supposed to be going out for a meal," David said.
"I suppose it will have to be next week or so – that's if we
can find a baby-sitter at short notice."
Sheila just smiled.
"Mum, you look all in. I think David had better take you
home. Can you come in tonight? Would Dad come?"
"Oh, Eleanor, I am sorry, but it I don't think he will. But I
will!"

David took Sheila back to his house, and from there she
drove to work. David decided to go back to school for the
rest of the day. There was nothing for him to do at home
– he had already decided to buy a take-away meal that
evening, and by going back, he relieved his colleagues
who were standing in for him. David went straight to the
maternity unit from school. Eleanor was sitting propped
up in bed.
"Hello, Sweetheart, how is Mummy doing then?" he
asked, as he kissed her.
Eleanor laughed. "Am I really a mummy?"
"It's a good feeling, isn't it?"
"Can you remember?"
"Eleanor, I've just become a daddy again! Wow!"
"I wonder how Grandma is," Eleanor said. "She could
have hurt herself this morning."
"Do you know what caused it?"
"Yes. If I'd have known, I wouldn't have done what we
did."
"So what was it?"
Eleanor took a deep breath. "I knew mum was pregnant
before she was married, and I knew that she was
expecting twins. That's all, and remember, Mum would
not talk about it. Well, her twins were delivered by
caesarean section. There was a reason. They were
conjoined."

361

"Siamese twins?"

"Well, yes, that's the everyday term. Conjoined twins are identical twins and approximately half are stillborn."

"And your mum's"

"They were alive, but with no hope of surviving. Mum had a breakdown, a serious breakdown, and she decided never to have another baby. Well, I think I was a mistake. But then there was the danger of Mum having another breakdown. They even considered a termination. However, once they knew I was not a twin, they stopped worrying. I think we were right to keep our twins a secret, but if I had known, we could have told her before she came. The look on Mum's face when she saw me holding them both – it was horror, probably at what might have been, or maybe it took her back. Anyway, it's in the past now."

Len Jenkins did not visit that evening, although Sheila did. David brought Eleanor and the twins home on Sunday afternoon. He took three days of paternity leave, and then Sheila took two days off work. David's mother and father came the following week, by which time, Eleanor was thinking about and planning for Christmas, despite David telling her to slow up and not excite herself. They did manage to have Eleanor's birthday meal, with Sheila looking after the twins. It seemed that Len was going to ignore their existence.

Christmas arrived. David and Eleanor decided to celebrate their wedding anniversary after Christmas. Daniel and Stephanie came the day before Christmas Eve, in order for Stephanie to help Eleanor. Keith, Jill, James and Naomi came for the day.

"You know I used to talk about feeling properly married?" she said to David in bed that night "Well, I have that feeling again."

They celebrated their first anniversary between the two holidays, with Sheila baby-sitting. Not long after the New Year, it was time to remember Jenny's life and funeral. David's children came, and they all went to the cemetery, but then Eleanor, Stephanie and Keith stood back, with the four children, leaving David alone with his two older children. Then life continued as normal. David teaching, and Eleanor housekeeping.

Easter arrived.

"I know the twins won't be walking, but what about going back to Wales in the summer? I talked to my colleague, and the cottage is free for a couple of weeks. I think we should try and get away," David said.

"Instead of the Canaries?" Eleanor said with a smile. "I fancy going back to our hotel."

"Adults only. No children. Remember?"

"Yes. At the time it did seem a good idea, I mean, having no children around. So, yes, let's go back to Wales again."

June arrived.

"Just think, a year ago I was doing my examinations," Eleanor said, over breakfast one morning.

"And we were preparing for the extension," David added.

"And now I'm feeding two children."

"Hang on, we're feeding one each!" David said. There were two high chairs; David and Eleanor were in position by each and spooning mush into little mouths.

"I meant with these," Eleanor said, patting her chest.

"And easy to take on holiday," David said with a smile.

"I'm looking forward to getting away."

David returned home that evening with a long face.

"David! You look as if you've lost a pound and found a penny," Eleanor said, after they had kissed.

"It's worse than that, Sweetheart. The holiday is off?"

"Are you joking?"

"No. There's been some kind of problem. A stream overflowed and then flooded the cottage."

"But it will be dried out in a month's time, won't it?"

"It took one of the walls with it!" David said.

"Oh!"

"Exactly"

"Never mind," Eleanor said, trying to sound positive.

"There are lots of other places."

"Like the Canaries?"

"I'm not leaving the children with Mum for a week!" Eleanor exclaimed.

"I was joking. Mind you, we once went to Menorca with the children."

"And how old were they?"

David grinned. "Much older. Mind you, there were babies on board, and at the hotel. It catered for kids. And it's only two hours away!"

"I am tempted! But, oh wise one, the twins do not have passports."

"Yet," said David.

"Are you serious?" Eleanor gasped, staring at him.

"I don't know. What do you think? It would mean getting them a passport each. Hassle. And then looking for a last minute deal. We could get them a passport and then find there are no last minute deals!"

"David, they will be eight months old!"

"Fair enough," David said.

David was late home the following evening, and feeling tired. There had been an after school meeting.

"How was the meeting?" Eleanor asked, as she greeted him.

"Boring. And a waste of time," he grumbled. "How was your day?"

"Good. Mum popped in at lunchtime, and I told her how we had discussed taking the children to Menorca."

"And she said we were mad? Right?"

"Pretty close," Eleanor agreed. "But, she said that if I wanted to apply for passports, she would help me."

"And how exactly would she help?"

"Stop being all superior. I phoned the passport office and we could apply in the normal way by post, or," she paused, "or apply in person. I would have to book an appointment and then take the twins with me."

"Eleanor! Come on, be serious!"

"I am! I've booked an appointment for next week. And Mum will take me."

David stared at Eleanor. "You're nuts," he said at last, shaking his head.

"David, even if we don't go, I want to do it. It will be a day out with Mum. All I need are the two signed photographs, and a letter from you, witnessed, to say that you are in agreement."

* * * * *

"I hope this is going to be worth it," David whispered to Eleanor. He was holding Adam, Eleanor was holding Matthew and the plane was descending to Mahon. Both children were suckling on a baby-feeding bottle of diluted apple juice. They didn't like feeding bottles, but they did like sweet apple juice. The reason was to try and keep them swallowing, and thus relieving the pressure in their ears. Further back, there was a crying child who was already suffering, and thereby making the people around suffer! "I think these two will yell when we take the juice away," he added.

"I'll switch them to me if necessary," Eleanor replied.

"What, on the plane. It's not very private, and anyway, is there room?"

365

"Look, if someone wants to stare, tough! Anyway, there will be much more flesh displayed on the beach. And we'll make room. It will only be for a minute or two, just to get them off the juice. And to answer your first comment, it's got to be worth it after all the hassle I went through."

*   *   *   *   *

Eleanor's mother had taken Eleanor and the twins to the Newport passport office for a ten o'clock appointment. They had left at seven, and stopped for breakfast near Monmouth. Eleanor had a letter from David, witnessed by his headmaster, and stamped with the school stamp. There was also a letter from his headmaster to vouch for him. She had David's passport as well as her own, plus her personal bank statement and their joint bank statement. Sheila had identification as well, although it was not required. Following their first interview, they were told to return in five hours time. Fortunately the weather was kind, but even so, by four o'clock, they were all fed up. They wheeled the buggy up and down inside the office, hoping that their presence there might act as a catalyst. At four thirty they were told that their application had been approved, and that the passports should be with them within a fortnight. They stopped in Monmouth to buy fish and chips, and to feed the twins. At one stage, Sheila was feeding chips to Eleanor, sprawled on the back seat with both babies latched on and gurgling. Then the three of them slept as Sheila drove them home.

Eleanor wanted to start looking for a holiday immediately, but David, ever cautious had insisted that they wait for the arrival of the passports. They arrived a week before the end of term, but with David at work, she could not get into the travel agents. Instead, she scoured the internet, becoming more and more depressed with what appeared to be the non-availability of anything suitable. The first chance they had to go looking together was on the Saturday. It was far from ideal; David was tired, the babies were grumpy, and it was raining. By the time they reached their third holiday shop, David wanted to give up.

"Darling, please! I spent a whole day in Newport, you've only spent half a morning," Eleanor said.

"Okay," David said.

They sat in front of the agent, told her their wishes, and then watched and waited as she started searching.

"Ah, Menorca, half-board, one week, family room, er, yes. Next week. Thursday."

"We'll take it," David said.

"Hang on," Eleanor said. "Is it suitable, I mean we'll need two cots. We can hardly fly with two travelling cots. Then what about stairs, lifts, pools, shops for nappies, let alone near a beach."

The agent swung the monitor round. "Cots are available for a small fee. There are two pools, and the beach is a hundred metres away. And there's a supermarket nearby because there's a lot of self catering around here."

"Flying from?" David asked. "Somewhere in England?"

"East Midlands. Ten thirty departure. Two and a half hours to Mahon."

"Two and a half hours. East Midlands. That's okay, but booking in at eight thirty. Rush hour."

"Then stay overnight at a hotel," the agent suggested.

"We'll take it," Eleanor said.

By Wednesday they had bought and packed mini-wetsuits for the twins, arm-bands, extra nappies, and the other paraphernalia needed. Because they would not be free to eat in the evening, they had packed no formal clothes. They were planning to have early dinners, eating in the family area with other families. They travelled late on the Wednesday, hoping that the journey would tire the babies. It did. The next morning they left the travel cots and car at the hotel and took a taxi to start their holiday. Having babies meant they embarked first, leaving their double buggy to be stowed below. The journey itself was grim – they both had to hold a baby, and David was relieved when they finally started to descend. Things had to get better, he thought, assuming they could persuade both babies to stop drinking the apple juice.

The next hour was hard. Queuing, waiting for luggage, and then sitting on a hot bus. However, on arrival, they quickly undressed, undressed the babies, and stood under a cool shower holding the babies. For a moment, they both wondered if they had made a mistake. When they finally dried and dressed, the air conditioning had kicked-in. There was time for a dip in the pool, making sure that they and the babies were not over-exposed to the sun. They rested until their dinner time and then finally took a walk in the cool evening pushing the twins in their buggy. It was very different from their honeymoon hotel, but they did expect that. In reality, it was far from ideal. The twins were too young to know what a sandcastle was, although they did enjoy bobbing around in the sea. The twins' day revolved around an early breakfast, water play in the sea – that is, when not under a sun shade. An early lunch of baby-meals from the supermarket, then sleep in their air-conditioned room! After an early dinner, they were taken out in their buggies so that their parents had some exercise. Then they were put down to sleep, leaving David and Eleanor to spend their evening in the main bedroom. Not ideal, but after a stressful term, David was happy to do very little but eat, sleep, read, and play with the twins, and forget about the stressful journey home at the end of the week.

There was a knock on their door at eight o'clock on Sunday morning. David, wearing only boxer shorts, opened the door slightly and peered out. It was Sandy, one of the two holiday representatives.

"Hi, Sandy," David said. "You haven't come to sell us a tour, have you?"

"No, of course not. Are you up yet?"

"Of course! Come in. The twins are having breakfast." What David meant was that Eleanor was feeding them both. She was sitting up in bed with a twin on each breast.

"Oh, sorry," Sandy said, obviously embarrassed, and backing away.

"Sandy, if Eleanor was sitting topless on the beach, you wouldn't turn a hair, would you? How can we help you?"

"I have some bad news, I'm afraid."

Thoughts began flashing through David's head. Tour company had gone bust – no flight home. Mum or Dad had died. Jill or Daniel had been killed. He waited.

"It's Mrs Anderson's father, he's been in an accident."

"What about my mother?" Eleanor asked.

"No, just your father. Something to do with cranes – at work on Saturday."

"He doesn't work on Saturday. David, switch your mobile phone on."

David and Eleanor used pay-as-you-talk and they had brought one phone in case they needed to send or receive a text. They switched it on every morning just in case there was a message. David switched it on and they waited. Eventually there was the double bleep of an incoming message. David read it.

"Eleanor, dad is in hospital serious injury on Saturday more to follow."

David looked up. "Did Eleanor's mother contact you, Sandy?"

"Not me personally. No, apparently it was his employer. Once they found out where Mrs Anderson was staying, they have asked us to arrange for her to go home, well, to the hospital." Sandy paused, and looked at Eleanor. "I'm sorry to bring you bad news, Mrs Anderson, but your father is in intensive care, and has been asking for you."

Chapter 23

So Sorry

Eleanor looked at David, back to Sandy and at David again. Adam and Matthew kept suckling at Eleanor's breast.

"What do we do, David? I can't leave the twins," she whispered.

"Right now we do nothing. Sandy, I'll see you at your desk in ten minutes. Sweetheart, finish feeding the twins, and wait for me here. I will be back in time to take you to breakfast."

David showered, skipped shaving, and then dressed in five minutes. Eleanor was already crying as he came out of the bathroom.

"Sweetheart," he said, bending over her and kissing her, "Try not to cry too much. The babies might sense it."

"How dare he ask for me," Eleanor said. "After the way he's treated me. I've a good mind to text Mum and say so!"

"Eleanor, Eleanor," David said gently. "I feel the same. But what should we feel?"

"I don't want to go!"

"I know, Sweetheart. We'll talk about it after breakfast. Let me go and see Sandy first."

Sandy was sitting behind his desk looking very worried. He stood up as he saw David approaching.

"Mr Anderson," he began.

"Hang on. Up to now I've been David. Especially when you wanted me to sign up for the Mahon trip."

Sandy laughed. Part of the representative's job was to encourage holiday makers to sign up for the various trips.

Sandy had begun his sales pitch before he realised that David was the husband with very young twins.

"Sorry," he said.

"Right, what exactly do you know?" David asked.

"I had a phone call from London and an e-mail. Mr Jenkins was working on Saturday, and was involved in an accident. He was rushed to hospital, and taken to intensive care. It was touch and go apparently, and still might be. He's been delirious and asking for his daughter, and the doctors think that by having his daughter, it might make the difference. So, his employer has said that they want her home as soon as possible. Oh, and they will pay."

"Don't they know she is a nursing mother of twins?" David asked.

"Nothing was said about that," Sandy replied.

"Right, can you phone London?"

"Yes, of course."

"Right phone your boss and tell them that Mr Jenkins' daughter is in fact married, with eight month old twins. Oh, and how did they expect Eleanor to go. Are there flights today? And vacancies?"

"I don't know, Mr, er, David."

"I'll leave you to do that then. I'm going to calm my wife and take her and my sons to breakfast. The last thing I want is for her milk to dry up."

"That was embarrassing," Eleanor said when David entered their room. She was pulling on a skirt, and both babies were lying on the bed.

"What was," David replied, thrown by her comments.

"Me sitting topless."

"For you or him?"

"Both of us! I won't be able to look him in the eye. You do realise that I was totally naked," Eleanor pointed out, raising her voice slightly.

"But under a sheet," David said

"Thank goodness!"

"All right, all right. I'm sorry."

"So what now?" Eleanor asked, pulling on a tee shirt.

"We go and feed our little ones and we feed ourselves."

"And what then?"

"I don't know."

Eleanor suddenly turned to face him, her eyes wide.

"David," she whispered. "Is it serious?"

David hugged her. "Yes, Sweetheart, it is. Very serious. It was touch and go. The doctors think that you could make a difference."

"Which means I've got to go, doesn't it?"

"It means that we all have to go. But not until after breakfast."

"David, I didn't mean what I said," she whispered.

"So you didn't text your mum?"

"David, you had the phone!"

"Oh yes. Right, come on. Let's squash a banana," David said, referring to the baby's breakfast. Breakfast was a major undertaking. The kitchen kept a banana for them, and a jug of warm milk. David squashed a banana while Eleanor mixed up some baby cereal. Then one of them would rush off and bring back two bowls of cereal. It was a juggle as they fed themselves and one baby each. The other person would then go and bring two plates of English breakfast. However, with the added stress of the bad news, neither David nor Eleanor felt hungry.

"Eleanor, we should eat something, even if it's only toast." David said, after they had prepared the baby cereal course. The mashed banana came after.

"Okay, you go while I hold the fort here."

When David returned with four pieces of toast, Eleanor
was still feeding alternate mouths with cereal. He buttered
and spread two pieces with marmalade.

"Give me a spoon," he said, and then taking bites of his
toast between spoonfuls of cereal being offered to one
twin.

"I could do with some cornflakes now," Eleanor said,
after a minute or two.

"Eleanor!"

"Sorry!" she said, grinning.

"It's your turn now."

Eleanor pushed her plastic bowl of cereal towards David,
handed him the spoon, and stood up.

"While you're there, get some for me, please," David
said, smiling. She pulled a face at him, and went. David
managed to crush the banana as well as feed both babies
and himself before Eleanor returned. It had to be done in
such a way that the twins could not see – once they
spotted the banana, they lost interest in their cereal! As
she returned, David saw Sandy hovering. He called him
to come and sit with them.

"Well, any more news?"

"I'm waiting for a reply," Sandy said.

"But you're not there to get it!" Eleanor pointed out.

"One of the hotel staff is helping. And Angie has been
called in as well," (Angie was the other holiday
representative for the company.) "But I have made a few
enquiries."

"Go on."

"There are no available seats on any of today's flights,
nor tomorrow's, but there are seats from Barcelona on a
scheduled flight."

"But Barcelona is in Spain," Eleanor said. "How do we
get there? Swim?"

"There are ferries."

"Are you serious?" David asked.

"It's just a suggestion," Sandy said.

"So you're suggesting that we take a ferry to Barcelona, and then fly home from there? And how do we go about arranging that, let alone get to the ferry? Oh, where is the ferry, anyway?" David asked.

When Sandy didn't reply, Eleanor spoke again. "Sorry, Sandy. It's been a shock and it's hard to take in. Look, when do you expect an answer? Did you tell them back home about your ideas?"

Sandy nodded, still feeling that David had been too blunt.

"There is one thing you could do for us," David said gently, to Sandy.

"What's that?"

"Let us phone Eleanor's mum from your desk. We've only brought one mobile between us, and it won't cope with a long conversation."

Sandy looked confused.

"Pay-as-you-go, Sandy," Eleanor said. "We weren't expecting to call home."

"Oh, all right. Sure. Come to my desk as soon as you finish here."

As soon as Sandy had left, Eleanor's composure cracked and David thought she was going to cry again.

"Sweetheart," he whispered. "Come on, where's the girl who was kicked out of home? You got through that, you'll get through this."

"Only because I had you."

"You've got me now."

"Physically! It's my mind. I'm very angry, as you have probably guessed. But I know I shouldn't be. If you really want to know, or it wasn't for Mum, I probably wouldn't go."

"I think you would, Sweetheart. I know you're hurt and angry about being rejected."

"It's not just me, David! It's you, and it's our children. Now he wants me, am I'm supposed to go running?"

"Sweetheart. You know the answer. Tell, me, would you have run if you were the father of the prodigal son."

"David, that's not fair!" she burst out.

"I know it isn't. But if you didn't go, and not for your mother's sake, you would for ever regret it if he didn't survive."

"How do you know?"

"I don't know personally, but I know what people say, and I know you. That's one of the reasons I wanted to marry you."

"David, I need a hug," she said through tear-filled eyes.

"You'll have to wait until after breakfast. Come on, the kids want their banana."

They managed to hug in the lift during the short ride between floors. As they approached Sandy's desk, his countenance told them that he had heard from London. "It's not office hours in London, but someone must think that this is important; I have had an answer," he said to them. "Right, yes, all four of you must go. And it's how I suggested. There's a ferry from Cuitadella at midday. Arrives in Barcelona before six. Hotel for the night, and the eight-thirty flight to Heathrow."

"Are we in the same time zone as mainland Spain?" David asked.

"Yes, one hour ahead of England, why," Sandy replied.

"Time of arrival at Heathrow," David said. "We will need to be met. My car and the car seats are in the Midlands. We flew from the East Midlands airport."

"Ah!" said Sandy. "Good point!"

"And how do we find the hotel in Barcelona?" Eleanor asked.

Sandy smiled. "It's in the same group as this one. You

will be met at the ferry terminal, and taken to the airport tomorrow. I don't know which flight, but I imagine that whoever is dealing with it in London will know. Can I text you if I find out?"

"Yes, of course. Thank you."

"Is there anything else you need right now?"

David shook his head.

"Yes. I was going to go to the supermarket for more nappies, oh, and lunch for the twins. Will there be food, I mean proper food on the ferry," Eleanor said.

"Ah, here comes Angie. She doesn't know it yet, but she's been assigned to you until you leave. I'll put her in the picture and then she will be with you." He grinned. "You might even fit in a quick swim,"

"That was tactless," Eleanor muttered as they left Sandy. "I think he's just trying to distract us. But I think he had a point. What are we going to do? Pack and then sit and worry?"

"David! I was going to phone Mum." Eleanor said. "Back to his desk, come on!"

As they drew near to the desk, Sandy paused from telling Angie, and turned to Eleanor.

"Mrs Anderson?"

"You said I would be able to speak to mum, that's if she's at home," Eleanor said.

"Sure, sorry."

He picked his phone and dialled some numbers. "Right, just dial the number; I'm already connected to the UK."

"What time is it in England," she asked as she waited.

After letting it ring, she put the phone down again.

"Then she's at the hospital," David said.

"Or on the way – driving," Eleanor replied.

"Send a text. Say we're on the way, arriving tomorrow or say she should contact your dad's boss."

Eleanor took the phone from David, and began to punch the letters. Finally she pressed send, and handed the phone back to David. Within seconds, it began to ring. David was surprised and looked at the screen.

"Unknown number," he said before putting the phone to his ear. "David Anderson speaking."

He listened for a few moments, before handing the phone to Eleanor. "It's your dad's boss."

Eleanor took the phone, and apart from a few yeses, she listened. At one stage she asked for a pen and paper, and wrote down a number. Then she told them where their car was, and said that they would need two baby carrying seats to get them home.

"He had been waiting to get our mobile number from Mum," she said to David, as she gave him the phone.

"It's as you say, Sandy. Ferry. Hotel. Plane, and we'll be met. And he hopes we will be in time." She turned to David. This time he felt her shaking as he held her. Sandy had been talking to Angie while Eleanor had been texting and then talking on the phone.

"Mrs Anderson," she said gently, "Sandy said you needed some shopping. Shall I come with you?"

"How long have we got?" Eleanor asked.

Sandy looked at his watch. "I'll book a taxi for ten-thirty. Angie will come with you, and see you onto the ferry."

"You'll need a big taxi," David said.

"Okay, I'll book two," Sandy replied, with a shrug.

"So shall we go shopping," Angie repeated.

Eleanor looked at David. "What should I do? I can't think straight."

"You know what you need, so you should go shopping. If Angie could help me with the twins, would you be all right on your own, or do you need us all to go?"

"It would be easier on my own!" She turned to Angie. "Would you mind helping David? I think he would like to take them to the pool."

Angie smiled. "That could be fun, but I don't have a costume."

"That's fine. As far as I'm concerned, it's another pair of hands."

Eleanor helped David change the twins into their water outfits, that is, waterproof nappies! Then she departed leaving David and Angie to carry the twins to the pool. The twins loved being in the water. They bobbed around for over half an hour, with David in the water and Angie sitting on the edge until Eleanor arrived back.

"Hi, Sweetheart, do you want to come in?" David called.

"Have I got time? And what about all the wet stuff?"

"We're not flying today, and we have an extra pair of hands," David said, indicating Angie. "Go on, ten minutes. It will do you good."

As soon as Eleanor returned, David went up to his room to shower, dry and change leaving Eleanor in the water. He was right, it was good for Eleanor. After ten minutes she said she did feel less stressed, and Angie helped her take the twins back up. Eleanor showered while David and Angie washed, dried and changed the twins, not easy when there was only one sink for two babies. Eleanor then gave the twins a quick top-up, her milk first, then some water. Then it was walking time – David took them in the buggy while Angie helped Eleanor pack.

By half past ten, everyone was ready. There was a six-seater taxi with baby seats already fitted waiting. Angie joined then as they were driven to the ferry. She then helped them carry their luggage on board, and into a small cabin which had been acquired. Eleanor hugged her as they said their goodbyes. There was still forty minutes or so before it was time to leave, but because Eleanor knew that eventually they would have to spend time inside the ship in the air-conditioned atmosphere, they took turns in walking the buggy round and round the deck. Unfortunately, it was now becoming very warm and Eleanor worried that the twins could overheat and dehydrate, so they were given frequent top-ups of water.

Once the ship left the harbour, they went to the restaurant. Eleanor produced a jar of baby food, and a banana. Then it was milk time. Most women find it reasonably easy to feed one baby discreetly – the baby's head being part of the visual barrier, and her clothes being the rest. Eleanor sat in the corner of the room, and with her chair facing the corner, lifted her top, and attached both babies after adjusting her feeding bra. David went to the hatch and bought some sandwiches, some yoghurt, and two coffees. They drank the coffee in the restaurant, but kept the sandwiches for later. Once back in their cabin the twins at first seemed very lively, they had experienced a significant amount of stimulation over the preceding four hours. There was no cot or proper bed, just two long padded benches, with cushions. Eleanor thought the twins would roll off them, so she used the cushions to make a bed on the floor. Once down, the purr of the engines seemed to have a soporific affect, and the twins dropped off to sleep. David looked at his watch.
"Another fives hours," he muttered. "Maybe a bit less. Whose idea was this holiday?"
"You asked that before," Eleanor replied, quietly.
"If that cottage hadn't flooded, we would have been in Wales."
"And it would have been raining!" Eleanor added.
"Now I feel much better," David said, smiling at Eleanor.
"Mind you, it would have been easier to get back from Wales!"

"Meanwhile, what do we do now? These benches are very narrow."
"Not if we cuddle up tight."

Five hours later they were in another taxi on their way to another hotel. The crossing had not been easy. Although it was cool inside their cabin, once the twins had woken up, they needed to be entertained. That meant pushing them around in their buggy. The problem was it was now very warm on deck, with very little shade. They needed to be in nothing but a nappy, but they needed to be out of the sun. On the bright side, most of the passengers were interested in them – a form of entertainment in itself for the twins and which helped pass the time. Eleanor knew the twins would be late to bed that night, so she tried to get them to have another sleep before they disembarked. But it did not work and Eleanor gave up. Their next hotel did not really cater for children; however, it seemed that their last hotel manager had telephoned his colleague about their needs. On arrival, they were taken first to their room, and then to the restaurant. The restaurant was not due to take customers for another hour, but they were offered a simple meal, and help in preparing the twins' meals. Their accommodation consisted of two separate but joined bedrooms which allowed Eleanor to put the twins down immediately after eating, and still have a room for their own use. Although they both had brought books with them, neither felt able to read. The English speaking channels on the television kept them amused until an early bedtime.

Monday started in a totally different way to the previous day. On Sunday morning, they had been woken by the twins. Apart from satisfying their immediate needs for food, they had expected a stress free day. On Monday, they were woken at six o'clock by the hotel reception, and they knew it was the beginning of a stressful day. Eleanor's first job was to feed the twins while David sorted out their clothes for the day and packed their overnight things. Eleanor was hoping that her milk would keep them happy until they reached the airport, where they then planned to have breakfast after checking in. The plan worked. At six thirty-five they were in a taxi for the twenty minute ride to the airport. By five minutes past seven, they were struggling across the concourse with a buggy, two cases and two backpacks. They had to collect their tickets from the Iberian airlines desk in order to proceed to the check-in desk. This was worrying David – would they be there? They were. Check-in was smooth, the only hiccup was the two bottles of water Eleanor had for the twins as they went through security.

"Madam, this is too much!" the official said.

Eleanor was furious. "Then I'll drink some myself!" she said. She unscrewed the teat, took a big draught, refitted the teat, and then put it in Adam's mouth. "Now you take the bottle from him," she said glaring at the official.

"It's okay, Madam," he said, seeing the funny side.

"What about Matthew's bottle. Do you want my husband to drink some?" Eleanor asked.

"No, Madam. You can go through."

Once in the departure lounge, the made their way to a breakfast bar area.

"I don't feel hungry," Eleanor said, still feeing cross.

"I do, Sweetheart. Come on, you don't know when we eat next. Go and ask for some warm milk, and look at the breakfasts at the same time."

Half an hour later, both twins had been fed with their breakfast cereal – made in their plastic bowls and using the warm milk. The banana had then been mashed in the same bowl. David had eaten a bacon and cheese roll. Eleanor had nibbled at another one, and now had it wrapped in tissue to eat later. Both had drunk coffee.

"There, that feels better," David said. "I assume that we will be met in London. Isn't it time to text your mum saying where we are?"

"Yes. I'd better hurry. I think they'll announce the boarding gate soon. Can you walk the twins up and down, but don't go out of my sight? I don't want to lose you now!"

At eight fifteen they were high in the sky, and heading for Heathrow.

"How about a glass of wine?" David said, as he saw a steward taking food and drink orders.

Eleanor giggled. "David, it's early morning!"

"So what? I think we deserve it. Just for getting up at six o'clock."

"Don't be silly."

"Well, I'm having one."

Eleanor giggled again. "A man shouldn't drink on his own, should he?" she whispered.

David ordered two plastic glasses of wine.

The sign read "ANDERSON FAMILY" Eleanor spotted it first, and grabbed David's arm.

"I wonder if that's us?" she said.

"Let's go and ask him" David replied.

"I'm to take you straight to the hospital," Malcolm, their taxi driver, said. "Then, when it's convenient, Mr Anderson, I'll take you up to get your car. East Midlands, isn't it?"

"Yes, thanks, Malcolm."

"Do you know how my father is?" Eleanor asked.

"Sorry, Mrs Anderson. All I know is that I have to convey the Anderson family from A to B, then Mr Anderson on to C."

"But you do know we're going to a hospital? "

"Yes, Mrs Anderson. I assumed it was a family emergency."

"It's my father. He was hurt in an accident on Saturday morning,"

"I'm sorry, Mrs Anderson. Where have you come from?"

"Menorca, via Barcelona."

Eleanor's mother met them in the corridor. Eleanor rushed into her mother's arms.

"Thank you for coming, Darling," Sheila said.

"How is Dad? We're not too late, are we?"

"No. He's steady, still delirious at times. Tubes everywhere. He's still asking for you. We said you were on your way. Come along, he's just up here."

Sheila paused outside the doors. "I don't suppose you can take that in," she said, indicating the buggy.

Eleanor was already bending over it, and releasing Adam. She straightened up and handed him to David. Then she released and picked up Matthew.

"Are you taking them in?" Sheila's asked.

"Mum, he threw me out alone. But now I'm not alone – I have a family. It's me and David and the twins," she paused, "or nothing!"

"Eleanor," David gasped, but quietly. "No!"

Eleanor looked at him. "Yes, David." She looked at her mother. "You understand, don't you?"

Sheila nodded.

"Take us in, then," Eleanor said.

Eleanor hardly recognised her father. He was propped up on pillows, bandages round his head. His right arm was in plaster. His eyes were closed and there was a drip leading up to a bottle and going to his free arm. Eleanor walked up to the bed and took his left hand.

"Dad, it's Eleanor," she said quietly.

Len opened his eyes, first looking ahead, and then to his left. His eyes focused on Eleanor.

"You've come," he whispered. "Thank you."

"No, Dad," she said. For a moment he looked startled.

"Dad, we have come," she said, stressing the word we. "David, my husband brought me. And our twins." She turned to David. "David, come closer."

David stood by Eleanor, and Eleanor continued

"Dad, you know who David is, don't you?"

Len looked at David, then back to Eleanor. "Yes," he whispered.

"Dad, is there anything you want to say?" Eleanor asked quietly.

A tear rolled down Len's face.

"I'm sorry, Eleanor."

Eleanor bent down. "Dad, I'm Mrs Anderson now. Isn't there anything you want to say to David?"

Len pulled his hand away from Eleanor and tried to reach out towards David. Because of the drip in his arm, his movement was limited. He looked up at David and there was pleading in his eyes. David suddenly turned and thrust Matthew at Sheila. Then he dropped onto one knee by the bed and took Len's hand. The man's mouth was moving as though the words were stuck. Then he spoke. "David, I am so sorry."

Eleanor arrived in time, but were these his last words?
How did David react to the apology?
Was their family complete?
And what is the worst thing a teacher can hear?
Read the continuing story of Mr and Mrs Anderson in
Testing Times